THE GREEN YEARS

KAREN WOLFF

THE
GREEN
YEARS

a novel

bhc
press

Livonia, Michigan

Editor: Flannery Wise

THE GREEN YEARS
Copyright © 2019 Karen Wolff

Published by BHC Press

Library of Congress Control Number: 2018959723

ISBN: 978-1-948540-89-6 (Hardcover)
ISBN: 978-1-948540-50-6 (Softcover)
ISBN: 978-1-948540-51-3 (Ebook)

For information, write:
BHC Press
885 Penniman #5505
Plymouth, MI 48170

Visit the publisher at:
www.bhcpress.com

In memory of my father

THE GREEN YEARS

1

BETWEEN IOWA AND South Dakota, the Sioux River makes a bend to the west as if to escape its eventual disappearance into the muddy waters of the Missouri River. It can't go far, and soon curves back to its southerly flow. On the South Dakota side, about a mile from the river's westernmost point, a settlement called Richmond took root in the 1860s. It was the merest speck on a map, home to a handful of families who lived a hand-to-mouth existence and didn't expect much more. It's where Gram and Granddad Didier operated a one-room grocery store and barroom.

Dad plunked me down with my sister Polly in that sorry place before he enlisted in the army in 1917. I was eight and Polly was eleven. My three older brothers went to stay with Uncle Lyle and Aunt Hazel on a farm a ways off.

I knew I was supposed to be grateful to Gram and Granddad for giving us a home, but I didn't like it much. Especially in the beginning. The first time I saw their place it took me about two minutes to explore the whole thing. The house had just one bedroom. "Where will I sleep?" I asked.

Gram said she and Polly would sleep in the bedroom. "And you, Harry, will sleep with Granddad on the foldout daybed in the living room."

I soon knew why. Granddad snored. He farted in his sleep too, but, once I conked out, I didn't notice much.

Gram ran the household. She was stout with straight, gray hair fastened in a tight bun on the back of her head. Everything about her was big—her feet, her hands, even her hawkish nose. She wasn't mean, but when her black eyes fastened on Polly or me, or even Granddad, there was no use arguing. She didn't go in much for hugs and stuff, but that was all right with me.

Polly didn't want to stay at Gram's any more than I did. "She just wants me to be her hired girl," she said. If that was so, Gram was in for a surprise 'cause Polly didn't like to work.

The day after President Wilson declared war, Dad showed up on our doorstep whistling "Yankee Doodle." He was the best whistler for miles around, and I could always recognize his sound. I ran outside to meet him.

"C'mon, Harry," he said. "I'm gonna sign up. Want to go with me?" Off we went to the county seat so he could register with the Selective Service. Dad whistled all the way there, and I tried to whistle just like he did. He'd say, "No, like this," and demonstrate again. Finally we both wound up laughing at my efforts.

There must have been a hundred men on the grounds outside the courthouse, standing around talking in excited voices. They'd formed a long line from the street all the way up the marble steps of the building. Some wore suits and hats. Others, like my dad, had on overalls and work boots. Dad got in line and I stood close to him, listening to the men talking.

"Did you hear what happened to John Pankkuk?" one asked. "He almost got a beating the other night."

"How come?"

"That Kraut's so rich. Folks thought he should buy more Liberty bonds."

"What's a Kraut?" I whispered to my dad.

"Just a nickname for a German," he said. "'Cause they eat a lot of sauerkraut."

I was puzzled. We were mad at the Germans, but I thought they lived across the ocean, not around here.

The line moved slowly in the hot sun. Kids marched around the grounds pretending the sticks they carried over their shoulders were rifles. Dogs barked, and a little brass band began to play patriotic songs. We finally made our way up the marble steps and went inside. I remember the thrill of that building, the grandest place I'd ever seen with its high-domed ceiling and wide staircase hung with red, white, and blue bunting. Posters were plastered on the walls. One pictured a huge boot about to smash something with the words "Help Stamp out the Kaiser."

A big American flag hung over a table set up in the lobby. Behind it, several men sat in shirtsleeves. Dad seemed to know the man with suspenders who wore his hat tipped back over his head.

"You know, Calvin, with that passel of kids and no wife to look after them, you could get a deferment. You don't have to be the one to save us from the Kaiser."

"I know, Gus, but the country needs every man, doesn't it? And I want to help." Gus smiled and said, "You're a good man, Cal." He handed Dad a paper to fill out, and, just like that, Dad was in the army. The men shook hands, and I swelled up with pride, wishing I could sign up too.

Back outside we passed a ladies' aid stand that offered free lemonade to every man who enlisted. Someone behind us said, "Did you hear about Bill Vogelzang? That damn German got a deferment. Said his dad was too sick to run their farm. When he came through here, the ladies wouldn't give him lemonade. I bet his mailbox gets painted yellow." Dad just shook his head.

When our turn came, a chunky woman in an apron handed a glass to Dad. "We're proud and grateful to you for helping our country. Would your boy like some too?" I nodded and we drank it down. On the way home I asked Dad why those men wanted to paint the man's mailbox yellow.

"I guess they think he's a coward," he said. "Yellow-bellied."

DAD CAME TO tell us goodbye before he left for the army. He and Polly and I sat on the bare boards of Gram's side porch, our legs dangling over the edge. I could tell he was nervous. He wiped the sweat from his forehead and tried to smooth down the tufts of his red-brown hair. It was useless. His hair was coarse as a horse's tail, and the tufts went whichever way they wanted. He gave it up and his blue eyes crinkled tightly as they always did when his hair got the better of him.

"I know you kids aren't too happy about these arrangements," he said, "but it's not going to last forever."

"A year's a long time, Dad," Polly had said softly.

"It'll go fast, and we'll write letters. You'll be busy in school."

I hadn't been so sure about that. "Please don't go, Dad. It scares me. What if Gram gets tired of us and wants to get rid of us?"

He'd put his arm around me. "That won't happen, Harry. I know Gram's tough, but you're her daughter's kids. She really cares about you." He'd turned to smile at Polly. "You remind me so much of your mother, Polly. You look just like her with your black hair and big brown eyes. Just as beautiful." He'd looked at her a long minute like he was trying to memorize her.

He'd pulled me to him. "Come here, towhead. I'm afraid you got the short end of the deal 'cause you look like me with your big green peepers and all those cowlicks."

I'd managed a little smile. Back then there was nobody I'd rather look like than my Dad. I'd done my best not to cry as we hugged, and he kissed us goodbye. Polly had blubbered a while, then Buster, Granddad's silly, lop-eared dog, brought his ball for us to throw, and Dad was gone.

❖ ❖ ❖

THAT FIRST MORNING after Dad left for the army, I heard Granddad get up from the daybed we shared. When I opened my eyes, Buster was staring at me, his head level with mine and his tail thumping on the floor. I reached out to pet his silky black ears, and he licked my hands.

"Breakfast's ready," Gram called. "Better wash your face, Harry."

I got right up and went to the kitchen. Gram fixed us fried eggs and pancakes with butter and syrup. After we ate, Granddad went to his store, and Gram and Polly got busy doing dishes and making beds.

I went outdoors and stood on the side porch where we'd said goodbye to Dad. Dark clouds rolled across the sky, and the air smelled like rain. I didn't know what to do with myself, so I sat down where the three of us sat the day before, and I thought about Dad. He wouldn't be coming home today after work like he always did before. He wouldn't walk in all grins, and say, "Well, if it isn't my boy Harry. How was your day? Did you make a lot of money today?"

I could picture how he'd go to the washstand and roll up his sleeves. He'd scrub his face and arms with our homemade soap and dry himself with an old blue and white towel.

I'd tell him I made forty-nine dollars selling neckties. Or thirty-five dollars picking corn. Something silly. He'd say, "That's good money, Harry. Someday you'll make a lot more than that."

"Will I ever make a hundred dollars, Dad?"

"Yes, I expect you will."

"Really, Dad?"

"Sure, Harry. I bet you'll make a thousand, but you'll have to dress up in a suit and tie. And I know you don't like that very much." Then he'd laugh.

That wasn't going to happen today. Maybe it would never be like that again. As those thoughts sank in, my whole body hurt. I felt so low. At first, the idea of Dad joining the army was exciting, but it sure wasn't anymore. It was awful.

The rain began to fall gently, and then came down harder and harder. I slipped off the porch and crawled underneath where I could sit cross-legged in the half darkness. Cobwebs stuck to my face and hair, and sow bugs scurried around in the loose dirt. I spied bones scattered here and there where Buster had left them. Pretty soon he found me and crawled under the porch too. He put his head on my lap, and we sat there together watching the rain. I let the sad, lonesome feelings come down over me like thick, gray fuzz. I felt more alone than I'd ever felt in my life.

What would happen if Dad never came back? Or if he got killed? What if I had to stay here for my whole life? And my brothers. Ty and Gabe and Eddie. When would I see them again? I chewed on these unhappy notions for a long time, missing Dad, missing my brothers, until the rain finally began to let up. The squeal of the screen door spring interrupted my low feelings. I heard Gram's heavy tread on the porch boards above my head.

"Harry? Harry? Where are you?"

I crawled out from my hiding place. "Here, Gram."

"Just look at you. You're filthy."

I tried to brush myself off.

"Harry, I need you to take this jar over to Aunt Lida's and get some fresh milk. Mine has turned."

I took the jar, feeling a little relief to have something to do, and I set off walking the three blocks to my great-aunt's house. On the way I met a group of six or seven boys with their bikes in the middle of the road. One called out, "Hey, kid. What's your name?"

I stopped. They seemed big, older, a little threatening.

"Harry Spencer," I said.

"You live here? I ain't seen you before."

"I just came to live with my grandmother."

"How come? Where's your folks?" They moved closer to me, and one of them tried to grab the jar I was carrying. I pulled back.

"Don't," I said, fear making my voice weak.

"What's the jar for?"

"I have to get some milk."

"Oh, the little boy has to get some milk," one kid said in a taunting voice. "Little Harry needs his milk."

The others started saying, "Little Harry. Little Harry," in singsong voices.

The tallest boy came over to me. He shoved his face close to mine and said, "Who'd you say your folks were?"

"My dad's Calvin Spencer. He's in the army. My mother's dead." The others shut up when they heard that.

He said, "Your dad's in the army? How long's he been gone?"

"He just left yesterday."

His blue eyes bored into mine for a long minute. Then he said, "I'm Wes. My brother Clete joined up too. He left this week." He grinned. "You miss your dad?"

I nodded. He pointed at the other fellows and said, "This here's Billy, and that's Bucky. Over there is Don Beaubien and Skinny Nelson and his little brother."

I said, "Hi."

"Look here, Harry. We've got a clubhouse over back of Billy's barn. We meet there every afternoon to talk and plan things. You can come if you want to."

"Okay," I nodded. "Thanks."

"All right. Maybe we'll see you over there."

They climbed on their bicycles, and I watched them ride off. One of them called back, "So long, little Harry," but it didn't sound mean this time.

After that, I spent every minute that I could with those boys. Playing with them was like being with my brothers. Lots of fun and plenty of mischief. One time we caught ancient Betty Sykes's cat and put it yowling in a box on her front porch. Another time we tied a string to an old pocketbook and laid it on the main road. Then we hid in the tall grass in the ditch and waited for it to be spotted. When a driver got out to pick it up, we'd yank on the string, and the pocketbook would be gone before he could get to it.

These boys were tough and sure of themselves, and I wanted to be just like them. They had bicycles and fathers who took them fishing. And mothers. I'd never had a chance to know mine, 'cause she died when I was a baby. I yearned with my whole heart for all the things they had, but mostly for a house where our family could live together. What I remember today is how at night in bed I'd make up stories for myself and fall asleep dreaming I had everything they had.

It didn't take long before I got in trouble because of those boys. I gave myself a good scare too.

2

I T HAPPENED ON a sweltering day that summer. The boys were sitting around practicing their cussing and trying to smoke a pack of Lucky Strikes that Billy had filched from his father. It was daring and risky stuff when I was eight, and the others were eleven or twelve. They'd all had a few puffs when Wes said, "Let's go swimming in the Brule," and off they went, leaving me behind.

Every one of them had a bicycle except me, and I boiled with jealousy. I tore down the road after them, my bare feet afire from the sunbaked dirt and gravel, my lungs burning. They left me like that all the time, but today I'd made up my mind I wasn't going to be left behind anymore. Not this time or ever again if I could help it.

Panting and breathless, I broke through the willow trees that hung over the water, cloaking the swimming hole from the road. Cooler air hit my face, and I smelled the dampness. The pond was huge, the water dark and deep, and I wasn't supposed to be there.

Ever since we'd moved to South Dakota, my grandmother had warned me. "Don't ever let me catch you at Brule Creek, Harry. I'll tan your hide. The current's too fast, and whirlpools can suck you under. You hear?" Her eyes never left my face. "Your mother'd tell you the same thing if she were alive. You stay away from the Brule."

But here I was in spite of Gram's threat.

"Can you swim, Harry?" Wes asked.

"I dunno."

"Well, it's time you learned." He picked me up by my overall straps and threw me into the water before I had time to take a breath. I sank fast, and the cold rose up my pants leg to my crotch; the cold, cold flowed into my ears. Fear grabbed me hard when my mouth and nose filled with water. I couldn't breathe.

Just when I thought I couldn't stand it any longer, I came to the surface, choking, my arms thrashing. I snatched a quick breath before I went down once more, convinced I was drowning for sure. After another panicky time below, I bobbed up long enough to hear somebody yell, "Kick your feet, Harry, or you'll drown yourself." Well, I kicked like a crazy man, and, to my everlasting astonishment, my head stayed above water.

Breathless and coughing, I looked around and spied a branch hanging over the water. I aimed for it with no idea how to propel myself. Somehow, instinct took over, and I made it to the edge where I grabbed on to that stick for dear life. Oh, it was sweet to know I hadn't drowned! I hung there for a long time, catching my breath and giving my poor heart a chance to slow down.

The others had stripped down to their skivvies and were jumping and splashing, paying no attention to me. I was glad 'cause otherwise they might have been able to tell how scared I'd been. I dragged myself out of the water, my clothing heavy. I took off my wet overalls and laid them over a bush to dry. Gram would kill me for sure if I came home in wet clothes.

I sat in the sun for some time, warming myself, marveling that I'd been able to swim, or at least dog paddle. Then it dawned on me that I'd ended up on the bank opposite the path that led home. Terror gripped me again. I'd have to swim across the pond in order to get back. I watched the others cavort in the water. Maybe I could sneak across the creek upstream through the woods. Downstream it was all rocks and falls. Yet, in my heart I knew I had to swim back or the boys would think I was baby. They'd call me "Little Harry." I couldn't let that happen.

For some reason a conversation I overheard the night before popped into my head. Gram and Granddad were discussing the shaky finances at their grocery store. I wasn't paying much attention, but I heard Granddad say, "It looks like we'll either sink or swim this summer."

Gram said, "Well, let me tell you, Alfie. I have no intention of sinking. We're going to work hard. We'll persevere."

Persevere? I wasn't sure exactly what that meant, but I knew it was what I had to do. I'd swim back across that pond if it killed me. I felt resolve in my belly, and I wasn't so afraid this time. Wes carried my overalls over his head so they weren't quite so wet when we got to the other side. He even gave me a ride back to town on his bike. I knew I'd be in big trouble, but I didn't care. It was the first time I'd made myself do something that terrified me, and I was proud of it.

I waited as long as I could before going home for supper. My hair was still damp, and my pants were far from dry. I sat down with Granddad and my sister Polly at the big, round kitchen table, hoping Gram wouldn't notice my pant legs. She was at the black cook stove, dishing up our food. She came to the table and stood over us, holding a platter of golden fried catfish, her bulky figure wrapped in a spattered apron. My stomach reminded me how hungry I was, and I made to grab a big piece.

"Just a minute, Harry. Your hair is wet. Where have you been?" Gram started right away. "Did you go to the Brule? I've told you and told you to stay away from that place. You can't swim."

"Yes, ma'am."

"Is that where you were?"

"Yes, ma'am."

"I'm going to whip your backside."

"But, Gram. I can swim now. Good as anybody. I swam across that swimming hole twice."

Granddad laughed. "It's okay, Bess. A boy has to try it some time. He'd have done it sooner or later."

I was grateful to the beery-smelling old man, smiling his toothless grin, his devilish eyes fixed on me. He wasn't my true grandfather, but a little Frenchman Gram married after her first husband died. His name was Alphonse Didier. He played fiddle at the dance hall on Saturday nights and liked to tell stories that made me laugh even though Gram didn't always appreciate them.

Gram didn't let go of my disobedience as easily as Granddad. She decided that Polly and I could put our time to better use. "You kids can help out at the store," she said. "Take over when Granddad comes home to eat dinner." She hustled Polly and me across the big side yard of the house to their grocery store on the corner. A sign above the door said *Alphonse D. Didier, Proprietor.* The smell of coffee beans hit me the minute we walked in.

"Here, Harry, see if you can turn the crank on the coffee grinder," Gram said. "Polly, you can straighten out the produce bins. Get rid of the bad stuff."

I struggled, but I could turn the crank. Polly poked her fingers at the bins in the center of the room that held onions and potatoes. I could tell she didn't want to touch that stuff, but she had to do what Gram said.

The store was just one room with a yellow, linoleum-covered counter where the gold cash register sat. It had big, round number keys that were hard to push down. Tall windows faced the road on one side, and shelves for canned goods and baking supplies filled the other walls. A small oak icebox held cheese, eggs, and cold meat. Candy and cigarettes were arranged under the counter in a glass-front cabinet.

"Don't you kids get into the glass case, or let anybody else in there," Granddad said. "I keep it closed up so nobody can swipe cigarettes."

A door cut through one wall of the store opened into a windowless room with a bar and some stools. It was dark and smoky and smelled of beer—beer spilled on the floor, beer leaked from barrels, and beery belches from the men who gathered there. Ashtrays overflowed until Gram couldn't stand it anymore and emptied them. Underfoot we crunched on the shells of the peanuts Granddad provided.

"That bar will be the death of him. Or me," Gram would say because he enjoyed the bar more than he should. Gram would roust him out of bed in the morning to open the store. If one of his friends came in, like as not, they'd go into the bar and drink. If more friends came, he'd drink some more. At noon Gram would send Polly or me to the store, and he'd come home for dinner. Granddad's teeth were almost ruined from chewing tobacco, and it took him a long time to eat. Then, if he'd been drinking beer, he couldn't do much but sleep, so Gram would have to take over at the store. Or one of us would do it. Sometimes she forgot about me being there, and I stayed for the whole afternoon. Though I didn't realize it at the time, I got an education in that store. Over the years I worked there I learned how to put our best stuff forward, how to encourage folks to try new things, and how to smile and be polite even when people griped about the prices. I'd put it all to good use later on.

Ory Gabel, who was my Sunday school teacher, was a customer. He came in one day and wanted a few groceries. I could add up the prices and wrap the packages. I could even write up a bill for a charge account, but I didn't know how to make change for the five-dollar bill he gave me. There weren't any other customers so he said, "Would you like me to show you how, Harry?"

I was mortified, but I nodded.

"If somebody's bill is $4 and he gives you a five-dollar bill, how much change does he get?" I knew the answer, so he asked harder questions.

"What if the bill comes to $3.40 and he gives you a five? What if it's $7.42 and he gives you a ten?" When I got the right answer, he'd say, "That's great, Harry. You're a sharp boy." He taught me how to count the change into the customer's hand to make sure it was correct.

Between arithmetic problems, he talked about God. He said I was born to be a Christian warrior to help people find Jesus. I didn't know exactly what he meant, and I wished he'd leave that business alone. It embarrassed me, and I didn't have much of an answer for him.

I got my fill of Ory every week at Sunday school at the Methodist Church. And I had to attend church service with Gram. The preacher always prayed for "our boys overseas." He said about the same thing every Sunday, and I got so I didn't listen much until Gram's sister, Great-Aunt Lida, with her greenish stained false teeth, poked me on the shoulder and whispered that I should bow my head and pray for my dad. So I did. I also prayed for a bike.

3

I WAS DESPERATE FOR a bicycle of my own. I imagined myself riding with the boys, visiting the cave where they said Jessie James hung out. I just couldn't figure out how to get one. Once Dad sent me a dollar, and I hid it away to save for a bike. As I remember it now, it was the only dollar my dad ever gave me in my entire life.

Summer was half over when I found a comic book at the store with an ad for selling medicinal salve. Sell a hundred tins of Rawleigh's Antiseptic Salve for Man and Beast within one month and you'd win a free bicycle.

It was risky to send away for the salves without knowing if I could sell them, and I wondered what Dad would think. Dad had said he thought I'd make a lot of money someday. Maybe that was now. My plan was to comb my hair and go to every house in town and try to sell two tins—one for people and one for their animals. In a week I'd go back to see if they needed more.

Gram had a conniption when the package came. "What's this?" she said.

I explained I was going to sell salve and earn a bicycle.

"In a pig's eye! Who do you think is going to buy all this? One hundred cans? Who'll pay for this if you can't sell them?"

"Don't worry, Gram. I'm pretty sure I can sell them."

"Yes, but what happens if you can't? I'll tell you right now, I'm not going to pay for it."

I was scared silly at what I'd gotten into. Just the same, I stuck to my sales plan and started making the rounds, selling the cans for a dollar a piece.

I tried Mrs. Miranda Phelps first. I knew her from church and she was always nice to me.

"Hi," I said, my voice oddly stiff and high. The words poured out of me.

"I'm-selling-some-salve-and-if-I-sell-one-hundred-I-can-get-a-bike— it's-wonderful-salve-and-will-cure-everything."

"Oh, Harry," she said, laughing. "Take a breath." She put her arm around me and invited me to sit on her front step. "Now tell me all over again what this is. And don't forget to breathe!"

She made me say it twice. Then she bought one can and sent me on my way. I got much better at my sales talk, and by the end of the day I'd sold eight cans. Only ninety-two to go. I asked Gram to keep my money safe because I knew that she wouldn't let Polly or Granddad get into it.

After a week, I was down to forty-seven cans. By the end of the next week I was down to twenty-two. Then the going got rough. I had to go around to the same houses where I'd made my first sales to see if they needed more. Not many did. One old woman yelled, "Don't come around here again, or I'll take a switch to you."

I knew I was a pest, but I kept asking people to buy. Some did just to get rid of me. With only a week to go, I was down to eight tins. I'd worn out my welcome in town and had to try something new. I went over to the bar and worked on Granddad's drinking buddies.

Pug McCormick, who drove a chicken truck, usually came in the daytime. Polly and I had to time his visits 'cause, if he left the crates of live chickens in the sun too long, they'd die. Pug was an easy sell with bites and scratches all over his hands from the chickens. He bought two cans.

Squint Pickard was a half-witted old man, stumpy, with one eye that didn't open just right. He didn't need my salve any more than the man in the moon, but I told him how much better his feet would feel if he'd rub salve into them. He bought a can, and I felt guilty 'cause I knew he didn't have any money to spare.

Bill Nelson was there too. He said, "I don't have any cash on me, but if you come to the house Saturday afternoon, Jalmer and I'll buy some of your salve."

I was pretty sure he'd be as good as his word. Bill and Jalmer were bachelor brothers, and Granddad said their credit at the store was like gold. I wanted to ask how many they'd buy, but I didn't dare.

Now I was down to five cans, and my month for selling them was up on Monday. My body prickled all over in bed at night as I worried about losing the bike after all my work. I'd tried to sell to everybody in town. Except one. Gram. But I'd have rather sucked eggs than ask her to buy. I wanted to prove to her that I could do it, and I wanted that bike.

Saturday finally came, and I walked to the edge of town where the Nelson brothers lived. I was so scared I could hardly breathe for fear they wouldn't buy. Pretty soon I heard a hullabaloo coming from their place. A bunch of men were standing around some noisy machine yelling and laughing. Every so often a fluffy white glob flew into the air, and they whooped harder than ever.

Jal's face was red, and his eyes squeezed up with laughter. "Look at this, Harry. We're washing our clothes." Sure enough, their washing machine was sitting out in the yard, going like a son of a gun.

"The belt broke on the washer," he said, slapping his leg.

A steam threshing machine sat a few yards away, going full throttle. They'd hitched the belt of the thresher to the washing machine, making the washer spin so fast there were soapsuds shooting all over the yard. Everybody howled with laughter when a sock flew up with the suds in a big burst.

I wasn't a bit surprised to see Granddad there, laughing with the rest of them. Nobody loved a good time more than he did. When I walked up, he put his arm on my shoulder and grinned his gap-toothed grin. "What do you think of this, Harry?"

"Bill promised to buy some salve if I'd come out here today. Do you think he'll remember?" This was fun, but I had business to do.

"Just wait 'til things quiet down some. Then ask him," he said.

I saw a couple of farmers who, by the looks of their heads, had come to town this Saturday for haircuts. I ran up and gave my sales talk. They scarcely paid attention, but one gave me a dollar and stuck a can in his pocket. I approached two others, but they pushed me aside. One said, "Look out, kid. We wanna watch the action."

Then I saw old Walter Trometer and hesitated because I'd already sold a can to his wife. I asked him anyway, and I sure didn't remind him about his wife. He thought for a minute, then pulled out a dollar. Now I had only three cans to go. It seemed like a half a day before things settled down at that place. Finally, most everyone left, and I went up to Bill to see if he'd remembered.

"Harry, I gave you my word. Here's a buck." Bill took a can of salve and yawned. "Now I'm gonna have me a nap."

"What about Jalmer?" I said, my voice high as a girl's.

"I think he went up to Yankton with the Snyders," he called back through the screen door.

I stood in disbelief before the closed door. Jalmer was my very last chance, and he'd slipped away without my seeing him go. I clutched the bag with the two cans that I hadn't sold, never imagining I'd have to carry them home. How could this happen after all the weeks of my selling salve and telling everybody about the bike? I'd tried and tried, but it'd all come to nothing. I'd have to admit to my friends I wasn't going to get one. My face squeezed up as I started for home, and I had to bite the insides of my cheeks to keep from bawling. Sweat ran down my neck, and I wiped it away with a grimy hand.

I could picture Gram standing over me with her "I told you so" face. I kicked at the dirt in the road, sending up whorls of dust over my pant legs. I didn't want to face her yet, so I headed over to the store.

Noisy laughter poured from the bar, and I heard Granddad telling a big story about the Nelsons and their washing machine. I slunk behind the counter in my misery and sat down on a stool we kept back there, grateful there were no customers.

A few minutes later Granddad stepped out of the bar and saw me. "Harry. Get me a couple dollars worth of dimes and nickels, will you? So I can make change for these fellas." He turned and went back inside the bar.

I opened the till, counted out the coins he wanted, and took them to him. When I came back, the thick stack of bills in the drawer I'd left hanging open spoke to me. Without even forming a thought about it, I reached into the till, took two dollars, and slammed the cash drawer shut. The bills went into my pocket with the rest of my money, and the two unsold cans of salve went under the counter.

My heart thumped against my chest, and my palms got sweaty. I was shocked at myself. I was a thief! I'd stolen money. Gram always said there was nothing worse than a thief. I should put the bills back right now before I got caught. But I couldn't do it. I wanted a bike that much.

"DID YOU SELL all your salve?" Gram asked the minute I got home. I nodded. "Well, you sure don't seem very thrilled about it."

"I'm just tired, I guess." I bent over and tied my shoelace to avoid looking at her. I wondered if she could tell what I'd done.

"Hmph." She waited like she expected me to say more, then something boiled over on the stove, and she went back to it.

I was miserable the rest of the day. I wished I'd never thought about a bicycle. That evening Granddad and Polly cheered and patted me on the back for my success.

Gram said, "I didn't think you could do it, Harry, but you sure showed me."

"You're quite a boy, Harry. A real go-getter," Granddad said.

I pretended to be excited, but shame made my heart heavy as stone. Guilt burned through me, but I couldn't think of a way to give the money back. And the truth was, I didn't want to.

On Monday morning, Gram helped me get a money order for one hundred dollars for the Rawleigh Company, and we sent it off. She smiled and said, "Looks like you're gonna have a bike, Harry." I felt myself let go a little, still not quite believing the ordeal was over.

That afternoon Polly came running into the house after spelling Granddad at dinner. "What are these?" she said, waving my bag with the salves. "I thought you sold them all, Harry."

"Those are mine," I yelled, grabbing at the bag. "What are you doing with them?"

"I found them under the counter."

"Give them to me," I screamed even though I knew I was caught.

"What's going on here?" Gram hustled over. "What's this? Didn't you sell them, Harry?"

My face heated up, and the tears I had choked back the other day now burst out. She grabbed the front of my shirt. "What's wrong with you, Harry? What did you do?"

I sobbed and sobbed, tears sopping my shirt, my nose running, and I couldn't speak.

"I want to hear it, Harry. Right now." She shook me until I choked out a few words.

"No...nobody wanted them."

"Now you stop this crying. Right now! What are you talking about?"

Of course the dreadful truth had to come out, how I thought I could sell all the cans, and when I couldn't, how I'd taken two dollars from the till and pretended I'd earned it. How I let us mail in the money order and all the rest.

Gram sent Polly outside and sat me down at the kitchen table. Her black eyes were as sharp and mean looking as an eagle I'd seen once. I was terrified.

"I thought you were an honest boy, Harry. Someone I could trust. This makes me mad. Stealing from your own family. What would your dad say? Answer me. What would he say?"

I cried louder, trying to talk. "I dunno." I choked. "He...he'd say I was bad." It hurt so to picture Dad's face twisted up with disappointment in me.

She went after me a long time, and my crying finally slowed down. The thing I remember most was when she said, "Listen to me, Harry. Of all the people in the world to hurt, you don't ever want to hurt your own family members. You only get one set of them in this world, and you better treat 'em right."

Then she marched me over to the store and made me tell Granddad I had stolen money from him. It was humiliating, my eyes swollen from crying and people staring. I whispered my wickedness to him as softly as I could. He said, "Aw, Harry, you could've asked me for the money, and I probably would have given it to you. You didn't have to swipe it." His kindness made me start crying all over again.

Gram said, "Go on home, Harry, and don't you dare leave the house. I'll deal with you later."

FOR THREE WEEKS I washed dishes, pumped water, swept the floor, and pulled weeds in Gram's garden. She wouldn't let me spend time with the other boys in the afternoons, and if I slacked off on the chores, she said she might sell my bike when it came. I earned those two dollars back and then some, but I didn't complain. I'd done something I wasn't proud of, and in my heart I wanted to make it right.

Toward the end of August, my ninth birthday came and went without much notice. The leaves had just begun to fall and school would start soon. Granddad came home for dinner one noon and said, "Harry, go outside and sweep the leaves off the porch, will you?"

"I'm hungry, Granddad. Can't I eat first?"

"No. You go on and do it now."

I went out, slamming the door, and started to sweep, my head bowed over my work. When I raised my eyes, I froze and couldn't do anything but stare. A thrill started in my fingers and shot through me until my whole body tingled. Then I let out a holler they could've heard in the next state. My bike! Dark green with steel wheels and spokes, shiny handlebars, and a horn. I don't think I ever ate dinner that day. Granddad came out on the porch to watch me ride and stood proud as a little banty rooster, his felt hat cocked to the side, and a grin spread over his face. Even Gram came outside in her apron to watch. I rode all over town so folks could see that I finally got my bike. I just wished my dad could see it. I think he would have been proud, though its glory was always a little tarnished for me by what I had done to get it.

It didn't take long for all the boys to hear about it. Every one of them wanted to ride it, to honk the horn, and feel its sleek paint. I let them each have one turn. After that we did trades. A stick of gum was good for three blocks; a nickel for a ride to the school and back. They soon had enough of that and I was glad. I wanted that green beauty for myself.

4

THE TOWN WHERE I spent my childhood was called Richmond after the man who founded it, and it was an apt name. The land is flat, with deep, black soil left by a millennium of silt deposits from the flooding river; yet just to the north, less than half mile away, stands one of the geographical wonders of the world—the Loess Hills. These high bluffs, overlooking the Sioux and the Missouri rivers all the way to Council Bluffs, are formed of silt and clay and they erode into shelf-like formations of great natural beauty.

According to Aunt Lida, who knew everything there was to know about it, the town had ninety-five houses, one church, one school, and our store. In spite of the town's name, Granddad liked to say, "Nobody in Richmond is really rich 'cause nobody has enough money to be rich." Then he'd cackle at his joke, even if no one else thought it was funny. The great thing about Granddad was that I didn't have to understand his jokes for him to make me laugh.

I entered the Richmond school that September in the fourth grade. It was a country school and had only two rooms with grades one through four on one side and grades five through eight on the other. A wide hallway separated them. The two teachers left the doors open so they could go back and forth across the hall. Mrs. Sawyer taught reading, spelling, and penmanship. Miss Foster taught arithmetic and geography. They both taught current events. The war was always on everybody's mind, but even we kids heard talk around town about Prohibition. Miss Foster decided we should learn about it, as she said, the "right way."

A group called the Women's Christian Temperance Union invaded our school. I knew what all those words meant except for "temperance," which I figured related to your temper—being mad about something. These women came in their feathery, flowered hats and took right over. They were mad, all right. They talked about how wicked it was to drink alcohol and how we must never do it and how we must talk to our parents so they wouldn't do it either. They blabbed on and on, handing out pamphlets for us to take home and looking us right in the eye so we couldn't escape swearing we'd never taste the stuff. I wondered if they knew we sold beer in our store. They'd have had a conniption if they knew I sometimes served it to customers. You better believe I didn't say anything about it.

After all that, they invited Gladys Welles, who was an eighth grader, to give a speech about drinking. She'd won an oratory prize at the county contest; so we had to listen to this sappy girl go on. She waved her hands and rolled her eyes. At the end, she pulled a wine glass from her pocket, raised it high, and smashed it on the floor saying, "I've never touched a drop, and I never will." Some of us squirmed, but the feathery ladies clapped and clapped. Wes made the mistake of laughing out loud, so the teachers had him sweep up the broken glass. I was glad I kept quiet.

At home my grandparents talked a lot about Prohibition. Gram said, "There's a big argument coming. The 'dries' want to get rid of alcohol entirely. That Mr. Holsapple up in Mitchell with the Anti-Saloon League wants to close all the saloons. Make South Dakota bone-dry."

"That'll be the day," Granddad said. "What do they want to do? Put me out of business?"

"They think drinking causes too much trouble, Alfie. Men spend all their money on it; their kids go hungry; and all the rest."

"Aw. A little beer never hurt anyone, Bess." He was grouchy about it all evening.

Even my Sunday school teacher, Ory Gabel, talked about the evils of drink. I told him I didn't think he needed to worry much about us. We were only in the fourth grade.

"You're never too young to take the pledge," he said.

ONE DAY MRS. Sawyer, whose own boy was in the army, asked how many had family members serving, and I raised my hand proudly along with a couple of others.

"If anyone has letters they'd like to share, please bring them so we can learn more about what it's like over there."

I wanted everyone to hear how my dad got wounded. Gram wasn't so sure Dad would've wanted me to have others read it, but I begged and pestered her until she let me take his letter to school. I read it to the class.

> *Dear Family,*
>
> *Well my good luck finally came to an end a few days ago. I took a lousy German bullet in my right arm. It didn't do too much damage, but I can't shoot, so I'm behind the lines sitting around while it heals, and I can write a little. At least I'm satisfied that I caused the enemy some trouble before I got hit.*
>
> *So many men were taken in this battle it turns my stomach. But it's even worse to see the injured fellows. Missing their arms or legs, blood everywhere. The smell is terrible. I'm alive and I suppose I should be grateful for that. Sometimes I don't know. I just hope this thing ends soon.*
>
> *Your father,*
> *Calvin Spencer*
> *Somewhere in France*

Everyone sat big-eyed and quiet after I read, and Mrs. Sawyer smiled kindly at me. "Your father must be a brave man, Harry. You should be proud of him, making this sacrifice for us."

I nodded, awed and proud. I wanted my dad home, but his glory had touched me, and I liked the feeling.

DAD HAD BEEN gone nearly nine months when Uncle Lyle surprised us one day by coming to visit. He had a telegram from the army that said dad's arm wound wasn't healing right, so they were sending him home. I couldn't get my head around this big news for a minute, but oh boy, when I did, I could feel the goose bumps come out. Dad was coming home! Now we'd have a house and live together like we used to. We'd talk to him about hunting and fishing, and all the other stuff. I would show him my bike and tell him how I got it. And he would tell us what it was like to fight the Germans. I would be able to play with my brothers. Everything would be all right again.

Gram slicked us up so we could go to the train station. She pulled Polly's hair back and tied it with a big bow, and she found a necktie for me to wear with my Sunday shirt and pants. Uncle Lyle and Aunt Hazel came with my three brothers, Eddie, the oldest, Gabe, and Ty. We hadn't seen each other for quite a while, and everyone seemed bigger. I guess we were excited, because we just danced around in the yard, punching each other on the shoulder, so wound up we couldn't stand still.

"Stop that," Gram yelled. "You're going to get your clothes dirty." But we just couldn't.

When it was time to go, we piled into the back end of Uncle Lyle's truck for the ride to Beaverton, shivering with the cold and huddled together for the ten-mile trip.

At the railroad depot all of us jumped out and stood on the brick platform, jabbering while we waited. Uncle Lyle and Aunt Hazel sat on the black iron benches, but we were too excited to sit.

"I bet I see him first," Ty said.

"No, you won't. I'm taller," said Eddie.

Polly thought Dad would get us a house right away. "We'll need at least three bedrooms, one just for me."

"You can't have a room by yourself," Gabe said. "You'll just spend all day in there combing your hair." She pinched him.

We were all grins and happy teasing. At last we heard the train whistle and its mighty roar as it pulled into the station, steam making a cloud around the hot engine and the smell of burning coal coming from the smokestack.

"I'll bet he'll try to hug all of us at once, just like he used to," I said.

The passengers began to step down from the train. First came some women who'd been shopping, and they were all mixed up about whose bags were whose. It took them several long minutes to get everything sorted out. Next came two men in uniforms. My heart gave a jolt, but neither one was Dad. The men's wives rushed up to them with hugs and kisses, and the other passengers had to wait until that was over. Then there was a tottery old couple who walked like every step took them closer to the grave. Finally they got out of the way, and Dad appeared. He stood on the top step a moment, pale and thin, the last person off. The porter set his bags on the ground, and Dad stepped down and looked around like he wasn't too sure where he was.

We ran to him yelling, "Dad! Dad! Here we are."

I thought he'd throw his arms around us. Instead, he put his left arm out straight and laid his hand on my shoulder. The others stopped dead in their tracks, puzzled by this strange behavior. He extended his left hand to each of us in turn and shook our hands. That's when I noticed that his right sleeve was pinned up.

Eddie said, "Dad, your arm."

"Gone." It was the first word he had uttered to us since he went away.

Our aunt and uncle came up to him all smiles.

"Lyle. Hazel." He nodded soberly to them and extended his hand to Uncle Lyle for that strange handshake. I saw their faces change, their smiles fold up and disappear when they noticed his sleeve.

"My God, Cal. We…we didn't know about…" Uncle Lyle's words trailed off. "You should have told us."

"It got infected."

Aunt Hazel hesitated a sad minute while she took it in. Finally she reached up and kissed his cheek. "I'm so sorry, Cal. I'm just glad you're home."

I stared stunned at Dad's sleeve. I wondered what was inside. He looked so white and strange, his hair cut off short. I'd never seen him so serious. Uncle Lyle said, "Get his bags, boys," and motioned for us to leave. Gabe and Eddie raced to grab them, and we headed for the pickup, no one saying a word. I felt like somebody had hit me in the stomach, and I'd gone all hollow and empty inside. I couldn't figure it out. Dad's arm was gone, and it seemed like he didn't care about us anymore.

Once more we got into the truck. Dad rode in the cab with our aunt and uncle. We crowded together and peered through the window. I guess we just wanted to look at him, to see if he was talking to them, and to imagine what he was saying. But we couldn't tell much.

When we got home, Gram and Granddad greeted us full of smiles and big hellos, but that changed fast when they saw our serious faces and Dad's arm. Aunt Hazel took Gram aside and whispered to her, and then she helped lay out fried chicken, mashed potatoes and gravy, tender new lettuce dressed with cream and sugar, and rhubarb custard pie, always Dad's favorite.

Folks tried to talk, but their sentences came out in jerky lumps. Sometimes there were several minutes of silence. They mentioned others from Richmond who were in the army, how the war was going, the weather, crops, anything they could think of, but Dad just sat eating his food with his left hand.

Polly sat next to him. She looked up at him, grinning. "I'm in seventh grade now, Dad." He just nodded. She flushed and stared at her plate.

Gram said, "Well, Cal. Do you have any idea what you are going to do now?"

He looked up from his food and said, "Maybe I'll try to find a job, one a cripple can handle, I guess."

"Do you still have your cut-off arm, Dad?" I blurted out without thinking. Eddie poked my ribs hard.

Dad glared at me. After a long minute he said, "No. Of course not. Why would I?"

My face heated up and my mouth went dry.

He said, "I expect it got dumped onto a pile of body parts with all the others that got shot up."

I could feel everyone around the table squirm and go silent. I hated myself for asking such a stupid question. I thought he was done talking, but he went on.

"They put the whole mess into a hole in the ground, and they burned them." He shuddered, laid his fork down and put his hand on his knee.

Gram jumped up and said, "Polly, help me clear the table. Harry, why don't you show your brothers your bike?"

We stood up and started to go outside. Dad stood too. He reached in his pocket, and silently handed Gram a hundred-dollar bill. I just knew, when I saw it happen, that he was going to leave again, and he wasn't going to take me with him. Sure enough, he went outside and got into the truck. We boys went to the shed, but grand as my bicycle was, nobody said much.

"What's going on? What's going to happen?" I asked Eddie.

"I don't know."

"He's so quiet," Gabe said.

We stared at my bike. "It looks great," Ty said. But none of them even felt like riding it. My brothers soon followed Dad to the truck.

Aunt Hazel and Uncle Lyle said their goodbyes, and I stood with Gram and Polly and watched them drive away.

"Gram, what's the matter with him?" I asked. "Why is he acting so strange? I didn't get to show him my bike. Why couldn't we go with him? He didn't even say goodbye." The tears started and I couldn't make them stop.

Polly stood sniffling, her eyes still bugged out from the dreadfulness of it all. "Why doesn't he like us anymore?"

Gram said, "Listen, kids. I think your dad is just plain shell-shocked. He lost his arm and he isn't over it yet. He's going to stay with your aunt and uncle for a while 'cause he needs to rest. Then maybe he'll seem like himself again."

"But I want to see him. We could take care of him. I want him to get us a house," I cried.

5

MONTHS WENT BY and finally a year, but Dad didn't get it sorted out. We never got a house, and Polly and I didn't see him much. I was sick inside for a long time because I wanted him so much. I'd always daydreamed about my mother, imagining her hugging me and telling me I was a fine boy, but I could let go of that because I had a father. Now I didn't have him either. While he was overseas, I'd told myself everything would be all right when he got back, but nothing was right, and I didn't know what to do. I longed more than anything for my family. Those feelings of being alone and abandoned are probably the reason I wanted kids and in-laws and all the rest when I got older. I imagined big holiday celebrations and birthday parties with aunts and uncles and cousins to make up for all the lonely times I had as a child. Sometimes the kids at school asked me if I was an orphan. That made me so mad that one time I socked Billy Snyder in the eye. I was mad at my dad too. Why didn't he act right? Why didn't he take care of us?

Mrs. Sawyer hauled me in after school for that business with Billy, but she seemed to know how I felt. "Your dad was your hero, wasn't he, Harry?"

I nodded. "He used to be. Before the war."

"You'll have to be extra strong, Harry, until he gets over his shell shock."

She was right. Dad had been my hero, and now I didn't have him anymore. I just wanted him to be like he used to be. I imagined sitting beside him and having him put his good arm around me and telling me things I needed to know. It didn't matter if he was missing an arm. I thought about him every night when I went to bed and tried my darnedest to stop feeling bad about him. I had to make myself stop thinking about him. It was hard, but I got so I could almost do it. Except that when I least expected it, he would pop into my head, and the hurt would start all over again. It took me a long time to realize that things weren't going to work out the way I wanted, and that I was going to have to grow up and live my life without him.

Dad stayed on with our uncle and aunt, so Polly and I remained at Gram's house in Richmond. As a fifth-grader, I moved into the school-room with the older students. Polly was in the eighth grade. I had friends at school, but still I was lonely a lot. I was glad we had Buster, a big, brown fellow with those soft black ears. He followed me everywhere. I loved him so much; sometimes he seemed like the best friend I had.

A STRANGE THING happened that year. I don't know how it started, but I found myself noticing girls. I'd never liked girls at all, and still didn't, but I began to pay some attention. Polly had gotten tits and her chest pushed out. At first she seemed embarrassed; then I think she started to feel a little proud. She'd sashay up the aisle to the blackboard or the teacher's desk, and the boys would grin and poke each other. I didn't like that much, but I noticed some of the other girls were chang-ing too. I looked at them plenty, but didn't say a word, not even to my buddies.

Mid-year a new girl came to our school. Carol Ann Bellwood wore her long, yellow hair in sausage-shaped curls with a ribbon tied on top of her head. The ribbons changed color every day to match her dress. Her eyes were blue and all sparkly when she smiled. Everybody liked

Carol Ann, and I thought she was the prettiest thing I'd ever seen. The other boys, even the older ones, thought so too.

In my imagination I talked to Carol Ann. I pretended she would tell me what a good ball player I was or notice when I got the answers right on an arithmetic paper. I would admire the picture she painted of her pet kitten. None of that ever happened. For some reason I couldn't think of anything to say when she looked my way, so I did dumb stuff like throwing a paper wad at her or bumping her desk to mess up her penmanship. I wanted her attention, and I got it, but mostly she just got irked at me. Sometimes I sat next to her when we changed seats for spelling class because she smelled so soapy and clean, though I always made it seem accidental.

One day we played a game of tag at recess, and I snagged her hair ribbon and pulled her hair.

"You are the meanest boy," she said as she tried to grab the ribbon from me.

Keeping it from her was great fun, but instead of staying at it, she said, "Come on, girls. Let's don't play with them anymore. They're too rough." Of course they all followed her to the other side of the playground.

That left me standing there holding the stupid ribbon. "I guess we got rid of those sissies," I said to the boys. But I hadn't meant that to happen. I dumped the ribbon in the trash.

After that, I was surprised when I got an invitation to her birthday party. It came in the mail, so Gram and Polly saw it before I did.

"Harry's got a girlfriend," Polly said in a singsong voice.

"I do not," I protested.

"You gonna get her a present, Harry? For your girlfriend?" Polly just wouldn't give up. It made me squirm.

I'd never been to a birthday party, but I wasn't going to miss this one for anything. Polly said I should take present. What could I get her? No money. No place to buy anything in this town. I had to make a plan.

I went to see Great-Aunt Lida. I told her I was interested in making some money and did she need any odd jobs done.

She said, "Why do you need the money, Harry?"

"I…I'd like to buy some new Sunday clothes to wear to church," I lied. I didn't like to lie, but I couldn't bring myself to tell her that I wanted to buy a present for a girl.

She seemed pleased. Anybody interested in church was in her good graces.

"My windows need washing. Do you think you could do that?"

I began counting up in my head the number of windows in her house. She had a big porch and had replaced the screens with windows so she could use the room all year. I started seeing dollar signs.

"I'll do it," I said, "for ten cents a window."

She narrowed her eyes at me. "Inside and out?"

I sighed. "Yes, ma'am. I'll start tomorrow after school."

It took three afternoons and about killed me, but I washed thirty windows and collected my three dollars. Now I had to figure out a way to get to town so I could buy Carol Ann a present.

Lots of folks went to Beaverton on Saturday night. All the stores stayed open so people could shop. We didn't go 'cause our own store had to stay open. If I wanted to buy Carol Ann a gift, I'd have to get a ride with someone. I started hanging around Bobby Granholm. He was kind of a pantywaist and not my favorite, but he was flattered when I suggested we play ball.

"Are you going to town tomorrow night?" I asked him after a long session of playing catch and him missing the ball half the time.

"Yeah, probably. We usually do."

"S'pose I could ride along?"

"Sure. I'll ask Ma."

Mrs. Granholm was so tickled that Bobby had me for a friend that she fell all over herself inviting me along for the trip. She even got permission from Gram.

I was nervous all the way to town, embarrassed to buy a present for a girl. It was silly to be so squirmy about picking out a gift in front of Bobby or his mother, but I couldn't help myself. I had to think of a way to ditch them for a few minutes.

We went to the variety store, and Bobby stuck to me like syrup on pancakes. We looked around for a long time, but I didn't see anything that would do for Carol Ann. I was beginning to panic. If I couldn't find something pretty soon, I was in trouble.

"Bobby," said Mrs. Granholm, "I think we ought to see if we can find some new shoes for you. They're on sale this week."

"Oh, Mom. We wanted to look at the baseball gloves and stuff."

"There'll still be time, dear. I think we'd better take this opportunity to save a little money while we can."

I was relieved and said, "It's okay, Bobby. I'll just look around while you try on shoes."

As soon as they went on their way, I started covering those aisles lickety-split. I saw piles of clothing, men's overalls and hats, women's purses and shoes. In the household section were frying pans and rolling pins. I fiddled for a minute with an apple corer, but that didn't seem right. Somehow I got into the sewing section and meant to leave in a hurry, but I saw rolls and rolls of ribbon. That would be it! I had ruined her hair ribbon, so I would get her a replacement. I bought a yard of wide yellow satin ribbon and a yard of narrow blue lacey stuff. The clerk rolled them up, and I managed to get them into my pocket before I met up with Bobby. I felt a huge surge of relief now that the gift business was settled, and I was ready to enjoy the rest of my night in town. We tried out baseball gloves and looked at fishing equipment. I didn't have to pay attention to girl stuff anymore, and I even liked Bobby better. He and I bought some wax candies with nectar inside and walked down the street chewing the sweet wax. At the last minute I decided I had enough money to buy myself a shirt for Sunday school. That would erase my lie to Aunt Lida.

ON SUNDAY, I cleaned up for church. Polly did her best to smooth out the cowlicks in my coarse hair. I put on my new shirt and tried to stay neat until Carol Ann's party. I walked to her house that afternoon nervous because I didn't know what to expect. It turned out to be fun. We played games—pin the tail on the donkey, musical chairs, and tag. Then it was time for Carol Ann to open her presents.

Her mother had put a big, blue-checked tablecloth on the picnic table in the backyard and stacked up the presents in front of Carol Ann. As she started to open them, my hands began to sweat. I'd pictured her smiling at me and "oohing" and "aahing" over the pretty ribbons, but now I was uncertain and worried about my present. All the others were wrapped with fancy paper and ribbon, even the ones from boys. Mine was in a plain white envelope. She got lacy handkerchiefs, bath oil, a set of watercolors, all kinds of girl stuff. My present seemed silly and cheap. I knew she would hate it and think I was a dunce. I got more and more nervous and could hardly sit still. When she reached for my envelope, I couldn't stand it anymore. I jumped up from the table and ran toward the front yard, around the house, and down the street for several blocks.

It felt good to run, but it didn't take me long to realize I was going to look like a complete fool to everybody. Maybe I should just go on home and forget about the party. Then I remembered the ice cream and chocolate birthday cake, so I headed back. By the time I got there, everybody was singing "Happy Birthday," and Mrs. Bellwood was serving the cake. I slipped into my place, and nobody noticed that I'd been away. I was sure glad. I spooned up some cake with fudge frosting and vanilla ice cream and forgot about the darned present.

When the party started to break up, Carol Ann came over to me and touched my arm. "I saw you leave, Harry. Why did you do that? I didn't get a chance to thank you for the hair ribbons." She smiled, and I felt my insides squeeze up. I sure couldn't tell her why I left.

"I think they're beautiful, and I can't wait to wear them."

I could only mumble. "You do? I...I didn't know what to get you." Another one of my dumb conversations, but this time it was real, not pretend.

"It was very thoughtful of you. I don't know which one I'll wear first." She played with them, looping them around her hair and twirling.

"I...I'm glad you liked them," I didn't want to leave, but I couldn't just stand there and stare, so I pulled myself away, figuring maybe she didn't hate me after all. In fact, I think she kind of liked me, and I thought she was the most wonderful girl in the world. I turned around as I walked away and looked back at her. She smiled and waved.

I GOT HOME just in time to say goodbye to Uncle Lyle and Aunt Hazel who had stopped in to see Gram that afternoon.

"Well, Harry. It looks like your dad will soon be living here in town."

My heart soared. "What? Right here in Richmond?" I could scarcely believe it. I would have my dad here where I could see him and talk to him. I was overjoyed.

"Yes. Your Uncle Lyle thinks it would help your dad to be around people. They think he's too isolated on the farm. He never goes anywhere, never sees anyone, and they don't think it's healthy for him. Besides, Hazel is going to have a baby after waiting all these years, so that's part of it too."

"Where will he live, Gram? Here? With us?"

"No, not here. There's not enough room. I'm going to see Sally McVay at her boarding house tomorrow. She usually has a room or two for rent."

"Does Dad know about this?

"Your Uncle Lyle is going to talk to him tonight," she said.

"Will it make him mad, do you think? To have people deciding these things for him?"

"Oh, I think Lyle will handle it well. Who knows? Maybe Cal would just as soon be living somewhere else."

I was thrilled. Surely my dad would start acting like himself and would care about us again. I ran to the store to find my sister.

"Polly, Polly. Guess what? Dad's going to move here to Richmond."

She was as stunned as I was. Her big black eyes bugged out as she stared at me and took in the news.

"We're going to get our dad back. I just can't wait. Isn't it terrific?" I expected her to be as thrilled as I was, but she was quiet for a moment.

"I feel like I've just gotten used to him being away," she said. "It hasn't been much fun to be around him since the war, the way he is. He's not like he used to be."

I hadn't really thought about that until she said it. My stomach, full of cake and ice cream, knotted up. What if he didn't change? What if he stayed so far off and uninterested in us? I didn't know if I could stand it to be around him every day and have him be so strange.

All that evening I went back and forth between relief and happiness that my father soon would be nearby, and then I'd think of Polly's words, and worry that things might not turn out so well after all.

I said to Gram, "How do you think it'll be with Dad here in Richmond?"

"Well, you shouldn't get your hopes up too high, Harry. He's not over this thing yet. It took your grandfather Preston a long time to get over all the ugliness in the Civil War, and he wasn't even wounded. He was just fifteen when he signed up, and he saw way too much death and destruction. It affects people. It may take your dad a while longer to recover."

THE NEXT DAY Gram and I walked out to Sally McVay's with Buster tagging along. The house was the nearest thing our town had to a mansion. It was a huge two-story affair with wide porches around three sides. There were apple and plum trees and a grape arbor out back, and we sometimes snitched fruit there. If Sally knew, she didn't seem to mind.

One of our schoolteachers, Miss Foster, stayed there. Sometimes families sent their overflow company when there was a wedding or a funeral, and occasionally Sally would rent to a traveling salesman.

Sally met us on the front porch and invited us in. She was a round, sweet-faced Irish woman who laughed and smiled a lot. Everybody in town knew her and loved her. While she and Gram discussed arrangements for Dad's board and room, I looked around at the high ceilings and golden oak woodwork everywhere. The doors even had crystal knobs. I thought Dad was lucky to live in such a house.

As we walked home I asked, "Does Sally have a husband?"

"No," Gram said. "I've heard there was somebody years ago, but it didn't work out. I don't know why, 'cause she'd make a good wife for somebody."

UNCLE LYLE BROUGHT Dad and his belongings to Richmond a few days later. When they pulled up in front of our house. Granddad greeted them, "Welcome back to Richmond, Cal. How're you feeling?"

"I feel like hell. What were you expecting?" Dad's wild hair had grown out and hung down over his ears. He stared straight ahead and made no move to get out of the truck.

Granddad didn't give up. "Bess just made some coffee. You want a cup?"

"No," Dad said. "I don't want anything."

His voice was ugly. I tried to figure out what he thought about this move. It didn't look good. Silent and afraid, Polly and I climbed into the back end of the truck and rode to Sally McVay's.

As we got out, I heard Lyle say, "Why'd you treat Alfie like that, Cal? He was just being friendly."

"I dunno. When I see him and remember he's a Frenchman, I get mad. He's just like them over there. They don't think about anything except having a good time and drinking wine. Only difference is that Alfie drinks beer. I hated the Germans, but they'd fight. Damn Frogs let the Yanks do their fighting."

"For God's sake, Cal. Alfie's lived in America since he was two years old. He and Bess have taken in your kids and given them a place to live. How can you talk like that?"

Dad said nothing. He watched as we hauled in his suitcase and a few boxes of things. His room was on the east end of the house next to the kitchen. It was like a sunroom, cheerful because of the big windows that faced the garden. The bed was made up and looked clean enough to please even Gram. Polly and I started unpacking his things, but Dad said, "I can do that myself. Leave it." So we stood back, feeling useless.

As Uncle Lyle started to leave, Dad snarled at him, "Is Sally a damn Catholic?"

Uncle Lyle said, "I guess so. That doesn't make any difference, does it, Cal?"

Dad snatched the crucifix hanging over the bed and shoved it into a dresser drawer. "I don't want to look at that thing," he said, his face an angry scowl. "At least Sally isn't French."

Lyle looked shocked. "You better get over it, Cal. You've got to live in this

world. You've got to get along with people."

Dad glared. "The hell I do."

Lyle threw up his hands, turned around and walked out. I didn't know what to do, so I said, "Do you want a glass of water or anything?"

"No. I don't. You can go now."

He stood awkwardly as if uncertain what he wanted. Polly said, "Why don't you sit in the rocker, Dad? It looks comfortable."

"I will. I will." He turned his back to us and stared out the window, so we crept out and went home not very happy.

"Well, at least we don't have to spend every minute with him," said Polly.

I nodded, but I was dejected and heartsick. Why did Dad hate Granddad, of all people, just because he was French? Or Sally because she was Catholic? I went outside to play with Buster for a while. He licked my hands and face, and that always made me feel better. I knew he cared about me.

6

DAD MADE ARRANGEMENTS with Gram to do his washing and ironing every week. For this he paid her twenty-five cents. Early on Monday morning, I'd hop on my bike and go to the boarding house to pick up Dad's dirty clothes. Often he'd place his laundry bag on the porch, and I wouldn't even see him. On Wednesday I would return with the fresh batch, the shirts starched and ironed to a fare-thee-well with the right sleeves folded up and fastened with a safety pin. He couldn't very well avoid me when I delivered the clean things. I usually found him in his room reading a magazine or newspaper. He'd say, "Just put them there, Harry," and go on reading.

I ached to talk to him, but I couldn't think of anything to say that interested him. One day I found myself whistling "Yankee Doodle" as I rode to his place. When I got inside I put down his clothes, and he handed me a quarter for Gram.

"Dad, do you remember how you tried to teach me to whistle when I was little?" He looked up. "Just listen to this," and I let forth with my best effort. He watched and listened to the whole thing and then stared at me when I was finished, his face expressionless. Finally he nodded and said, "Not bad, Harry," and went back to his reading.

I was thrilled. It was the first time he had paid attention to me for anything. Usually he made me feel like I was someone he didn't know very well. The moment didn't last long, but I thought it was a start.

I told Gram, "Dad liked my whistling. He said it wasn't bad!"

"Maybe you're making progress with him, Harry."

She took the quarter from me and tucked it into her rainy day jar without ever offering me anything for my efforts. It grated that she never paid me for my part in keeping Dad in clean clothes. I never had any money, and I was impatient to become rich. But that was the way she was.

The Monday-Wednesday routine continued all summer. Dad rarely said much to me and didn't seem to care about hearing me whistle any more. Yet one day I found him sitting in a rocker on the front porch with Sally McVay. She always greeted me with a big hello, and today was no different.

"Your dad's been helping me in the garden picking the everlasting beans. I thought we needed a rest."

"That's what Gram has had me doing too." I smiled at him. "Gets tiresome, doesn't it?"

He nodded, looking almost cheerful. "It feels good to be outside doing something useful."

He reached in his pocket for the quarter for Gram and, instead, fished out another coin. It looked like a quarter but it had a hole right in the center of it.

"What's that?" I asked.

"That, son, is a souvenir from the day I drove a spike through the Kaiser's head."

"What?" I couldn't imagine what he was talking about.

He went on. "I was out on a detail to pick up the fallen after a battle. We found a German soldier, just a boy really. How he got so close to our lines was a mystery, but we loaded him onto the wagon just like the others. When I lifted him up, some coins fell out of his pants pocket. I picked up this one and saved it."

He stared at the coin like it had a secret message on it. At last he said, "I looked at that boy's face and my blood boiled."

"You mean because he got so close to your lines?"

"No. I got mad at the high and mighty person who sent this kid to the front to get killed and left on the field. Mad because we had to go in there and get our American boys killed. When I got back to camp, I took a good look at that coin. One side had a profile of the Kaiser on it. When I saw it, I wanted to kill him."

I dreaded to hear what came next. I couldn't figure out why he was so upset over a coin.

"I walked over to the blacksmith who took care of our horses, and I asked him if there was a way to put a hole in it. He probably thought I was crazy, but he showed me how to heat it up and pound a spike through it."

"How come you wanted to do that?" Sally asked.

"It just gave me great satisfaction to know I had put a spike through the Kaiser's head," he said.

I hardly knew what to say.

"I guess you figured you got even with him," I said as I looked at the strange coin.

"No. I never got even. Not ever."

I NOTICED THAT Dad kept a stack of gun catalogues and hunting magazines in his room. I wondered why a one-armed man would be interested in guns. He'd been a good shot before he went into the army, but now? I wasn't brave enough to ask, but one day he showed me a picture of a rifle in one of the catalogues.

"Just look at this beauty, Harry. It's a Savage Bolt Action Repeater. I'd sure like to have a gun like that. It costs $21.00. I may just order me one."

"You would? What would you do with it, Dad?" I said that too fast, and was afraid that I'd touched a sore spot with him.

His face took on that distant look he got when he relived something in his past. "I had a good eye, Harry. The best in my unit. I could plug the ace of spades at fifty paces."

"If you'd get a shotgun instead, maybe you could let me use it, Dad. You could teach me how to hunt." I got to thinking that, at long last, I might get to handle a gun, go hunting with it. I'd wanted one for a long time. Lots of the other boys had guns. And after all, what could my father do with it?

Still lost in his thoughts, Dad didn't answer right away. Finally he snapped out of it and said, "Nah, not likely Harry." Then he got up and left the room.

Even though Gram had warned me not to get my hopes up, this was one of those times when I did. I so much wanted a father who would take me hunting or fishing, or even talk to me about it. I had to keep telling myself that it wasn't going to happen. He was never going to be like my old dad, and I had to quit hoping he would change. I moped around for a while, riding my bike all over town, going nowhere in particular, Buster following with his tongue hanging out. Then I remembered I had to relieve Polly at the store so she could eat dinner.

"Dad's talking about getting a rifle," I told her.

"Whatever for?" she said. "What's a one-armed man supposed to do with a rifle?"

I shrugged. "I don't know, but I wish he'd teach me how to shoot."

"I don't know, Harry. He's so peculiar anymore. I'd hate to see him with a gun. No telling what he might do. You just never know which way the wind will blow with him."

It was true. He seesawed back and forth between being somewhat normal, and then going off on one of his rants about the Germans, the French, or the Catholics. Polly had pretty well separated herself from Dad. She didn't go to see him. Once in a while Gram invited him for Sunday dinner, but Polly didn't even try to talk to him. She was disgusted with him.

My sister had finished the eighth grade and had no interest in going on to school, so she quit, and Gram made her clerk in the store every day. It wasn't very good for the store. Polly didn't clean the blade after she sliced meat. She didn't sort the produce so the rotten stuff wouldn't spoil the rest. She never did learn to make change very well, but most folks bought on credit, and she could get that written down okay.

That day, between customers, I started cleaning up the mess she'd left. It gave me a chance to chew on my talk with Dad. He was being selfish and mean to me, and it made me sore. I was his boy. Why couldn't he help me the way other dads did? I needed to be able to hunt, and I needed him to teach me. It wasn't so much to ask. I griped to Polly about it when she came back after dinner.

"Harry, you've got to quit thinking about it. You'll just get yourself into a stew."

She was right. I was going to have to get over it, force myself to forget and let it go, but it was hard.

"Maybe I can talk Vince into taking you hunting this fall," Polly said in an effort to cheer me up.

Vince LeBeau was a tall, dark-haired fellow, part Indian and part French. He'd been hanging around the store all summer, buying Coke or cigarettes, but mostly flirting with Polly who was supposed to be working. Polly pretended she had no interest in Vince, but I could tell she liked him. She kept her eyes on him and made sure she was the one to wait on him, all smiling and friendly.

Vince and Polly began to see a lot of each other that fall, and nobody was too surprised when they ran off and got married after Polly turned sixteen. She and Vince stopped by the house the day after they eloped to tell us about it and to pack up her things. They couldn't keep from grinning and blushing as they told their news.

I thought Gram would be upset, but that didn't seem to be the case.

"Where are you going to live?" she asked.

"We've got a couple of rooms in a house near Vince's folks down in Jefferson," Polly said. She described the furnishings in her new home, the little stove and two rocking chairs. Her mother-in-law had given her a set of pretty dishes and some pans. When she heard that, Gram, not to be outdone, dug out some embroidered dishtowels and pillowcases.

"But the wedding. Where was it? Did you have a minister, or what?" Gram asked.

"St. Joseph's," Polly said. "Father Calhoun married us. She ducked her head and went on. "I didn't say anything about it before, but I joined the Catholic Church a while back."

"Really," Gram said. "You joined the church?"

"Dad doesn't know about this," Polly said. "I'm afraid to tell him. He'll be mad about me joining the Catholics. Will you tell him for me, Harry?" Her cheeks were pinked up from the excitement of it all, and I thought she looked really pretty.

I didn't look forward to doing that, but Gram thought I should. I never knew Gram to be chicken-hearted before, but it was plain she didn't want to face my dad over this. I thought about it for a while after they left, and then I got out my bike, dreading what I had to do. As I rode to McVay's, I practiced the words I would use. Sally answered the door, drying her hands on her apron. She gave me her sweet smile.

"C'mon in, Harry. I'm glad to see you."

I took a big breath and crossed the threshold.

Dad was sitting in her kitchen finishing his dinner. I went up to him, but I was so nervous I forgot my planned words and just blurted out the news.

"Polly got married, Dad."

"What? What did you say?"

"I said Polly got married. To Vince LeBeau."

"Who? LeBeau? That's a French name. Did she marry a French-man?" He jumped up, his eyes wide, and came right at me. A fright went through me, and for a second I thought he might hit me.

"I think he's just part French, Dad, and part Indian."

"Is he Catholic?" He clenched his good fist.

I was too scared to answer, so I just nodded.

"She married a Catholic? And a Frenchman to boot? Doesn't she have any sense? Why did Gram let her do that?"

My voice was shaky, but I managed to say, "She ran away, Dad. Anyway, Vince is a pretty good guy."

"I don't believe it. Not for one minute. They're never any good. No damn good, whatsoever. This would never have happened if her mother were alive."

Sally put a hand on his arm, but he shook her off.

"I hope she had sense enough not to join the Catholic Church."

I didn't have the courage to tell him about that, so I kept my mouth shut.

He commenced yelling and stomping around the kitchen. "Will you tell me why she did that? Why would she marry a damn Frog? One of those bead mumblers?" Sally retreated to a corner of the room, twisting her apron, a look of shock on her face.

"Probably gives his money to a man in a dress to buy more statues. And candles. And they probably sit around drinking wine after that."

He carried on about the Catholics and the French, and about everything else for several minutes, saying the same ugly things over and over. Finally I just stopped listening. I didn't pay much attention to him anymore when he got like this because he had such a big chip on his shoulder, and I was tired of it. I turned around and let myself out the door. He was still muttering to himself as I left.

I rode by Great-Aunt Lida's house. She always had fresh baked cookies, and I figured she'd offer me some. Then I saw through the kitchen window that she and Gram were drinking coffee and, no doubt, gossiping about the elopement. I'd had enough of that, so I went to the store where several of Granddad's pals were standing around. Ory Gabel was there too. They were talking Prohibition. Granddad said, "I don't see how the government can spend money trying to shut down a little place like mine."

"The 'dries' got the upper hand," Walter said. "They got so stiff-necked 'cause the WCTU goaded them into it. You watch. We'll all pay more taxes for this mess." "Wait a minute, gents." Ory spoke up. "Maybe it's part of God's plan to help us get rid of the temptations that make us do evil things. Did you ever think of it that way?"

The men groaned and looked away. After a minute, Bill Nelson said, "That's not

the only problem. I hear the Ku Klux Klan is getting organized. Somebody burned a cross up by Plankinton."

"Is that right?" another said. "I hate to think what that bunch might do."

That sounded like scary stuff, and I wanted to hear more. Just then, some women came into the store. The men said no more and began to clear out.

I finally found some of my buddies, and we went over to Harold Swanson's pasture for a game of baseball. We didn't have enough kids for teams, so we played workup. Pretty soon a bunch of girls came to watch. I wanted to bat a home run to show off in front of Carol Ann, but I couldn't hit the broad side of a barn that day. Instead I tapped a little foul ball that landed in a fresh cow pie, and I had to clean it off while everybody laughed.

That was the way this day had been, and I was just as happy when it ended.

7

SCHOOL WAS BECOMING tiresome, and I felt relief when I finally made it through the eighth grade. My teacher, Mrs. Morris was cleaning up her schoolroom on the last day of the term, and she'd asked me to stay after.

"I just want to ask, Harry, what your plans are now that you've finished eighth grade." She stretched her substantial figure and began to erase the blackboard. I jumped up to help her as I had done so many times before.

"My granddad is anxious for me to work in his grocery store, so I guess that'll be it."

"Harry, you're a smart and enterprising boy. I realize your grandparents need you right now, but have you thought about what you want to do? In the future?"

"I think about it all the time, Mrs. Morris. I'd really like to make something of myself, but I can't figure out how to do it.

"Have you thought about high school, Harry? You've got a good head for figures. I can imagine you doing something in business, maybe banking, when you're older. You need to go further with your education, though, so you won't be stuck."

I tried to imagine myself going to high school. Most of the boys I knew quit school as soon as they finished the eighth grade, and that's what I assumed I would do too. My brothers and Polly all left school the minute they could, and it seemed like they were living more grownup lives than I was. I envied that. Still, I could see that whatever they were doing now was about what they would be doing the rest of their lives. I wondered if high school could make a difference for me. Maybe it would be right thing.

THE EIGHTH-GRADE GRADUATION ceremony would be at the Beaverton High School for all the schools in Union County. Of course Gram and Granddad couldn't go because of the store. My dad wasn't likely to show up either, so I wouldn't have any family there like the other kids. I decided not to go.

Carol Ann stopped by the store a couple of days beforehand to buy a Coke. "Are you ready for graduation?" she said.

"Oh, I think I'll skip it."

"Harry, you have to go to graduation. Everybody else is going. You don't want to be the only one to miss it, do you? It'll be fun."

"Maybe for you."

"Oh, come on. Please go. You can ride with us." She came over and grabbed my arm, pulling me toward her. "Pretty please, Harry?"

I couldn't resist her. "I swear, Carol Ann. You could talk me into just about anything!"

The next day I got dressed up and rode with the Bellwoods to the Beaverton High School. We graduates sat in alphabetical order in the front of the assembly hall chattering nervously. Three men stepped onto the stage and the room got quiet. One of them prayed a while and then another one, who said he was the principal, made a speech. I didn't like the looks of that man. His eyes were small and set close together. His mouth twisted into a sneering expression, I was bored with his speech and glad when he finally quit.

We lined up backstage and, I have to admit, I was eager as we stood waiting to walk across the stage to receive our diplomas. I heard the superintendent call out "Carol Ann Bellwood" and I could see a little bit of her in her new pink dress way ahead of me. I was happy for her and glad I'd decided to come.

Then everything changed. I didn't mean for it to happen. Just before my name was called, I started to feel pressure in my lower regions. I was mortified and my face went hot. I wanted to fold myself into those black velvet curtains and never be seen again. But the line kept moving forward and I had to move along with it. Finally I heard the superintendent say my name, "Harry Lyle Spencer." I bent over some and walked as fast as I could. I grabbed the diploma from the man's hand and used it to cover up my embarrassment, and scooted off the other side. I was sure everyone in the audience had noticed. The Bellwoods. Carol Ann. Everyone. Why did this have to happen today, of all days? It had been a problem lately, especially if I was up in front of the class. But why today?

I made a beeline for the restroom and just stood around for a while waiting for my body to settle down. I didn't want to leave, but I couldn't stay in there all day. Finally I made up my mind to act like nothing had happened.

People had gathered in the lobby where some of the mothers had arranged cookies and punch for a party. I slipped in among them, and nobody said anything except Carol Ann who wondered where I went.

"Where do you suppose I went?" I said all smart-alecky.

"Oh," she said, and changed the subject. "Let's look around. The principal said we should if we were planning on high school." We spent the next hour looking into classrooms, the gym, and especially at all the typewriters. I was impressed.

WHEN I GOT home that afternoon after the ceremony, I asked Gram, "What would you think if I decided to go to high school?"

She turned quickly. I could tell I'd surprised her.

"I don't know about that. Nobody in this family has ever done it." It sounded like she was buying time to think it over. "I thought you were sick of school. Couldn't wait for it to end."

"I was. I was tired of this little country school, but we looked at the high school today. There's a shop where they teach wood working, and an indoor basketball court. I think it might be fun to go there."

She gave me one of her stern looks. "Well, it better be for more than fun." Then she was quiet a moment. "It would sure be different from what your brothers did."

"I know, but I'm not like them." After Eddie and Gabe quit school they found a couple of sisters and started courting them. I liked Ramona and Esther. They were farm girls who loved to dance and have fun. It seemed in no time, they planned a wedding and got married in a double ceremony.

"No, you're not like them. I feel kinda sorry for them, living over there in Iowa on that ramshackle rented farm," she said. "No money for cattle or equipment. They wouldn't have been able to put in a crop if their Uncle Lyle hadn't loaned them some money. Pretty soon they'll start having babies, and it'll be hard for them to get ahead."

She went on. "I don't know what to say about high school? We'd kind of assumed that you would spend more time in the store once you got out of school. Because of Polly going off and getting married."

Gram didn't exactly discourage me about high school, but I could tell she was thinking about what to do if I couldn't work so much at the store. Then I had an idea. Ty was the only one of us left with Uncle Lyle and Aunt Hazel. He was a shy, bashful fellow, and I felt sorry for him staying there.

"Gram," I said. "Could we ask Ty to come here to live? I'd really like to be with him. Maybe I could fix up the shed where he and I could sleep."

She glared at me. "I've already had two of Calvin Spencer's children dumped on me. I'm not taking another one."

"It's not really our fault, Gram. With Dad the way he is."

"I know that, Harry, but Granddad and I are too old to be raising kids."

I thought that was pretty selfish of her. We were just about grown and didn't need much "raising" as far as I could see. But her word was law. I let her chew on it for a while, hoping she would change her mind.

We had just finished supper that night when there was a knock on the door, and there was Carol Ann still in her pretty pink dress.

"Well, this is a surprise," Gram said. "Come on in."

Granddad couldn't have managed a wider grin if he had stuffed a whole corncob in his mouth. "Let's give this pretty girl some of your strawberry shortcake, Bess."

I pulled out a chair for her and Carol Ann said, "I brought your diploma, Harry. You left it in our car."

"That's right. I forgot all about it. Thank you."

Gram set out a plate of shortcake heaped with strawberries from her garden and sweetened whipped cream.

"Oh my, Mrs. Didier, I don't know if I can eat all that."

"Sure you can," said Granddad. He couldn't take his eyes off her. I couldn't either.

"Did you tell your grandparents about the high school, Harry?"

"No. Not really."

She proceeded to tell them about every detail of everything we had seen—the little kitchens where girls learned to cook, the classrooms for every subject. I didn't see how she could remember every last thing that way. I sure couldn't.

"I'm so excited about going to school there," she said. "I just hope Harry decides to go too." She smiled at me.

"Only people I know who went to high school are bankers," Grand-dad said. Granddad hated bankers 'cause he had to borrow money from them once in a while. "You aren't planning to be a banker, are you Harry?"

"No, I don't think so," I said.

"I just don't know how he'd get to school," Gram said.

"Dad said that if he decides to go, he could count on us for a ride," Carol Ann said. "You'll do it, won't you Harry?"

When she looked at me like that, all sweet and smiley, I was ready to do just about anything she wanted. But more school? I still wasn't sure.

"I'll think about it," was all I would agree to.

She got up to leave and Granddad said, "Where's your manners, boy? It's dark out. You better walk this girl home."

I wanted to do just that, but had been too shy to say so.

We ambled slowly down the road on this pleasant, warm night. The moon was out and it was easy to see our way. I put my arm around her waist. When we got to her house she grabbed my hand and said, "This was a special day, Harry. Would you like to kiss me?"

I reached over and gave her a little peck on the cheek. It was the first time I had kissed her, and that one little peck didn't seem like enough. So I kissed her again, this time on the lips. She kissed back and it was pure bliss. Then I felt it again—that pressure rising down below. I stepped back before she noticed anything.

"Is that you, Carol Ann?" her dad called from the doorway.

"I'm coming," she said and ran to the door. "Think about school, Harry."

Oh boy. It was hard to leave after that. I could have stayed for hours. I finally turned around and headed home. The moon was still bright and I figured I knew what "moonstruck" meant.

At home Granddad grinned at me. "That's a mighty pretty girl you've got, Harry. Did you get a kiss?" he cackled.

"Oh, Alfie. Leave him alone," Gram said.

8

G RAM WASTED NO time putting me to work first thing after graduation. "The store needs to be cleaned top to bottom," she announced at breakfast. "I've been waiting for school to be out so you could help."

I wasn't very excited about this, but it felt good to be doing something different, and I knew she was right. The store needed attention. I carried buckets, brooms, mops, rags, soap, and Clorox over there. She gave the orders, and I did the work. I brushed down the ceiling to get rid of cobwebs, dead bugs, and the like. I quit every time a customer came in so as not to advertise the dirt. Then she got me started on the windows.

I peeled off announcements and advertising signs faded from the sun, notices of auctions and sale items, some posters so old they advertised Liberty bonds even though the war was long over. I cleaned out the dust from the sills and scrubbed the woodwork till its clean ivory color was restored. Finally I washed the windows inside and out with vinegar and water.

I stood back to admire my work, but Gram took one look at the windows and said, "They're still dirty, Harry. You'll have to do them again."

I groaned. This job was going to take all summer. Just as I was starting over on the inside, the door burst open and three of the Beaubien kids came in. Don, who was a year behind me in school, came over to me.

"Have you heard the news, Harry?"

"What news?"

He looked around and spoke in a hushed voice. "They say the KKK is coming. It could be any time now."

"What do you mean? The Ku Klux Klan? Who told you?"

Rumors had been bubbling up the last couple of months. People had heard that the Klan was getting organized and was planning to make trouble for the Catholics and the "wets," but we hadn't taken it very seriously.

"Father Calhoun told us last Sunday," Don said. "He said there might be trouble, that they might come after us."

"What do they do?"

"They get dressed up in long white robes and pointed hats that cover their faces so you can't see who they are. Then they come to your place and burn big crosses to scare you."

Don's news sent a shiver up my spine. Not much in our town scared me, but I had never dreamt of anything like this.

"What are you going to do?" I asked.

"The priest said we should pray for them, but my dad says we'll just have to fight if they come to our place. He's got a gun."

My eyes widened at that thought. If the Klan came after Don's family, they might come after us too. Would Granddad shoot them with his old shotgun?

That night I asked Granddad about what Don had told me, and he said, "Aw, I don't think that talk is going to amount to anything. Don't worry about it."

I did worry though, as I washed down the walls. I wondered what my dad would think, the way he was so down on Catholics and the French since he got back from France. I hoped he wouldn't hear the news. Then I thought, why should I care what he thinks? He doesn't care about me.

I had to move on, so the next day I started on the produce bins. They were filled with onionskins, here and there a shriveled potato, dried juice from fruit that had been left too long, and some things I couldn't identify. I washed them out and disinfected them and filled them with good, fresh fruit and vegetables.

One thing this kind of work did for me was to give me time to think about my future. As a little kid I planned great things to do when I got big, but it was just daydreaming, pretend stuff. For a while I wanted to drive a chicken truck like Pug McCormick. Then I decided it would be fun to work for the railroad, be a train engineer and go places.

That all seemed childish now, and I began to count up what my real options were. I could keep working at the store for the foreseeable future. Spend my life cleaning up Granddad's messes and making no money. Or maybe I could find work on a farm. It didn't appeal to me much, but that's what most boys did at my age.

I wanted to make something of myself. I thought of men in our town whose lives I could study and emulate, and that's where I ran into trouble. Dad sure wasn't that person any more. Granddad was fun in his way, but I didn't admire him much. I thought about every man I knew, and I just couldn't find much to admire. No one I knew seemed to have much ambition or interest in bettering himself. They just went on, day after day, doing about the same thing as they had done the day before. Never planning ahead. Yet I knew there were people out there somewhere who had made big successes of themselves. How did they do it? That's what I wanted to know. It sure wasn't by washing down a country grocery store.

The most admirable person I could think of was Great-Aunt Lida. Now there was a woman who knew how to get ahead. She made cheese and sold it; she peddled her garden produce. Anyone who wanted to have a special dinner got one of Aunt Lida's chickens. They were that good. She did all that and tithed religiously to the Methodist Church. I admired her gumption but couldn't very well follow her pattern.

I talked to some of the men who delivered goods to us. Bud Johnson drove the beer truck. I asked him if he thought he had a good job.

"Are you kidding, Harry? The government revenuers are breathing down my neck, and I've got a knot in my stomach all the time watching out for them. Then I get out here in the country and find out two of the barrels are leaking, and I'll have to make another trip. Or your granddad doesn't need as much as I brought. I lose my day's profit from stuff like that."

I could see what he meant. His job wasn't so great. That brought me right back to the idea of going to high school. I remembered all those typewriters I'd seen in the business classroom. People who learned to type must be able to find jobs somewhere. I remembered the time my dad told me I might work at the courthouse someday, and how I'd have to wear a suit and tie every day. Maybe that was for me. The problem was that I didn't have a very clear idea what kind of work those men, who wore suits, did.

Still pondering, I removed the meat and cheese from the meat cooler. I washed out that case with Clorox water, let it dry and air out. Then I trimmed the dried up cheese and cold meat and rearranged all the food so it looked fresh and appetizing. I thought the worst of the cleaning was over, but, no. Gram wanted me to do the floor. It was filthy, but I didn't know how bad it was until I started scrubbing. The floor was just raw boards. Granddad threw a little sawdust on it every day and swept it up now and again. When I got rid of the sawdust, I discovered the wood was black with mud, grease, dropped food, and who knows what. I scrubbed with Gram's stiff brush over and over. The floor turned a nice yellow-white color, and folks really took notice when they came in.

"What have you done here, Alfie?" someone would say looking around in admiration.

"Got my grandson home from school. That's what."

I was pleased with my work, but I did wonder how long it would stay clean. If it were my store, I knew I would paint the floor so it could be cleaned easily. I went home every night tired and slept like the dead, but I still didn't have any spending money. I set my long-term plans aside for the time being and decided to ask Gram how she would feel about paying me a small salary. Well, she didn't feel too good about it.

"What are you talking about, Harry? You have a place to sleep and three meals a day. Did you ever figure out what that was worth? And all those years when you were too little to do much work."

So that was it. I'd get my board and room, and I'd better be grateful for that. I would have to figure out something to do about this situation because I couldn't go through life with no money. I couldn't even go roller-skating with Carol Ann and the other kids unless I got some cash.

After the store was cleaned up, I told Gram that I'd like to find some farm work to make a little spending money. She didn't object because she understood my problem—she just wasn't about to give me a handout. That's when she began to back down about Ty coming to live with us. I guess she figured that if I were going to work elsewhere or go to high school, she'd need him for the store.

I CONSIDERED THE farmers I knew and who might be willing to hire a greenhorn like me. Also, which one had enough money to afford help. I settled on Ole Tollefson. He was a bachelor who had inherited his parents' farm. Ole was known for being stingy beyond belief, but he had quite a bit of money as a result.

I rode my bike out to his farm. It was so quiet I thought he must be in the fields, so I called his name several times. He finally poked his head out the door of the tool shed where he was working on something.

"Harry! What a surprise. I'm just sharpening my axe so I can cut down some brushy trees. What on earth brings you out here?"

"Hello, Ole." Talking to Ole was always hard for me 'cause I didn't know where to look. He'd had an accident years ago when he rode a load of hay under a bridge with a low iron superstructure. Before he knew it, one of the girders had sliced off the end of his nose. Of course it had long since healed, but folks said you could pretty near see Ole's brains when you looked at him because he was all nostril. I didn't want to stare, but I wanted to look him in the eye to make my pitch. I did my best to focus somewhere on his forehead.

"You probably don't know it, Ole, but I just graduated from the eighth grade, and it's time I found some work to do. I hoped you might have something for me here on the farm."

"Shucks, Harry. I'd think you'd be working at the store."

"I do work at the store, but that's for my board and room. I need to make some cash money."

He eyed me up and down. I wasn't a particularly big fellow, but I thought my average size would be all right.

"You don't look like a farmer, Harry, but looks ain't everything. Can you drive a team of horses?"

"I don't know. I've seen lots of others do it. It doesn't look too hard."

He laughed. "It's not if you know what you're doing. It's real hard if you don't."

"I wish you'd give me a try, Ole. I'll do my best."

Ole decided to try me out cultivating a cornfield with a team of horses. He helped me hitch up the cultivator and the team, told me where to go.

I got on the seat and took the reins, then had a thought.

"You didn't tell me what you'd pay me, Ole. Would three dollars a day be all right?"

"That's highway robbery, Harry. You go cultivate a field, and, if you do it right, there'll be money for you."

So I slapped the reins against the horses the way I'd seen others do, and we started down the road, the curved blades of the machine turning, ready to till the soil between rows of corn. It was a beautiful sunny day, the air was clean and fresh, and I was going to make some easy money.

I turned the horses onto the field road and stopped when we got to the gate. It was made of three strands of barbed wire wound around an old wooden post and held tight to the fence post with a twist of heavy wire. I got down from the cultivator, opened the gate, and drove he horses through. I jumped down to close it, feeling confident about this job and happy.

As I dragged the gate across the opening, the rotting gatepost suddenly snapped in two and all hell broke loose. The barbed wire came off the post and flew up in the air like an angry snake, and then came bouncing down on the cultivator with a metallic racket that broke the peaceful quiet of the day. I jumped back, startled by the noise. It spooked the horses, and they took off running with the cultivator dragging behind, flipping this way and that. Stunned, I watched as they went all the way to the far end of the field not stopping until they reached the fence, the cultivator twisted behind them and nearly upside down. A wide swath of young corn plants was torn up and mangled in their wake.

I was sick. I went down the field to the horses who were now calmly munching grass at the side of the field. If I could right the cultivator, I could turn the horses around and still do the work. I tried every which way, but couldn't manage the cultivator by myself. I knew the horses should be unhitched from the machine, but if I did that, there was no telling where they would go while I went to get help. I finally decided to leave them where they were.

I walked that long, hot mile back to Ole's place practicing what I would say to him, ashamed of my failure. I knew one thing. There wasn't going to be any easy money. Not today.

Ole walked back to the field with me. I think he realized the accident wasn't entirely my fault, but when he saw the damage to the field he said, "I don't believe you're cut out for farming, Harry."

So there it was. I was hired and fired all in one day. It galled me, but I didn't want to be a farmer anyway.

Gram noticed how I was moping around that afternoon and asked if Ole had hired me. I figured I'd better tell her what happened before Ole told it all over town.

"It wasn't really my fault, Gram. The post was so rotten it barely held the gate shut."

"That may be true," she said, "but the accident happened while you were using it just the same. Maybe you ought to get ahead of the game and go out there and put in a new post for Ole."

"What? Fix the thing after he fired me?"

"If you fix it, he'll be so amazed that he'll tell people about that, instead of how you broke his gate."

Well, that sure put a new slant on things. Ole was a big talker and I didn't look forward to the ribbing I'd get about ruining his corn crop. Gram was pretty smart.

I went out to the storage shed and found some posts left over from fencing the garden. I got the wire cutters and managed to balance a post across the handlebars of my bike and rode all the way out to Ole's cornfield again. I forgot to take gloves with me, so I took off my shirt to protect my hands from the barbed wire. It was a hot, nasty job, but maybe it would save my good name. I stood back when I finished, and was proud of my work. I hoped Ole would appreciate it.

THAT EVENING I went over to Carol Ann's. We sat on the front steps of her house, and I told her about everything I'd been doing, including my failure on the farm.

"Poor Harry. I wondered what you were up to."

"Yeah, Gram had really saved up some chores for me. It gave me time to think. I don't want to work in that country store forever for no wages, and I've made up my mind about one other thing for sure. I don't ever want to be a farmer."

She laughed. "I don't blame you after what happened today."

"I'm going to go to high school, Carol Ann. I figure it's about the only way left for me if I want to make something of myself."

"Oh, Harry. I'm so glad that's what you've decided. I really hoped that's what you would do. We'll have a great time. You'll see."

She was so pleased with me that I started thinking I might be able to kiss her, but Mr. Bellwood came out and sat down in the porch swing. He chatted a bit about the nice evening and gave no sign of leaving. In fact, I was pretty sure he intended to stay there until I went home, so I finally gave up my good idea and said goodnight.

I told Gram the next morning about deciding to go to high school.

She said, "I'm not too surprised. That girl really wants you to do it." She paused. "We'd better ask Ty about living here in that case. For the store."

"Really Gram? That'll be wonderful. Shall I fix up the shed for us so we can sleep there?" I could imagine the two of us out there staying up half the night, talking and laughing.

"No, I don't think so. It'll be too cold out there in the winter. Granddad will have to come back and sleep with me. You and Ty can have the daybed."

I was so happy to have Ty coming to live with us that I decided not to argue.

A few days later, Uncle Lyle's truck came bumping down the road, I nearly died of shock. Ty was driving! Ty, my brother, who was only a little over a year older than me, was driving the truck and Uncle Lyle was in the passenger seat. I was so jealous I thought I would bust right open. I had never even sat behind the steering wheel of a car or truck, and here was my brother driving. He jumped out so casual about it, and I was green with envy.

"Hi, Harry," he said. "Isn't this great? Me coming to stay here."

I couldn't even say hello. Instead I said, "When did you learn to drive? Does Uncle Lyle let you drive all the time? Can you show me how?"

"Hold on, Harry," Uncle Lyle said. "I needed Ty's help with some things on the farm, and it made it easier to have him drive once in a while."

I turned to Granddad. "Are we ever going to buy a car? Everybody knows how to drive but me."

"I don't know if that's a very good reason to buy a car," he said.

"I could take you places, do errands for you and Gram. It would save a lot of time. Please, Granddad. We need a car."

"I'll think about it," was all he would say.

I finally remembered my manners and helped Ty move in, and I made him promise to teach me how to drive if we ever got the chance.

9

THE PALETTI FRUIT and Vegetable truck from Sioux City arrived with our produce order, and Tony Paletti himself burst into the store where Ty was learning how to run the cash register. Tony waited for Granddad to finish with a customer, then said, "Alfie. I have some news for you." He looked around to make sure no one was listening. "Bud Johnson asked me to pass this along to you."

"That crazy devil!" Granddad said. "Where's my beer? He's missed his last two deliveries and the bar's about dry."

"That's what I'm trying to tell you. He isn't going to deliver beer this week, and maybe not for a while after that. The Prohibition agents are making raids in Union County, and Bud doesn't dare deliver 'til they clear out."

"How do you know?"

"They hit the Tip-Top Tavern in Burbank and closed it down, and a bootleg place in Jefferson. Richard Hart led the raid. You know, the one they call 'Two Gun?' You're lucky they haven't been here."

"'Two Gun Hart," I said. "Isn't he the one with pearl-handled pistols?"

"Yeah," Tony said. He's led bootlegging raids all over Nebraska. Even in Sioux City. I haven't heard of him in South Dakota 'til now."

Granddad stood slack-jawed with this news, and I felt a ripple of fear go down my backbone. This was something, to think the Feds might come to our store.

"How am I supposed to keep my customers happy?" Granddad said.

"I don't know, Alfie. I guess you'll just have to wait."

Within two days, the beer barrels in the store were dry, and Granddad had to turn away the regulars, himself included.

"Damn it anyway," he said. "This isn't right. They're going to ruin my business." He swore and groused around for another day. Truth be told, I think he wanted the beer for himself as much as for the store.

"I'm gonna borrow Lyle's truck and go down to Sioux City and get the beer myself," he announced at dinner.

Gram was appalled. "You can't do that," she said. "You don't know your way around down there. Sioux City's a rough place. It's wide open," she said. "They don't call it 'Little Chicago' for nothing. All those mobsters. What if 'Two Gun' Hart finds you there?"

"We'll stick to the back alleys. Nobody will even notice us."

The thought of all this stirred me up. We'd heard plenty about how wide open Sioux City was. How the mobsters came out there on the Chicago, Milwaukee, and St. Paul railroad when things got too hot for them back east.

"You remember what happened to that minister, don't you?" Gram said.

"Well sure. Everybody knows that, but he was a 'dry' and I'm not."

The shooting of Reverend Haddock was legendary. He went around preaching about the evils of drink, so the saloonkeepers hired two thugs to give him a whipping. They didn't count on the minister fighting back, and John Ahrensdorf ended up shooting him dead. There was a famous trial, but somehow the jury decided the shooter was innocent. He was so proud of his success he had his picture taken with the jury just for bragging rights.

That tale didn't stop Granddad though. He wasn't determined about much in this world, but he wanted his beer. Next thing we knew, he had recruited Uncle Lyle and his truck to go to Sioux City. He asked me if I'd like to go too! I was scared to death, but I wanted to go along as much as I'd ever wanted anything.

"You're not taking this boy to do your dirty work," Gram said.

"I'm going to need him, Bess. It'll give Ty a chance to run the store with your help. Lyle will drive, and Harry and I can get the barrels loaded up and out of town quick as anything."

"You are a crazy fool, Alphonse." She never called him Alphonse unless she was really mad.

But Granddad won out, and the next day the three of us got in Uncle Lyle's truck and headed for Sioux City. We crossed the Big Sioux River into Iowa and took the river road that ran south alongside the bluffs. I'd never been to Sioux City and couldn't wait to see it. The danger we might face from the revenuers pumped me up even further.

"Do you think they'll catch us?" I asked.

"Hope not," Granddad said. "I don't want to go to jail."

"This is a damn fool thing, Alfie," Uncle Lyle said.

"Well let's wait and see," he said.

The thirty-mile trip took a little over an hour on that dirt road, but it felt like a whole day to me.

"How do you know where to go, Granddad?"

"I'll probably have to ask."

"Will we ride a street car?"

"I doubt it."

"Will we eat in a café?"

"We might. Now just hush up for a while, Harry."

When I had about given up on us ever getting there, the road took a big bend to the east. The tall clay bluffs stood on our left, and on our right the Big Sioux River met up with the Missouri. Our teacher had showed us on a map where this happened, and she told us how big the Missouri was, but I never dreamt there could be this much water. The river was a beautiful deep blue color and sparkled in the sun. It was so wide I could barely see across. There were barges loaded with barrels and crates and all kinds of fishing boats on the water. Riverboats with their paddle wheels were docked on the Nebraska side of the river.

"There it is," Granddad said, and I tore my eyes away from that magnificent river to look at the buildings rising on our left and gawked open-mouthed at what lay before us. It was a large city with about seventy thousand people, but until I saw it, I just couldn't imagine any one place in the world with so many buildings.

Uncle Lyle pulled off the road near the river where the ferry operation was located. Granddad got out to get some directions, and I went with him into the little lean-to building. Inside were a half dozen men sitting around, drinking beer and eating sandwiches. They were a rough, unshaven lot, their pants so filthy they could have stood up by themselves. They turned to stare at us.

"That beer looks mighty fine," Granddad said, grinning. "Wish I had time to join you." When he got no answer, he said, "Do any of you know where I can find Davy Berman?"

They looked at each other and didn't say anything for a minute.

"You here to cause Davy a problem?" one man asked with a gravelly voice.

"No. I'm here to do some business with him, "Granddad said.

Once again there was a long silence. These grizzled men looked like pretty tough characters, and I worried about what they might do.

"Oh hell, Mike, they don't look like the law. Tell 'em where Davy is."

The first speaker stood up, twice as tall as Granddad. He went to the window and pointed. "Take a left out there at the crossroads and go north to Fourth Street. Go east on Fourth until you come to the Chicago House Hotel. You'll likely find Davy there." He paused and looked directly at Granddad. "I don't want to hear about no trouble for Davy, you hear?"

"I sure do," said Granddad. "Thanks for your help."

I was more than happy to climb back into Uncle Lyle's truck.

We followed the directions and soon found ourselves in the middle of the downtown area. Cars and trucks moved in all directions. There were horse-drawn wagons and more people than I had ever seen in my life. Brightly painted streetcars jammed with folks moved up and down the streets, their bells clanging. I stared at Pelletier's Department Store six stories high, its windows filled with women's finery of every description. Next to it was Morris's Hat Store, and I marveled at a store that sold only men's hats.

Uncle Lyle drove in low gear as he wound his way through the traffic. I was watching a nimble newspaper boy trying to sell papers to people in moving cars when suddenly I was thrown forward as Uncle Lyle braked hard to avoid hitting a little kid who ran out into the street ahead of his mother. I saw the sweat on Uncle Lyle's upper lip and figured he must be nervous about driving in all this traffic.

Fourth Street began to go downhill, and ended in just a few blocks. We followed it all the way to a wall that kept us from driving into another river. Somehow we missed the Chicago House Hotel on the first pass, so Uncle Lyle turned the truck around, and I watched with Granddad as we went back. The hotel sign, painted in white letters, was half hidden under a wide green awning. Its four stories gleamed with high arched windows on the upper floors and a fire escape zigzagging down the side.

Uncle Lyle found a place to park, and we all breathed a sigh of relief to come to a stop.

"Well, gents," Granddad said. "What would you say to some dinner before we do our business?"

That was fine with me. I hadn't realized how hungry I was until he mentioned food. We got out and looked around. Granddad stopped a fellow to ask, "Any good eating places around here?"

The man jerked his thumb toward the side street. "You might find somethin' down there in the Sudan."

We started walking. I spied a sign that looked promising—Madame Shaw's Maple Grove. Across the street was Minnie Kern's Place. There was loud music coming from both of them, and a bunch of fellows were standing around, laughing and smoking big cigars.

"I...I think we're in the wrong place, Alfie," said Uncle Lyle.

"I believe you're right," Granddad answered.

They turned abruptly and headed back the way we had come.

"Why couldn't we stop there?" I asked.

"Just wasn't right," Granddad said without looking at me. "I'll explain later."

That puzzled me some, but I was so busy looking around, I let it go. I sure was hungry.

We finally came to a little place called Uhler's Saloon and Food and went inside.

The man behind the counter said, "You fellas here for poker or food?"

"We'll take some food," Granddad said.

Next thing I knew, there was a big plate of chicken fried steak, mashed potatoes and gravy, and green beans floating in bacon grease sitting before me. I piled into it. To top it off, Granddad ordered apple pie and coffee for us, and I felt terrific when I'd cleaned it up.

We stepped out to the street and walked to the Chicago House Hotel. The three of us stood peering through the big window for a minute, then Granddad hitched up his pants and we went in. It was very dark inside and full of smoke. As my eyes adjusted, I made out the green and black square-tiled floor and the walls covered in dark gold shiny paper. There were men sitting around talking, smoking, trying to read the paper. I became conscious of piano music coming from a big upright in the corner.

The piano player was a tall woman wearing a red silk dress with black ruffly stuff around the neck and down the front. Her shoes on the pedals were shiny black lace-up boots, and she had her hair pulled up on top of her head. Her heavy silver earrings and bright red lipstick made her look as fancy as anything I could imagine, as if she were ready to go to a party right there in the middle of the day. I had never seen the likes of such a woman before, and I stared plenty.

Granddad went up to the desk and asked the man where to find Davy Berman.

"I think he's downstairs," he said, "but if you're doing business with him, you better leave the kid up here. Davy don't like kids around when he's workin.'"

So Granddad and Uncle Lyle left me. I found a chair and prepared myself to sit back and enjoy looking at the fine woman and listening to her music. She saw me watching her and said, "What would you like to hear, cutie?"

"I don't know much about music," I said, mortified.

"Well, how about a rag?" And off she went with a fast, bouncing piece. I hoped she wouldn't ask me any more 'cause I wouldn't know what to say.

Three men sat at a round table in the center of the room. One of them had a wild shock of white hair. He looked over at the piano player and said, "Pipe down, will ya, Lettie. I can't hear myself think."

She made a face at him and played softer. Now I knew her name was Lettie.

I sat listening for fifteen minutes or so when suddenly a boy my age came running in saying, "The preacher's comin'. The preacher's comin'."

I was astonished to see the men at that big round table push it aside, lift up the carpet, and open a trap door underneath it. A whoosh of dank, coal smell hit me. They lowered two crates of hard liquor from behind the desk into that opening. Two of the men jumped down with it, one of them being the man with the white hair. The third fellow closed it up fast, dropped the rug, and pulled the table back over it. He and a couple of others sat in chairs around the table looking like they'd been there all day. And it all happened so fast, I thought I hadn't seen right.

In another minute about six policemen and a man in preacher clothes rushed in. A policeman blew a whistle and the preacher fellow yelled, "This is a raid. Where is Whitey Larson? Where's the liquor? I know he's been selling it here."

The preacher was tall with stringy yellow hair down over his ears. He wore a black suit and tie and a wide-brimmed black hat. He looked around the room at all the men, but nobody said anything. Then his steel-gray eyes fixed on me. My heart rose up and was pumping so hard I could feel it in the ends of my fingers.

"What are you doing here in this den of evil, boy?" He pointed a long finger with a grimy nail in my face.

I could barely squeak anything out. "I…I'm just waiting for my Granddad."

"Young man, your direction is hellward for certain when you frequent this pestilential place. This is where the scum of God's dirt suck the young men of this country into eternal damnation." He stared a long minute and fear tore through me like fire. "You'll feel the devil's flames if you persist." I believed I could already feel them burning me, shriveling me into a pile of ashes.

"Get out, boy, while you can. Get out before you're ruint."

Finally his eyes let go of me, and I took a big, ragged breath and sagged into the chair.

He turned to the woman at the piano. "Where are those sinning devils, Lettie? Where's that snake Whitey?"

She shrugged, then smiled up at him. "I have no idea, Preacher Simms. I'm just practicing the piano a little bit." I was awed that she didn't seem afraid of him.

The preacher signaled to the policemen. "Let's have a look upstairs." As they were disappearing up the steps, I saw, out of the corner of my eye, the white-headed man run past the window and down the street. I figured that must be Whitey Larson. Two policemen, who had remained outside, chased after him.

A commotion from the basement drew my attention. A short, pudgy man in a summer straw hat and a wrinkled ivory-colored suit came up the stairs. He was smoking a cigar and had a big gold pin stuck in his tie. He looked like somebody to fear with his scowling face and beady eyes darting around the room. Granddad and Uncle Lyle followed behind. Uncle Lyle's face was white as Gram's flour, but Granddad looked like he might be enjoying things. I was never happier to see anybody in my whole life than I was to see him at that moment.

Granddad said, "C'mon Harry. Let's get out of here." We headed for the door but were stopped by an officer just outside. He said, "Get back in there. Nobody leaves till we say so."

The man with the gold pin walked up to him, reached out, and shook his hand. "How's the family, Chester?" he said.

"Uh, fine, Mr. Berman."

"That's good to hear. Very good. Chester, I want you to let these two friends of mine and their boy leave," he said in a low, whispery voice. "They're just visitors from out of town. They're of no interest to the preacher."

Chester looked uncertain, but I saw the bill sticking out of the policeman's hand as he opened the door for us to leave, and I knew how it got there.

We hurried back to the truck and collapsed inside.

When he could get his breath, Granddad said, "Well if that don't beat all. Your first trip to Sioux City, Harry, and you get mixed up in one of Preacher Simms's raids."

I didn't like to admit to him how scared I'd been. How scared I still was. I said, "That was something to see, all right, but I'm sure glad it's over."

Granddad said when Davy Berman heard the police come in, he just pulled on some kind of bell cord so everybody upstairs knew to leave by the fire escape. Davy had a big poker game going on, and he never stopped playing for one instant. But when he heard everyone go clomping upstairs, he decided it was time to get us out of there.

"Now, Lyle. Davy said to go down to the Sudan 'til we come to Blanche's Bower and turn into the alley. There's supposed to be a guy named Jerry there. He'll show us where to get our beer."

"You sure don't mean to do that, do you Alfie? I think we should just get on home," said Uncle Lyle.

"Not on your life, Lyle. I paid for that beer and I mean to get it."

Blanche's Bower was a fancy house with a wide side porch where several pretty women and some men were playing music on a Victrola. It was a hot day, and the women had their skirts pulled up to their knees. While I gawked, Granddad went to the door and rang the bell. A plumpish woman with long blonde hair answered. "Hello there, Pops," she said, smiling and pulling her silky robe around her. She held a cigarette in a long holder. They talked a minute, and then she hollered back to someone inside. "Send Jerry out here, will ya?" Her robe fell open when she turned, and I got an eyeful of her lacey underwear. She wrapped up again, leaving me in a daze. Pretty soon a runty fellow showed up. He took us to an old barn where we loaded six barrels into the truck as fast as we could and covered them with a tarp.

It was a long trip back because the truck wouldn't go over twenty miles an hour with its heavy load, so I had plenty of time to think. It began to trickle into my senses what the Sudan and all those gaudy places might be about. This was brand new to me, all those beautiful women, laughing and having fun with the men standing around, not a bit shamed by the skimpy clothes they wore. I wondered what went on inside those houses.

We got home after dark, got the beer unloaded, and I dropped into bed. I replayed the whole day in my head before I went to sleep and made up my mind to find out more about that Sudan place.

THE NEXT DAY Wes and Billy and the other fellows rode by on their bicycles. "You want to go bike riding with us, Harry?"

"Yeah, I do," I said. I wanted to tell them about the Sudan in Sioux City. Maybe I'd get answers to the questions that were plaguing my mind.

"Okay, fellas. I'll see you as soon as I eat dinner."

I caught up with them mid-afternoon. We decided it was too hot to ride, so we sat out back of Billy's barn where it was cool and shady, and I told them about my trip.

"You mean you actually saw a mobster?" Billy's mouth hung open, his eyes bright with excitement. "Did he have a gun?"

"I didn't see one, but maybe he did." They were impressed, I could tell. I went on to tell them about all the sights, the women's silky clothes, how they pulled their skirts up over their knees, how they smiled and winked at me. I may have exaggerated a little bit, and the boys were really interested.

"What were they doing?" Don said.

"Just sitting around on the porch, eating sandwiches and drinking beer, laughing and talking like it was a party. Then every once in a while a couple of them would go indoors." It excited me to tell them about it. "I couldn't see what went on inside, but it seemed like they were having a good time."

Wes jumped up and yelled. "I know what they were doing in there." He bent over and brought his voice down to an excited whisper. "My brother Clete told me about it. When he was in the war in France, they went to these places where women would let the men get in bed with them, and, you know, do stuff. I'll bet that's what was going on in the Sudan."

We sat wide-eyed and silent at the thought. The image of Lettie flashed through my mind, and I felt the familiar heat rise in my body. This had been happening to me plenty since my trip. I liked it, but it made me feel bothered, stirred up.

"Did you see anything like that, Harry?" Mike asked.

They all were looking at me, and I wanted to be able to tell them that I had seen it. I wished I *had* seen it, but all I said was, "I couldn't do anything like that with my granddad around."

"Oh," Billy moaned. "I'd have given anything to have been there."

"Me too," Mike said. "You're so lucky, Harry."

10

WHEN GRAM HEARD the account of our trip to Sioux City, she was madder than a wet hen.

"Ye gods, Alfie. You could have gotten this boy into serious trouble. It's one thing for you to take a big risk, but you shouldn't have gotten Harry involved." She paused for breath. "I'll bet Lyle was fit to be tied."

"I took care of Lyle, Bess. Don't worry about him."

"Don't worry about me either, Gram," I said. "I came through just fine, and I had a great time."

I told her about the streetcars and the fancy clothes in Pelletier's window. I didn't mention Lettie or the sights in the Sudan, even though those things were taking up quite a bit of space in my mind. I wondered if these were unclean thoughts. I was pretty sure they were. Preacher Simms's eyes boring into mine stayed with me too.

I thought I might feel better about everything if I went to church on Sunday and cleansed my mind of the wickedness I had seen and thought about. It also bothered me that I helped Granddad do something illegal. An hour or two in church, neat and sitting up straight, might put things right.

We arrived at the church, and my old Sunday school teacher, Ory Gabel, gave me a wide smile when I walked in. Reverend Sayles showed a little more life than usual. His sermon was about being our brother's keeper.

At the end he said, "I hope you'll come back to the church tonight and hear our guest speaker. You'll learn more about how we can protect ourselves and our children from unnatural outside influences." I wondered what that was about, but was so grateful his sermon was short that I forgot about it. We prayed a while and sang another hymn, and I felt a lot better. I went up to Carol Ann with a clear conscience, happy to see her, and told her about my trip, but nothing that would shock her. After we talked that over, she said, "Are you coming to the convocation tonight?"

"Convocation? What's that?"

"That's what Reverend Sayles was talking about. The Men's Club from the church has invited this minister from Grand Forks to talk about a group he's starting. My parents think it will do wonderful things for our town. We're going, and I think you should come too."

"Maybe I will."

I walked home with Gram who was all corseted up in her good navy blue dress with the lace collar, her black straw hat from Sears and Roebuck squarely on her head, and immaculate white gloves even on this warm day.

"Are you going to the convocation tonight?" I asked.

"I think maybe I will," she said. "Lida says he is a fire-breathing speaker. He's a Prohibitionist, so I know Granddad won't go. You want to go?"

I nodded. If Carol Ann was going, I was going to be there too.

GRAM AND I went back to the church that night at 7:00. We were a few minutes early and were lucky to get a seat about halfway toward the front. In no time every pew was filled, and a few people even stood in the back. I spotted Carol Ann in the first row and was sorry we hadn't gotten there earlier so I could sit with her.

Our minister, Reverend Sayles, usually so stiff and sober, stood up and gave us a bigger smile than was normal. He shouted in a hearty voice, "Welcome, Americans! We'll begin tonight by singing 'Columbia, the Gem of the Ocean.' It's on page 272 in the hymnal. Don't be bashful. Let's stand and sing out. Show our guest how we feel about the U.S.A."

He waited while everyone got up and the rustling stopped. He looked at the pianist and said, "All right, Olive."

She swung into a powerful introduction, and we all sang. Our fervent voices filled the church. By the smile on our guest's face, we must have made it clear we loved our country.

"That was very fine indeed," Reverend Sayles said. "I am pleased to see so many of you here tonight because we are going to hear from a brilliant speaker who has come all the way from Grand Forks to be with us."

He introduced Reverend Halsey Brooks. Reverend Brooks was a big man, one whom Gram would call portly. I'd call him just plain fat. His black suit was so tight, I figured he must have bought it before he got so portly. His heavy jowls rolled over the starched collar of his white shirt and made his face red.

He began, "I am appreciative of this opportunity tonight to present several matters of interest to all good Americans." He looked at the ceiling prayerfully as if he were having a private word with God. Then he stared straight out at us.

"Let us remember the sublime principles instituted by Christ for the guidance of man in all his endeavors..."

Oh no, I thought. Two sermons in one day was one too many for me, and my mind wandered away. I hadn't known what we'd hear, but I'd hoped it wouldn't be "churchy." I wondered what Carol Ann thought. Even Gram seemed to nod.

Reverend Brooks gave the congregation another stern look. "There can be no laxity of devotion..." He went on. "Today our American unity is threatened by hordes of people, a polyglot mob of more than eight million, who have burst upon our shores from foreign lands. People of every color and persuasion—Hebrews, Moors, Papists…"

"Polyglot" was a new word for me. I had a fleeting thought of my sister Polly. I would call her "polyglot" next time I saw her just to get her riled up.

He went on. "Why? You may ask. Why do they come here? Well, I'll tell you. They come because they want to reap the rewards of what our ancestors sowed for us. They want to take our inheritance. Folks, take a minute to think about it. Was it THEIR forefathers who built this country? No. It was ours. Was it their intelligence that created a great democracy? No. It was ours. It was the superior brain power of our founders who formed our government, and now these foreigners want to change it, take away what is our birthright."

I didn't know any foreigners. I yawned. I'd hoped for more excitement.

"Right now, as we sit here, there are Jews in New York City who are trying to create a worker's union to usurp the rights of good business owners. Men whose know-how built the factories and plants all over this land. What right, I ask you? What right do these interlopers have to grab wealth that is unearned?

"Right now in this state, your Treasurer is a member of the Roman Catholic Church. A Roman Catholic handles your tax money. Can you believe that? What do you suppose is his priority? Where does his loyalty lie? Is it to you, the citizens of the state? Or could it be to the Pope?"

My dad hated Catholics. I thought he was a little off, but maybe he knew something I didn't. I thought of the Catholics I knew. Don Beaubien, Sally McVay, Vince, and even Polly. They seemed all right to me, but maybe there was something wrong with them. I wanted to hear what it was.

"You know, folks, back in Ireland, the Church of Rome exacted a tax on every household, and it went straight to the Vatican. That hasn't happened here. Not yet. But God help us, we need to protect ourselves by making sure that these people do not succeed as politicians. We cannot trust that their priests and bishops won't have their hands in the politicians' pockets."

Then he lowered his voice and spoke as if he were confiding a secret to us. "Have you thought about your own sheriff here in Union County? What is his religion?"

He looked around expectantly. I saw Miranda Phelps who was sitting in front of us look at her husband with raised eyebrows. Others stole quick peeks at each other.

"I'll tell you if you don't know. He is a Catholic, and even if he is unknowing, he is a part of the worldwide plan to take over this country. Ask yourselves. Does he take power unto himself that is not his? Do you know what he does with the fines he collects when someone gets crossways with him? Have you considered that?"

A shock went through me as I listened. People squirmed and turned around to look at each other. Our sheriff was Bernie Beaubien, Don's father. Mostly he was a farmer, but once in while there was a ruckus, somebody missing a stray cow or losing a pocketbook, and Mr. Beaubien handled it. What did this preacher know about him that we didn't? What had he done? Nobody had to tell me to pay attention now. This was right here at home.

The minister's voice rose, and his jowls shook as he continued. "It is time to take action. We must counteract these wicked influences— idol worshippers, bootleggers, gamblers, violators of the Sabbath."

And just when everybody was sitting up and ready to hear what we should do, Reverend Brooks made us wait. He pulled a white handkerchief from his pocket and wiped his forehead, his face, his mouth. He took his time refolding it and returning it to a pocket. Then he went on in a calmer voice.

"I want to share with you the thoughts of a great American, Colonel William Joseph Simmons, founder and first Imperial Wizard of the revival of the Ku Klux Klan."

Mention of the KKK made a little shiver go through my body, and the hair on my arms stood up a bit.

"Colonel Simmons has planned a new Klan, a Klan of great works. He intends to establish universities and a trust to aid failing farmers. He wants to provide homes for families and jobs for everyone. He will build medical centers and a chain of hospitals. Doesn't that sound grand?"

Yes, I liked this very much. Especially the idea of a house for every family. For such a long time I had ached for a house where our family could live together. Maybe Dad would've recovered from his shell shock if we'd had one. Even now, maybe the KKK could find a job for him. I was thrilled and uplifted by these words. I didn't know such possibilities existed.

"Colonel Simmons's Klan has given money to those in need— widows whose fatherless children were hungry, breadwinners who could not afford a doctor. It has built parks and playgrounds. Its members are men who care for their families and their fellow citizens, men who work hard and swear to forego spirits, gambling, and unclean living. His Klan is an organization with allegiance to no foreign power, to no Pope in Rome, but only to God and country."

This did not sound like the Ku Klux Klan that burned crosses and wore white sheets and pointed hats, the one that Don Beaubien was so scared of. These were fine things that the Klan meant to do. I could hear people around me murmuring their approval.

Reverend Brooks paused again, and his voice dropped in pitch. "Folks, I know many of you had husbands, sons, and fathers who served in the recent war in Europe…and when they were in those distant lands, they longed for America and loved her more than ever…" His lips trembled as his voice rose higher and louder.

"When at last they laid down their arms, bound up their wounds, and headed for home, they wanted to find the same country they remembered. They wanted their country to be worth the sacrifice of broken men and bodies. As they reached these shores, they were so overcome with emotion and gratitude, they fell to the ground and kissed the sweet earth of their beloved homeland."

Then, right in front of us, Reverend Brooks dropped down on his hands and knees, his butt in the air, looking as if it might split the seam of his pants, and he kissed the floor of the church, I heard some people suck in their breath at this drama. When he rose up, tears were running down his cheeks. He continued to preach, his soft, pink palms outstretched like Jesus on the cross.

"We must honor these men…" He choked on his tears. "We must honor these men by assuring that the country they fought for is as strong and unified and God-fearing as it was when they went abroad."

A surge of patriotism rose in me as I thought of the men he described. Men who fought for America. Men like my dad. His words lit a fire in me, and I wanted to help keep our country safe and strong just like Reverend Brooks said. I wanted the Klan to do all those grand things he talked about.

The air in the church was thick and hot. People were leaning forward hypnotized by his words, nodding to each other, some blinking back tears as he reminded them of those who were wounded or died. A few "Amens" could be heard. By now everyone was wound up in his cause, and I was ready to join up too. In a powerful voice he said, "Hear me now! What I propose tonight is the establishment of a KKK Klavern right here in Richmond, a Klavern to join with those a few miles away in Beresford and in Canton as a means of assuring that our great United States remains a unified, God-fearing country."

When at last he finished speaking, his voice hoarse from the effort, there was a moment of silence, and then everyone stood up and clapped. We'd never heard anything like this in our little town before. Reverend Brooks gave a bow, wiped his face, and sat down. People talked excitedly, fired up by the minister's words. Reverend Sayles invited men to sign up on the spot at a table near the door. As Gram and I turned to make our way out, I was astonished to see my father in the back of the church. Before I could reach him, he ducked outside and disappeared into the night.

"Did you see that?" I said to Gram. "Dad was here."

"He was? That's a surprise. He never goes anywhere."

We stood around outside the church for a while, cooling off in the evening air and listening to people talk. "This is wonderful," I heard. Or, "Just wait till this thing gets going. Things will be a lot better around here." Gram didn't say a word, just smiled and nodded to her friends, and then we walked home together. As we approached the house, I ran ahead eager to tell Granddad what we had heard.

I started talking almost before I was through the door. "They're starting a Klan here," I said. "My dad came tonight. Maybe they'll get him a job and a house for us."

"Whoa, Harry. Slow down. What are you talking about?" He looked up expectantly as Gram walked in. "What's going on?"

She smirked. "We've had some real entertainment tonight, Alfie. Promises like you wouldn't believe. This fellow's a stem-winder, all right. Made the Klan sound like the best thing ever to come down the road. And folks bought the whole package." She shook her head. "I couldn't believe it."

"Hmph. I suppose that includes turning everybody into a 'dry,' doesn't it?"

"'Fraid so. Might not be all bad," she said as she unpinned her hat. "Not only that, he set his sights on the Catholics." She related what he had said about Bernie Beaubien.

"Bernie? I never thought there was anything wrong with him."

"He's also after Negroes and Jews," she said, "but I don't think he'll find any around here."

"Yes, but he talked about some wonderful things that the Klan means to do, Granddad," I said. I ticked off the list—houses, hospitals, universities, and all the rest.

"Well, don't hold your breath," he said. "We'll have to see it first." He gave us a big, toothless grin. "But wait a minute. I haven't had a chance to tell you. Harry, you're an uncle."

"Polly?" Gram said.

"Yup," he said. "A baby girl and she named her Mary Josephine. Vince's mother and dad stopped by to tell."

This was turning into quite a night. My sister Polly so grown up she had a baby. Right away I wondered what Dad would have to say about it. I'd already planned to ask him about tonight's meeting when I picked up his dirty clothes in the morning, but before I had it all thought out, Gram said, "You better let your dad know about this when you see him tomorrow." I dreaded telling him about Polly's baby worse than a toothache.

GRAM SENT ME to the store first thing in the morning with a basket of tomatoes from her garden for Granddad to sell. His customers were talking about the meeting.

"I paid 'em my fifteen dollars and signed up right on the spot," said Walter Trometer.

"So did I," said another. "I couldn't believe what he said about our sheriff. I always thought he was all right."

"You just never know, I guess," said a third.

"Are you going to join, Alfie?"

Granddad stood behind the counter, fiddling with the charge book. "Can't do it, gents," he said.

"Why not?" Walter said. "Are you just cheap?"

"Nah. That's not it."

They looked at him expectantly. Granddad wasn't usually shy about talking.

"You seem to forget," he said. "I can't be a member. I'm what you're supposed to be fighting against. Did you forget I was born in France?"

They all got very quiet.

Finally Walter said, "They didn't mean you, Alfie."

"They sure as hell did," he said. "I was even baptized a Catholic." He waited a minute and added, "And I sell beer."

This rocked me back on my heels. I had gotten so wound up last night about what I heard, it had never even occurred to me that it could affect someone like Granddad. I stopped to think about others who wouldn't be welcome in the KKK. Bill and Jalmer Nelson had come from Sweden with their parents when they were just little kids. And the McVay's, who ran Dad's boarding house, were from Ireland and Catholic to boot. None of them could join. I just couldn't make things jibe with this whole KKK business.

When the customers cleared out, Granddad shook his head. "Those fellows signed up and still don't even know what they've done."

11

I GOT ON MY bike and rode over to see Dad. Sally wasn't home, so he and I sat at the kitchen table. I had Polly's big news to tell him, but I was scared to say anything after the way he'd acted when he heard about her wedding. This might be worse. I decided to work up to it gradually.

"I saw you in the back of the church last night, Dad. What did you think of that preacher?"

"He was long-winded, but I thought he had some good things to say. We can't let this country get overrun with foreigners. Especially the damn Catholics."

"I thought he was kinda hard on Mr. Beaubien, didn't you?"

"Maybe. Maybe not. Maybe he deserved it."

"Gram and Granddad don't think so," I said. "His boy is my friend from school."

He just grunted.

"Do you think you would ever join the KKK, Dad?"

"I might. Depends on what they plan to do. There's a fellow staying here at Sally's who talks about it a lot."

We sat for a minute. I stretched my legs, then my arms. I couldn't seem to find anything else to talk about, and I couldn't put off my news any longer. "Dad. I thought...I mean, Gram thought...well, we all thought you should know." I swallowed hard.

"Know what?" he said.

I let it pop out. "Polly had a baby yesterday, Dad." His head jerked up, and his eyes bored into mine. I thought I might as well finish what I had to say. "It's a girl, and they named her Mary Josephine."

It seemed like it should be good news that he had a grandchild, but, oh boy, did that set him off. He pulled his mouth up in a tight knot and his lips turned white. His eyes grew huge, and he let loose.

"My God! Isn't it bad enough that my only daughter ran off and married a Frenchman? She must have joined the goddamn Catholic Church down there in Jefferson." He stood up and banged his good fist on the table. "Now, here she is with a French Catholic brat! She even gave this kid a Catholic name." He got up and paced around the room, yelling, "I think I'd rather it'd been born dead. You hear me, Harry?"

I stood up open-mouthed at his hateful words.

"Dad, take it easy. Calm down. I think Vince and Polly are getting along fine. They're happy."

He went over to the kitchen door and yanked it open. For a moment I thought he was going to stomp out, but he wheeled around and came toward me.

"I can't stand it. I'm never going to speak to her again. In fact, I don't ever want to lay eyes on Polly again. Or her kid. Ever."

His extreme words were hard to take. I didn't think he had any business criticizing Polly. She mostly had to raise herself, and he'd been no help to her. I wanted him to stop talking so hatefully about my sister.

"Dad, I don't understand. Why do you hate the French and the Catholics so much? What is it that makes you so mad at them? They fought with us in the war. They were on our side, weren't they?"

"You might have thought so, but they didn't want the Americans there. All they cared about was themselves. The damn fools didn't seem to know they couldn't have won the war without us. They acted so superior and arrogant. They thought they were so much better than us. It made my blood boil." His words twisted his face into an ugly mask, but at least he'd stopped talking about Polly.

I said, "Come on, Dad. Did they do something to you?"

"I'll tell you what they did," he said all angry-like. He turned and stared out the window for a minute as if reminding himself of what had happened. When he spoke, his voice was quieter, almost as if he were talking to himself. "It was terrible there on the Marne. So many got wounded. Or died. The trenches stunk so."

"It must have been awful, Dad. We couldn't tell from here what it was like. How bad it was for you."

He nodded, calmer now. "After I got shot, they put me in the field hospital. Nobody had time to pay attention to my wound. It didn't seem all that serious. I figured it would heal right up, and I'd be sent back to the trenches. Then it got infected. I could feel it getting hot. My arm turned red, and pus poured out of it. When the nurse saw it, she said, 'I don't think you'll be going back anytime soon, Cal.'"

Dad returned to the table and sat down. I was almost afraid to move, wanting to hear his story and hoping he'd finally tell something about being over there even if it was terrible.

"The field hospital had to be moved, so they took me behind the lines to a French hospital that was run by a bunch of nuns." He grimaced. "I can see those whey-faced women yet. No wonder they were nuns. They were so plain and ugly, no man would have wanted them."

I risked a little smile. "Yes, but I'll bet they took good care of you."

He snorted. "Not so. They put me in a room with another Yank and proceeded to ignore us. We were lucky if we got food once a day."

"They let you go hungry?"

"That's right. The other fellow was in bad shape, out of his head a lot. He'd already been there a couple of weeks, and he wasn't getting any better. One time he told me that the nuns used all their medicine on their own wounded men, and there wasn't anything left for us Americans."

"That's terrible. How could they do that? Was it true, do you think? Did you ever find out?"

"Not really. One morning I looked over at the other bed and I saw that Buck, that was his name, was dead. I had a little bell beside my bed so I rang it and rang it, but nobody came. I was so weak from the infection and no food that it was all I could do to get to the hallway. I just stood there leaning against the doorway and yelled and yelled. It took a long time, but finally one of those pasty-faces showed up. She said, 'Oh, Mister Spencer. You must stay in bed.'

"I said, 'For God's sake, woman. You've let that man die. He's lying over there dead since last night.' She looked in and crossed herself, and then started mumbling some prayers. Oh I was pissed.

"'I'm going to die too if I don't get some care,' I said. 'I haven't seen a doctor. Nobody has changed my bandages, and this wound stinks. I want some food and new bandages, and I want some help getting this cleaned up.'

'Yes, Mr. Spencer,' she whispered. They all whispered."

I listened in horrified silence as Dad went on.

"She went away, and finally some boys took the body out of the room. Nobody came to help me until after dark. Finally that same sickly looking woman came back. She had no food. No bandages. She said, 'You must pray Mr. Spencer. Pray to Our Lady. Pray to St. Joseph to help you get well.' She handed me a little Jesus statue. It was like a kid's toy. I looked at the silly thing, and I took it in my good hand and threw it out the window. We heard it hit the paving below. I screamed at her, 'Goddamn it. Get me some food.' She squealed and scurried away like a little mouse."

"Dad, I can't imagine anything so awful. How could they get by with ignoring you like that? There must have been something you could do. Wasn't there a doctor around?"

"Oh, Harry. You don't know anything. Not a goddamned thing."

Dad stood and tried to pour himself some coffee. He was still clumsy with his left hand, and the cup teetered on the counter and fell to the floor. He was silent and watched while I picked up the broken pieces and dumped them in the wastebasket. I found a rag and wiped up the spilled coffee. I wondered if I should leave. A part of me wanted to get out of there, away from him, but another part of me wanted to hear his story, and he seemed to want to talk.

"They sent a doctor all right. The next morning. He was an old man, too old to be in the army. He had a thin little mustache and a mean face. He couldn't speak English, so they found somebody to translate. He wanted to put me out and cut away the rotten flesh on my arm, put in a tube to drain it, if necessary. He thought it would heal up fast. I was so tired of the whole thing. What he wanted to do sounded all right to me after all this time, and I told them to go ahead. But first I wanted some food."

"Did they feed you?"

"Finally. I got a bowl of oatmeal and a piece of bread. And can you believe it? A cup of coffee. I thought things were really turning around. They came mid-morning and gave me something to knock me out before they started work on my arm.

"When I woke up in the middle of the afternoon, I was all alone. My arm was bandaged up, and it hurt like hell, but I figured I could tough it out. I finally got my eyes to stay open, and that's when I saw it. Across the room there was a table about as high as my bed where they had put their instruments. Only now there was a white enamel bowl on it. And, oh God, Harry. My arm was in it."

I felt my stomach churn.

He put his good hand over his eyes before he went on. "I just stared and stared at my own hand over there in that bowl. I couldn't make sense of it. How could my arm be over there? Then it came to me. That sonofabitch had cut off my arm."

I STUMBLED OUT of Dad's place, my head spinning with what I had heard. I had to get away by myself to think. I started running without knowing where. I ran and ran all the way to the edge of town and across the main road. I started up the tall bluff on the other side and climbed in the hot sun until I was out of breath and had to stop. I fell to my knees and felt my stomach sicken as I replayed the story in my mind, shuddering with the thought of the cut off arm, the saw, all the blood, and the pain. I imagined what it would be like to wake up with the limb still in the room but not attached. It was horrible, too horrible to bear.

The strange man who told me this. This man whose bent and twisted thinking sickened me. He was so bitter and filled with hate. Was he my father? I didn't know him anymore. I didn't like him much, and that made me feel guilty and ashamed now that I'd heard his story.

I sat there on that hill until I could breathe again, the wind whipping the tall grass and drying my sweat. I let the sun bake into me. After a long time, my body quieted and I was able to get to my feet. I stood on the high clay bluffs that marched alongside the Sioux River all the way to the Missouri. Below me Richmond lay on the flat flood plain. Occasionally a child's cry could be heard, or the slamming of a door. Nothing in that peaceful scene could have foretold the misery that I knew was down there.

I didn't want to think about my father. I was angry with him and felt cheated by him. I was the one who had gotten hurt. I didn't have a regular family anymore; my brothers and sister were gone; our home was gone. And it was all his fault. He had brought on all this misery. Yet I couldn't forget the horror in the hospital, the meanness and the callousness of those people. What if it had happened to me?

No. No. I didn't want to feel sorry for him. I didn't want to feel his agony. If he hadn't left us, this would never have happened. I stood on that high place trying to empty my head of all I had heard and felt. Still, the thought of my father's misery wouldn't leave me alone. It kept sneaking in from the corners of my mind. It niggled at me, and I tried to put it away from me. I'd taught myself to forget about Dad, not to care about him, not to think about him. But his agony and the shame he must have felt for what had happened to us kept coming back to me, circling round and round in my mind like the great red-tailed hawk flying over my head. Finally I could deny it no longer. His pain spiked itself through me. I sat down again, and great choking sobs overtook me. My father. My father.

I wanted to put a fist down Ory Gable's throat. Every Sunday he told us that God loved us, that He cared about each one of us, that we were His children. We just had to put our faith in Him. Put our lives in His hands. Well, Ory Gabel was wrong. This God hated our father and hated me. Otherwise He wouldn't have allowed the butchery that crumpled my father. Oh, I spent a long, hot afternoon hating God. I sat up there on that high bluff until the sun began to go down, and I blamed Him and hated Him. I stayed until that great western sky went from gold to purple as evening came. The hot wind died down, and I could feel the clay dust of the bluffs, finer than sand, in my mouth and in my hair, inside my clothes. I was spent now, my anger gone, my mind empty, only wanting to go home.

Gram, who was sometimes hard to love, saw me come in and brushed the hair from my eyes.

"Where have you been, Harry?"

"I went to see Dad. Then I needed to get away for a while."

She looked into my eyes. "He must have talked to you? Did he tell you his

story?"

I looked at her in disbelief. "Did you know all that stuff?"

She nodded.

"Why didn't you tell me?"

"I don't know," she said. "You were so young. We wanted to protect you."

"You shouldn't have kept me in the dark. I needed to know." I felt the heat of anger boil up in me again. "Why did you treat me like a child? Everyone knew but me. It's my dad. You shouldn't have kept it a secret from me."

"I'm sorry, Harry. We thought it was the right thing."

I slammed out of the kitchen.

❖   ❖   ❖

THAT NIGHT AS Ty and I were going to bed I asked him if he knew about Dad and what had happened in France.

"Dad didn't tell me directly, but I heard bits and pieces when he told Uncle Lyle and Aunt Hazel. He talked about it over and over again so I figured out most of it. I think they got sick of hearing his story."

"Is there anything to do for him, Ty?"

"What could we do, Harry? Uncle Lyle did his best to get him beyond it, but he wouldn't listen. What could we do that would be better?"

"I don't know," I said.

"Aw, Harry There's nothing we can do. It's just the way he is. We just have to forget about it and let him be."

12

DREAMS OF BLOOD, dead bodies, and severed limbs disturbed my sleep that night. Sometimes men in white masks armed with saws were so real that I woke up rigid with fear and trembling. In my dreams I looked and looked, but could never find my father, though I could hear him calling for me. Ragged, wailing calls.

Gram must have known how it was because she didn't get me up at dawn like usual. The sun was high and hot when I awoke. As I opened my eyes, my dad's dreadful story came back to me, and I curled up in my sheets trying to escape the memory. It held me in its grip until finally I could stand it no more. My thirst won out and forced me out of bed. I went to the kitchen for a dipper of cold well water.

"Good morning, sleepyhead," Gram said. She looked at me kindly, like she felt sorry for me. I had been pretty sore at her the day before.

"I'm just on my way over to Lida's," she said, "to get us a chicken. You better get dressed and get to the store so Granddad and Ty can come home for dinner."

I nodded, still groggy.

"Harry, I have a little something for you." She reached for my hand and pressed a fifty-cent piece into my palm. I stared at it blearily.

"After you finish at the store this noon, maybe you and Carol Ann would like to go roller skating."

I looked at her flabbergasted. She had never given me money out of the blue like that. And she never encouraged me to go somewhere just for fun.

I managed to mumble, "Thanks, Gram."

"Have a good time, Harry."

I watched out the window as she hurried down the road still in her apron. My mind emerged from sleep, and my dark feelings began to lift. Carol Ann. I needed to see her. I had so much to tell her. I managed to pull on some clothes and hop on my bike to ride to her house.

We made our plans to go to River Sioux to skate as soon as I could leave the store.

She said, "I'll pack a picnic lunch to eat in the park."

"Great," I said. "I'll be back about one o'clock."

IT WAS A hot, late-summer day and we walked slowly the mile or so to River Sioux carrying the picnic basket between us, talking about nothing in particular, just happy to be together someplace away from home. Our shoes scuffed up the dust, and the wind lifted it into small whorls. Grasshoppers popped up now and then surprising us. The grass in the ditches alongside the road was dusty and dry, and the smell of summer's end was in the air.

We passed through the big stone archway for River Sioux Park, and the air to became cooler. We smelled the dampness of the river. Huge cottonwood trees provided shade for the campground where several tents were pitched. Noisy vacationers filled the rental cottages this time of year, their clotheslines waving with towels and bathing suits.

I had always loved the playground with its swings and merry-go-rounds, and my favorite when I was younger, a tube slide, its slick surface sending you to the ground in a split second. Picnic tables stood in the grassy areas. We set our basket on one to reserve it and walked down to the water. White, sandy beaches lined the river where the water was crystal clear and moving rapidly, even for this time of year. I took my shoes and socks off and waded for a minute to cool myself from the long walk.

"Try it," I said to Carol Ann. "It feels great."

"I can't do that," she said. "Parade around in my bare feet."

I wondered at that, seeing as how we had both spent our summers barefoot when we were little kids. She had sure gotten fussy.

"Oh, come on," I said.

Finally she could resist no more and joined me, holding up her skirt and grabbing my arm to steady herself. I splashed my hot face with the water, shooting some at her too.

"No, you don't, Harry. I don't want to get all wet before we go skating." She ran back and sat down in the shade, leaning against a big tree and watching all the little kids trying to swim. I got our picnic basket and sat with her. We laughed out loud when fat Mr. Tom Crill, the owner of River Sioux, came floating down the river on his back, puffing on a big, black cigar. After a bit, he turned over on his stomach and swam upstream, his cigar still clamped between his teeth. Then he rolled over and floated downriver again. Everybody clapped at his performance.

"Shall we eat before we skate?" Carol Ann said.

"Yeah, I'm hungry." We devoured the hard-boiled eggs, the fresh whole tomatoes warm from the sun, and homemade cinnamon rolls that Carol Ann had packed.

"My mom made these rolls for Dad to take to the KKK meeting tomorrow night," she said. "He's still talking about the convocation and how good this Klavern will be for the town."

"Hm. So he joined up?"

"He sure did. Right there that night. He thinks it's a wonderful idea. He got his white robe and a big pointed hat. They're going to meet every Wednesday night at the old pool hall."

"What does he think about Sheriff Beaubien?"

"Oh, I don't know if he bought into that. He just thinks the KKK will do some good things for the town."

"My dad was at the convocation," I said, "but he was one of the first ones out the door."

"Really. I didn't see him. Did he sign up?"

"I don't think so, but I don't know. I sure don't like the way he hates the Catholics. I wish he didn't."

The whole sorry scene yesterday with my dad replayed itself in my mind as we sat there. I began to tell Carol Ann bits and pieces of it. I didn't mean to, but I just couldn't help it. The story kept pouring out and pretty soon I had told her the whole thing.

When I was finally finished, she said, "That's dreadful, Harry. I feel so sorry for your poor, poor father." Tears stood in her blue eyes. "He must be miserable."

My dad miserable? I hadn't really thought about it that way. I was the one who was miserable. Sure, a terrible thing had happened to him, but I hadn't considered his feelings after all these years. We were half mad at him most of the time because he wouldn't act like he used to. It seemed like he'd made up his mind to be hateful and not behave like our dad.

"Maybe that's why he acts the way he does. 'Cause he just feels so awful inside," she said.

I wondered if that kind of misery could make a man turn away from his family, from those who loved him. We would've done anything in our power to help him if we had only known what to do.

"Maybe he needs some happy things to think about. Maybe you should tell him funny stories, jokes," she said, smiling. "That might get his mind off his trouble."

"What kind of jokes?" My mind had been so far away from funny stuff, I couldn't think of a single one.

"Oh, I don't know." She thought for a moment and then said, "What about this one? When somebody asked Rosie how she cured her husband of biting his fingernails, she said, 'Oh, it was easy. I just hid his false teeth.'"

I groaned, but I had to smile. Then I thought of one too. "Do you know about Sven? He had a son who came home one day from school and said, 'Dad, I have the biggest feet in the third grade. Is that because I'm Norwegian? No, Sven said. It's because you're nineteen.'"

We sat there and told each other the silliest jokes we could think of until we were both laughing so hard we had to hold our stomachs. We had about run out of them when the whistle blew at the skating rink meaning it was time for a new round of skating to begin. We gathered up our picnic things, put on our shoes, and headed across the road to the pavilion.

It was a high-roofed, open-air building that could be closed quickly during rainstorms by bringing up wooden shutters over the screened window openings. What started out as a dance floor had been expanded for roller-skating. A boardwalk under wide eaves provided a walkway where skaters could go to cool off. I marveled how the whole thing was built around a huge cottonwood tree in the center with openings in the roof for its branches.

I paid our admission and we put on our rented skates. I had been to River Sioux many times, but I never had enough money to skate, so I had just watched the others. But now was my chance, and I didn't waste a second. We got out on the floor with all the others and began skating counter clockwise around that tree. Carol Ann was pretty good at it and laughed at my awkwardness, but it didn't take long to get the hang of it.

Every so often they would call out a change. "Ladies turn," or "Gents only." Sometimes it was for couples, and I put my arm around Carol Ann's waist and we skated together, leaning into each other and matching our footwork. Late in the afternoon we made a whip. Everyone took hold of hands and formed a long line. We began slowly with the one in the center of the floor barely moving. As we got going, the one on the outside end had to skate faster and faster. Sometimes he had to let go because he just couldn't skate fast enough. I loved the feeling of the air blowing through my shirt as we picked up speed and got going so fast it seemed like we might take right off into the air.

Our two and one-half hours were up before we knew it, and we moved breathless to the side to remove our skates. The exhilaration was still with me when we went to the fountain for a long drink of cold water.

"That was fun," Carol Ann said.

"Yeah," I said. "I'm glad we came out here today 'cause I've got a surprise! Guess what? I've got a job!"

"What do you mean? How could you get a job here?"

"While you ladies were skating, I got an idea, so I went over and talked to Mr. Crill. I asked him to hire me to be one of the fellows who helps people put on their skates. I could hardly believe it when he said he could use me. I'm supposed to come back tomorrow so he can teach me what to do. It'll pay ten cents a pair. Maybe I'll finally have some money for things."

"That's wonderful, Harry. Good for you. Maybe I'll come out and see you while you're working. You can put my skates on." She looked at me with her pretty, flirty smile.

"I'll do it," I said.

When we had cooled down some, we got our basket and began to walk home. The sun was low and directly in our eyes as we headed west. We took turns walking backwards to avoid its rays.

Somehow we got onto the subject of my father again.

"You know," Carol Ann said, "If he could get some kind of a job, it might improve his outlook. He might meet people and make some friends."

"I don't know what kind of work he could do with one arm," I said. "He's really pretty clumsy with it."

"Harry." She stopped walking and looked at me. "I have an idea. What if he got an artificial arm? You know, the kind that has a hook instead of a hand?"

I felt a little tingle go through my body. I hadn't thought of this before, and I wondered if we could make it happen.

"That's a great idea," I said. "I'm going to ask Gram about it. Maybe we can help him get one." I felt uplifted by this notion. Here was something that might make things better.

We walked to Carol Ann's house where I had left my bike. I was so grateful to her, and I liked her so much, I wanted to kiss her. But it was broad daylight, and her little brother, Jerry, was outside playing. So we said a slow goodbye, and I headed home, my mind full of this new idea for Dad.

As I rode by the school, I saw a little knot of boys and heard some shouting and crying. I rode up and jumped off my bike. "What's going on?" I yelled. Don Beaubien was on the ground and Corky Burris was on his back, punching him. Howie Mines was urging him on. Both of them were awful bullies.

"That'll teach you, you dirty mackerel snapper," Corky said.

"You took care of him," Howie crowed.

A couple of Don's little brothers were standing nearby crying.

"What are you doing?" I said. "Get off him, Corky."

"Oh, mind your own business, Harry," he said, but he got up. He and Howie got on their bikes and high-tailed it away.

I helped Don get up. His nose was bleeding and it looked like he'd taken a hit on the side of his head.

"Why were they beating on you, Don?"

He looked at me, and tears started to roll down his dirty face.

"They said my dad stole money. They said the preacher told everybody at the church last Sunday night. My dad never stole anything from anybody, Harry. I was so mad I punched Corky, but I couldn't handle the two of them." He wiped his face and turned to his brothers. "C'mon, boys. Let's go home."

I remembered what the minister had said and was sickened by the ugliness his words had caused.

"Don," I called out to him. "That's not exactly what he said."

He waved sadly at me as he walked away. "Thanks, Harry. It doesn't matter."

But it did matter. What that minister said about Don's dad wasn't right, no matter what good things the Klan meant to do.

13

AFTER SUPPER THAT night, I raised Carol Ann's idea of an artificial arm for Dad.

"I don't know, Harry," Gram said. "He fights everything people try to do for him. I know Uncle Lyle tried his best."

"But he didn't try this."

"That's right," Ty said. "He didn't, but how in the world can we get one?"

Granddad sat working a toothpick in his mouth. "I expect you'll have to write to the government. If you can get it from them, it won't cost anything with him being a veteran."

"That's true," Gram said. "I guess there's nothing to lose by trying. You might as well go ahead."

I found a piece of school tablet and sharpened a pencil with my penknife. Ty and I sat at the kitchen table and worked out the wording of a letter to the government. We asked for an artificial arm for our dad, Calvin Spencer, whose arm had been amputated in France during the war.

Gram looked it over and said, "You'll have to give them more information: you should tell them which arm it is. Put in his birthday so they can look him up. How about his middle name?"

Ty and I stared at each other. Neither of us could think of his middle name. Ty drummed the pencil on the table for a moment and then popped up with it. "I remember," he said. "It's Edward. Calvin Edward Spencer. That's how our brother Eddie got his name."

He added that to the letter.

"You know, boys," Gram said, "Maybe we should send the letter to Dr. Brunner to see if he can help."

It relieved me to hear her say that because it meant she was with us on the whole idea. Dr. Brunner knew Dad and would surely know what to do. Anyway, we didn't know any addresses in Washington, D.C. It seemed like such a vast, faraway place. I doubted if anybody would even read our letter if we sent it there. My handwriting was better than Ty's, so I copied it over as neatly as I could. Gram signed it, and I addressed an envelope to Dr. Brunner in Portlandville. The next morning I took it to the store for the postman.

A stranger stood facing Granddad across the counter. Well, not a stranger really, but someone I didn't know personally. It was the man who sat behind the table at the convocation, signing up members for the KKK. He was staying at Sally McVay's, and I had seen him on her porch talking to my dad. He was big, mean looking, and he seemed to be all one color. His curly hair, cut short and plastered to his head with pomade, was tawny brown, the same color as his eyes. His skin was rough and weathered tan with deep pits from smallpox or something. Even though it was a hot day, he wore a long-sleeved shirt and a necktie, but it was plain to see how well muscled his arms were.

He looked at Granddad standing behind the counter. "The sign outside says Mr. Alphonse Didder, Proprietor. Is that you?" There was a sneer in his voice.

"It's Didier, sir. How can I help you?" Granddad said.

"Well, Mr. Alphonse Didderer." Again he taunted with the tone of his voice. "I need a pound of coffee."

Buster, who was sleeping behind the counter, came out to sniff, and the hair on his back rose up a little. I went to the coffee grinder and commenced grinding.

Granddad, who stood behind the counter, said, "You can just call me Alfie."

"What kind of a name is Alphonse Didderay, anyway?"

I slowed down the grinder a little bit to listen, and when I did, the man turned to me, his tawny eyes flecked with gold. He looked bold and nasty.

"Just keep grinding, kid. I'm in a hurry." He turned back to Granddad. "What did you say it was?"

"It's French, I guess," Granddad said.

"You born there?"

I could tell Granddad didn't like the way this conversation was going. He kept fiddling with the charge book and his pencil.

"Yes, but my folks brought me here when I was just a kid."

"So you're not really American, I guess."

"I figure I am." Granddad inched toward a baseball bat he kept behind the counter.

"What goes on in the back room over there?" the man asked, jerking his thumb toward the bar.

"Oh, I sell a little beer to my friends. Do you want some?" Granddad looked up with a sickly smile on his face. He was trying to be his usual friendly self, but his voice sounded nervous.

"No, I don't want any beer," the man said. "It's illegal to be selling beer. Don't you know that? Haven't you heard of Prohibition?"

Granddad didn't answer. I finished with the coffee and packaged it up. "That'll be fifty-two cents," I said, hoping he would pay up and leave. I stepped behind the counter and stood with Granddad.

"Listen here, *Alphonse*. Have you joined the KKK yet?"

The way he said Alphonse, I could tell he was still trying to belittle Granddad. I burned with resentment at his words.

Granddad shook his head. "No, I haven't. Hadn't really planned to."

"Well, I think it would be in your best interest to join. This movement is big, and I'd think you would want to be a part of it. You being a businessman and all. It'd be better for your store and your family, don't you think?" He leaned across the counter, his huge figure making Granddad shrink into himself. After a minute, he picked up his package of coffee and paid for it.

"I'll stop back in a couple of days and get you signed up. It costs fifteen dollars to join."

"Fifteen bucks. Where am I going to find that? I don't think you need to come back. I don't plan to join."

The man opened his eyes wide. "Well, Mr. Alphonse Didder whatever your name is. We'll just see about that," he said, and went out the door.

I let out a big whoosh of breath from the tension. "Who does he think he is to talk to you like that?" I said.

"He's the organizer for the Klan, Harry. Walter Trometer told me they sent him in from Indiana to get this thing going here. His name is Rufus Laycock. He's been around pestering everybody to sign up, and he kind of threatens them if they don't."

"Will he try to do something to you? Will he hurt you?"

"Nah. It's all just bluster, I think."

I wasn't so sure. I hated to leave Grandad alone in the store after that, but I had to see about my new job. What I had seen that day gnawed at me all the way to the skating rink. The more I heard and saw of this KKK business, the less I liked it. I couldn't forget Don Beaubien's fight with the bullies at the school and the report I'd heard of the cross burning in Alcester. So far I hadn't seen anything good come of the KKK, and I was beginning to doubt they would ever do those great things the preacher talked about.

BEFORE LONG, GRAM heard from Dr. Brunner. The Veterans Bureau had checked the records, and Dad was entitled to receive an artificial arm. The letter said that he'd been offered one before he was discharged, but he had turned it down.

"I wonder why he did that," I said.

"I can't imagine," Gram said. "I suppose he was already feeling mulish."

"Makes me wonder what he'll do when he finds out about this," Ty said. He was nervous about everything, and I felt a little niggle of worry too.

"We have to try," I said. "Otherwise his life is just going to go on and on with him not able to do anything and feeling awful about it."

We figured out how the thing worked by poring over the *Marks Manual of Artificial Limbs* that came with the letter. The artificial arm was held in place with straps that went under the arms and around the chest.

"I'll bet that's a hot contraption to wear," Granddad said. We nodded.

A flexion strap controlled the arm movement, and a hook was attached in place of a hand. The manual described the hook as "the most desirable and useful implement for the laboring man." It could close or spread apart in order to grab hold of things and was managed by flexing the bicep. A picture showed a man digging his garden with a spade using both his good hand and the hook. Another featured a man throwing a ball with his artificial arm.

This sounded almost too good to be true. Surely Dad would want to have such a thing, but the questions haunted me. How would we raise the subject with him? Who would do it? What if he wouldn't even try it on? What if we got it on him and his bicep wouldn't work?

We hadn't figured out any of that, but all of us thought we should move forward. Gram wrote to Dr. Brunner that night and asked him to make the arrangements to get the arm. She put down Dad's height and what she guessed his arm length would be by measuring his shirtsleeve. We decided she should let Sally McVay know what we were doing so she might help us when the time came. Now we would just have to wait and hope for the best, but my insides knotted up every time I thought about what Dad's reaction would be.

14

MEANWHILE, I WAS learning my job at the skating rink where I was to help people put on their rented skates. Being the newest boy, I was assigned the Number Four position. As customers came in, they'd start with the Number One position, and, if there was a crowd, they'd work down to me. At first I was clumsy, handling their shoes and all, but it got easier every day. Part of the job was to keep all the skates in good working order, oiling them and replacing the straps when necessary. It made me feel important to go around with the skate key on a piece of string around my neck. I was proud that folks saw me as a member of the staff. It made me feel like I belonged. Maybe I was on my way to being somebody.

The head boy was named Russ Popken, and he was sixteen years old. I admired just about everything about him. He was tall and wore his dark hair slicked down and shiny. His face was tan and showed off the whitest teeth I'd ever seen. The thing that got me the most was that he had a car to drive. I couldn't believe that somebody that young could go anywhere he wanted. Sometimes he and the other boys took off after work and went to Beaverton. I don't know what they did there, but I was impressed and hoped they would invite me to go some day.

I worked every chance I got and saved just about everything I made. It was only three weeks until high school would start, and I got jittery when I thought about it. I looked down at my old, worn work boots and knew they wouldn't do. I wanted new shoes and some long pants. I figured if I could put by five dollars, I could manage. That would mean putting on fifty pairs of skates at ten cents a pair. It would be close, but maybe I could do it.

Just when I got that figured out, it seemed like people only came in twos and threes, and I didn't get any customers. I prayed for a herd of people to come all at once and make me rich, but I had to be patient.

Russ noticed my frustration. One day he said, "I'm going to go get some cigarettes. Sam, you want to come with me?" Sam was the Number Two boy.

Sam jumped at the chance, so Russ told Harold, the Number Three boy, to move to first position and me to move to the second. That day I made two dollars. That was more like it, and I was grateful to Russ whenever he gave me a chance to get ahead like that.

Mr. Crill said the skating rink would close after the first weekend in September, so I continued to work as much as I could. The money started to add up. Gram was dumfounded when I gave her $25.00 to order my new school clothes and shoes from the Sears and Roebuck catalogue.

"Harry, I'm real proud of you. I had no idea you were making this kind of money."

I grinned. It was a powerful feeling to know that I wouldn't have to ask Gram for anything, and I made up my mind that, no matter what happened in the future, I was never going to go without money. My success made me want to strut, to holler, to tell everybody how good it felt. Why, I could even buy myself a coke or a candy bar if I wanted. I prayed Gram wouldn't think she needed a cut of it.

Russ and the other boys included me in their group regularly now. Sometimes we just drove around, talking and laughing, looking for something fun to do. They all bragged about their girlfriends. Whose was better looking, whose was the better dancer or kisser, and they kept hinting at a big IT. I was pretty sure I knew what they meant, but I wasn't about to ask.

"Did you ever kiss a girl, Harry?"

"Oh yeah," I said, casually, like it was an everyday event, but I was quick to change the subject. The only thing I could brag about was that I'd visited the Sudan in Sioux City, and they liked hearing about that. Maybe because I fudged a little on the truth of it just to keep it interesting.

I told Russ I was going to start high school.

"Good for you, Harry," he said. "I wish I weren't so lazy. That's what I should be doing. You gonna play football and all that stuff?"

"I dunno. Gotta wait and see."

"I suppose you'll be going to dances and parties."

I hadn't given that a thought, but I said, "I suppose so."

"You got a girl?"

"No. Well, sorta, I guess." I didn't know if Carol Ann was my girl or not, but I kind of thought of her that way.

"Well, she'll want you to take her to dances. You just wait and see."

My heart plummeted. I didn't know the first thing about dancing. "I...I don't know how to dance," I said, feeling lower than a snake's belly. "Do you know how?"

"Oh, I'll say. My girl Darlene and I go to all the dances. She's a great dancer. We go everywhere, especially when there's a good band. River Sioux, sometimes to the Rigadon in Sioux City, or to the Tromar Ballroom in LeMars." He lit up a cigarette and blew the smoke out the window. I thought he was the smoothest, most sophisticated fellow I'd ever met.

"I'll tell you what, Harry. I'll talk to Darlene and see if she'd teach you how to dance. Then you'll be ready for high school."

RUSS TOOK ME to Darlene's house several times that summer so she could teach me. How different her home was from mine. A bunch of younger brothers and sisters poured out of the house whenever we drove up. They didn't care about the loose, unpainted house siding or the tall weeds in the yard. They were too busy having a good time, everybody laughing and talking.

Inside, we pushed back the worn furniture in the living room, tables with no varnish left on them and a battered couch that could hold four or five of the younger kids. Darlene's mother, Pearl, dropped her housework for these occasions and took a seat at the big, black piano, and we danced on the blue-flowered linoleum floor. Pearl played the piano by ear, and she knew all the latest tunes. Sometimes she just made things up so the music would be right for whatever step we were working on.

We started with the box step. Left foot forward, right foot slide. Right foot forward, left foot slide. I did the steps by myself several times, then Pearl started the music and Darlene and I danced as a couple. At first I was shy about putting my arm on her waist, but Russ didn't seem to mind, and I finally got used to it. He danced with one of the sisters while Darlene was teaching me. Something about the music seemed to infect all the kids. The minute it started, they were up and dancing with each other, not embarrassed if girls danced with girls, or boys with boys. They just had to move.

Darlene showed me how to use my left hand to guide my partner to do turns. This was the most amazing fun I had ever had. We danced till we were out of breath, then someone made popcorn and we relaxed for a while. Eventually we moved on to the two-step with its quick, quick slow, slow movements, and then I learned the waltz. Darlene told me to listen to the music and let it tell me what to do. She said I was a "natural." I couldn't wait to show Carol Ann what I had learned. After a few sessions, I knew I was ready for the first dance.

ONE RAINY DAY the rink wasn't doing any business so Mr. Crill told us all we could leave. Instead of going home, Russ drove us to Beaverton where we walked up and down the streets, looking in store windows, talking about what we would buy when we had some real money. The others all wanted to see a Buster Keaton movie at the new Hipp Theater. I felt guilty spending money for a ticket, but I'd never seen a movie, and I couldn't have resisted any more than I could have turned down a free hundred-dollar bill. I had to do it.

The movie was called *Sherlock Jr.*, and I almost made myself sick I laughed so hard. Everything Buster Keaton tried was wrong, and he had to put it right to win his girlfriend and keep her away from the sheik. In one scene he hung off a ladder on a big water tower at the railway station. The water poured out and washed him down onto the train track. It's a wonder it didn't kill him.

I had a fine time and couldn't wait to tell Ty about it. We started for home after dark, replaying the scenes and laughing at them all over again.

"That was so funny, I'd like to see it at least one more time, maybe twice," Sam said.

We all agreed we'd go again after the next payday. Contented with our plans, we settled down for the ride home. As we got near Richmond, we noticed flames high on the bluff just north of the town. We got quiet pretty fast because it wasn't just any old fire. A huge cross was burning up there. Russ slowed down and stopped. We sat, petrified with fear, staring at the sight. I shuddered because I knew what it meant. The KKK cross burnings meant that the Klan was after somebody, or that someone had done something they didn't like. Who was it? Anybody I knew? I thought of that Rufus Laycock, and I was scared for Granddad.

When Russ parked in front of my house, we could see people standing around outside their houses looking up at the high bluff. A few of the men were members of the local Klan. They acted sheepish and claimed to know nothing about the burning. So far as I could tell, nobody could say who was responsible or why it had been done. We watched for at least another hour, grateful to see the fire begin to sputter out. Folks talked quietly among themselves, and then started returning to their homes. Russ took off with Harold and Sam.

Ty and I stood outside in the yard with Gram and Granddad. "That scared the bejesus out of me," Ty said.

"Me too. I wonder who did it," I said.

Gram shook her head. "I don't like this a bit. That Klan stuff is no good."

"A bunch of fools," Granddad said as we turned and went inside. We still felt upset about it and talked until late that night. I don't think any of us slept too well. I know I didn't.

15

A COUPLE OF DAYS later Gram reported that she had seen Sally McVay about the new arm that was coming for Dad. "I asked her to tell Cal that the doctor and Uncle Lyle would drive out next Tuesday, but not to tell him about the arm. Just tell him there'll be a nice surprise."

"That's good, Gram," I said. "He won't have time to work up a head of steam about it."

"Sally said she'd try to get that Rufus Laycock out of the house before we arrive.

It sounded like she'd be glad to see the last of him."

"I'd think so," said Granddad. "After the way that guy talked to me the other day, I can't think of anybody who'd want him around."

"She said he talks to Cal about the Klan all the time. That he's putting the pressure on Cal to join," Gram said.

"I wish he wouldn't do that. I hope he doesn't join," I said. Dad had enough hateful ideas in his head without the Klan adding to them.

"Well, he never leaves the house," Ty said, "so maybe it doesn't matter one way or another."

Uncle Lyle and Doctor Brunner showed up as promised, so Ty and I went to Sally's house with them. Dad sat at the kitchen table. His eyes were big, and I could see him jiggling his feet under the table. He didn't get up to greet us as we came in. It had never occurred to me that my dad might be nervous about our coming. He was always so sure of himself, but he looked downright scared now.

"Hello, Cal," Dr. Brunner said. "I haven't seen you for a while. How are you feeling? That stump giving you any problem?"

"No. It's just useless. That's all." His voice was high pitched and jittery.

"Well maybe that's going to change today," said Uncle Lyle, grinning broadly.

"Look what we brought you." He put the big box on the table and proceeded to open it.

"Wha... What the hell?" Dad said.

I was so excited I piped up, "It's an artificial arm, Dad. So you can do more things."

Dad looked over at me and then stood up and stared into the box. Even though it was a hot day, my hands felt like ice, waiting to see his reaction. I was afraid he'd get mad, stomp out of the room or something. He just stood there looking at it.

Uncle Lyle said, "C'mon, Cal. Let's try it on," and started to help Dad out of his shirt.

"No, I don't think so. They tried to give me one of these things when I was discharged. They're no damn good." He backed away from Uncle Lyle.

"Well, let's just try it and see. Doc here will make sure it fits right."

Before he could say anything else, Sally got the rest of his buttons undone and whipped his shirt off his left arm. I hadn't seen Dad without a shirt since he came home from the war, and my throat closed when I saw his stump. It was a horrid, withered looking thing, a deep reddish-brown color, and it got narrow as it came down to where his elbow had been. I felt my insides curl up to think of how much pain it must have caused him. Maybe it still hurt.

We stood quietly, scarcely breathing, while Doc fixed the straps around Dad's chest and buckled them. Then with great care, he attached the arm to the stump and rigged up the flexion strap.

"Now, Cal. You have to use your shoulder to lift this arm up. Can you try it?"

"I can't. I can't move it. I want to take the damn thing off."

"Your shoulder is weak, Cal, 'cause you haven't been using it. It's gonna take a while for you to get your strength up."

"No. No, this isn't going to work. I already know that." His eyes darted around from person to person.

Sally walked up, stood in front of him, and looked him straight in his eye. "You need to try it, Cal. I know you can do it. You just have to try really hard." She went around behind him and moved his shoulder for him, and the arm jerked.

"That's it," we all said. "You can do it."

My every muscle was in a knot, I was so anxious for this thing to work. I tried to make my shoulder feel like Dad's must have felt. Every time Sally moved his shoulder, mine moved too. His lips drew tight over his teeth, and his forehead wrinkled with the effort. She continued to pump his shoulder until, after several tries, he finally was able to make a small movement himself.

Ty and I yelled and danced around. "You can do it, Dad. We knew you could."

Dad let go a big breath, and I realized he'd been holding his breath too.

Doc said, "Now the next thing is to get your bicep to work 'cause that's how you open and close the hook. It's gonna be hard. You haven't used the thing except to cuss at it for a long time. Let's just try it."

The kitchen was hot on this August afternoon, and perspiration was running down Dad's face. Sally stepped up to wipe it off. "You're doing fine, Cal," she said. His eyes followed her as she backed away.

"I can't make it move. I want to quit this."

"Pretty soon," Doc said. "I want to make sure this thing works. Try real hard."

"Please, Cal," Sally said.

He looked down at the hook, took a deep breath, and strained to make his arm muscle move. Every time he tried to squeeze his arm, I squeezed mine too as if I could transfer my effort to him. He tried over and over, but nothing happened.

"Rest a minute, Cal," Doc said. "Just think in your head about the motion you need to make. Practice it with your left arm so you feel what it's like to move that bicep."

He did what the doctor said.

"That's it. You have to make it feel like that on the right side. I'm going to wrap my fingers around your arm and squeeze, and I want you to squeeze back with that muscle. Do you see what I mean?" Dad nodded.

I was glad it was Doc doing it and not me. It made me squeamish to think of putting my fingers around his stumpy arm, and I turned my head away, ashamed of being such a coward.

They tried over and over, and my mouth was mealy with fear that it wouldn't work. I lost count of how many times they tried. It was at least fifteen or twenty before the hook finally moved a little, and we all yelled again. Dad sat down, gray-faced, exhausted by the effort.

"When they tried this with me in the army, I was so weak, I could barely hold the thing up," he said. He sat breathing heavily for a moment and then raised his left hand to cover his eyes.

"Who did this? Whose idea was it?" he asked, his voice gruff.

"Your boys did it, Cal. They got the thing in motion," Uncle Lyle said.

Dad raised his head and looked straight at Ty and then at me, his eyes blazing. Fear tore through me and I squirmed. I thought he would tell us we should mind our own business. Stay out of his affairs. I was scared he would take off the arm and fling it at us. Then I realized it didn't matter if he got mad at us, if he just kept working the arm. I could take that. What I couldn't take was if he went into a sulk and didn't even try to use it.

Ty said, "It was Harry's idea, Dad, but I sure went along with it. And Gram helped too."

Dad looked at the arm in his lap and blinked back tears. "Harry," he said to himself. "My youngest boy."

Sally handed him a handkerchief. He took it and wiped his eyes.

"I've been no good to you, Harry."

"It's all right, Dad," I said. "I'm getting by all right." I felt my eyes start to water too, but I wasn't going to let myself cry. I wanted to pop with joy now that it seemed this new arm might work and he wasn't going to be mad.

Dad turned to Uncle Lyle and the doctor. "When Sally told me you were coming to see me, I thought you were going to take me to the insane asylum or the county farm, Doc."

"Oh Cal," Sally burst in. "I told you it'd be a pleasant surprise."

"If I were going to do that to you, Cal, I would have done it a long time ago," Doc said.

"I think we should celebrate," Sally said. "Cal's got a new arm, and he's going to be able to make it work." The tension broke in the room, and I sagged with relief. She brought out a pitcher of lemonade and some brown sugar cookies. We all sat at her kitchen table, finally able to relax a bit. We laughed and talked, and it was almost like it used to be with Dad.

"Where did you get the idea for this, Harry?" Sally asked.

I had a fleeting vision of Carol Ann on our walk home from River Sioux. "I...I guess it was that pirate story, you know the one about Captain Hook," I said. Boy, I made that one up in a hurry.

Sally turned to Dad, "I sure hope you don't get as mean as Captain Hook, Cal."

"I don't think I will."

With Sally listening closely, Doc explained to Dad how to take the arm on and off and how important it would be to exercise every day to build up his strength. After we finished our refreshments, it didn't seem like there was anything more to do, so we thanked Sally and left together. Dad walked to the porch with us still wearing the arm, his eyes red-rimmed.

When we were out of sight of the house, Ty and I shook hands, so happy with our success. But that wasn't enough. We grabbed each other in a big bear hug, banging each other on the back in our jubilation. I wanted to sing and shout, I was so relieved and happy. I couldn't get to Carol Ann's house fast enough. Her little brother, Jerry, was playing in the front yard.

"Hey, Jerry. Where's Carol Ann?"

"Mama's got her out back in the garden, pickin' tomatoes and string beans."

I hightailed it around the house and saw Carol Ann bent over the rows of beans, a sunbonnet shading her face. She straightened up when she heard me coming.

"Harry. My goodness. What are you doing here?" Then she remembered what was supposed to happen that day. "How did it go?" Her anxious face was rosy with the heat and the freckles on her nose stood out.

"It worked, Carol Ann. It worked." I wanted to grab her and swing her around. Mrs. Bellwood looked up just then from the tomato plants, so I held back.

"Dr. Brunner brought the artificial arm out today just like he said he would, and Dad actually let him put it on, and he tried it out."

"Oh my. That's wonderful news, Harry." She pulled her sunbonnet off, and I could see where the perspiration had darkened her hair. She turned to her mother.

"Mama, I want to talk to Harry for a minute."

"All right, but don't run off. We're nowhere near done with this job."

She led me over to the apple tree, and we sat down in the shade while I told her about the whole thing. "He teared up when it was

over. I thought maybe he'd be mad, but he wasn't. Sally really helped
get him to try it out, and he was able to move it up and down. He
was even able to make the hook move a little bit. His arm is weak and
he'll have to work hard at it." I burbled on and on, talking about how
the arm worked with a flexion strap and how Sally served cookies and
lemonade.

"He actually laughed out loud." I paused. "You know, this never
could have happened without you, Carol Ann. It was all your idea. I
just can't thank you enough. Dad doesn't know that it was your idea,
but I plan to tell him one of these days. Maybe I'll take you over there
to meet him."

"I'm thrilled it worked. It's wonderful, but you're the one who
followed through and got everybody going on it. It's a fine thing you
did, Harry."

Mrs. Bellwood was bent over her tomatoes so I decided to lean
over and give Carol Ann a kiss.

She laughed. "Harry, I'm so hot and sweaty. I don't think you want
to come near me."

"Yes, I do. I'm just so happy." I took her face in my hands, feeling
her damp, glowing skin. We had a long kiss, and she kissed me back. I
loved the hot salty taste of her, her soft lips, even her grubby hands. I
loved the way her sunbonnet hung around her neck all tangled up with
her hair. In fact, I knew then that I loved everything there was about
that girl.

16

MONDAY MORNING WAS the start of high school. I went very early to Sally McVay's to pick up Dad's laundry before leaving for school. He was on the porch, and my eyes lighted immediately on his right arm. I was reassured to see his hook in place.

"Hi, Dad. Didn't expect to see you out so early this morning. What are you doing?"

"I'm just fooling with this darned thing." The worry lines on his forehead were puckered up. "I can't control the hook, and if I can't control that, I might as well throw the thing away."

"Doc said it would take a while. Remember? Want me to squeeze your bicep like he did?" I didn't mind doing it so much with his long sleeve covering the bare stump. He waved me away impatiently. Just then someone rattled by on the road in a Model T. I smiled to recall Carol Ann's advice.

"Dad. Know why a Model T doesn't need a speedometer?"

He looked at me frowning, a question in his eyes.

"It's 'cause if you're going twenty miles an hour, the trunk rattles. If you're going thirty miles an hour, the hood rattles. If you're going forty miles an hour, the transmission falls out."

He stared at me and finally a tiny grin showed up in the corner of his mouth. Relief. He got the joke.

"I've got a big day today, Dad. I'm going to start high school."

He nodded. "I suppose you're gonna try to make something of yourself."

"I sure hope so. That's my plan."

He smirked. "Plans don't always work out, Harry. I can tell you that."

"I've made up my mind to try, Dad."

I grabbed his bag of dirty clothes and left. I wasn't going to let him get me down.

EVERYTHING WAS FRESH and clean at the school. The floors were waxed to glossy perfection. The teachers were dressed up and smiling. Bright signs welcomed the freshmen and directed us to the assembly hall. Carol Ann went to sit with some girls, so I talked to Billy Snyder and Jim Blankenship and several others I knew. I hadn't seen them since last May, and they'd all grown taller. Their faces were tan, their hair bleached from the summer sun. We were all slicked up, combed, and ready for the year. My new clothes felt stiff and hot, but they seemed just right as I compared myself to the others. I was glad I had a job at the skating rink so I could buy them.

Mr. Lyman, the principal with the pinched, mean-looking face I remembered from eighth-grade graduation, welcomed us to the school and explained how the class schedule worked. As freshmen we would take English, math, history, and science. We would also have calisthenics three times a week. Then we were divided into four groups, each led by a teacher. I was assigned to Miss Birde Baldwin. Birde, I thought, what a silly name. She looked like her name, skinny with a twittery voice, overly cheerful.

"You are going to have such fun," she told us, "because learning is fun."

Oh brother. I could only take so much of her. I hoped she taught sewing or something. She repeated all over again what Mr. Lyman had just told us. Then we filled out schedule cards. Each of us had a short conference with her while she checked our cards.

I said, "What about the shop classes? Can I take something there?"

"It's 'may I,' Harry," she said, smiling as if that were the funniest thing she had ever heard. "Shop classes come when you are a junior, and you have room for electives in your schedule."

"Well, how a business class? That's really what I want to learn."

"No, those are electives in the commercial track. You won't be ready for those for a couple of years."

"A couple of years," I said in disbelief. I didn't like the way this felt, and I hoped I hadn't made a big mistake starting high school. I wanted to talk to Carol Ann to see what she thought, but she was in a different section.

We started our abbreviated class schedule. I felt some relief when I got to algebra class. I was good at arithmetic. The teacher, Mr. Hummel, had a relaxed way of explaining things. He gave a big assignment due the next day and I was eager to start on it.

History began with a long talk about the cradle of civilization, whatever that was. The class might be all right, but I was glad when it ended because it was noontime, and I was starved. We followed our noses to the lunchroom where the smell of hot cooked food made my mouth water. I could hardly stand to pass it by, but I had to save my money and eat what Gram had packed for me—a sandwich of thick slices of chicken on her homemade bread, two hard-boiled eggs, a tomato from the garden, and two molasses cookies. I spent two cents for milk. It was a perfectly good food, better than most, but I craved the hot stew and biscuits. The counter with its luscious looking pies and cakes was hard to pass up. It seemed like the older, savvier kids ate the hot meal, and we sorry freshmen brought ours from home.

I looked around for Carol Ann and saw that she was eating with some of her girlfriends. I sat with some of the boys I knew and wolfed down my food. Sam and Bucky invited me to go outside and play ball before the next class, but I decided to take a walk around the school.

I went up to the third floor where the business classes were taught, hoping to see the teacher to plead my case. Through the window of the typing room, I could see students busy at their machines and the teacher explaining things up in front. I wanted to be in there with them, learning how to do that too.

Mr. Lyman came by at just that moment and said, "What are you doing here, young man?"

"Just watching the typing class, Mr. Lyman."

"What's your name?"

"Harry Spencer, sir."

"Well Harry, I don't know why you are up here, but it's time you went to your next class." He checked his watch. "You'd better get a move on. Don't just wander around the building like this anymore."

I left in a hurry. By the time I found my English class and sank into a seat, I was well aware of my new shoes, for they were sending some painful messages to my toes. I was also sleepy. Mrs. Kleinsasser had us start right out by reading the essay "On Pragmatism" by Ralph Waldo Emerson, after which there was to be a discussion. She'd written questions on the board. I tried and tried to read, but my eyes grew heavy; I couldn't make sense of the words. My head drooped and I jerked upright. I felt it droop again a couple of times, and then I slept. I don't know for how long, but when I came to, I was alone in the room except for Mrs. Kleinsasser who still sat at her desk.

"Are you Harry Spencer?" she asked.

"Yes, ma'am." Oh, did I feel sheepish.

"Well Harry, I suggest you go to bed tonight with the chickens because you may not sleep in my class ever again, tempting as it is after you have eaten lunch." She glared at me a moment and then softened.

I sighed. "I'm sorry, ma'am. I don't know what came over me." I was embarrassed to have this happen on my first day.

"I'll tell you what, Harry. You read the Emerson essay tonight. Answer the five questions about it, and we'll call it square. But don't you dare sleep in my class again."

"Yes, ma'am." I struggled to collect my things and leave the room as fast as I could.

"Goodbye, Harry. I'll see you tomorrow. Don't worry. We're going to be friends."

I wondered about that. She must think I was a dolt.

Somehow I got through the rest of the day. When classes were over at four o'clock, I caught up with Carol Ann at the front door. We said goodbye and waved to all the other kids as they hurried by us, headed for home. Finally we were the only two left. We sat down on the bench to wait for her dad to pick us up.

I told her about the disaster in English class.

"I can just imagine," she said. "You must have felt so embarrassed. Our English teacher said we were supposed to read the Emerson essay too, but she thought we weren't ready for it. We read some poems out loud instead, and then she read some Mark Twain to us. It was fun."

"That sounds better to me. I wish I was in your class."

We sat idly. "They won't let me take any shop or business classes until I'm a junior," I said. "That's really what I want. I don't know if I can stand to wait that long. How am I ever going to make something of myself if I can't find out about that stuff? That's why I signed up for high school."

"Maybe after they know you better, they'll let you do it. If you do really well in your other classes."

"I'd like to play football too, but they practice every day after school until 6:30, so I guess that's out unless I can find a ride with somebody else."

"I'm sorry, Harry. We've got to find something that you will really enjoy about high school." She sat thinking for a moment. "I know. What if we try out for chorus? They rehearse from four to five every day. That'll give us something to do while we wait for Dad."

I turned that idea over in my mind. I liked to sing, but I wondered what the other boys would think if I joined the chorus.

"Oh, Harry. It's a mixed chorus, both boys and girls." She laughed at me. "You won't be the only boy."

So I agreed to think about it, and then her dad showed up to take us home.

EVERYTHING WAS EASIER on the second day. I managed to cadge a cup of coffee from the cooks at lunchtime, hoping it would keep me awake during English class. Mrs. Kleinsasser gave me a smile when I handed in the Emerson assignment.

"Did you get some sleep, Harry?"

"Yes, ma'am. I'm ready to go today." I could tell I was going to like her as a teacher even after my rocky start.

After school, Carol Ann and I went to the music room where Miss Dysart listened to each student sing individually. I had never been nervous about my singing before, and it took me a few tries before I got going so she could find out how high and low my voice would go. Then she asked me to sing any song I wanted, anything I knew. I wondered about popular songs, but thought maybe she wouldn't approve, so I sang a hymn, "The Old Rugged Cross." I saw her stifle a grin, but when I was finished, she said, "You have a really nice voice, Harry, and I'd like you to sing baritone in the chorus. Everybody is going to have to work hard at learning to read music. You won't be the only one."

17

FOR PURE FUN, nothing beat the calisthenics class. Freshmen boys met just before lunch on Monday, Wednesday, and Friday. It was great to get outside in the warm fall weather and cut loose for a while. The calisthenics coach was Mr. Hummel, my algebra teacher, whom I already liked. He showed us lots of strengthening exercises—pushups, sit-ups, jumping jacks, and he did them right along with us. We tried hard to please him because he was so good at everything and set a fine example.

One day, during our second class, the lady, who lived on the other side of the schoolyard fence, began calling, "Mr. Hummel. Mr. Hummel."

He turned around to see who it was, and she beckoned him to the fence. Her face was red, and her voice was loud enough that we could hear most of what she said.

"Mr. Hummel. Every morning I put my baby boy in the yard in his buggy for a nap, and every time you hold this class, the noise wakes him up, and he starts to cry."

Mr. Hummel's back was to us and we couldn't hear what he said, but we heard low, soothing sounds like he was trying to calm her down.

She went right on. "I've read all the baby books that say a child needs to be out in the fresh air and sunshine, and that naptime is a good time for that. But my little McDermott can't sleep with all the noise. Can't you get those boys to hold it down?"

Mr. Hummel said a few more quiet words to her and then turned to us, looking very serious. He said, "Mrs. Carmichael is having trouble with her baby boy's naps because our noise keeps him awake. Do you think we could quiet down a bit so little McDermott can get his sleep?"

"What did you say his name was?" Alan Klemme asked.

"I believe she said it was McDermott."

This struck me as funniest thing I had ever heard of. A gurgle of laughs came up from inside me and burst right out. Sam was standing next to me, and he started to laugh too. Then the others started. Mr. Hummel tried to be serious, but pretty soon his mouth was twitching, and his shoulders shook. He had to wipe the tears from his face he laughed so hard.

"Okay, boys," he said when he got control of himself. "Let's see if we can tone it down some and make Mrs. Carmichael happy."

We went on with the class, trying not to yell, even doing the counting for our exercises in a half voice. It sure wasn't quiet, but we did our best. At the end of class Mr. Hummel made us run around the perimeter of the schoolyard four times without saying a word, and then we went inside to eat lunch.

We were abuzz with what had happened. "Why can't the kid sleep inside the house?" someone asked. "Because McDermott needs fresh air," another answered. We howled at the silliness. The Baby McDermott tale spread through the school in a flash. The girls would say, "Don't wake McDermott," each time we filed outside for class. Every time we started a session, we'd hear McDermott set up a squall. And every time Mrs. Carmichael came running out to yell at us to quiet down.

We made halfway attempts to do it, but when we ran relays or worked on the rings, there was no holding back the cheers and yelling. Mrs. Carmichael never gave up, coming out to the fence to shake her fist at us, but we got so we more or less ignored her.

Frank Halverson was the biggest kid in the class and the meanest. He had a fat pink face with little piggy eyes, and he went out of his way to play nasty tricks on people. One day when Mrs. Carmichael came out, he yelled at her. "Leave us alone, old lady, or I'm gonna sic the KKK on you. My dad's a member."

He turned to us and said, "I'm gonna tell my dad about her, and I'll bet the Klan will come and kick down the door of that mackerel-snapper's house."

Mr. Hummel grabbed him by the collar and hauled him to the principal's office, and we didn't see Frank for a couple of days. I felt a sour taste in my mouth after that. Frank had made a funny thing mean and threatening. If the Klan went after silly Mrs. Carmichael, there was no telling what else it would do. Nobody would be safe.

Then I had an idea. I skipped lunch the next day and walked down the street to the Methodist Church and studied the building for several minutes. When I got back to the school, I drew a sketch of the church. It sat in the middle of a large churchyard with no houses close to it. A little peaked roof held up by two pillars made of rocks, the same as the church foundation, sheltered the front steps. I judged it to be about twelve feet off the ground. On the main roof of the church was a square, box-like structure, open on the sides, with short columns on each corner, creating a space where the church bell hung. Above the bell, the tall, shingled steeple, topped with a gold cross, rose straight to God.

I NEEDED RUSS. The October weather was nippy, and I was grateful for a short bike ride to River Sioux. Russ worked for Mr. Crill in the off-season, and I found him in the boat shed where he was painting rowboats.

"Hey, Harry. What are you doing here?" he said, wiping his hands on a rag that smelled of turpentine.

"I came to see if you'd like to help me with a little job Friday night. It's Halloween, you know."

He laughed. "Well, sure. What do you have in mind?"

I told him my plan.

"That's about the funniest idea I've ever heard of," he said.

"It *is* funny, but Frank Halverson is just mean enough to get the KKK involved, and I don't want that to happen. I figure if we pull this off, we haven't hurt anybody, and old lady Carmichael will get the point."

We talked over the details, and Russ agreed to help.

"All we need is a good long rope," I said.

"Looks like you came to the right place." He pointed to the shelf on one wall of the shed where coils of rope were stacked up.

"Do you think Mr. Crill would let us borrow a rope?"

"I don't think he'd care. In fact, I don't see why he'd even have to know about it. We can bring it back to him afterwards. He's not going to need it any time soon."

So the arrangements were made. Russ loaded my bike in his car and gave me a lift home in time for supper.

The next day at school I let Sam and Harold in on my plans. They danced around grinning, excited about the idea and eager to help.

"Don't breathe a word of this to anyone," I told them. "Meet us at the church about 10:30 Friday night."

WHEN FRIDAY CAME, I told Gram that Russ and I were going to town to see a movie.

"You're going to a movie on Halloween? I wonder about that." She watched from the door as we walked to the car. "Now listen here, boys. You stay out of trouble, do you hear? Don't go pulling any crazy pranks."

"We're too old for the kid stuff, Gram. Don't worry about us."

We drove to downtown Beaverton and parked on one of the side streets off Main. About a quarter to ten we started walking slowly toward the school.

Russ said, "Nervous about this, Harry? Want to change your mind?"

I was plenty scared, but I said, "I want to do it, Russ. It's gonna be great."

The town was getting quiet as the little kids wrapped up trick or treat fun. We met no one the last couple of blocks. From the schoolyard, the back porch of the Carmichael house appeared to be in dark shadows. The buggy had been there that afternoon, and I prayed Mrs. Carmichael hadn't taken it inside. No lights showed in the house and, while I had seen a couple of cats around, I was pretty sure she didn't have a dog. We were lucky to have a bright moon and enough wind to cover the sound of our footsteps.

"Okay," I whispered. "We better start." A little shiver went through me.

I went to the front of the house and stole down the side yard near the school. I could hear Russ breathing on the other side of the fence. I got down on my hands and knees and crawled slowly to the porch. Every little noise spooked me; I was almost afraid to breathe. It felt like I crept along for a mile before I came to the edge of the porch and stood up slowly. The dark shape of the buggy was now just a couple of feet in front of me. I reached for the handle and tried to pull it toward me, expecting it to roll on its quiet rubber wheels. It wouldn't budge! What did she do? Tie it to the railing?

My mind raced. The porch was about waist high, so I laid down on it with my feet on the ground. The floorboards groaned with my weight and I froze. I waited a long minute, then reached out quietly and felt each of the buggy wheels to see what was holding it there. Finally I found a brake on one of the back wheels. It made a little clicking noise when I released it, and I lay dead still, listening and waiting. Nothing. I stood up and took hold of the handle again and slowly rolled the buggy toward me. As soon as it was free of the porch, I picked it up and carried it to the fence. It was made of wicker and weighed practically nothing. I was able to hand it over the fence to Russ without much trouble. Then I joined him and we hustled down the street toward the Methodist Church, carrying it between us.

When it was safe, Russ whispered, "Man, I thought you'd never get back to me. What happened?"

I told him about finding the brake.

We were nearly to the church when a couple of dogs set up a ruckus. We dove into some bushes with that buggy on top of us, my heart thumping away in my chest.

A man came to the door of his house and called, "Red. Spike. Shut up before you wake the whole neighborhood."

We heard his wife say, "Must still be some Halloweeners out there, Ralph." He stood on the porch a minute and finally went back inside.

The dogs' noise died down at last, and we crept out of the bushes and hurried the short distance to the church. Sam and Harold emerged from the tall grass at the side of the building and whispered excitedly, "Where have you been? We've been waiting and waiting."

"It took us a little longer to get the buggy than we thought," I said, "but now we can go to work."

I had hidden my school tablet with the plans inside my shirt before we left home so Gram wouldn't ask any questions. I took it out now and laid it on the church step, groping around in the dark until I found a rock to keep it from blowing away. Then I pulled a candle stub from my pocket. Russ lit it, and we crouched around the drawings to review the plans.

"First, we have to get onto the porch roof. Russ will stand over there next to the pillar. I'll go up first and, when I get up there, Russ will toss me the rope and I'll tie it…" A sudden shock rocked my whole body. I stopped whispering and looked at Russ.

"What? What's the matter, Harry?"

I managed to squeak out, "The rope. We forgot the rope."

He looked at me for a second while he took this in, then clapped his hand to his forehead.

"Oh my God, Harry. You're right. We left the rope in the car. We're skunked without it. What'll we do?"

I sat right down on the ground. There was no way we could do this without the rope. We'd have to give it up because of my stupidity. But as I sat there, I thought, *no*. We'd come too far for that. I was all for running back to the car myself, but Russ said, "I think I should be the one to go. People might see you and think it's odd you're getting into my car." I saw the sense to that.

"Okay," I said, "you go."

He took off running quietly. The three of us went back into the tall grass at the side of the church, taking the buggy with us, and we settled down to wait.

Harold said, "My folks are going to skin me alive when they find out I snuck out the window."

"Mine probably will too," Sam said. "I hope this is worth it."

The waiting got on our nerves, and I could tell they were losing some of their enthusiasm. "It won't take him long to get back," I reassured them. "And finishing up won't take long either. We'll be out of here in about twenty minutes, I bet." I didn't feel all that sure of it myself, but I wanted to keep them bucked up. "It'll be worth it. Just think what everybody will say when they see what we've done. What'll old lady Carmichael think?" They chuckled, and I prayed Russ would get back soon.

I was about to give up the whole thing myself when I heard the loping footsteps of someone running down the middle of the road. I rose up from the grass, and relief washed over me. There was Russ panting from the run.

"There are still a few folks walking around downtown," he said gulping for air. "I moved the car so they didn't see me getting the rope out of it."

"Good," I said. "Let's go to work."

As I had shown them on my drawing, Russ, the tallest and strongest of us, stood at the side of one the stone pillars with his legs spread apart and his arms braced against the stones. Harold, as the next largest, climbed onto Russ's shoulders and wrapped his arms around the pillar. When they felt secure, I climbed on Harold's shoulders and managed to pull myself onto the porch roof, scraping my belly in the process. I inched over to the peak, got my knees astraddle it, and whispered, "Toss me the rope." It came up from behind me, but I caught it. I scooted forward until I was smack up against the box-like structure that held the bell. I got a handhold on the box and pulled myself up to a standing position. From there I was able to wrap the rope around one of the columns and knot it tight. Then I threw it down to the ground for Sam who came up next using the rope to help pull himself up. Next it was Harold's turn. Sam and I pulled the rope taut to take some of the weight off Russ, and Harold came grunting all the way onto the roof.

The three of us clung to the belfry while Russ tied the rope to the back axle of the buggy. Then the hoarse whisper came, "Okay, pull it up."

The three of us began to pull the rope hand over hand with Russ on the ground. The wind had come up and wanted to catch the buggy, so Russ had a job to keep it from twisting and banging into the church. We got it to the edge of the porch roof where it got hung up, and we couldn't move it. The angle of our rope was too flat to get the wheels over the edge.

"We gotta get the rope higher," Sam said.

I saw what I would have to do. The sill around the belfry box where the columns were mounted was about eight inches wide. If I stood on that, it would raise the angle of the rope. I told the others what I was going to do.

Sam said, "You better be careful, Harry."

I said, "Harold, wrap your left arm around that column and your right arm around my leg when I get up there. Sam, you do the same thing on the other side. Hang on tight."

I felt no fear as I climbed up there, but oh did my stomach buck when I looked down. The rising wind dried the sweat on my body making me suddenly very cold. I stood for a few seconds to calm myself.

"All right," I whispered. "Hand me the rope."

I looked straight ahead and felt for the rope with my hands. When I got hold of it, I began to pull. My first tries were poor weak things that didn't accomplish anything. I thought for a moment. If I were going to make anything happen, I'd have to raise my arms, hold the rope over my head, and pull from that position. I wondered if I could keep my balance. Did I have the guts? I had to try.

"Don't let go of me," I said. I took a deep breath and slowly raised the rope above my head and began pulling harder and harder. Nothing happened for a long time, but I kept pulling hand over hand until at last the buggy bumped up over the edge and rolled right up to us. The rope went slack, and I wobbled dangerously for a minute, but the boys held on to me. I hung on to the rope so the buggy wouldn't slide back and then got down from my perch, shaky from the ordeal. I handed the rope to Sam and squatted there for a moment to collect myself. My heart was pounding like a drum. It had been a scary few minutes.

By now Russ had been able to climb the rock pillar and was waiting on the porch roof. We maneuvered the buggy over the belfry and leaned it against the steeple. Then, with each of us positioned at one of the columns, we began winding the rope around and around the buggy and the base of the steeple, passing it from hand to hand until the buggy was secure and there was only enough rope left to knot it around a column. The deed was done.

Harold said, "By golly, we did it!"

All of us took a look. He was right. We *had* done it! We pounded each other on the back, tickled with the results of our work.

Now we had to get ourselves down from there. Russ being the tallest went down first. It was a scary thing to lie on your belly with your feet dangling over the edge of the roof, searching for a foothold on the pillar. Russ tried to help from below, but mostly we slid down, bumping and banging ourselves on the rocks in our rush to get out of there.

When we were all on the ground, I said, "Good job, everybody." We were grinning like jack-o-lanterns in the moonlight.

"Can't wait to see what happens tomorrow," Sam said.

"My folks are going to wonder how I got so scraped up," Harold rubbed the rope burns on his arms.

Those two took off for home, and Russ and I ran for the car. We climbed in and collapsed exhausted, breathing hard and not saying anything. Finally, Russ laughed and said, "Dammit, Harry. That was a fine thing." I looked at him in disbelief, and then I laughed too. It was, indeed, a fine thing.

18

A T HOME, I got out of my clothes and ready for bed, chuckling to myself. I'd have given anything to see the looks on people's faces when they spied the buggy up there on the steeple. It was tempting to wake Ty to tell him what we had done, but he was snoring away on our narrow daybed. My legs moved like they were in molasses, they were so tired from all the climbing. Buster usually slept at my feet, but he wasn't around, so I knew Granddad was still at the store with his beer-drinking buddies. I lay down as quietly as I could, still thinking about our fine prank, but my eyes were gritty and soon fell closed.

I don't know how long I slept before the sound of men's voices crept into my consciousness. They weren't talking loud, but they sounded excited. I thought I was dreaming, but Ty woke up, too.

"Who's out there?" he said.

"Must be Granddad."

"Yeah, he was drinking again tonight. He's probably closing up."

We rolled over and went back to sleep. It couldn't have been more than fifteen minutes when I roused up again. I heard fierce barking followed by a long wailing sound I'd never heard before from Buster. I sat up and pulled on my pants, rubbing the sleep from my eyes.

"C'mon, Ty. We better see what's going on."

I went to the kitchen while he got into his clothes. I pulled the curtain aside to look. A light flickered through the window, and my throat closed up. A huge cross burned on the hill in back of our house and the store. I stood frozen, unable to speak.

"Oh my god," Ty said. "They came after us."

We watched men in white robes and tall hats disappear around the store. They ran to their cars idling on the road and drove away fast. The noise awakened Gram who came out in her white nightgown, her hair undone, and asked, "What's going on?"

I opened the door, and smoke smelling of fuel oil filled the room.

"Is Granddad here?"

"No, he hasn't come home," she said.

"We've got to find him," I shouted.

With only the light of the burning cross, Ty and I ran to the store, calling for him. The door stood open to the darkened interior. My heart was pounding in my chest, my mouth dry. We felt our way inside, both of us so familiar with every inch of it that it was easy to get around. We didn't find him. We pushed on through to the windowless bar with its familiar smell of beer and peanuts. Only now it smelled of smoke. Granddad wasn't there.

Outside, we hurried around the building and found the back wall of the bar on fire. A kerosene can stood nearby. By now a few neighbors had heard the commotion and were coming out in their nightclothes. Aunt Lida's husband Carl had put on his pants and was pulling up his suspenders as he hobbled toward us on his arthritic knees.

"Start pumping, boys," he yelled. Two or three others came running with buckets and pails and soon organized a line to throw water on the burning wall.

Where was Granddad?

I raced to the store again and climbed the four steps to the porch that ran across the front of the building. I heard a low whine from Buster and followed the sound. He was on the ground off the far end of the porch. Granddad lay beside him, his body still as death.

"Granddad!" I yelled. "Are you all right?"

He gave no answer. His left leg was twisted crazily under him. My hand on his chest found a heartbeat. I ran back to the men carrying the water, my own heart thumping in panic.

"I found Granddad. He's hurt." Ty came running, and someone made a torch so we could see.

"We need to get him inside." I looked at the side of the store where we had propped a ladder to do some repairs on the roof. "Tell Gram to bring some quilts," I yelled. One of the men headed to the house, and soon she came running heavily, still in her nightdress.

"You found him. Is he alive?" she asked.

"Yes," I said, "but he's bad off."

Ty and I dragged the ladder to Granddad and covered it with the quilts. We lifted his small body onto the ladder, careful of his damaged leg. It dangled loosely, and he moaned with pain when we tried to straighten it. My hands shook, but somehow we got him covered. I grabbed one end of the ladder and Ty the other. We made our clumsy way across the grass. Granddad moaned again when we laid him out on the bed, and I was relieved when Gram took over. My heart still hammered; my jaw was clenched, and my teeth wanted to chatter, but I stopped them.

"Harry," Gram said, her voice high and tense. "Ask somebody to get Doctor Brunner. We're going to need him. I think he's broken his leg. And look at this. His back is bleeding."

I went out again and asked Ed Daniels, who had a car, to go to Portlandville for the doctor. "Sure, Harry," he said and left at once.

Ty went to the icehouse and began chipping a bucketful for Gram to use with Granddad. I went back inside and watched as she washed his face and hands ever so carefully, muttering to herself. "You crazy old man. Why didn't you come home and go to bed tonight? Now look at the fine mess we've got." Her words were harsh, but her hands told a different story. He didn't seem to be conscious. I saw two long scratches on his back, oozing blood onto the sheets.

Then I thought, *Buster*. I had to get back to Buster. Outside, the men pumping water had gotten the fire put out and were standing around, talking in the light of the cross that still burned.

I ran to the dog, dropped to my knees, and petted his head. "Come on, boy. Can you get up?" He licked my hand and tried, but he couldn't do it. I ran my hands over his body. His legs seemed okay, but his back wasn't right. He whined when I touched it. He must have broken it jumping, or being pushed, off the porch. I held his head in my lap, trying to think what to do for him. But in my heart of hearts I knew there was nothing. You can't mend an animal whose back is broken.

Uncle Carl came over and put his hand on my shoulder.

"His back is broke," I said.

He knelt down as I had and felt Buster's body. You know we'll have to put him down," he whispered. "I'll go get my shotgun."

No. Not Buster. Not my best friend through all these lonely years. I wept into his head, and that sweet animal tried his best to lick away my tears. I sat doubled over, sickened, in agony to think I must lose my dog. I couldn't bear for him to be shot. Why did this hideous thing have to happen?

"I don't think you want to watch this, Harry," Uncle Carl said when he returned.

I got to my feet, my legs shaky. "Yes, I do. I'm not leaving." I stood while he cocked his gun and fired, the blast huge in my ears. Buster's body rose up as though he had decided to get up and walk. Then he fell back, trembled, and lay still.

A fierce, sour anger roared up in me and pounded in my head. I hated the men who did this evil. I wanted to hurt them, to make them feel what I was feeling.

"I want to kill them," I screamed at Uncle Carl.

"I know, Harry. This is as mean as it gets." He waved his arm to take in the whole scene. "I don't understand why they did this. There's just no reason on earth." He turned to join the other men and then, looking back, said, "You best get a shovel and bury him, boy."

I nodded and waited until he left, my mind filled with loathing for the perpetrators of this viciousness. I sank down again beside the bloodied corpse of my dog. Who did this? Why us? Why did God let it happen? I did not love God. He didn't deserve our love if He could allow this to happen. I'd learned that once before, and now I had to learn it again.

I felt my face knot up, my teeth grind together when I looked at the gory mess of tissue and bones that had been my dog. "Buster, my poor Buster." I said it over and over. And I grieved. In my mind I could feel the soft, silky hair of his ears, his muzzle. I thought about how he followed me everywhere I went, how he would fetch his ball to play, and how he would curl up next to me when he knew I was low. The pain jumbled together with all the other old hurts; the mother I never knew, my brothers grown and gone, my father who was lost to me, and now the dog I loved. I let the tears come, and after a while, the heat of my anger drained away, leaving me tired and sad. I stayed beside Buster, saying goodbye until the first of the sun's pink rays began to show through the gray, and Ty came looking for me.

"Better come in, Harry. Dr. Brunner is here, fixing up Grand-dad's leg."

I got up slowly and looked at the store. Someone had painted a black KKK sign on the front wall, and the cross was still burning up on the hillside. Never again would I believe that there was anything good about the Klan. What a fool I'd been to think they might make things better. I despised everything about them.

I started to go for the shovel when I saw a human body lying in the ditch beside the road. I went over and looked down into the sleeping face of Squint Pickard. He was snoring lightly, most definitely alive. He must have gotten drunk last night and stumbled into the ditch to sleep.

I gave his shoulder a shake. "Wake up, Squint. You need to go home." His one good eye came open and then fell shut again. "Get up Squint. It's morning. Time for you to go home."

He groaned. "Harry. Izzat you?"

"Yeah," I said. "Are you all right?"

He groaned again. "Too much las' night. Too much beer." He sat up slowly and looked around, getting his bearings

"Okay, but now it's time for you to get up." I reached down and helped him stand.

"Saw 'em," he muttered.

"What? What did you say? What did you see, Squint?"

"Whole thing. Saw the whole thing."

He started to walk away. I grabbed his arm. "What did you see?" He tried to mouth some words, but I couldn't understand him. I yelled. "Damn it, Squint. Tell me. What did you see?"

He raised his head and looked at me as if he didn't know me. I knew his mind went fuzzy sometimes. There'd be no sense coming from him when he was like that. I let go of his arm.

"Saw the whole she-bang," he said as he started walking toward his house.

TY HELPED ME gather up Buster's remains and wrap them in newspaper and an old towel. We went up the little rise back of Gram's garden and took turns digging the hard clay until we had a proper hole. As we piled the dirt over his body Ty said, "Do you want to say a prayer for him?"

"No," I said. "I don't feel like it."

I put the shovel away, and we headed for the house where Dr. Brunner was about ready to leave.

"Your granddad is going to take time to heal, boys. That was a bad break in his leg. Both bones snapped, and I think his thighbone might have a crack in it. I've given him something so he'll sleep a while, and I'll come back in a day or two." He scratched his head as he looked around at the still smoldering cross. "Who did this? Was it the KKK?" We nodded. "Those Klan ideas are crazy." He shook his head and climbed into his car, muttering, and drove away.

Ty went inside, but I had one last job I wanted to do. I got Granddad's ax, and climbed the hill where I began chopping down that cross. I hacked and hacked at it until it fell with a heavy crash, scattering fiery embers over me. Then I cut it into pieces. I chopped every chunk, chopping until all of it was in tiny bits. I chopped until my hands were bloody and raw. Then I shoveled up the pieces, still hot to the touch, and put them in the metal barrel we used for burning.

When I was finished, I flopped down exhausted on the side of the porch. Gram brought me some coffee, and I drank it right down. My mind circled round and round with what had happened. I wanted to get even with those bastards. How? How could I do it? I didn't even know who they were for sure. Exhaustion finally got the better of me, and I laid down on those hard boards and fell sound asleep.

19

THE MIDDAY SUN bored into my eyes. I awoke and threw off the quilt someone had tossed over me. The pain in my hands hit me. They were red and swollen with blisters in the palms, and my arms were covered with blood and grime. Last night's scene filled my mind as I sat up. The horror of what I had witnessed, what I remembered, didn't gibe with the clean fall air and the amazing blue October sky. Yet, there on the hill were the burn marks and ash left from the cross.

I stood up stiffly and went into the house for a drink of water. All was quiet, so I tiptoed back to the bedroom. Granddad was sleeping, his mouth open, his left leg huge in its white cast. He looked puny and sunken in, somehow. Gram sat in the rocker beside his bed, dressed now, but dozing. She seemed older, her face wrinkled and sagging. Even so, her black eyes snapped open at my sound, and she got up and followed me to the kitchen.

"How is he?" I asked.

"It's bad, Harry. The doctor gave him something to keep him comfortable, but I'm afraid he's got some hard times coming before this is over." She shook her head and stared out the window to the place where the cross had stood, her face pale and tired looking in the daylight. "It makes me so mad. It's so stupid."

"Gram, I'm gonna get those sons-a-bitches if it's the last thing I do. I'm gonna track them down and burn them out."

"You're angry, Harry. We all are, but we don't even know…"

"I'll find out. I don't know how, but I will. I'm not helpless." My voice rose as my anger rekindled.

"Take it easy, son."

"No, I won't. I'm gonna make somebody pay for this. Nobody can do this and get away with it." I slammed the chair into the table.

"Shush, Harry. I want him to sleep." She straightened the chair then turned to face me up close. "Look at you. You're soot and grime from head to toe. I'll heat some water so you can wash up."

"I don't care how dirty I am. It doesn't matter."

"I know," she said, but she put the teakettle on anyway. She got me some clean clothes and left to give me privacy.

I was sorry I'd yelled at her. She didn't need any more trouble than she already had, so I peeled down to my skin and washed my body, slow work because of my hands. When I was dressed, Gram came back to the kitchen. She took one look at my palms and got some Unguentine and gauze to wrap them up.

"Thanks for everything you did last night," she said. "I don't know where we'd have been without you boys."

"They killed Buster, Gram."

"I know. Ty told me." She tied the last piece of gauze. "I'm sorry, Harry." She put her hand on my cheek and smoothed back my wet hair, her face all puckered up. "He was a good dog. I'll miss him."

"Why'd they do this, Gram? What did we ever do to them?"

She heaved a tired sigh. "I don't know why, Harry. Maybe 'cause Granddad wouldn't join up. You were there when that organizer guy threatened him."

"Oh, yeah. Rufus Laycock." I recalled the ugly episode at the store, and the anger hit me all over again. "I was glad he didn't sign up. Who was that guy to come in there and try to force him to join?"

"He stood up to them all right. Maybe he shouldn't have."

I was appalled. "Do you really believe that?"

"No, I guess not. Not really, but I hate this kind of trouble." She stood twisting her apron with her big, gnarly hands, her shoulders sagging. "If they'd seen Alfie all bloody and his bones broken…" Her voice trailed off.

After a minute, she straightened up. Her lips squeezed together, and her nostrils flared as she said, "It might have made them think. Made them wonder if that's what they really meant to do with all that Klan business. It burns me up that folks around here would stand for this stuff."

"Me too, Gram."

She poured herself a cup of coffee and leaned against the counter. "He won't be able to work for I don't know how long. The store'll be hard to manage. Lord knows, we already had all we could handle around here without this." She shrugged and muttered almost to herself, "We'll just have to handle it. We don't have a choice. That's just the way it is. That's the way it always is."

Gram was tough. I wondered if anything could make her cry. I'd never seen it. I remembered something Mrs. Kleinsasser had told us in class. When she moved west with her husband, she was struck with the difference in the people out here compared to back home in Pennsylvania. She said people here took things the way they came. All the difficulties, the hardships, the hardscrabble life. All the things that people complained of back home, felt sorry for themselves about, cried and fussed over, and wrote to Congress about. Out here she thought people were stronger, more able to endure the bad things. They didn't complain much. They didn't fight much. They chalked up their afflictions to fate and moved on. She said they were stoics. Well, if that was so, I knew Gram was a stoic. I admired her for that. I wanted to be like her, but my blood was hot and I had to get revenge.

"I can't see why they'd try to burn the store down just because he wouldn't join. What kind of reason is that?"

"Well, there's probably more to it. Some folks didn't like it when Granddad added the beer hall onto the store. And they don't think much of the men who sit over there drinking at night. Pug and Squint and the rest of them. Alfie drinks more than he should too. Folks thought Prohibition would bring an end to all that, but it didn't."

"They didn't have to bust him up for that, did they? He wasn't hurting anything. He could have died." I winced when I thought of him lying back in the bedroom, helpless in his big cast.

"Some folks don't like it that Alfie's a Frenchman, not born in this country. They think he's too flighty, just wants to have a good time. Not serious about things. Some of them know he was baptized a Catholic, and the Klan hates Catholics."

"So they try to burn him out? Is that what this is about? They ought to think about what this town would be without a grocery store."

"I'll say! They wouldn't like that very much. Especially one where they can get credit."

She fussed around fixing me something to eat that I could manage with my bandaged hands. Then she went back to Granddad. Neighbors had brought food just like they'd do for a funeral—Aunt Lida's apple cake, somebody's potful of chicken and noodles, some good brown bread. I ate till I was full, drank a cup of coffee, and went outside to look things over.

At the store, someone had pinned a note on the door, saying we'd be closed for repair until Monday. Ty was hard at work, painting the front side. When he turned to face me, I saw his tired eyes and knew he must not have slept much either. He painted with a ferocity that didn't surprise me. Whenever the least thing upset him, he tore into physical work—sweeping, scrubbing, hoeing the garden. Today was no different, only the upset was bigger.

"I wanted to get rid of those KKK letters," he said. "I had to go over and over it to cover them up, so I just decided to keep going. This whole front needed paint anyway." He glanced at my hands and grimaced. "I was glad to see that damn cross gone when I woke up."

"What are we going to do, Ty? We can't let them get away with this."

"What can we do, Harry? The two of us can't fight off a bunch of men we don't even know."

"We've got to find them and raise hell with them. I'd like to kill them for what they did."

"We might want to get even, Harry, but I don't see how we can do it."

Ty avoided controversy if he could, but this was too big. I wanted to get even, and I figured he'd want that too. But he turned back to his painting as if that would cover up the whole ugly thing. I gave up on him.

Around back, the wall was charred black from the ground to the roof. It was ugly and raw, but the flames hadn't gotten going well enough to cause a lot of damage. Gram would have to call Claude Tucker, our local handy man, and have him take the siding off and check the beams.

The air was foul with smoke inside the store. Weak light in the beer hall made it difficult to tell, but I couldn't see any fire damage on the inside. The place needed airing out. For now I closed the door on the barroom. If only it were that easy to shut out all the trouble the place had caused.

The food in the icebox was still cold, so I figured Ty must have seen to the ice. Finally, I walked back to the garden and the new mound where Buster lay. It looked so small and insignificant today. That poor creature. I wondered if he'd felt a lot of pain, if he'd felt it when Uncle Carl shot him. The anger churned in me again, and I tried to imagine how I could find the scum who did this. I was so tired I couldn't figure out what to do.

I sat down beside the grave, my mind in a muddle, hurting and mad, everything going round and round in my head. I looked up just as Carol Ann came walking up the rise, and I felt a surge of pleasure to see her. I wanted her with me. Then I remembered. Her father was a member of that hateful Klan. Was he here last night? Was he part of this thing?

"I've been looking for you, Harry. We heard what happened. Is your granddad okay?" I nodded, and she came closer.

She saw my bandaged hands. "What happened to you? Are you hurt?"

"Burnt my hands." I knew I sounded gruff and unfriendly.

"Oh, no." She sank down beside me, her face all knotted up. "I'm sorry, Harry. I feel so bad about all this."

I didn't answer right away. Finally, I had to ask. "Was your dad here last night? Was he in on this?"

"Oh, Harry." Her eyes opened wide. "How could you think that? My dad wouldn't do anything like that."

"All I know is that he joined up with them, didn't he?"

"Yes, he did, but Dad says this ends it for him. All this KKK business." She turned to me. "But what about your dad? He joined up too, didn't he?"

"My dad! What do you mean?"

"He's been going to the meetings, Harry."

This news hit me like a punch in the stomach. "That's a lie. I don't believe it. He wouldn't do this to his own family," I said, my voice shaky.

"It's not either a lie. I heard my dad tell Mother. He wondered why your dad had joined up. He doesn't go to church or participate in anything else."

I exploded. "I don't think my dad joined, but yours sure did. He was here last night. Helped do all this damage. I hate him and the Klan."

She started to cry. "You can't accuse my dad of this, Harry. He told us it wasn't the Richmond Klavern behind what happened here. It was somebody from out of town."

"I bet he was part of it, but now he won't admit it. Nobody will. They'll duck and hide. Play innocent when they realize what they did. Your dad too."

"Harry. Stop saying things like that."

She was really bawling now, her eyes red and running. Some part of my brain knew I shouldn't blame her for what happened, but I wanted to blame somebody, I was so filled with hatred.

"I won't stop. I'm gonna find them and burn their houses down. I'm gonna hurt their animals. I'm gonna…"

Her hand came up and smacked my face good. "Stop it," she screamed. We looked at each other in disbelief, and then she turned and ran toward the road. I stood stunned, my cheek stinging. I felt weak and sank to the ground again, anger whooshing out of me like air from a balloon. I didn't know whether to be mad at her or not. She wasn't to blame, but her father sure was. And maybe mine. I hated them.

After a while, I got up and walked toward the house. Ty was putting away his brush and paint and met up with me.

"I saw Carol Ann come whizzing by. What's the matter with her?"

"Aw, I don't know. Everything I guess."

"Well, I'm going inside. People keep coming by to ask what happened. I'm sick and tired of telling the thing over and over." Ty wasn't very talkative on the best of days, so I knew this was hard on him.

I went in with him, and we found Granddad propped up in his bed, eating some chicken and noodles.

"You're awake," I said. "How's your leg?"

He laid back in his pillows and said, "I guess I'm gonna live, but I sure can tell I'm stove up."

"Phil Beaubien stopped by a while ago," Ty said. "He wants to come over and hear just what happened so he can file a sheriff's report."

Granddad snorted. "Lotta good that'll do."

"Well, I'd like to hear the story too," I said.

A couple of hours later when Sheriff Beaubien showed up, we gathered in the bedroom.

"I don't see what good this'll do," Granddad said.

"Might not do any, Alfie, but it's something I have to do. So why don't you just tell me what happened? Maybe start by telling me who was in the store that night."

"Oh, let's see. Bill and Jalmer Nelson were there, but they left early, about ten or ten thirty. And Ole Tollefson. Charlie Wendt, and a young fellow I didn't know. I think he said his name was Tom, and he was down here from Beresford doing some farm work for his uncle."

"Who's his uncle?"

"He didn't say."

"When did Ole leave?"

"Right after the Nelson boys. I heard him drive away in that old noisy truck of his."

"How about this Tom fellow?"

"He stayed quite a while. Charlie Wendt too. We all drank quite a bit. Somebody said it was after eleven, so I told them I was going to lock up. That fella Tom went first. Charlie hung around for a while, and then he left too. Squint and I were the only ones left."

"That's Squint Pickard?"

"Yeah, he's there most every night. Anyway, I started collecting the glasses and wiping off the bar. Squint and I may have had another glass or two. I can't quite remember. Finally I told him he better leave."

"And did he go?"

"Yeah. I have to kick him out almost every night at closing time, so that wasn't unusual."

"Then what happened? Did you leave?"

"Well, I remember turning off the lamps, and I went to the front door. I think I was trying to find my keys so I could lock up." Granddad looked sheepish.

"I'd had too much to drink, and I stood there on the porch, fumbling around in my pockets. It was dark as hell. Next thing I knew a whole crowd came rushing at me from the west end of the porch. They were wearing those white things with the tall hats, masks on their faces, and a couple of them had torches."

"How many were there?"

"I don't know. It's kind of a blur. All I know is that it scared the bejesus out of me. I just couldn't figure out what was going on. I heard fire crackling. Buster was barking, and cars were running. They came on me so fast. I heard somebody say, 'There he is. Now we can get him.' It was so noisy, I didn't know if I heard right. I tell you, I was afraid for my life. I didn't know what they meant to do. They were talking kind of excited like, 'should we beat him up?' 'let's tie him up,' stuff like that. They got up close and held a torch up to my face. Somebody said, 'He's drunk.' And something about me being a damn Frenchman. They crowded up next to me, jostling and pushing me around there on the end of the porch. Somebody grabbed my arm and twisted me around so I was facing the door. Buster was right beside me."

"Did they hit you?"

"I can't say for sure. I kept trying to get my hand out of my pocket. Seems like there wasn't enough room to move. I stumbled. Then another really big one of them came up the steps there in front of the door. I think he might have grabbed at me. I don't know. Next thing, I lost my balance and fell with Buster all tangled up in my legs. I went down on top of him, and I heard him yowl. I must have hit my head 'cause I don't remember any more."

Mr. Beaubien leaned back. "Did you recognize any of them?"

"No. Not a one. I couldn't tell anything. I was too woozy."

"I can't figure how he got these long scratches on his back," Gram said. Granddad said he didn't have any idea. After a little more conversation, the sheriff left, but we continued to talk.

"I should have guessed what would happen," Gram said. "Yesterday there were so many cars. They came in two's and three's, driving by real slow. Then they would turn around and come back the same way. I was busy, and I just didn't pay much attention."

"Carol Ann says Dad joined the Klan. He's been going to meetings," I said. "She heard her folks talking about it."

That was news to them, and we chewed on the possibility that Dad might have helped the men last night. Ty didn't believe he'd do that to us, but Gram and Granddad didn't seem to know what to think.

"I can't figure out Cal anymore," Granddad said.

"We have to find out who it was. We can't let them get away with it."

"Not much we can do tonight," Gram said at last. She yawned as she gave Granddad a couple of aspirins.

"We'd best get to bed."

I sat for some time by myself in the kitchen. My insides writhed to think of the trouble with Carol Ann. I felt again her stinging slap on my face as we stood by Buster's grave. How did that happen? What did I say to her? I remembered the shattering news she had given me about Dad. It had driven me, made the anger rise up, and I had boiled with it. I had raged at her, my poor, sweet Carol Ann, and I had blamed her for her father. But I could see now, it wasn't just about *her* father. It was also about my father. I couldn't blame her for her dad any more than I could blame myself for my own father. I was ashamed. I sat heavy and sad, wanting nothing so much as to run to her house, to find her, to hold her and kiss her and tell her how sorry I was. Nothing mattered to me so much as her sweet forgiveness. I had hurt her, and I loved her. I had to make it right between us.

20

ON SUNDAY MORNING Gram emerged from her bedroom and announced that she was going to church. Her hair was freshly washed and done up in a tight bun. She wore her heavy, dark Sunday dress and her polished black shoes with their silky ties.

I looked up, surprised. "I figured you'd be too tired to go."

She harrumphed. "I'm not going to let people think that they can get me down, especially those fools who joined the Klan." She straightened her shoulders. "We have to stand up to them. Which one of you wants to go with me?"

I implored Ty with my eyes to speak up. He figured out what I wanted and said, "I'll go, Gram. Harry's still got bandages on his hands."

I loaned him a pair of my school pants and breathed a sigh of relief when they set off. I needed time by myself. Granddad dozed off after he finished eating breakfast, so I poured a cup of coffee, pondering all that had happened, and then I made a plan. I would try to talk to Carol Ann and make up with her. I would need to think about my words so she'd believe how sorry I was. But that was for tomorrow. Today I'd go over to Sally McVay's and ask Dad, outright, if he'd been in on this terrible thing. If he'd helped the Klan.

I took a big breath and got up to leave, but something pulled me right back to my chair. It surprised me. Maybe I was a coward. Maybe I was afraid to face my own father. Maybe I had a big yellow streak in me. It wasn't that I was scared of him. After all, what could a one-armed man do to me? Maybe the truth was that I just didn't want to know. What would I do if he denied it? Would I believe him? What if he said he *had* been at the store that night? Then what? Hit him? Kill him? No. No, everybody said it wasn't the local group. Some men from out of town, they said. One of the other Klaverns.

Just then Granddad called to me from the bedroom in his weak, croaky voice, and I left off planning to see my dad.

"Harry, are you here? I'm really dry."

I went to his side with a glass of cold water.

"God, this thing hurts," he said. His face with its two-day stubble was contorted as he twisted around, trying to find a comfortable position in the bed. He drank thirstily and sank back into his pillow. "I've don't see how we're going to get by. Me laid up like this."

I nodded. "We'll figure it out, Granddad. Don't worry."

"Bessie can't look after me and run the store too. Ty sure can't run the place by himself fourteen hours a day."

I knew what was coming, and I didn't want to hear it.

"We'll manage somehow," I said in an effort to stall him.

"No, Harry. I think you'll have to stay home from school and run the place. You know better'n Ty how to do it."

There it was. Just what I feared, and I felt sick to hear it. In the back of my mind I knew they were going to need me, to want me to stay home. I also knew he was right about Ty. Running the store didn't come natural to him. He was so bashful around people.

"You want me to drop out of school?"

"Well, my God, Harry," he said, his voice testy. "You've already had eight years of school. I don't know anybody who needs any more than that."

"I don't want to give it up, Granddad. It's my only chance to make something of myself. I need to graduate. Maybe we can figure out something else to do."

"I don't think we can make it otherwise, Harry. We need you." His eyes pleaded with me.

I wanted to get away from him, his pathetic face. Finally the words I didn't want to say came out. "You know I'll do whatever I have to do."

But just saying that tore me up something awful. I didn't want to drop out. I was used to high school now, and everything was going so well. I knew what Mrs. Kleinsasser and Mr. Hummel would think about it. They'd say I was destroying my future to solve a short-term problem. And Carol Ann. She'd be so disappointed. Carol Ann. Would she care what I did? I had to see her. I knew she was in church today, and the Bellwoods would have their big Sunday dinner afterwards. Then they'd all go back to church tonight. I'd just have to wait.

Back in the kitchen, I tore the bandages from my hands in frustration. No more going around like a little kid with all that gauze. My hands still hurt, but I didn't care. My other troubles seemed bigger.

I stepped outside onto the porch and felt a shiver until the sun began to warm my body. I glanced at the store where Claude Tucker had removed the burned siding and some of the inner wall so the beer hall could air out. Ty and I planned to wave towels around inside there to get rid of the smoky smell. Gram wanted the bar closed for the foreseeable future, and I was just as happy about that. Granddad groaned and said he'd probably go broke. She said we might go broke, but it wouldn't be because of closing the bar, and at least we wouldn't have to worry about the federal agents coming around.

Just then I saw Russ's car drive up the road to our house, and I cheered up when he stepped out and waved. He came up on the porch where I stood.

"I heard what happened, Harry. Is everything all right?"

"Yeah, I guess so, but they got us for sure." I pointed to where the siding was missing. "Tried to burn the store down."

He looked at it, scratching his chin. "What's the matter with those people?"

I shrugged. "Granddad says I'll have to quit school to help out. I sure don't want to." We stood silent for a moment.

"I wish I'd gone on to school. I should have." Then he brightened up. "But things are working out okay, I guess. Maybe you don't need to finish high school."

"But I do," I said. "I don't want to work in a country grocery store all my life. I want something better than that."

"You're really serious, aren't you?" He patted me on the shoulder. "Don't worry. Your grandmother'll work something out." Then he changed the topic. "Hey, Harry. Do you have any cigarettes in the store you could sell me? I'm out."

"Sure. I was just gonna take these towels over there. We have to air the place out." I got the key off the nail by the door, and we went to the store. I rang up a pack of smokes, and then Russ said, "I can wave a towel. I'll help you."

That was fine by me. With the front door and the barroom door open, Claude's ventilation system began to work. When we were finished, Russ and I put the inside wall back in place to avoid an army of mice taking over the groceries, and then I walked to the car with him.

"Look Harry," he said. "Maybe I could come out after work and keep the store open evenings a few nights a week. Would that help?"

I nodded. "It sure would. Thanks, Russ." His visit had bucked me up, and I was grateful he'd stopped by.

THAT AFTERNOON, AFTER Sunday dinner, folks started coming over to see Granddad, to visit, to get all the details about what had happened. I was nervous at first, looking at each man, wondering if this fellow or that one was a member of the Klan. One after another they came, each assuring Granddad that nobody from Richmond had been involved in the thing. Some of them were people who charged on their accounts at the store all year long. Generally, if we reminded them, they paid up in the fall when their crops were in, and today, a couple of them brought cash to the house to settle their bills early. That's how remorseful they were about what happened. Gram kept the coffee pot going all afternoon.

His last caller was Walter Trometer, one of Granddad's oldest friends. Once more we had to hear about the Richmond Klavern's innocence in all this.

"Alfie," he said. "It wasn't any of us. Do you know that Rufus Laycock fellow skipped town and took all the money he had collected from us? We held all those meetings and decided to use our money to buy some playground equipment for the school. But he just took it and cleared out. We disbanded the thing."

I let out a big sigh of relief when I heard this news. If it was true, it surely meant that Dad couldn't have been here that night. If only the men in town hadn't started this up, he wouldn't even have been a member. Still, I doubted we'd heard the end of the story. Even if the local folks didn't do this to us, who did? What would stop the KKK from trying it again? Walter's words didn't remove the fear I felt.

AFTER SUPPER I told Gram that Granddad said I'd have to quit school. She frowned. "He had no business making that decision without talking to me. I've been thinking about it, Harry. I hope you don't have to quit, but I'm not sure. I've got a little money put aside—your dad's laundry money. If there were somebody to hire for a few weeks, I think we could afford it. Business has been pretty good lately. Of course we have to pay Claude Tucker for his work. I suppose he might be willing to wait a little while. We've done that for him plenty of times."

"Russ is done at River Sioux this week. He needs a job. He offered to help us out for a while."

She looked at me with narrowed eyes. "Do you trust him, Harry?"

"I do, Gram. He's a good worker."

She nodded. It looked like I'd be going back to school. Now I had to see about my girlfriend. I decided to wait for her to come home from church that evening.

I'd wrestled all day with the words I'd say to her, searching for the best way to let her know how sorry I was. I huddled in the dark and cold at the Bellwood's front gate waiting for their car to arrive home, waiting to talk to her.

Mr. Bellwood jumped out of the car first. He spoke first. "Hello, Harry. I didn't expect to see you here." He came over and extended his hand. "I wanted to say…I hope you know…about what happened Friday night. Well, what I mean…what I wanted to say…we're so sorry. We didn't do it, Harry." He finally got it out, a sick, sad look on his face.

I just nodded and said, "I believe you, Mr. Bellwood. Thanks."

The family got out. Carol Ann, a scarf knotted around her head against cold weather, wasn't so friendly. "What are you doing here?" she asked, her eyes cold and hard looking.

"I…I want to talk to you."

Mr. Bellwood gave us a puzzled look but shrugged his shoulders and went inside with his wife and Jerry.

"I don't want to talk to you, Harry Spencer," she said her voice cross. She turned to walk up the path to the front porch. "Anyway, it's too cold out here."

"Carol Ann. Don't go in. Please don't go in." I sounded like a sick calf. She turned back to me. "Did you tell your dad what I said about him?" This wasn't the way I planned to start the conversation, but the words just came out. "I didn't mean it. It was an awful thing for me to say. I was so upset."

"I didn't tell him, Harry." Her voice was almost a whisper compared to my noise.

"Oh, please Carol Ann. I'm so sorry about all that."

"Yes, I suppose you are." She tossed her head, her manner still icy. She must have hated me.

"I was so shocked to hear about my own father, to think he might have done something so dreadful. I lost control of myself. I deserved what you did to me. I'm glad you did it. It brought me to my senses."

"Well, that's something, I guess," she said. "I was horrified you would behave that way. I couldn't stand to hear what you said. It hurt me."

I moved up the path to be closer to her. I longed to touch her. "Oh, please forgive me. Please Carol Ann," I begged. "I love you so."

She looked at me with a sad expression. "I thought that I loved you too, Harry. But now I wonder. I couldn't believe you would say those things."

"It was awful of me. I'll never do anything like that again, I promise. Please, can we go back to the way we were? I'd give anything."

"I don't know, Harry."

I reached out for her hand, and she let me take it. Our fingers were freezing, but my body tingled at the touch of her. I brought her closer and put my arms around her. She rested her head on my shoulder, and I could have held her there forever.

"Let me try to make it up, Carol Ann. Please let me try."

"I can't stay mad at you," she murmured into my collar.

She turned her face to mine, and I kissed her lips and her cold face over and over. Then she ran up the steps. At the last second she said, "Will I see you in the morning for school?"

"You bet," I said. She went inside, and I stood a moment holding on to the warmth I felt spreading through me. She was my girl again.

21

NOW THERE WAS just my father to face. I offered to pick up his washing early on Monday morning. Sally welcomed me into her warm kitchen. The breakfast things were cleared away, and Dad sat at the table with a school tablet and a pencil in his left hand. He frowned.

"We heard about what happened, Harry," Sally said. "Are you all right?" Concern showed on her face.

"We're okay," I said, watching my father. He shoved away the tablet and pencil like he was embarrassed to be caught with it. Finally he said, "Granddad doing all right?"

"As well as can be expected, I guess." Was he just saying that to cover himself? I couldn't tell.

He looked away.

Sally squeezed my arm. "I'm so terribly sorry. I just don't understand what makes people do the things they do," she said.

"I appreciate that, Sally." I waited for Dad to say something else, but he didn't offer anything. It was an awkward moment.

Sally jumped in. "Look at what your father's doing, Harry." She held up the tablet where he had written his name about ten times in letters that looked like a little kid's. "He's teaching himself to write with his left hand."

I said, "That's good, Dad. Good job." But my heart wasn't in it. I headed for the door. Dad got up and walked out to the porch with me.

When the door closed behind us, he said, "I'm real sorry about what happened, Harry. Granddad and Buster and all."

I was so relieved to hear him say that. Surely Dad couldn't have been involved in this hideous thing. In that moment of torment, I wanted to hug him, to believe in him, to let my suspicions fall away, but something held me back. I grabbed the laundry bag and took off afraid I would break down if I stayed.

I HURRIED TO Carol Ann's house eager to get to school, to see my friends, and to leave the troubles at home.

"Harry, how are your hands today? Let me see them," she said.

"They're fine," I said. I wasn't about to show them to her and have her fuss over me in front of her dad.

As we neared the school, we saw a large group of kids bunched up in front of the door waiting for the bell. They were talking a mile a minute. It didn't take long to find out what they were buzzing about.

"Hey, Harry. Did you hear about Mrs. Carmichael's baby buggy?" Bucky said. "Somebody tied it to the church steeple on Halloween."

Our prank seemed ages ago after all that had happened. "The church steeple! Really?" I pretended surprise. "Who did it, I wonder?"

"Nobody knows for sure, but I think it serves that old lady right. Don't you?"

I nodded. "I guess so."

Rumors ran through the group with everyone speculating on who did it. Somebody heard it was a gang from Sioux City; others thought maybe it was the Ku Klux Klan. I avoided looking at Harold and Sam, afraid I might give away our secret. Or afraid they might.

Bucky called to Frank Halverson who stood off to the side, always an outsider in this group. "Hey, Frank. Did you get your dad's KKK guys to hang up that buggy?"

Frank's little-bitty eyes lit up when someone talked to him. "No, it wasn't them," he said. "They had bigger fish to fry last weekend." A flash of anger went through me. Was he talking about what happened to us? Could my father possibly be associated with his dad? Frank preened and strutted around just begging someone to ask what his dad's KKK bunch had done, and, of course, someone did.

"I'm not supposed to say," he said, but it was clear that he was busting to tell and had to work hard to keep his secret. When attention shifted away from him after a few minutes, he said, "I might tell if somebody'd give me a dollar."

"Nobody's gonna give you a dollar to hear your stupid secret," Sam said.

The bell rang just then, and we went inside.

I was still thinking about Frank's words when, halfway through algebra class, the school secretary came into our room and spoke to Mr. Hummel. He listened a moment, then said, "Harry, Mr. Lyman would like to see you in his office. You can go with Mrs. Tate. Take your books with you."

Mr. Lyman must have heard about the Klan attack on the store. He probably wanted to ask how Granddad was. Everyone's eyes were glued on me as I followed Mrs. Tate out of the room.

The principal was standing behind his big, bare desk, holding a wooden ruler in his hand. His face, always mean looking, was red and more bunched up than usual. I figured out that this was not about our store. He said nothing for a few moments, just slapped that ruler into the palm of his other hand from time to time while I stood. When he had made me thoroughly nervous and uncomfortable, he laid the ruler down, reached into his desk drawer and pulled out a tablet.

"Harry, do you recognize this?"

Oh God! It was my tablet. A rush of heat raced through my body. My heart thrummed in my head, and I felt a desperate need to urinate. I knew exactly what this was about, and it wasn't the Klan attack.

"Answer me, young man. Do you recognize this?"

I croaked out a raspy "Yessir" and swallowed hard, my mouth dry.

"Well, what is it?"

"It's a tablet, sir."

"I know that, Harry. Don't be fresh. Whose tablet is it?"

"It's mine, sir."

He nodded in agreement. "Yes, I thought so since it has your name on it. How do you suppose I got it? You must have left it someplace." He gave me a sly look. We both knew I was cornered.

"I dunno, sir." But I did know. I'd left it on the steps of the church. I knew it the instant I saw it. We'd been so pleased after we got the buggy up, I forgot all about the tablet. Now someone had found it, and I was in trouble. I felt stupid, stupid, stupid.

"It has some interesting drawings in it." Mr. Lyman thrust a page with a church sketch in my face. "Did you make this?"

"Uh, yessir."

"And this one?" He flipped to the next page.

I nodded.

"Speak up, Harry."

"Yessir."

"Why did you make these drawings of the church?"

"I dunno."

He leaned toward me, his cheeks aflame. Bits of spittle glistened on his thick lips. I had never noticed the wart beside his nose before. Now, as I stared, it seemed to grow larger and larger. Some part of my brain wondered if it would pop.

"I think you do know why you drew those pictures, Harry. You planned the whole thing with Mrs. Carmichael's buggy, didn't you?" His voice thundered in my ears. "Answer me, Harry. Did you plan that thievery, that cruel trick?"

I gulped, swallowed, and said nothing.

"You will not leave here until you tell me."

At last I whispered, "She yelled at us all the time." I felt weak in the legs and wanted to sit down, but I didn't dare.

"Is that any reason to steal her property? To show such disrespect for the church? To put other people at risk? Those men had to climb up there and undo your prank. That was dangerous. What kind of boy are you to be so thoughtless?"

I hung my head, hating every minute of this.

"You've probably gotten other boys in trouble with your schemes. Their parents won't want their sons to be in school with such a trouble-maker. What will your grandparents think? They've sacrificed a lot so you could attend high school."

I felt his words pelting me like bits of hail in a thunderstorm, but they didn't register anymore. I stopped listening and stood there dumbly, waiting for him to stop, just like I'd learned to do with my dad when he ranted. In my misery I scarcely noticed when the room went quiet.

He finally quit, his temper used up. He lowered his voice and said, "What do you have to say for yourself, Harry?"

I shook my head. "I don't know what to say."

"Well, I have an idea. Since you don't know what to say, I'm going to give you some time to think it over." He pointed to a small anteroom to his office with a table and two chairs.

"I want you to go in there and think about what you've done. Then I want you to write a letter to Mrs. Carmichael explaining it to her. You and I will deliver it to her. We're going to talk about this some more, Harry. We are not done with this thing. You're going to tell me who else was involved and exactly how you did it." He handed me paper and pencil and turned to leave.

"Please, Mr. Lyman, sir. Please, I...I need to use the restroom."

He turned back, a look of disgust on his face, but he must have realized my need was real. He pinched a piece of my shirtsleeve between two fingers as if he were holding up a dead mouse, and said, "March."

And march we did, down the long hall to the restroom with him holding on to me all the way. Classes were letting out and people stared at us goggle-eyed. It was the most humiliating thing I'd ever experienced, but I needed relief. The restroom was blessedly empty and I hung on to the washbasin a few extra seconds trying to get myself calmed down. Then we went back to his office, and I sat alone at the table with the paper and pencil.

I thought about what to say and finally picked up the pencil and wrote the date, *November 3, 1923.* I knew I should write *Dear Mrs. Carmichael.* Why did I have to do that? She wasn't dear to me. I hated her. I hadn't before, but I did now. After a minute or so, I swallowed hard and wrote.

> *Dear Mrs. Carmichael,*
>
> *I am the boy who took your buggy last Friday night. I heard you got it back with no damage to it, and nobody got hurt. It was a Halloween joke is all.*
>
> *Harry Spencer*

When Mr. Lyman returned, he said, "Well, Harry. Is this your letter?" He picked it up from the table and read it, then let me have it. "Listen here, young man. This won't do. Your letter expresses no regret, no apology of any kind for what you did."

"You told me to explain it to her, sir. I thought that's what I did."

"You are an insolent, intractable boy." The color rose up in his cheeks again. "You will sit here until you write an acceptable letter if it takes you the rest of the day. Do you hear me?"

"Yessir."

He slammed out of the room, and I enjoyed myself for a minute or two, knowing I had gotten under his skin. Then I thought about my situation. Everything was a mess at home after the store attack. I still worried that Dad had participated, and now it was a mess at school. I sure didn't want to spend any more time here, so I decided to write the letter he wanted and get it over with. But I felt something harden in me at the same time. I resolved that I would not tell him the names of the other boys, no matter what he did to me. That much I knew for certain.

A little later, the two of us walked to the Carmichael house, Mr. Lyman carrying my satisfactory letter in his hand. When she came to the door he said, "Mrs. Carmichael, this is Harry Spencer. He has something he wants to say to you." She turned to me with cold, unfriendly look. I didn't want to say it, but I finally did.

"I'm sorry I took your baby buggy." The words came out in a hurry. "It was a joke for Halloween."

"Hmph. You had your nerve. Stealing my property right off my back porch."

I wanted to say, "You got it back, didn't you?" but of course I didn't.

Mr. Lyman said, "Harry's written a letter of apology, and, on behalf of the school, I offer my apologies too. I want you to know that we don't approve of this kind of behavior." He handed her the letter. She stood, her mouth open like she had a lot more to say, but all that came out was a weak, "Okay." She shut the door, and we turned and left.

Back in his office, I figured I was to get another grilling, but Mrs. Tate stopped him as we came in, and they had a whispered conversation. He seemed uncertain what to do, but finally said, "Harry, get your things."

We walked down the hall together and he found a seat for me in the back of the library. He told me I was to stay there the rest of the afternoon and that I was suspended from school for three days. Then he hurried off.

I had steeled myself for all the "who" and "how" questions, but it seemed like it wasn't going to happen. I took out my English book and tried to read the assignment. I would read a paragraph or two, and then I would relive Mr. Lyman's scolding. I would try it again, then I would think about what I was going to tell Carol Ann. My folks. It was a very long afternoon.

When the bell finally rang at four, I gathered up my belongings. Mr. Hummel came in and motioned for me to go with him. I followed him to his classroom and he told me to have a seat. He said, "Mr. Lyman had to leave this afternoon and take the train to Omaha. His mother is very sick and may die. He left me in charge."

That was good news as far as I was concerned.

He sat down on his desk, his feet dangling over the side. "I understand you've had a pretty terrible time lately, Harry. I'm sorry."

I hung my head. These were the most sympathetic words I'd heard in a while.

"You performed quite a prank, you fellows." He smiled a little. "It was dangerous and dumb, but, in my book, it wasn't evil. It was mischief." He held up a hand to stop any word from me. "Harold and Sam told me what happened. They didn't think you should be the only one punished for it. They also told me why you did it. To keep the KKK from going after Mrs. Carmichael. Is that right?"

I nodded, grateful for his understanding.

"Now, about this suspension thing. I think that, under the circumstances, a three-day suspension isn't warranted. I've told Harold and Sam to stay home tomorrow, and I want you to do that too. Let this thing blow over."

"Thank you, Mr. Hummel." It seemed like a knot inside me loosened when he said that. I wanted to hug him, but I didn't figure it was the right thing to do.

"There's just one last thing I'd like you to know, Harry. It's about Mrs. Carmichael. I know you fellows think she behaves oddly, but listen. About two weeks before school started, her husband had a bad accident. He's a brakeman for the railroad, and he fell off the train somehow. They thought he was going to die. They took him to St. Paul where he had an operation. He's lost one leg, but he's going to live and will be home soon."

I put my hands over my eyes. "I feel like a real jerk, Mr. Hummel. I'm really sorry for the dumb thing I did."

"I knew you would be, Harry. I knew you would be." He patted me on the shoulder and told me I could go. "Thanks," I said and took off like a scared rabbit afraid I might break down.

❖ ❖ ❖

THERE WAS NO getting around it. Carol Ann had heard the whole tale of my shenanigans from her friends, and I knew I would have to confess everything at home to explain why I wasn't going to school in the morning. Ty listened to my story and seemed to think it was hilarious. Gram had a different take on it.

"Harry Spencer, I'm ashamed of you. I knew you and Russ were up to no good on Halloween, but to rope those other boys into something so dangerous." She shook her head. "You were foolish. That Mrs. Carmichael could've had you arrested. Taking the poor woman's buggy right off her porch. What were you thinking of? This, on top of all the trouble we've had the last few days."

She turned around to glare at Ty who was laughing so hard he had to wipe his eyes. I stood in embarrassment and misery, waiting for her to stop. I was worn out with the battering I had already taken, and now this. But I had made a plan for what I would say.

"I'll work at the store, Gram. You and Ty can have the whole day off." I pleaded hoping to get away from her.

"You better believe you will," she said still angry. Yet, I got the feeling that she liked the thought of a day away from the store.

When we went to bed that night, Ty made me tell him the whole thing over from beginning to end. About baby McDermott. How we got the buggy up the steeple, and all the rest. I imitated Mr. Lyman and punched up the story quite a bit. He loved it and had to smother his laughs in his pillow.

"You have an exciting life, Harry. How do you do it? Mine is so dull."

I felt a little sorry for him because I knew it was true, but I said, "You seem to forget that we've all had about as much excitement as we can handle this past week."

22

WHEN I RETURNED to school on Wednesday. I was a hero. Everyone knew that I'd planned the baby buggy prank, and the kids admired me for it. They told me how clever I was, how they wished they'd thought of it, and how glad they were that we'd gotten even with Mrs. Carmichael. They'd heard about my trouble with the principal, and I got whispered questions from every direction.

"What did Lyman do to you?" "How'd you get your hands on the buggy?" "How'd you get it up there?" "Were you scared?" All day long they pestered me. I was torn because I liked to have the boys look up to me and want to be pals, but I'd made a vow to myself I was not going to do another thing that would get me in trouble with Mr. Lyman. I gave the barest answers I could, but that only made them ask more questions. All the talk enlarged the whole thing in their minds and made it more mysterious than it was.

Some of them had heard about the KKK attack on our store, and I got a lot of questions about it, too. I told them we'd found out that a KKK gang had been pestering the Catholics down by Jefferson, burning crosses and making threats. They got caught, and Sheriff Beaubien was trying to find out if it was the same bunch that attacked our store.

By a week later, the questions had quieted down and I was glad. I wanted to talk to Carol Ann about the fall homecoming dance. Notices had been put up around the building, and I knew that a band called Two

Hits and a Missus had been hired to provide the music. We would have cider and cookies, and Gram had even offered to do some of the baking for the refreshment table. It'd be my first dance, and I was both eager and a little nervous about it. My dancing instructions from Darlene and Russ made me confident that I would be all right, and I was pretty sure Carol Ann would be surprised at how skillful I had become.

The girls had been chattering for days about what they planned to wear, new clothes, shoes, and all that. So, as Carol Ann and I sat in the foyer that afternoon waiting for our ride home, I asked her if she was ready for the big dance.

"Um...uh, yes. I guess so," she said without much enthusiasm.

"Well, what are you going to wear? Did you get a new dress?"

She turned away from me and said, "My mother's making something for me."

Now this was peculiar. Usually she told me more than I wanted to hear about her clothing or someone else's. What was the matter with her today? I went in a different direction.

"What do you think I should wear? Do I need a necktie?"

She stood up and moved to the door to look out the window.

"I wonder what's taking Dad so long?"

Puzzled, I repeated my question. "Should I wear a tie, Carol Ann?"

"Oh Harry, I don't know what you should wear." She sounded upset. Finally she turned around to face me, but she couldn't lift her eyes to look at me directly. "I...I guess I'd better tell you, Harry."

"Tell me what?" She gave no answer, so I got up and took hold of her arm. "Tell me what?"

"I...Harry, I'm sorry. I'm going to the dance with Billy Snyder."

"Billy Snyder!" I shouted. "What do you mean?"

I was dumbstruck. How could she be going to the dance with Billy Snyder? It had never occurred to me that she'd go with anyone but me.

"He invited me, Harry. A long time ago."

I stood there unbelieving. "Why didn't you tell me? Why are you doing this?" My chest felt like a heavy brick was stuck inside.

I saw tears start to well up in her eyes. "My folks think I spend too much time with you. This baby buggy thing didn't sit well with them."

"It was just a joke. Nobody got hurt." I tried to read her face. "I thought you cared about me."

"Oh, Harry. I...I..."

Just then a horn honked and she ran out the door to her father's truck. If ever there was a time when I didn't want a ride home with Mr. Bellwood, today was it, but I had no choice. I followed reluctantly and climbed in.

"You two are sure quiet today," Mr. Bellwood said as we drove along. "More trouble, Harry?"

"No sir. Just tired, I guess." The rest of the ride home was silent.

THAT NIGHT WAS the longest evening of my life. I didn't understand why she would do this. Was it the Halloween trick? No, that couldn't be the only reason. Billy had asked her a long time ago, she said. How did he dare? I seethed at the thought of him. He knew she was my girl. I couldn't wait to get my hands on him. Then I felt like an idiot. Why didn't I know you were supposed to ask a girl to a dance? Why hadn't I asked her instead of just assuming we'd go together?

I paced around the kitchen, trying to sort it out. Ty was at the store and Gram had gone to a church meeting, so I was alone except for Granddad. As I stood staring morosely out the darkened kitchen window, he interrupted me.

"What's the matter, Harry? You got more troubles?"

Something about his sympathetic face got to me and I said, "Yeah, girl troubles." I told him what had happened. "I guess I'll just skip the whole darn dance."

"Oh, you poor boy." He chuckled. "Happens to all of us, you know. Tell you what. Just remember this. What's good for the goose is good for the gander."

I looked at him, puzzled.

"Look, dummy. If she's gonna go with somebody else, so can you."

Oh, man! I sure didn't want to do that. I couldn't imagine going with anyone but Carol Ann. But I didn't want to stay away. I had to be there to see if she really went with Billy, to see how she acted with him, and I didn't want to go stag and stand around staring at them. Maybe I *should* invite someone else after all. I thought about the other girls I knew. Norma Peterson, Dottie DePrato, Annette Garrett. I didn't want to ask any of them. They were nice enough girls, but they were homely as all get out. I just couldn't do it. I thought and thought. And finally I remembered Phyllis Porter.

Phyllis had missed a whole year of high school because of rheumatic fever. She had just returned this fall and was a grade behind. She didn't know her classmates very well yet, and she seemed alone a lot, maybe lonesome. She was pretty in a strange way, pale, with sad gray eyes. She seemed helpless, but I liked the slinky way she walked and her whispery voice. Tiny white teeth showed when she smiled. Yes, I would invite Phyllis. I'd show Carol Ann and Billy, too.

I FOUND PHYLLIS first thing in the morning and made my invitation. She smiled her pretty smile and said, "I'd just love that, Harry." She reached out with her thin fingers and squeezed my hand. "I didn't think I'd be going to the dance. Thank you." She squeezed my hand again. "But what about Carol Ann? Doesn't she want to go with you?"

I jerked back. "Carol Ann doesn't own me. I want to go with you." I wasn't sure what to make of this girl, but now I was committed.

Gram gave me a haircut and insisted I shine my shoes. I'd bought a new necktie, and by the time I was ready to go to the dance, I thought I looked pretty good. I figured Phyllis was a lucky girl to be going with me. I was that cocky. Then I thought of Billy Snyder and what a big, blonde fellow he was. How he played football and had muscles to show for it. That took me down a bit.

Bucky and Skinny Nelson were going stag to the dance, and I got a ride to Beaverton with them. They dropped me off at the high school, and I walked the two blocks to Phyllis's home, arriving exactly at eight. A sign in the front yard read *Marguerite's Beauty Shop for Women and Children.* Marguerite must be Phyllis's mother. I knocked on the door, and a slim, faded woman answered and introduced herself as Mrs. Porter. I could see that Phyllis resembled her. They both had the same wispy way about them.

"I'm glad to meet you, Harry. Phyllis has told me so much about you. You surely do look nice." She invited me to sit down on a fancy, wine-colored velvet chair.

"Thanks Mrs. Porter. I'll just stand."

"It'll be just a minute, Harry. I think she's about ready."

I looked around at the room the likes of which I'd never seen. Everything was frilly, a couch covered with ruffly pillows, little tables with curving legs that held flowery knickknacks and ashtrays. Photographs of handsome people hung on the walls, all dressed up, like they were in a show. I was so busy gawking, that I didn't hear Phyllis come in.

"Hi, Harry. I'm finally ready."

I turned. My knees nearly failed me. She didn't look the same. It took me a minute before I realized that it was her hair. She had bobbed her hair! It looked like a dark, fitted cap, combed smooth with shiny curves over her cheeks and a fringe over her forehead. None of the high school girls had bobbed hair. In fact I had seen only a few grown women in Beaverton with bobs.

But that wasn't all. She had put some red stuff—rouge, I think, on her cheeks, and bright red on her lips. Her dress was silvery blue, the color of her eyes, and a rope of about a million black shiny beads hung around her neck. Her high-heeled patent leather shoes made her seem taller. I was awestruck and stared at her. This was amazing! She was stunning, gorgeous, and she looked at least twenty years old.

Her mother helped her into her coat while I stood there like a lump. She said, "Now don't overdo it, Phyllis. We don't want you to get too tired." Phyllis rolled her eyes, and I knew her mother's words would be ignored. We had started walking toward the school before I was finally able to speak.

"You look beautiful, Phyllis."

She took my arm and pulled herself as close to me as she could get. "You can call me Phyll," she said in her whispery voice. Every nerve in my body jangled. For some reason I thought of Lettie, and I was aroused. Wow! This was going to be some night! A great night.

As soon as we walked into the gymnasium and shed our coats, I could feel everyone's eyes on us. Conversation stopped as they took in Phyllis's looks. She smiled shyly and never let go of my arm for one minute. Even the older boys stared, their mouths hanging open. Girls peeked at her and started patting their hair and straightening their dresses.

We found a table and chairs and sat down for a moment. Fellows beat a path to get their names on her dance card. I wrote my own name first, last, and a couple times in the middle just like Russ had told me to do, and her card was soon filled up. The band started to play, and we went onto the dance floor and began a slow two-step. I had practiced so much and felt so ready for this, but I sure wasn't ready for what she did. Instead of laying her hand on my shoulder, she put it on the back of my neck and pressed her body against mine. She clung to me, all soft and pliable like another skin. I could feel her beads and soft bosoms against my chest. We didn't talk. I couldn't. I was transported and couldn't believe this was happening to me. The feeling was so intense that I shuddered in relief when the number ended. Johnny Harris, who had come stag, came to claim her for the next dance, and I was grateful. I needed to sit down and pull myself together.

My friends came up one after another and said, "Where'd you find her, Harry?" "She's really classy." When I danced with the other girls, I couldn't keep from looking around at Phyllis, I mean Phyll. I noticed she didn't move quite so close to her partners as she did with me, and I was pleased. Frankie Halverson came up and said, "Wow, Spencer. I can see why you dumped Carol Ann for her. Question is, can you hang on to her?"

Why did that guy always make me want to hit him? But Carol Ann. I hadn't even thought about her until now. I looked around the crowded gym and spotted her dancing with Billy, and I smiled smugly. He couldn't dance for sour apples, and Carol Ann wasn't smiling. That was fine with me.

At intermission Phyll sat down, and I made my way to the refreshment table. I managed to snag a few cookies and wrap them in a napkin, and I took two cups of cider. Just then Carol Ann came up to the table. She wore a green dress with puffy sleeves and a big tie in back that made her look like a little girl. But it was her face that startled me. She looked as though she had been crying. Bright red splotches had erupted on her cheeks, and her pupils were large and dark.

"Harry. I…" she said, her voice hoarse.

I said, "Oh, hi, Carol Ann," as though I had just noticed her. I turned my back to her and headed for our table, but not before I heard Billy say, "C'mon, Carol Ann. I can't wait all night." That was odd, but I didn't really want to know what was bothering her. The boys were hovering around Phyll, so I hurried over and pushed the cider cup toward her.

"Thank you, Harry. I was so warm and thirsty." The other boys began to fade away, and she said, "Do you know the Charleston, Harry? It's fun to dance."

I shook my head.

"Well, if the music is right, I'll show you."

Apparently it was right the next time we danced, and she began doing the steps and kicks of the Charleston. I'd never seen it before, and I just stood moving a little to the music while she danced by herself. When it was finished, everyone clapped. She looked around with her shy smile and nodded. I was proud to be with her.

"I'll have to teach you the steps, Harry, so you can do it too."

"I don't know about that. It looks hard." I said, but I made up my mind that I'd learn that dance if it killed me.

At the end of the evening we danced a last waltz, and I was sorry the night had to end. We moved slowly with the others to the cloakroom to find our coats, and I helped Phyll into hers.

"Oh my, that was fun," she said, "but I'm feeling a little tired."

Bob Hollister, a senior boy, was standing nearby and overheard her. He came over eagerly. "Phyllis," he said, "I'd be glad to give you a ride home in my dad's car if you're tired."

She stood considering his offer. "Thanks, Bob." I thought she was going to accept, but she said, "It's just a short walk. Harry will take me home."

Bob looked at me, surprised she would choose to go with me rather than him.

We walked slowly with Phyll hanging on to me as before. I was more relaxed now, and we were able to talk easily. I asked her how she learned to dance.

"My dad loved to sing and dance. So did my mother. They taught me the steps when I was a little girl. My mother and I dance together sometimes because she misses it so much."

"Where's your dad? Doesn't he live with you?"

"No, he doesn't." She offered no other information.

As we approached her house, I began to wonder if she would let me kiss her. I figured she might because of the way she had clung to me all night, so I planned to do it when we got to her porch. I would turn and look into her eyes. I'd give her a little kiss and hope it would heat up before we were done.

It heated up all right. Before we'd even reached the front steps, she turned and wrapped both arms around me and raised her lips to mine. We had the biggest, wettest smooch I could imagine. What a night! I was just getting used to the kissing and liking it a lot when she broke away. She ran up the steps, opened the door and stepped half way inside. I could see her mother sitting in the living room.

"Good night, Harry. Thank you. I had a great time." She smiled her pearly smile and said. "I'm going to invite you over so we can practice the Charleston." And then she was gone.

I stared at the closed door, surprised and chagrined. She thrilled me. But in the back of my mind, I thought I should be the one in charge of things like kissing.

BY THE TIME Gram left the ladies in the vestibule at church Sunday morning, she knew every last thing there was to know about the dance. What Phyllis wore, her bobbed hair, the way she hung on me, how the other boys went for her, and all the rest.

She entered the house, put down her pocketbook, put her hands on her hips, and started right in.

"Did that girl really bob her hair for the dance?"

I shrugged. "I don't know. Maybe she was going to do it anyway."

"I hear she danced the Charleston." Her black eyes pierced me, and I looked away.

"So what if she did? She's going to teach me how to do it too."

"Humph. I'm not sure I approve of a girl who does that dance," she said.

"The Charleston is fun, Gram. There's nothing wrong with it. I bet you've never even seen it."

"Nor do I want to." She unpinned her hat and put on her apron, then turned to me again, her face stern.

"Sounds to me like you were out with a hussy."

"Phyllis isn't a hussy, Gram."

"I think Carol Ann suits you better. You better make up with her."

"It's not up to me," I snapped.

"I'll bet she'll be ready. I don't think she had a very good time at the dance. Miranda Phelps said she heard that Billy and his friends had gotten hold of some bootleg."

That surprised me. "I don't know anything about that," I said, wanting to hear more but unwilling to ask.

"I guess they kept ducking outside for a nip during the dance. Tried to get Carol Ann to drink some too."

So that was why Carol Ann had looked so upset. Served her right. But I was annoyed with all this gossip and Gram acting like I had done something wrong. I stomped out the door in exasperation and headed for the store to relieve Aunt Lida who had been helping us out on Sundays.

She grinned when I walked in. "Hear you took a real beauty queen to the dance," she said.

"Who've you been talking to?"

"Mrs. Trometer was in. She'd heard about it. Sounds like you had a good time. Right?"

"I did, Aunt Lida, but I can't see why everybody is so busy talking about it."

"It's the Bellwoods. They're mad as heck about Billy Snyder and the bootleg whiskey. I guess they're gonna talk to the principal."

That was sweet music to my ears. Billy Snyder would surely catch it when Mr. Lyman got hold of him. I knew Carol Ann wouldn't go out with him again. I began to think about the ride to school in the morning. How would she behave? Should I be mad at her? And her father. Should I be mad at him? Then I smiled to myself. Neither one of them could take away the fine time I had at the dance.

AFTER THE DANCE, Phyllis had every boy in the school buzzing around her. She invited me to her house a couple of times to learn the Charleston, and I finally got the hang of it. Those sessions weren't as much fun as I thought they'd be. The trouble was that Phyll talked about all the dates she had with other boys, Bob Hollister among them. She'd go on about the movies they'd seen and stuff like that. I couldn't figure out if she was trying to impress me, or what. I finally decided she just liked to talk about herself, and I was handy. The memory of our one magical night returned often, but somehow it wasn't the same now, and I gradually lost interest in her. That was just fine. We'd had our fun, and I was happy to let Phyllis go her way.

Somehow Carol Ann and I managed to patch things up. It took a while. We had to wait together every afternoon at school for her dad to pick us up, and, eventually, we just started talking. Neither of us said a word about the dance, and, after a while, it seemed natural to talk like we always had.

23

I T TOOK SOME time, but Granddad's leg began to heal. That's when he got restless and cranky about staying home every day.

"I think I'm okay now. I want Dr. Brunner to take this darn cast off. I need to get to the store."

"Alfie," Gram said for the umpteenth time. "The doctor told you the cast has to stay on for six weeks. Don't you remember?"

"My leg itches. I can't stand it anymore."

"It itches 'cause it's healing. Do you want some more apple cake?"

"What I want is something you won't get for me. I want some beer."

"I should've known. I had Bud Johnson come with his beer truck and take the barrels out of the store."

"You did what?" His eyes widened. "Why on earth would you do that, woman?"

"You know perfectly well that the bar has been closed since the attack. We couldn't just leave those barrels sitting there to mold."

He sighed. He did know it, but he wanted to complain. I felt sorry for him and all of us, too. Ty and I helped him to the kitchen table, propped his injured leg on a chair, and then helped him back to bed so many times every day that we were sick of it, and he was too.

One morning at breakfast he said, "I want to get out my fiddle and practice a little so I can go to the dance Saturday night at the pool hall."

Gram rolled her eyes. "Just how were you planning to manage that?"

He shrugged. "I don't know, but I'm gonna do it."

"I've got an idea," I said. "Ty and I can borrow Uncle Carl's horse and buggy and load him into it. We can deliver him to the pool hall and pick him up when he's ready to come home."

Her look let me know what she thought of my suggestion, but Granddad latched onto the idea and spent several hours over the next few days with his fiddle "warming up," as he said. His carping eased off as he planned for his first outing since he'd broken his leg.

Gram decided to cooperate and dug out a pair of my old knee britches. She cut the elastic in the left leg so it would slide over his cast and let him wear pants instead of the long nightshirt that was his daily garb. He was so small and had lost so much weight, the pants were a little large for him, but he was happy, and his eyes danced as he looked forward to the event.

Saturday came, and the skies opened up with a cold, late November rain that didn't stop all day.

"I think you better give this thing up, Alfie. You'll catch your death," Gram said.

"Not on your life, Bess. This'll quit before tonight. You wait and see."

The rain never let up even for a minute. His eagerness was so pathetic that, when the time came, I didn't argue, but put on my coat and hat and went to Uncle Carl's to get the horse and buggy.

"Surely he isn't going out tonight, is he?" Aunt Lida said in a worried voice.

"'Fraid so. He's determined."

"He's too old to be out in this kind of weather, and so is poor Rollo," Uncle Carl said. "Just be sure you rub that horse down good when you get him back to the barn."

I drove the horse and buggy to the house where Gram had Granddad bundled into his coat and hat. Ty and I carried him to the buggy easily. He couldn't have weighed more than ninety pounds. Ty ran back and got the red flowered oilcloth off the kitchen table, and we covered Granddad's cast with it because Gram was afraid the rain would melt it right off his leg.

It was pouring hard, but we set off for the outskirts of town where the old pool hall was located. We drove right up to the front door and carried Granddad inside, wrapped in the oilcloth, his fiddle tucked underneath.

People clapped and cheered when they saw him come in. The Meeves brothers had been trying to provide some music, but they weren't very good at it. Everybody knew Granddad played great music for dancing. The pinochle and poker games stopped, and people waited for him to get settled and tune up his fiddle. It wasn't long before they were sashaying around the floor and having a great time. In spite of being soaked through, I was glad we had made the effort for the old man. He grinned and seemed happier than he'd been for days.

Ty and I left and took Rollo home to get him out of the weather. We visited with Uncle Carl and Aunt Lida until it was time to pick up Granddad. Gram had said a couple of hours was plenty for a man just out of the sickbed.

We got to the pool hall right on time and went inside to find him, but Granddad was nowhere in sight. We looked everywhere and asked everyone. He couldn't move without help, yet nobody seemed to have noticed when he left. One woman said he took a break from the music, and she wondered why it never started up again. She said people had gathered around him to talk, and the next thing they knew, he was gone.

Squint Pickard was sitting near the door, and he said, "I saw him leave, boys."

"He left? How could he?" I asked.

"Arlo and Malcolm Fitch just picked him up and carried him out," Squint said. "They were going to take him for a ride in their Model T."

"On a night like this? Why?"

He grinned slyly. "I think they had some hooch. I wanted to go too, but they wouldn't let me."

Disgusted, Ty and I stood around for almost an hour, waiting for the Fitches to come back. Everyone was leaving the hall, and Bernie Beaubien, yawning and looking at the clock, was ready to lock up.

"Sorry, fellas, but I've got to close up now. Maybe they took Alfie home."

We didn't want to leave without him, but we couldn't very well sit outside in the rain with the horse all night.

"Maybe he's at home," I said.

"If he isn't, Gram's gonna pitch a fit," Ty said.

"Yeah, I know."

We stopped by the house on the way back. I tiptoed in. Gram had gone to bed, and there was no sign of Granddad. We had no choice but to take Rollo back to his barn and rub him down. We ran home, both of us sopping wet. Gram heard us come in this time and got up to see how the evening had gone.

She looked around. "Where is he?"

"He went off with the Fitches in their Model T before we got there," I said. She looked murderous.

"You boys get dried off and get to bed. I'll wait up a while for him, but if he doesn't show up pretty soon, I'm going back to bed." She scowled. "The durned fool can stay out in the rain all night for all I care. I knew this was a bad idea."

We left her in her rocking chair wrapped up in a quilt and were just as happy to go to bed. We'd already lost enough sleep over that old man.

THE NEXT MORNING, right after breakfast, we heard a knock at the door. It was Arlo Fitch looking as sick and sorry as a man can be who's been drinking bootleg whiskey all night.

"Ty, Harry, could you come out and help us get your granddad into the house?"

We got our coats and went outside, leery about what we might find. The rain had stopped, and the yard was thick mud. We had to squish through it all the way to the road. Granddad was sprawled across the back seat of their car, asleep under the red flowered tablecloth, his fiddle case clutched to his chest. He seemed unhurt but reeked of liquor.

"C'mon, Granddad. Are you all right? Let's get you out of here."

He opened his eyes enough to see us. "Oh, hello, boys. I had a fine time." His speech was slurred, and he closed his eyes again.

"We can tell," Ty said. "Sit up now so we can grab hold of you."

We pulled him up, and each of us took an arm and put it over our shoulders. We lifted and dragged his dead weight toward the house. His cast was spattered with mud, and a considerable chunk had broken off down by his ankle. Malcolm and Arlo followed us, handing the tablecloth, the fiddle, and a pair of crutches through the door. Then they beat it back to their car before Gram could get hold of them.

Gram's face was grim, but she was silent. I figured that boded worse for Granddad than if she yelled. We got his coat off and hauled him back to his bed.

"You're good boys," he said again. "Good boys, but Bess'll be mad." His eyes rolled shut.

Ty and I made a beeline for the store, not wanting to be around to witness what came next. We stayed away at the store all day, making bologna and cheese sandwiches for our dinner and helping ourselves to Coca Cola.

Russ showed up around four to run the store for the evening. Much as we dreaded to go home, we were hungry, and that was the only way to get fed. We entered quietly and were dumbfounded to see Granddad sitting at the kitchen table, a pair of crutches leaning against his chair.

"Hello," he said with a little grin, but with a face that looked whiter and sicker than when he broke his leg. "Your grandmother is pretty put out with me, and she let me have it after you left this morning."

I looked at Gram who stood at the cook stove, her back to us.

He spoke softly. "We just went out to Arlo's 'cause he remembered a pair of crutches in his attic." He paused and looked at her like he expected her to say something, but she just kept stirring the pot.

"She had a right to be sore at me, and I let her know I was sorry I went off with those fellows. Sorry they let me drink too much of their moonshine. Sorry my head feels big as a pumpkin. Sorry I worried everybody."

I wanted him to stop talking. We took off our coats and started to wash up, but he kept on.

"But, wow, boys!"

We turned around, stunned at the change in his voice.

"First time I ever rode in a Model T. It was great, even in the rain. Why, we just rolled along like nobody's business. Got where we were goin' in no time at all." He looked expectantly at the cook stove again, then back at us.

"So what your grandmother and I have decided this afternoon… well, the store has been doing pretty well and the Klan hasn't come back. So what we decided is that we're going to get us a car too." Now she turned around, spoon in her hand, looking like she was doing her best not to smile.

"Yessir," he went on. "We're gonna have us a brand new Ford Model T just as soon as I can get to town to buy it. What do you think of that?"

We stared open-mouthed. I doubt there were ever two fellows more surprised than we were. We'd walked in expecting a dark and angry scene, blame, excuses, the whole lot. Instead, everything had changed. Our world now had exciting possibilities, unknown for sure, but there just the same. As Granddad's words sank in, we looked at each other and began whooping and dancing. I grabbed Gram and whirled her around the room, and she laughed right out loud. I had no idea until then that she wanted a car too.

"Let's eat supper," Granddad said.

24

MY FRIENDS AND I often gathered at the store or on some-body's porch to talk. One time I asked them when they thought our lives would start. They looked at me like I was touched.

"Are you crazy? Our lives began the day we were born," Billy said.

"No, I mean when we really start to do things."

"Like what, Harry? We do stuff all the time."

I gave up and didn't raise it again. These boys were different from me. The future I'd conjured up in my mind, when I went places and became someone who amounted to something, stayed with me and never went away. I just learned to keep quiet about it.

But today was different. Ty and Granddad would come home this afternoon from Sioux City with a brand new Model T Ford. Surely that meant I'd be started toward whatever wonderful things were coming my way. My life would change; I'd be able to travel beyond Richmond, beyond my daily trip back and forth to school.

I fell to daydreaming about it in Mrs. Kleinsasser's class. I took trips to Chicago, the Rocky Mountains, and California before she called on me to explain the difference between a simile and a metaphor. I stammered and said something about substituting a long word for a short word. Everyone laughed. I knew it sounded ridiculous. My mind was so far away, I couldn't think of anything sensible.

Mrs. Kleinsasser said, "Harry, I do believe you were wool-gathering. Did I guess right?" I nodded, embarrassed. "See me after class. We'll get you straightened out."

I groaned inwardly. She always made those who didn't pay attention write an extra essay on some dull subject. I sure didn't want to do that, not tonight of all nights. I approached her desk nervously.

"You do know the difference between a metaphor and a simile, don't you, Harry?"

"I sure do. I don't know why I couldn't say it before. A simile compares two things using 'like' or 'as,' and, a metaphor. Well, a metaphor doesn't. What I mean is, it compares two things, but well, it uses different words..." I trailed off.

"All right," she said. "I think I know how to fix this. Read the section on similes and metaphors again. Then I want you to write six sentences, three that use similes, and three that use metaphors. That way I'll know you understand these figures of speech. Turn it in to me tomorrow."

I dragged myself out of the classroom. This sure wasn't the start of the new life that I was looking for.

The day crawled by. Classes seemed long, and then, when it was time to leave, Carol Ann's father was late. We had to stop for gas, and it was dusk before we got home. I craned my head out the window as we approached our house, but no new car was parked in front. My disappointment was huge.

"Gram," I said as I burst in. "Where are they? I thought they'd be here by now."

"So did I," she said. "I don't know what's happened."

She went back to heating up our supper, and I stared out the window, not knowing whether to be mad or worried.

"No use just standing there, Harry. They'll come when they're gonna come. How about pumping some water for me?"

I took the bucket and did as she asked. Then I tried to start my homework. One or the other of us jumped up and checked the window every couple minutes.

After what seemed like hours, I heard the chug-chugging of an engine, and I ran outside. Hallelujah! They were here at last. Ty honked the horn, and Granddad stumbled out of the passenger side, looking pale and exhausted.

"Longest day I ever put in," he said as he headed for the house.

"Why? What happened?" I asked. But he just waved his hand and went on.

Ty said, "It was a long ride. The dealer told us not to go over ten or fifteen miles an hour until we get her broken in."

"So that's why it took so long."

"Yeah. Granddad was nervous. Kept telling me to watch out for this truck or that car. Don't get too close to the ditch. That kind of stuff. Heck, he doesn't know how to drive, but he gave me directions the whole time. Then he wanted a drink for his nerves. Nothing would do, but I drive to Jefferson so he could visit Clancy's for some bootleg."

"Oh no," I said. "Not again."

"We got lucky, brother. Clancy's had the Feds breathing down his neck, and he hasn't made any for a while. Anyway, that's what took so long and made him grumpy."

I understood and said, "Let's don't say anything to Gram about it, okay?"

I walked all around that car, taking in every detail. Sitting in the driver's seat, I ran my hands over the sleek surface of the steering wheel. I pressed the three pedals and imagined changing gears out on the road and operating the hand brake. I turned the key in the switch from magneto to battery and tried out the windshield wipers, watching the fan-shaped motion they made from the top of the windshield. I stroked the pinstriped upholstery on the seats and sidewalls. Every last thing was slick and clean and worked perfectly.

The tank that held ten gallons of gas was under the front seat with a dipstick to measure the level. A spare tire was mounted on the rear, and under the back seat was a boxed set of tools with everything we'd need to change a flat and more. I recognized the jack and tire wrench painted black and spanking new. It was so dark I could scarcely see, but here came Gram with a lantern, her curiosity having gotten the better of her.

Finally I opened the hood. "Just look at that," I said in awe. "It's beautiful." And it was. Every part clean, with a purpose, and perfectly made.

"I don't have any idea what I'm looking at. Are those the pistons?" she asked.

I didn't know any more than she did, but I said, "Sure are."

She looked at it for a minute, then said, "Let's eat supper. This'll keep till tomorrow."

We went inside and sat down to our meal while Granddad described the haggling over the price.

"I offered him $269, but he wanted to charge me $65 more for the electric ignition. I told him I'd walk away from it, and we went back and forth a few more times. Finally we settled on $289, and he filled up the gas tank."

"What's that worth?" Gram asked.

"About two, two and a half bucks," Ty said.

"Seems like you came out all right, Alfie."

"I dunno," he said. "I still can't get over it. Most money I ever spent on anything in my life."

Ty and I couldn't resist visiting the new car again before we went to bed. Gram threatened us with our lives if we attempted to drive that night. We took a lantern, and I begged Ty to show me how to start the engine.

"First thing is to turn the key to the left for the battery and push the spark lever all the way up. That's the little rod attached to the left side of the steering wheel. Then push the throttle down about a quarter of the way." He pointed to another rod on the right side of the steering wheel.

"Okay," I said. "That's easy."

"Now jump out and grab the crank. Remember to crank clockwise."

I got down and put my right hand on the crank.

"No," he yelled. You have to crank with your left hand, Harry, 'cause if the engine backfires, that crank'll spin around counterclockwise and break your arm."

I was clumsy and tried the crank several times before the car started, but I finally got it going.

"Now get back in, and turn the key to the right for the engine, and push the spark lever down." It was so complicated, I had to try over and over before I could coordinate everything. Finally I managed it, and then! Oh how I itched to drive down the road somewhere, anywhere at all.

"There's a whole lot more to learn," Ty said as he explained the clutch pedal, but he thought it'd be easier once we had the car in motion. I hated to quit, but it was dark, and Gram would be after us if we didn't come in. I wanted to try one more thing. With the engine running, I turned on the headlights and hopped out to see what they looked like. Wow! They were powerful! That gave me an idea.

With that image in my head, I tackled my homework assignment for Mrs. Kleinsasser. I wrote:

The headlights were like the eyes of an owl in the dark.

I thought about the car and was able to come up with a couple more sentences.

A Ford horn was a donkey's hee-haw.
The spoked wheels were like the whirling pinwheels we got at the fair.
The raised hood was a ...

And then I got so sleepy I couldn't think anymore. I'd finish this assignment tomorrow.

AT FIRST TY and I were forbidden to drive unless Granddad or Gram were with us, but it wasn't long before they realized they didn't know anything about cars, and they had to depend on us. I didn't know much either, but I acted like I did, and they believed it. It made me feel grown up.

We did our best to teach Granddad to drive, but he never got the hang of it. He wasn't nimble enough with his bad leg to jump in and out of the car to start it, and the clutch flummoxed him every time. If he did get going, the car would jerk forward too fast. Then he'd brake hard, and the engine would die. He gave it up without ever admitting he had. Whenever he wanted to go somewhere, one of us took him. I didn't mind because it was just plain fun for me. It took a long time before the novelty of driving wore off. I'm not sure it ever did.

Gram was the biggest surprise. She was crazy about riding in the car. We went to town on Saturday nights because she wanted to go. Granddad was happy to stay home and mind the store. We'd clean up right after supper and head to Beaverton. Gram would wander through the general store, looking things over, not buying much, maybe some thread and sewing notions, but whatever she saw was a topic of conversation for the whole next week, especially the prices. I'd meet up with friends from school, and we usually finished the evening with ice cream at Mobley's Cafe.

Ty and I tried our best to get Dad to go for a ride, but he refused. "I've ridden plenty," he'd say. "I don't need to go riding around in Alfie's new car like somebody's poor relation." He was so tiresome anymore that it was easier just to forget about him and get on with life.

Before long Gram and Granddad loosened the reins and let us take the car without them. Ty and I went to Jefferson to see Polly and Vince, and I drove. I felt sinfully proud when I pulled up to their house and they came outside to admire the car. Their little girl, Mary Jo, was two years old, and Polly was expecting again. She was tickled to see us, and we had a long visit. Vince gave us a mess of catfish to take home to Gram.

What I wanted most of all was to take Carol Ann on a date in the car, but her mother put her foot down and wouldn't let her go.

"What's the matter?" I said. "Doesn't she trust my driving?"

"It's not your driving, Harry. That's not the problem." Carol Ann laughed. "She's afraid you'll use the arm heater."

"What's an arm heater?"

"That's when you put your arm around your girl to keep her warm."

I grumbled, and I wondered how Mrs. Bellwood was able to read my thoughts. How did she know what I had in mind? I wasn't sure myself.

The changes the car brought to our lives crept up on us almost unawares. If we'd stopped to think about it, we'd have seen how dependent we'd become on that wonderful contraption. We could go places, buy things if we had the money, visit people, see the world. I hadn't been to Chicago or California yet, but somehow I knew my life was bigger than it had been before. Maybe my life had started.

25

I DREAMED OF DRIVING the new car to school to show it off to my friends and let them see me driving it. I imagined what they would say. Some would be admiring, some jealous, and I figured I'd feel grand. But Gram wouldn't hear of it as long as Mr. Bellwood was available to give me a ride.

My chance finally came on the last day of school. We'd be dismissed after our picnic lunch, and Mr. Bellwood couldn't pick us up that early, so Carol Ann was to ride home with me. It was my first time to drive alone without Ty. I was nervous, but mostly just thrilled, hoping that nothing would go wrong, no flat tire or stalled engine.

Gram gave me a whole bushel of warnings and cautions, and then I heard them all over again from Mrs. Bellwood.

"Are you sure you have enough gas?"

"Don't go too fast. You don't have to hurry."

"Watch that bend where Abe Pollock lets his cattle cross."

You'd have thought I was leaving for Los Angeles, but I listened, not letting on how jittery I felt, how impatient I was to get going.

Once I got out on the road, I drove carefully, and when I reached the school without calamity, I let out a big breath of relief. I parked in front trying my best to look casual, like driving was something I did every day of my life. In no time, the boys gathered around to admire the Model T.

"When did you get a car, Harry? Is it yours?" Bucky said. "I wish we'd get one. Dad says maybe we will next fall."

Sam said, "Who taught you to drive, Harry? Could you teach me?"

"I wouldn't let him teach me," Frankie Halverson said, a sour look on his face. As usual, he hung back at the edges of the group, and most everyone ignored him.

The others walked around, touching the shiny finish, admiring the headlights, the slanted windshield with its little wiper, asking about the spark lever and the clutch. I'd never felt prouder in my life as I shoved the key into my pocket and tried to answer their questions. I'm pretty sure I strutted as I went inside with them for our last classes.

The teachers were as cheerful as we were about seeing the last of us for a while. We didn't do any serious work. They let us talk and kid around, and they joined in too. We cleaned out our desks and cloak-rooms, then helped neaten up the classrooms. We took down pictures and posters, got rid of trash, and washed the blackboards. When the moment came for us to get our report cards, I felt a small twist of worry. What if somebody gave me a failing grade? I thought I'd done all right, but maybe I was in for a surprise.

But I worried for nothing. I'd managed to finish the ninth grade with an A in algebra, a B in English, and two C's. Mr. Lyman had even written a few words saying how pleased he was that my deportment had improved over the year. All right. Now I wanted to have some fun.

We went outdoors to a picnic in the schoolyard, and Mr. Hummel saw to it that we had lots of games and races. Right in the middle of it, I spied Mrs. Carmichael hanging out laundry in her back yard with baby McDermott toddling around. I hadn't planned to do it, but I left the school grounds and went into her yard. Her eyes widened with apprehension. We hadn't seen each other since my clumsy apology last fall.

"Hi," I said. "McDermott is really getting big. Would it be all right if I held him up to the fence for all the kids to see? I'll be really careful with him."

She seemed uncertain but finally agreed, "Well, I...I guess it'd be all right."

I swooped up the little boy and called to my friends. "Look who I've got." Everyone cheered and clapped. They came running to the fence, and I thought the racket would make him bawl. But he just grinned a slobbery grin and stretched his arms out to them.

"He's darling. Let me have him," Ada Sue said. I turned around to look at Mrs. Carmichael. She nodded, so I handed McDermott over the fence. The girls all had a turn holding him, tickling him, and talking baby talk to him until he decided he'd had enough. His mouth turned down, and he started to whimper, so they passed him back to his mother. He buried his face in her shoulder and then peeked at me, his thumb in his mouth.

"Mrs. Carmichael, I'm really sorry about what I did last fall," I said. "It was mean, and it makes me feel like a fool now. I wish I'd never done it."

She took some time before she said anything. Then she smiled. "Thanks for saying that, Harry. It was a hard time for me with my husband laid up and all. I'm not too proud of my own behavior back then either. I'd like to forget about the whole thing."

We didn't have much else to say, so I shook her hand and said, "Bye, McDermott," waved, and went back to the picnic, feeling like I'd finished with that piece of mischief.

Carol Ann and I gathered up our school things and loaded them in the Ford. I started the car and let it idle for a few minutes. She climbed in, and we were about to leave for home when Frankie Halverson walked over with the usual smirk on his face. He kicked the front tire.

"How'd you get the money for the car, Harry? Did you get insurance after your store got hit?" His voice was unpleasant, taunting.

"No, we didn't. Not that it's any of your business."

"It doesn't make sense to me. The Klan tried to burn you out, and here you are with a new Ford. Some people I know had to pay big fines, but you got a new car."

206 | KAREN WOLFF

"That's not my concern, Frank, so just shut up, will ya?"

"You better look out, Harry. They're gonna try again. They're gonna get your store and that boozy grandfather of yours."

My blood rose hot. I wanted to punch him in his fat, pudgy face. He was nothing but flab, and I knew I could take him. I started to jump out, but Carol Ann put her hand on my arm.

"Don't do anything, Harry. It'll just make him worse."

It was all I could do to let Frank's words pass. My hands gripped the steering wheel, and hatred seethed through my body.

"I want to kill him," I muttered.

"Don't let him get to you, Harry. He's just trying to be a big shot."

I took some deep breaths and stared straight ahead, away from Frankie. After a minute, I put the car in gear. It bucked a couple of times. Oh God. Would I have to get out and start it again? Be embarrassed in front of him? But that blessed machine kept going, and we pulled away.

Carol Ann and I didn't say anything until we got out of town, and my breathing slowed down. Frankie's stupid meanness had sure taken the shine off our afternoon.

"What was he talking about," she asked, "when he said someone had paid a fine?"

"I don't know for sure, but you remember when Sheriff Beaubien told us about that KKK gang burning crosses down by Jefferson?. They got arrested and went to court. He's pretty sure it was the same bunch that attacked our store, but there's no proof. When Frank bragged about it at school, the sheriff figured out that his dad was a member."

She was quiet for a few minutes as she thought that over. I was calmer now and slowed down to make the trip last a little longer.

"I hope they don't come back," she said.

"They won't," I said with more confidence than I felt. "Gram says they're too yellow."

That seemed to settle it for her, and she talked about how nice it was to be outside in the middle of the day, out of school for a few months. We laughed about Mrs. Carmichael and McDermott.

"I love little kids like that," she said. "I'm going to take care of the Hubbard twins in the afternoons this summer. Their mother has her hands full, so I'm going to help her out. But how about you? Are you going to start right away at the rink?"

"It doesn't open 'til next weekend, so I have a little time. I'll have to work in the store every morning, but I'll make some cash money at the skating rink."

"Good for you."

"Russ got a full-time job as a butcher's helper in Portlandville, and Harold's dad is putting him to work at his new gas station in Beaverton. So I'll be the second boy after Sam this summer."

I took one hand off the wheel and covered hers with mine. I risked a look away from the road for a few seconds. She was so beautiful, her blue eyes wide and happy. "Are you going to come skating when I'm at work? Let me put on your skates?"

"Maybe. I suppose I might."

"I want to spend time with you this summer," I said. "I want to take you to a movie, or a dance. Do you think your mother would stand still for that?"

"I don't know, Harry. So far, she hasn't been willing, but I can ask again."

"Doesn't she know you're almost fifteen? It's time for her to let go."

She giggled. "I think she knows how old I am, Harry."

"I can't hardly stand it, Carol Ann. I've never even been able to dance with you." I pulled her nearer to me, and she didn't object. I wanted to put my arm around her, but worried too much about my driving to risk it. We continued to bump along, and it tickled me that every bounce seemed to bring her closer.

"I'd like that too, Harry. Maybe if we can think up a special occasion, I can talk her into it. Or if we go with another couple."

As we drove up to her house, she scooted back to her side of the car. "I think the way you handled Frankie was good, Harry. You were mad, but I'm proud you didn't get in a fight with him. It wouldn't have been worth it."

"I guess you're right."

I wasn't thinking about Frankie just then. What I wanted was to tell her she was my sweetheart. I wanted to wrap my arms around her and kiss the sweet place beneath her pink ear lobe. I thought I'd bust with frustration. When would I get my chance? I sighed as she got out. It sure wasn't going to be today.

But she had given me an idea. I knew Russ and Darlene would go out with us, and Russ would figure out how to give us some privacy. I drove away with that happy prospect in mind.

That night over the supper table I told what Frank had said at school about the Klan coming after us again.

"They better not," Gram said. "People won't stand for it."

"I don't know, Bess. They might try it again," Granddad said. "I've been thinking maybe we need to get another dog. A good watch dog that could stay in the store all night. Not one like Buster who'd rather lick your hand than bite it."

Buster. My throat tightened up. If he were here now, he'd be waiting under the table, ready to follow me wherever I went. Ready to play ball or just be my pal. Granddad could get a new dog if he wanted, but it would never be the same.

"I wonder when the high line will come through," Gram sighed. "If we had electricity, we could light up the store, and that'd be enough to scare them off."

"It'll just be another bill to pay when we get electricity," Granddad said.

"You sound like an old fogey," Gram said, "but until we get it, I think it's a good idea to find another dog."

And that's how Bruno came to live with us. He was a stout-chested fellow, black and white with a head the size of a basketball. We never did know what breed he was, but he had an arrogant way about him and a bark they could have heard in Sioux City. It didn't take him long to make himself comfortable behind the counter at the store where we had to step over him every time we went to the icebox. He had a way of looking at us that said, "You are an inconvenient nuisance. I've decided to let you pass, but I'm not about to move out of the way."

If it is a watchdog's work to announce intruders, Bruno was born for the job. What he would have done with them after that is hard to say, but it wouldn't have been pretty.

26

EVERY SUMMER I worked at River Sioux, and at summer's end I'd feel rich. I found out, though, I had to be careful with my money. Ty said I was a tightwad, and Russ told me I was just plain cheap. I didn't care. I knew what I had to do to make my money last.

I wanted so many things. Clothes. Not just the everyday stuff, but fancy sweaters and caps, a suit with a matching vest, and two-tone shoes to go with my outfits. I wanted to go to movies. I wanted to take Carol Ann to see shows and go dancing. I wanted to buy cigarettes now that Russ had taught me to smoke. I wanted to go to Sioux City. And the thing I wanted most, the thing that seemed most unattainable, was a car of my own, not one belonging to Granddad or somebody else, but my very own.

I needed money. I wanted money. The question was how to get it. I was prepared to work hard and to sacrifice to build up savings, but I hadn't figured out how to acquire funds in the first place. Maybe I got the horse before the cart, but I decided to set a goal for myself so I'd be ready when an opportunity came. A thousand dollars. I wanted to be worth a thousand dollars by the time I was twenty-one years old. I told Gram about it, and she just shook her head. "That's a tall order, Harry."

The tone of her voice told me she doubted I'd make it, but that was all right. I'd surprise her.

❖   ❖   ❖

THE SUMMER BEFORE my junior year, I became head boy at the skating rink and earned $20 to $25 dollars a week. I saved everything I could, and my bank account stood at $155 by the end of the summer. It was a start toward my goal.

At the skating rink, Mr. Crill talked a lot about electricity. He was very keen to have it at River Sioux so he could compete with the dance halls in Sioux City.

"Just think, boys," he'd say. "Imagine how this place would look with red and green and blue lights all around the eaves. And what if we hung globes high on the ceiling with soft lights for dancing?"

His plans sounded great, and we liked hearing him talk about them.

"I remember something I saw a couple of years ago at the Starlight Ballroom in Omaha," he said. "They had a revolving ball made of mirrors hanging from the ceiling. It caught the light as it turned and made patterns on the floor. It was spectacular, and I mean to have one at River Sioux. Soon as we get electricity."

"When will we get it, Mr. Crill?" someone always asked.

"I don't know. We have to wait for the politicians to decide. Soon, I think. My brother says it'll be soon."

Mr. Crill's brother was the state's auditor, and Mr. Crill made many trips to the capital to talk to the politicians.

"It's gonna change our world," he'd say. "If you boys are smart, you'll find a way to capitalize on electricity when it comes. There's gonna be money to be made."

The others didn't seem to have any idea what he was talking about, but I did, and I resolved to take action as soon as those wires came our way.

Meanwhile, as soon as he could get back to the store, Granddad restocked the beer supply even though the revenuers were an increasing problem in the county. One day Bud Johnson, who drove the beer truck, told Granddad he should take the beer barrels out of the store for a while until the Feds went somewhere else. While Granddad grumbled,

Ty and I helped load the barrels in Bud's truck, and he drove away with them late one night.

Sure enough, the next morning three men in dark suits showed up while Ty and I were alone in the store. They flashed their badges and demanded to talk to Granddad. Ty took off like a scalded cat to fetch Granddad, leaving me to answer their questions.

"You related to the Mr. Didier?"

I nodded. Even though I knew they wouldn't find anything, I was scared silly, and my heart was going to the races.

"You know why we're here, boy?"

"No," I said in a voice that made me sound like a little kid.

"We're here to make sure you're in compliance with Prohibition. You understand?"

I nodded again and was vastly relieved when Granddad walked in. I couldn't help admiring the show of innocence that old man put on.

"I have nothing to hide, gentlemen. Follow me." He unlocked the door to the empty bar and, with a genial wave of his hand, invited them inside. Even though the glasses had been removed from the counter, the peanut shells swept from the floor, and the ashtrays emptied, nothing could kill the telltale smell of beer that had soaked into the floor. Only a fool would fail to see that this was an operating saloon.

"Where do you keep it, Alphonse?" one of the men growled.

"What's that, gentlemen? Oh, beer? There's no beer here. You can see for yourself." Granddad's face looked innocent as a baby's.

"We heard you're open for business day and night. Where do you hide the stuff?" The questioner was a bulky, red-faced fellow who looked tough and serious about his work.

"Gents, look around. You can see for yourself there's no beer in this establishment." Granddad couldn't control his grin.

The three looked everywhere, behind the counter, in the ice-house, even in the cellar. They came upstairs, wiping cobwebs from their clothing.

"Alphonse, we're going to throw you in jail if we find out you're lying to us," the bulky man said.

"Don't see how you can do that, given there's no beer here," Granddad said.

"Don't get smart," the man said. They dusted off their hats, wiped the perspiration from their faces, and left the store. I prayed they wouldn't go to the house where I knew there was a pitcher of beer Granddad had poured off for himself before the barrels went away.

Granddad crowed all evening about how he had stared down the revenuers. It was beyond me to understand why he'd risk going to jail over beer, but that was Granddad. He seemed more interested in having a good time than running a business.

"They sure wasted their time," he said. "We hoodwinked them pretty good."

"That's easy to do when there's no beer around," Gram said. "It'll be a different story if they come back and find some."

They did come back the next two nights and found nothing, and again they threatened Granddad with serious trouble if they ever caught him with beer. The pitcher Granddad had taken home was empty by now, and I feared he'd insist on another delivery.

In a few days Bud Johnson stopped in to say that the Feds had left the county and gone to Yankton and Sioux Falls. We were safe for the moment, and Granddad opened the bar again. Things went back to business as usual, but I was pretty sure our worries weren't over.

27

ELECTRICITY CAME TO us the summer I was seventeen. The poles were shipped all the way from the Black Hills by railroad, and then two teams of horses pulled the wagonloads from Beaverton to Richmond. We watched as the drovers stopped at each block and rolled a big pine pole off the wagon to the side of the road. The younger kids climbed all over them as if they could find the electricity in them. We weren't much better. We stood around imagining the poles erect in the ground, promising something unbelievably glorious. Everybody was excited to think of what was to come, and everybody wanted in on every detail.

Crazy Betty Sykes, a white kerchief knotted on top of her head, stood with her hands on her hips to watch. We always wondered about that kerchief, whether it covered up a bald head. The only thing we knew was that we never saw her without it. Whether she was sweeping her porch or chasing dogs and kids out of her yard, she always wore the kerchief. Now her doughy face was screwed up in a frown as she yelled at us. "Lectric'll kill you. Get away from there." We laughed, but I could tell some of the folks wondered about it.

Mr. Crill had finally succeeded in persuading the legislature that it would be good for business if he could have electricity at River Sioux. The existing electrical line ran northwest from Beaverton to Plankinton, so several miles had to be run eastward to River Sioux. It was just luck that Richmond was in the pathway or we wouldn't have gotten power for years. As it was, we waited weeks before the crew came to set the poles.

School was out for the summer, and Ty and I were working in the store one hot, June morning when a horse-drawn wagon with "Castle Electrical Company" painted on the side showed up. Several men jumped down and started unloading picks, spades, shovels, and long pikes.

A tall fellow, tan, with penetrating blue eyes came into the store for some cigarettes. "Howdy," he said. "I'm Smitty." We shook hands. "That's my crew out there." He waved his arm in the general direction of the men outside. "I guess you know why we're here."

"We sure do," I said. "We thought you'd never come." He grinned. "Yeah, everybody's always anxious to get their electricity. Can't wait for all the fun." He turned as he went out the door and said, "We're gonna start digging, but it'd be helpful if you spread the word so people keep their kids out of the way. I don't want nobody to get hurt."

THE FIRST POLE lay on the corner across from the store. They hauled their tools to the site, and two men went to work with a pick and a long-handled shovel. After they had opened up the ground, Smitty sited the spot for the hole and the men started to dig.

"Damn it, Smitty. This ground feels like it's solid rock," one of them said.

Smitty laughed. "Quit complaining, Jake. You just ain't warmed up yet." He moved down the road and started two other men on the next hole.

It was hard, hot work. The men soon threw off their shirts, and their bodies, copper from the sun, gleamed as rivulets of sweat ran down their backs and dripped from their faces. The sinews on their necks and shoulders stood out in ridges as they strained.

Gram came outside to watch. After a few minutes she said, "Harry, you and Ty should pump a couple buckets of cold well water for those fellows."

We ran to do it, and they were grateful for the hospitality. The men were spread down the road now as they continued digging. At mid-morning they came back for the water and took a short rest.

I was full of questions, wanting to know how all this worked, how they got the poles up, when the line would be strung, how they'd get it into our house.

A grizzled old fellow said, "You just need to keep quiet and watch, kid. You'll learn something."

They were more talkative at noon when it was time to eat dinner. Smitty told us, "This is how it works. We use knob and tube wiring." He showed us the porcelain insulating pieces. "You gotta keep the electrical wire away from wood so you don't start a fire. We attach the knobs to the tops of poles before we raise them." He took a bite of his sandwich and a big slug of water. Then he picked up a couple of white hollow tubes and went on. "These here things are what we use in your houses. They keep the wire from touching the wood beams and walls. The wire that runs to a lamp or a switch has to be covered with cloth or rubber for insulation."

"Could I see one of those?"

He handed me a tube, and I rolled it around in my hand enjoying its smooth feel, cool, even in this heat. I was awed at how much he had to know to do his job.

The crew spent two days digging, but the real fun didn't start until they began to raise the poles. Smitty told us they'd use the piking method because the company was too cheap to send out a gin wagon for a town as small as ours.

The whole population turned out to see the first pole go up. Granddad even locked up the store so we could watch. Smitty assigned five men to the job. The butt end of the pole was positioned next to the hole where they'd dug a shallow trench so the pole would slide down it as it was raised.

Four of the men began to lift the top of the pole. As soon as it was up a few feet, another man, called the jinny, put a big brace made of two boards nailed together in an X-shape under the pole to hold it in place. Each time they lifted the pole a little higher, the jinny slid the X-brace closer to the hole. When they had gone as far as they could by hand, the men picked up their long pikes with v-shaped pieces of metal at the ends. They positioned themselves around the pole and used the pikes to continue pushing it to an upright position.

The men seemed small next to the thirty-five foot pole. I couldn't see how they could stand it up without it falling on them. Everybody in the crowd got very quiet as they watched. One women put her hand to her mouth. Others clutched their children, nervous about what could happen if something went wrong, but I was thrilled. I didn't know how they'd do it, but I couldn't wait to see it happen.

Smitty stood by the butt end of the pole and shouted orders to make sure the pole stayed lined up with the trench. "Left, go left a little, Jim. A little more. Whoa. Slow down. Take your time."

Oh, how that thing wobbled and trembled, but the crew seemed unafraid. They yelled at each other all the time too. "You're not working hard enough Jake."

"Hell, I could raise this thing by myself if you'd get out of the way," Jake responded.

It was a tense operation, and when the first pole dropped in with a satisfying thunk, everybody let out a big breath and cheered and clapped. It was a marvel to see that pole go into the hole just like it was supposed to.

Next thing, a man with a shovel began filling the hole around the pole with little bitty shovelfuls of dirt, and three others packed the loose dirt with tampers. Smitty said to the crowd, "It takes one lazy shoveler and three good tampers to be sure the pole is set right."

I thought about that and finally got the meaning. If they shoveled the dirt in too fast, it wouldn't get tamped hard enough and the pole might wobble, so the dirt got filled in slowly. They sure did know how to do things.

AFTER THE POLES were up, the crews went to each house to install interior wiring and a meter. Granddad complained. "Do you mean to tell me you're going to charge me four dollars before I use any electric? I thought the government was back of this."

Of course his arguments got nowhere, and in the end, our house got wired like everyone else's. Gram and Granddad decided they wanted a light in every room, so the crew installed a porcelain fixture with a clear glass bulb and a switch in each room. They ran a wire from the meter box to each switch, either through the basement or down the wall.

Only two households in town elected not to have electricity. Betty Sykes because she thought it was the devil's work, and Gus Granquist, an old fellow in his 80's who figured he wouldn't live long enough to get any use of it. Everybody else signed up and waited. And then waited some more. We waited so long people stopped asking about "when" and "what have you heard" every time they came in the store.

Instead they wore out their Sears and Roebuck catalogues, dreaming of what they would buy when the great day came. Women generally wanted irons so they could be rid of the heavy black flatirons that had to be heated on the cook stove. Some of the men thought about getting electric water pumps.

For me there was just one thing. I wanted a radio. I'd heard weak broadcasts on storage battery radios, but the signals busted up, and it was hard to make sense of what we heard. I wanted an electric radio so we could hear what was going on in the world outside Richmond. I wanted to hear the music and entertainment programs. I wanted a radio that we could listen to whenever we felt like it, day or night. I imagined all the sophisticated and up-to-date things we would hear. Yessir, I meant to get a radio.

I talked Ty into making a trip to Sioux City with me. He was always nervous going there, but decided the adventure was worth it. Smitty had told me the Castle Electric Company had the best inventory of electrical appliances and radios in Sioux City.

Ty was in a cold sweat driving in all the traffic in the city, and we had to stop a couple of times to ask where to find the store. Finally we located it in the Trimble block, one of the busiest shopping areas in the city. Ty was able to relax when we got the car parked, and we ventured inside.

Castle's was packed to the ceiling with electrical equipment for the home. Signs everywhere described how the housewife's work could be lessened with electricity. I saw things I never dreamed existed—Thor washing and ironing machines, bread toasters, fans, and lots more.

"Just look at this, Harry. This machine will wash your dishes." Ty and I looked at each other in wonder. Who could imagine such a thing?

"I can't wait to tell Gram about this. She'll never believe it."

Flame-shaped Mazda lights in several styles glowed from fixtures hung on the ceiling. A row of sewing machines attracted my eye, and I thought again of Gram huddled over the old treadle machine at home.

We worked our way to the back of the store, gawking at everything, but then I saw what I'd come looking for. A tingle of excitement went through me. I said. "Look, Ty! There they are."

"Oh, wow," he said. "Just look at that. There must be fifty of them."

Indeed there were. Rows and rows of shiny, handsome radios. I saw Crosleys, Philcos, and a half dozen other brands. Some were made of metal and others of wood. Some were designed to sit on a table or shelf, and others stood in fancy, carved wooden consoles. I couldn't imagine what all the knobs and dials were for. I itched to try one.

"Can I help you fellows pick out something? Maybe a new radio?" A salesman came up. "A lot of the young fellows are buying this one." He pointed to an Ozarka. "Would you like to hear it?"

I nodded eagerly, and he turned the switch on and twirled the dial.

"I'll find WNAX for you. That's the Gurney station in Yankton. It comes in clear all day long." He cocked his head as he listened. "Isn't that great? Shall I turn it up a little?" He twisted a third dial and it came in louder.

"It's wonderful," I breathed, and it was. An orchestra played polka music, and then there was an announcer talking about the Gurney Seed Company and how it wasn't too late to buy vegetable seeds for a bountiful garden. Next, a man's deep voice began a news report of a train that ran into a herd of cows near Kansas City. I was thrilled. I could have stood there all day listening to this magical box. I knew I was grinning like a fool.

"Of course we have lots of different models for you to try. Would you like to hear another one?"

I shook my head "no." I was smitten. I wanted that Ozarka.

"How much is it?" I asked. "

"It's $35 'cause it's on sale. It should be $67 but Mr. Steele, that's my boss, has ordered a lot of new ones, and he'll sell these at a bargain price."

I had to have that radio. I wanted to be ready the minute the electrical line came through.

"I'll take it."

Ty looked at me like I had taken leave of my senses. "That's a lot of money, Harry. We don't even have electricity yet."

"Don't worry. I can manage." I fished some bills out of my pocket to pay the salesman. Ty stared open-mouthed. "Where did you get that?" he squawked.

"From my bank account. Where do you think?"

He watched in wonder as the salesman took a new radio from the shelf, still in its box, and handed it to me. We headed out the door, and then I had a thought.

"Ty, would you take this to the car? I'll be out in a minute." I ran back to the store where I had a few words with the salesman and then with Mr. Steele. This time when I reached the car I had two more boxes of radios.

"Harry, what in the world? What have you done?" Ty looked flabbergasted.

"Well, I thought if I wanted a radio so much, other people'd want one too. So I asked what the price would be if I bought three radios instead of one. The salesman went to get his boss, and that's when I met Mr. Steele. He told me I was an enterprising lad and that he'd let me have the three radios for seventy-five dollars."

"But, Harry. What if nobody'll buy them? Then what will you do?"

"I'll sell 'em. I know I can, and I'll make ten dollars on each radio. Then I'll buy some more. Don't you see?"

And that's how my big business venture got started.

28

I SOLD THOSE RADIOS fast. Miranda Phelps and her husband always liked to be the first in town to get anything new. They bought the first one. My second sale was to Sally McVay.

"I'm stuck in the house every day," she said. "It would be nice to have the diversion of a radio, and your dad might enjoy it too."

I hoped she was right. He might hear things that would send him into a rant. If she was willing to chance it, I was keen to sell her one.

Those sales were easy, and I was eager to get back to Sioux City to buy more radios. Gram said, "You'd better wait until the line gets strung and we actually have electricity." She was afraid, if it never happened, I'd have a lot of merchandise to return. I grumbled, impatient, fretting that someone else might jump on my scheme.

Granddad put up a shelf on the kitchen wall where my own radio sat useless. Every time I looked at it, my frustration grew. When would it come to life? When would we hear all the exciting stuff I knew was in there? Sometimes I fiddled with the dials and pretended what it would be like. That tortured me even more.

We'd about given up hope when a truck rolled into town loaded with huge spools of wire. The driver pulled right up to each pole, and men with cleats on their shoes climbed up and strung the line. Then they ran a wire to each house and connected it to the wiring they had already installed. It was slow work, and another week passed before the job ended.

Late on a Friday afternoon, Smitty came into the store and said, "We've finally got the whole line done even out to River Sioux. The power will be turned on at noon next Tuesday."

Everybody in the store cheered and clapped and then rushed home to tell the news. Ty and I hung up a sign in the window so everyone would know. Then we waited through the long weekend, trying to go about our life normally.

"Harry, you're as jittery as water on a hot griddle," Gram said. "You better forget about that electricity till Tuesday. It might not work, you know."

"Oh, I think it will, Gram. It's just got to."

"I hope you're right, but don't let it break your heart if it doesn't."

On the appointed day, Gram and Granddad and I stood in the kitchen waiting for the miracle to happen. We counted down the minutes until the clock said twelve, the three of us staring at the light on the wall. Nothing happened. We waited, my hope lingering, but there was nothing.

Gram sighed and said, "We might as well eat our dinner while it's hot. No point standing here like fools."

"Well," Granddad said. "We've lived a long time without it. It won't kill us to wait a little longer."

I sat down at the table sick with disappointment and tried to eat. The food stuck in my throat, and I finally gave up. What could have gone wrong?

A few minutes later my brother burst into the house and said, "Isn't it wonderful! You can see every single thing in the store. Even in the bar." He looked around. "Why don't you have it on? Don't you want to see what it's like?" He walked over to the wall fixture and turned the switch. Light flooded the room.

I felt a thrill go right through me followed immediately by red-faced embarrassment. Of course. You had to turn on the switch. Why was I so stupid? We went through the house and turned on each light, looking all around as if we'd never seen those rooms before, marveling at the difference the lights made.

"The radio. Let's try the radio." I raced back to the kitchen, switched it on and spun the dial to tune in a station. It took a minute to warm up, and then we began to hear static and weak signals. I continued twisting the dial until a station came in loud and clear. A baseball game was underway and a male voice was describing every play. We figured out that it was St. Louis playing Cincinnati. I didn't care a whit about that game, but I listened as though my life depended on knowing every detail. I watched the clock, knowing I would have to leave soon for the skating rink. The hardest thing I ever did was to turn the radio off that afternoon so I could go to work. I groaned and complained, but finally did it. When I got out to the rink, I couldn't help showing off for the younger fellows. "It's the Reds five to three at the end of the third inning," I said.

"Wow, Harry. How do you know? Do you have a radio?"

I nodded proudly. "Sure do. Heard it for the first time today."

UNUSUAL THINGS OCCURRED in the coming days. The housewives in our town began to see dirt, cobwebs, chipped paint, peeling wallpaper, stains from water leaks, and every kind of shabbiness that you could think of. And they were ashamed. In no time they had their men trekking into the store to buy paint and brushes and turpentine.

"My wife says I have to paint the bedroom," one would say. Another might complain, "She says the kitchen ceiling is greasy and dark. I've got to clean it and paint it."

The women came in one at a time to peek at the book of wallpaper samples and pick new flowered patterns for their living rooms. Granddad got busy and ordered buckets of paint in yellow, lavender, blue, and lots of cream from Aalf's Manufacturing in Sioux City.

The whole town went into a frenzy of cleaning, painting, and papering, and our house was no exception. Gram didn't admit it outright, but would say, "I'm really tired of that forget-me-not flowered paper in the living room," or "I've thought for quite a while that we need to paint this kitchen woodwork."

We watched as the pot of wallpaper paste got mixed and the big brushes came out, the plumb line with its wooden knob at the end. Gram commandeered the kitchen table, spreading strips of wallpaper facedown and using a brush to smear on the paste. Then Ty or I would fold up one end and carry the strip to the living room, climb the ladder, and stick the thing to the wall. Gram checked to be sure each strip was plumb, that the patterns matched, and the overlap was just right. When she was satisfied, we used a dry brush to smooth out the lumps and bubbles, wiping up paste that oozed out the sides and trying not to tear the fragile paper. In the evenings, the women visited each other's homes, chattering about the merits of cornstarch versus flour to make wallpaper paste and admiring the fresh, new looks. Our town must have been the cleanest, shiniest place in the country, all of it due to those skinny wires that brought light to every corner.

29

A S SOON AS I could get away, I went back to the Castle Electric Company in Sioux City. This time I spoke directly to Mr. Steele.

"Sir," I said. "I've got a chance to sell a lot of radios in our town because we've just had electricity installed in everybody's houses."

He smiled at me. "Interesting. What's your name, young man?"
"Harry Spencer, sir. I live in Richmond."

"Well, I think we may be able to help you. Let's see what we can do."

I looked at all the radios again and decided to buy three more Ozarkas like I'd bought before, and then I picked three Crosleys. When it came time to settle on a price, I said, "Mr. Steele, do you think…is it possible…it seems to me that I should get a better price if I buy six radios."

His eyes widened as if he were surprised or annoyed at my nerve. I thought he might get mad, but after a minute he said, "Well, Harry. I guess maybe we could discount them some. How does $23 each sound?"

That was pretty good, but something compelled me to try for more. I said, "I was thinking more like $21, Mr. Steele."

"That'd be highway robbery, Harry."

I swallowed hard. "I think I can sell a lot more in the next few weeks." He thought it over, and I was sure the issue was dead when he said, "Okay, I guess we can let you have them for $22.00."

Wow! That meant I would make thirteen dollars on each radio. I was going to be rich.

Then I had another idea. "Mr. Steele, if I promise to come back in a week to settle up, would you let me have these radios on credit? See, I've got lots of possible customers, and nobody else sells this stuff in our town. I know I can do it."

"I do like your get-up-and-go, young man, but that's a lot of money to have tied up. I'd have to have a down payment. Have you got thirty dollars?"

"I've only got twenty," I said.

He sighed and said, "I guess that'll have to do."

I gave him the money and signed the charge before he could change his mind. We shook hands.

"I'll expect to see you in a week, Harry. You're quite a young business man."

"Thank you, Mr. Steele. I'll be here," I promised. And I was.

FOLKS WHO CAME into the store at home treated me like I was the expert on electric appliances. They asked me about radios, refrigerators, stoves, fans, and Miranda Phelps wanted to know about waffle irons. The attention puffed me up, and I played the big shot once in a while, making up facts when I didn't know for sure, like telling Mrs. Trometer that a refrigerator would make ice in twenty minutes or that you could get toast in a minute and a half. They believed me.

The next time I went to Sioux City, I bought ten irons in addition to radios. The regular price was $6.75, but I got them for $5.00 each. When I got home, I stacked nine of them in the store with a price tag of $7. I took the tenth one home and handed it, still in its box, to Gram.

"What's this?" she said looking at me, surprised.

"Open it, Gram. You'll see."

She pulled back the flaps on the box and peered inside. "Why, it's an iron. Harry. Is this an electric iron?"

"It sure is, Gram. Do you like it?"

"You mean it's for me?" She sat down in her rocker with the box on her lap, her surprised eyes on my face.

I laughed. "Well, *I* sure as heck don't know how to use it. Yes. It's for you. Now you can get rid of those heavy old flat irons."

She removed the shiny Hotpoint from the box, trailing the cord through her fingers. "I don't know what to say, Harry. It's so lightweight. I'm flabbergasted." She grabbed her hanky from her apron pocket and began to mop her eyes, and I realized she was teary. I had never seen Gram cry, ever. Even that awful night when the store was attacked. And yet here she was blubbering over an iron. I was tickled she liked it so much. I don't remember her getting a gift in all the years I'd knew her. Our family just wasn't one for presents, I guess.

Aunt Lida and Uncle Carl decided they'd like to try out a radio, so I took one to their house and set it up for them. Ever since I'd been selling electrical equipment, I'd kept a notebook, writing down names of customers, what they bought, and what I charged them. Sometimes folks had to stretch their payments over two or three weeks, and I had to keep track of that too. My notebook was a mess with crossed out information and erasures. Sometimes I forgot what I told people and had to make a guess. I'd laid that notebook on the table while I was hooking up the radio, and Aunt Lida saw it there.

"What's this thing, Harry?"

I looked up, hot and sweaty from my work. "My customer accounts," I said.

"Pretty messy, I'd say. How in the world do you know where you stand with this kind of bookkeeping?"

It was a good question. I didn't know. All I could say for sure was that I always sold things for more than I paid and figured I'd come out all right in the end. Even so, she was right about the sloppiness.

"I just don't have time to do it right," I said. "There's work in the store every morning until noon. Then I work at the skating rink from three 'til nine, so the only time I have for selling is in the early afternoon."

"I see," she said. "Yes, you do have a problem."

She said no more about it but paid me for the radio, and I left. That night when I got home, tired and ready to fall into bed, Gram said, "Lida stopped by tonight. She had an idea for you that might help in managing your business."

That's all I needed, I thought, was for those two old gals to get into my affairs.

"What would that be?" I asked, sourly.

"We were thinking. Now that Cal has learned to write with his left hand, maybe he could set up a system and keep track of your income and your costs so you know where you stand. It might be a good thing for him too. Help him feel useful."

I looked at her in disbelief. "My dad? You think he could do that?"

"Well, yes, I do. You know, he did bookkeeping years ago."

"He did? Nobody ever told me."

"Well, he did. That's what he was doing when he met your mother."

I could scarcely believe it. I didn't know much about Dad's life before I was born, but he'd been mostly useless since the war. I wasn't sure I wanted him involved in my business. I was afraid I couldn't count on him for much.

"He's a smart man, Harry. He just had a bad thing happen to him, and it affected him."

"I dunno, Gram. It doesn't seem like a good idea to me."

"Maybe you should just think about it, Harry."

I PONDERED GRAM'S suggestion for a couple of days, and after looking at my jumble of names and figures in my notebook again, I decided to go see my dad.

He sat alone at the table in Sally's kitchen, and his face lit up when he saw me. "Harry, I thought you'd be over to see me."

"What made you think that, Dad?"

He didn't answer but picked up a dusty, black ledger book from the table and waved it at me. "I found this in my things. Forgot I had it. I can use it to set up a system for your business. Help you keep track of everything."

I knew then that Gram or Aunt Lida had been here ahead of me. Nothing was private in this town, that was for sure, but I needed help. I laid my messy notebook on the table, and we went to work. He labeled one page INCOME and the opposite page EXPENSES. It was awkward for him to reach around with his left hand to write, and I was astonished at how quickly he grasped every detail. He began to enter the items from my notebook.

"Dad, how do you know how to do all this?"

"I was always good at numbers, Harry. I did bookkeeping when I first met your mother and married her. I thought we had a good life back then even with you kids coming along so fast."

"Why'd you quit, Dad?"

"I didn't want to. I didn't have much choice." He laid his pencil down, and put his good hand to his head. His eyes became cloudy and took on that faraway look he often got. I worried he'd forget what we were doing, and might get up and walk away.

"It was Rachel. Your mother. Just like that, she got sick, lost the baby, and then she was gone. Without her, I didn't know what to do. It was such a bad time." He stared off somewhere, not moving. Then he said in a whisper, "I miss her."

I swallowed hard at his words. They filled me with the old longing to know my mother, to have her love. Even though it couldn't be, I still wanted it. I shook my head to help me put the thought aside. Goodness knows, I'd had to do it often enough. After a couple of minutes I said, "Is that why we ended up at Granny Marigold's?" My question drew him back from his reverie. His eyes focused on me.

"Yeah." He sighed. "She offered us a place to live, and I jumped at it. She needed someone to help with her house, and I had all you kids. It worked out. That is, until she died and we sold her house."

He got up and poured us each a cup of coffee from Sally's graniteware pot. It was slow work for him with just one hand. As I watched him, some ornery thing, some old resentment, rose up in me, and I didn't get up to help him. He didn't seem to notice anything.

"The trouble was that Granny lived over by Westfield, and there weren't any businesses around there where I could get a job keeping books. So I went to work on Harvey's farm. Didn't especially want to, but that's what there was."

"That's too bad, Dad. I'm sorry you had to give up doing what you liked." The coffee had been sitting too long and didn't taste very good, but I was interested to hear his story. I realized he'd had plans once, just like me, but he didn't get to follow his. Still, he might have if he hadn't gotten mad and spent his time hating things he couldn't change. He joined the Klan and did God knows what. The old doubt about the store attack rose, and disgust churned in me for a minute before I was able to squash it down.

"I figured when I came back from the war, I'd look for a bookkeeping job somewhere, and we'd be set," he said. "It was this damn arm that screwed me up." His mouth twisted, and his words were choked with self-pity. "That was the end of anything good for me."

"It was hard on all of us," I said with some bitterness. I couldn't forget that he still refused to see Polly or meet his granddaughter. A few seconds went by, and I remembered I was here for business. I changed the subject.

"You know what, Dad? I'm good at numbers too. That's my best subject in school. Do you suppose I inherited that from you?"

"Could be, I suppose," he said.

"But I didn't know how to organize all this." I pointed to my notebook.

He straightened his shoulders and took a big breath as though to throw off his earlier thoughts. "This'll be simple, Harry. Stop by a couple times a week so I can keep current with your sales, and we'll be able to tell exactly where you stand." He looked at me with a hint of a grin. "Maybe we'll get you close to that $1000 goal."

So Gram had told him that too. I needed to learn to keep my mouth shut. Even so, I thanked him and left Sally's, feeling all right about my visit. I'd learned some things I didn't know.

30

MR. CRILL DECIDED to celebrate the new bright lights at River Sioux with a grand Fourth of July dance and fireworks. We boys helped him string the colored lights around the pavilion just the way he had imagined. He hired the Castle Electric Company to install the faceted revolving ball on the ceiling. You never saw a man so pleased with things. His chubby face shook with excitement as he looked around, a cigar clamped between his teeth, and we couldn't help but be happy for him.

"Let's turn everything on and see what it looks like," he said. We admired it all even though it didn't look like much in the daylight. What I enjoyed was watching his enjoyment of it all.

"A man should have dreams," he'd say, and I agreed, feeling a little sad when I thought of my father. Dreams were great if you had the ability to make them happen.

Because it was to be such a special holiday, Mr. Crill hired Lawrence Welk and his band, the Hotsy-Totsy Boys, to play for the dance. Everybody who had a radio listened to their polkas and waltzes on WNAX, and Mr. Crill even placed ads on the radio station so people would know about the celebration.

For my part, I made sure to invite Carol Ann to be my date so there'd be no unpleasant surprises like I'd had at the school dance.

"About time you asked me, Harry. Mother's already got a new dress half made for me. I was starting to worry you might forget, and there I'd be with a new dotted Swiss dress and nowhere to go," she teased.

I didn't know what dotted Swiss was, but I knew she'd be the prettiest girl at the dance, and I was proud to be her boyfriend. All our friends would be there, and even Gram and Granddad were going. It would be quite a night.

OUR WEATHER HAD been nothing but thunderstorms for several days, but we awoke on July Fourth to a clear sky and blistering hot sunshine. Steam rose from the muddy ground making it smell like the river, and the humidity left our clothes soaked with sweat from the smallest exertion. Still, the discomfort was small compared to our anticipation of the evening to come. We ate an early supper. Granddad locked up the store, leaving Bruno on guard, and went to River Sioux with Gram and Ty in the Ford.

Russ and Darlene picked me up and then Carol Ann. She was the most adorable thing I could imagine, just like a little doll. Her dress was fluffy, blue with tiny dots of white, and her hair was pulled back in a new style and fastened with pearly combs. I had never seen her wear lipstick before.

"Don't kiss me, Harry," she said when we got in the car. "I don't want to get smeared."

Later. I'd kiss her later.

Our excitement mounted as we drew near River Sioux. Cars and buggies were rolling in from everywhere. Young boys directed the traffic, sending automobiles to park west of the pavilion and horse drawn carriages across the road to the north. Smart. No chance of stepping in anything unpleasant if you arrived by car. The lawns were filled with people who'd come early with picnic baskets and were frying fish or roasting wieners. Hot, sticky children ran whooping and shouting, their mothers warning them to stay back from the riverbank.

Though the sun had not quite set, the lights on the pavilion were turned on, and it was every bit as beautiful as Mr. Crill had hoped. We heard the band warming up, and at eight o'clock they played the national anthem. Everybody sang, hands over their hearts, as they looked at the big flag Mr. Crill had put up. Then the dancing started. First we had a lively polka, and our fresh clothes were soaked through in no time.

"Ooh, look at that!" Carol Ann said when she saw the mirrored ball going round and round, lights glinting off it. "It's like magic."

I smiled at her pleasure. We danced waltzes, two-steps, and the schottische, sometimes trading partners with Russ and Darlene or other friends. We giggled a little when Gram and Granddad got out on the floor to dance a waltz. She was so tall, and Granddad so tiny. Yet they laughed together when it was over, walking to their seats, wiping their faces. Even Ty danced with some girls from school. He looked clumsy, I thought. I'd better arrange for Darlene to help him.

A couple of times we were so out of breath, we moved up close to the band stand and listened to Lawrence Welk play the accordion while we sipped Cokes. He wore his hair slicked back in a pompadour, but his face looked like a hardworking farmer's until he finished playing. Then his eyes lit up; he would smile and make a stiff little bow to the applause.

At ten o'clock, the musicians laid down their instruments and mopped their faces, and the dancers went outside to watch the fireworks show. I led Carol Ann to the back side of the pavilion where there weren't any people. Earlier in the afternoon, I had laid a ladder alongside the building. Now I stood it up and said, "Let's go up on the roof where we can see better."

"What? You expect me to climb onto the roof?" She stood with her hands on her hips. "No, Harry. What if I ruin my dress? I'm not sure I can do it."

"Sure you can. I'll help you."

It wasn't easy, but we managed to climb over the eave onto the wooden shingles. The roof was canted only a little on our side, and we felt the heat left from the afternoon sun on the rough, splintery wood. I wished I had thought to bring a quilt. Cottonwood trees that grew along the river made their whooshing sounds as they moved in the wind. I took off my shoes and socks and let the breeze play through my toes. We sat happily, waiting for the fireworks to start.

Carol Ann said, "You were right, Harry. It's nice up here. Lots cooler." Following my lead, she removed her shoes, rolled off her thin white stockings and laid them carefully beside her. Something about watching her actions, seeing her bare toes in the moonlight aroused me.

A huge boom announced the beginning of the show and we watched as colored rockets exploded in the sky. "If you lie back, you can see it better," I said. I put my arm around Carol Ann and pulled her down beside me. After that I wasn't so interested in the fireworks. I kissed her ear, then turned her face to me with my free hand, and we kissed a long time. I put my hand on her throat and gradually moved it downward. "I can feel your heart beating," I said. I touched her breasts through the dotted Swiss and, when she didn't stop me, I felt the roundness, the pillowy softness. A thrill went through me. Just what I had dreamed of. I rose up a little and put my hand on her leg.

She said, "No, no. Harry," but she didn't push me away. I held still for a moment and then continued stroking her leg, reaching up a little higher each time. The fireworks boomed and cracked. The red, green, and gold showers colored the sky, and I was blissful, in another world.

"What the hell? Who put this ladder here?" Mr. Crill's familiar voice roared from the ground below, shocking me out my dream state. I whipped my hand from under her skirt and sat up.

"Who's up there?" he yelled.

"It's me, Mr. Crill. Harry."

"Harry! What the devil are you doing up there?"

"Just watching the fireworks, Mr. Crill."

Silence held for a moment while my heart thudded in my chest. Then he said, "You're a damn fool, Harry. You could break your neck."

He paused. "You be sure to put this ladder away when you come down. I don't want every kid in the county climbing onto my roof. You hear?"

"Oh, I will, Mr. Crill."

We waited a minute and thought he had gone when he spoke again. "There's a white stocking down here. Does that belong to you, Harry?"

Carol Ann gasped and looked around frantically for her stockings.

"I...I guess so." Neither of us had noticed when a breeze had floated that stocking to the ground.

"Well," he said. "I'll just hang it over a rung on the ladder."

"Thank you." We sat like statues, Carol Ann holding her remaining stocking, my heart palpitating with fear and guilt. When we were certain he had gone on his way, I leaned over the eave and retrieved her stocking

"Oh, Harry. I'm so embarrassed," she said, her voice stricken. "What if he tells my folks?"

"He won't. He doesn't know who was up here with me."

"What if somebody sees us coming down? I'll die."

She started to snuffle, and I knew my ideas of romance were over for the evening. We put on our shoes and socks. I went down the ladder first and made sure no one was watching.

"It's safe. You can come down."

She almost slid down the whole length of the ladder. I hugged her close, not wanting to let go of the mood we had going up there, but she pulled away. I found her a seat inside the pavilion as people started to dance again, and I put the ladder back in the boathouse.

Carol Ann was painfully quiet as we danced. I kept reassuring her that no one had seen us, that no one knew we were on that roof, but I could tell she was scared.

"We mustn't do that again, Harry. Promise me?"

I grinned. "I don't know. I thought maybe you liked it. A tiny bit, anyway."

She colored, then said, "We just mustn't."

When we got home after the dance, all she gave me was a quick peck on the cheek and jumped out of the car without waiting for me to walk her to her door.

Russ looked at me and said, "What's the matter with her?"

I wanted to tell him in the worst way. I wanted to tell him about my audacious behavior. I was happy about it, but I decided to keep quiet. "She's just tired, I guess." I knew he didn't believe me, but he didn't press it. He just slapped me on the knee and said, "Attaboy, Harry" and laughed.

31

I BEGAN TO BELIEVE I was finally on my way to making something of myself. With predictable income from the skating rink, I'd
put over $500 in the bank; people still wanted irons and toasters and
radios; and, best of all, I loved a girl who loved me back. One more year
of high school, and I would be ready for the adult world. I rolled out
of bed the morning after the July Fourth dance, eager to face the day,
exhilarated by all the possibilities before me.

"Didn't expect to see you up so early this morning," Gram said,
"after that big night." She had hot coffee ready.

"It's a great day, Gram."

She gave me a wry grin. "Maybe you could get me a bucket of
water before your great day starts."

She had a way of pulling me down sometimes, yet tedious chores
like pumping water happened in everyone's life. I was soon on my way
to open up the store where I'd stocked some electric toasters. With luck,
today would be a good day for selling them.

I started grinding a few pounds of coffee for folks who had stayed
up late at the dance and needed an eye-opener. As I turned the crank,
my mind wandered back to last night with Carol Ann. I shivered to
think how thrilling it had been to touch her, to feel her softness, to feel
her responding to me. I was dying to try that all over again. She had said
we mustn't. She wanted me to promise we wouldn't. I wondered if she

really meant it, because I thought it'd kill me if she stuck to it. We had a date for Friday night. Maybe I'd find out then.

Somehow I got through the week. I was always busy waiting on customers and selling irons or sometimes a radio. I had meetings with my dad so he could bring the ledger book up to date, and before I knew it, it would be time to go to work at the skating rink, and I almost didn't have time to think about Carol Ann.

On Friday Ty relieved me at the store so I could go home to eat dinner. When I walked into the house, I overheard Granddad say, "If it's true, it'll be hard on him, I reckon."

"If what's true?" I asked.

He gave Gram a look, and she shook her head. "Nothing much, Harry. Just some idle talk."

I looked at them both, but they didn't say a word. I shrugged. "Well, what's for dinner? It's too hot to eat, but I'm starving."

Gram dished up a plate of fried eggs and garden peas. I slathered a couple of slices of bread with butter gone soft in the heat and poured myself a glass of milk. I'd just taken a few bites when there was a banging at the door. Looking startled, Gram got up to open it.

"Well, my goodness, it's Carol Ann. Come on in."

"No. I need to talk to Harry." Her voice was ragged.

"What? What's the matter?" I said as I got up. I could see she'd been crying. Her face was all blotchy and red, and her nose was dripping. A stab of guilt went through me. Someone must have found out about our escapade at the dance.

I went outside, and she threw her arms around me, sobbing like somebody had died.

"What's the matter? What happened?"

"I hate my dad," she blubbered. "I hate him," and off she went bawling and wailing.

"Come on, now. What happened? What did your dad do?"

"It's so awful, Harry. I can't stand it. He's so mean."

I'd never seen so much crying even when my sister Polly was carrying on about something. My shirt was getting wet from all the tears.

"Aw, Carol Ann. You've gotta quit crying. Tell me what happened." She slowed down a little bit and wiped her nose on her hand.

"He...he's making me...me...move."

She started crying and snuffling again. I tried to think what she meant. How could he make her move?

I stood there just rocking her in my arms for several minutes until the sobbing slowed down. She tried to talk but choked on her words.

"Kansas City. He says we're moving. To Kansas City."

I was stunned. No words came to me at first, but she was so torn up, I had to do something. "Come on," I said. "Let's find some shade." I took her hand, and we walked up the rise to the spindly Chinese elm near Buster's grave.

As she sank to the ground, she said, "Oh, Harry. It's so awful. He says we're moving on August first, and I won't be able to go to high school and graduate with you. And I won't know anybody in Kansas City, and, oh, I don't want to go. I just can't." She buried her face in her hands.

This couldn't be happening. I couldn't imagine my life without her. Never had it occurred to me that something like this could take place. "Why?" I kept saying. "Why is he doing this?"

At last her sniffling and hiccupping stopped, and she was able to tell me. Her dad had been offered a job as a cattle buyer in the Kansas City stockyards. It was a big boost for him, and he wouldn't have to drive around picking up people's cattle and hogs to sell at the stockyards. Now he'd be the one doing the buying.

"He's so happy about it," she said. "He doesn't care about me. How I feel."

"How's your mother taking it?"

"Oh, she puts a good face on it for him. But I don't think she likes it one bit."

"I don't know what to say. I just can't let you go, Carol Ann." My brain was rolling around in my head, and I couldn't think straight. I couldn't let her leave. I couldn't lose her. Life would be unbearable. I had to make a plan.

"I don't know what to do, Harry. I don't want to go, but I have no choice."

Her voice sounded so forlorn and sad, it made me ache to see her hurting so much. We sat without talking for a minute, my mind whirling as I tried to figure out what to do.

"Maybe you could stay here in Richmond this year and finish high school. I'll bet you could get a room at Sally McVay's."

"That's the first thing I thought of, but they won't let me do it. They don't think it would be good for me to be here by myself. I begged and begged, but it's no use. They won't stand for it."

The tears had stopped, but every once in a while as we sat there, she made little mewling sounds that broke my heart. She was hurting, and so was I.

Then I had another idea. A big one. "I know what we can do, Carol Ann. What about this? We can get married."

She sat up and turned her swollen face to me. "How could we do that, Harry? How would we live?"

"I don't know. I guess I'd quit school and find a job."

"They won't let me. I know that for sure."

"But you're sixteen years old. We could elope like Polly and Vince did. I love you, Carol Ann. I want to marry you some day. It might as well be now," I pleaded with her. "I just can't let you move away."

That brought on a fresh stream of tears. "I love you too, Harry, but you can't give up school. It just wouldn't be right. You'd never be able to do all the things you've planned on. You'd never get out of Richmond."

I turned my face to the hot wind that was drying the tears she had cried into my shirt. She was right, but I'd marry her in a minute it if it kept her here. It wouldn't be easy for us, but surely I could figure it out.

"Let's get a drink of water. We can't decide anything right now." I pulled her up, and we walked to the well where I pumped icy cold water. She took the dipper and drank, then splashed water onto her face.

"We'll figure this out, Carol Ann. There has to be something we can do"

BUT THERE WAS nothing. On the fateful day in August, I helped Mr. Bellwood and a couple of moving men load the family's belongings onto a truck. They didn't need me, but I wanted to be there as close as possible. I wanted to touch Carol Ann's things and remember every last detail. It took until the middle of that blistering hot afternoon to haul everything outside and pack it in the truck. Some of Carol Ann's girlfriends stopped by to say their farewells. I stood back, listening to their promises of letters and cards.

Then the moment came that I dreaded most of all. I held her in my arms and felt my eyes mist up as we stood there. I didn't care who saw me kiss her and hug her and stroke her hair. We didn't say much; we'd already said about everything there was to say in the past few weeks.

"Promise you'll write, Harry."

"I will. I love you, Carol Ann."

"I love you too, Harry."

I shook hands with Mr. Bellwood and got a hug from his wife. She called to Jerry to get in the car, and they drove away. Neighbors who'd come to see them off waved until they were out of sight. It was the saddest, loneliest feeling ever to stand in the yard of that empty house and know Carol Ann wasn't coming back.

Her girlfriends came over to me with long, sad faces. Pearl Goodman put her hand on my arm and said, "We won't let you get lonesome, Harry." Her round, chubby face creased in smiles that made her look just like her mother who was about the widest woman in town. Then Betsy Bonham said, "We like to roller skate, Harry. Maybe we'll come out to the rink to see you." She was a tall, scraggly-haired girl, all bones

244 | KAREN WOLFF

and big feet. They were Carol Ann's friends, and I knew they were nice enough girls, but right then they had no appeal for me. Didn't they understand how I was feeling? I just walked away.

Finally everybody left but me. I felt I was still connected to Carol Ann if I stayed. I wanted to think of her, to remember her here. I went all around that empty house, looking at the bare windows, the locked doors, and then I wandered out to the vegetable garden in back. Carol Ann's mother knew she wouldn't be putting up string beans, or corn, or tomatoes this summer, so she decided to let the garden go and left it untended. It was a forlorn place. Weeds had sprouted up in the hot dry weather and were taking over the crops. Rabbits had stripped the lettuce and pea plants down to nubs. Corn left unharvested hung heavily on the stalks. I walked up and down each row, unable to pull myself away, my mind haunted with the emptiness I felt.

I fell to my knees along a row of beans and began to weed, slowly at first, then faster and faster. At the end of the row, I was wet with sweat and tasted dust in my mouth. I wondered why I was doing this. Yet I kept cleaning up that garden. I even weeded the row of marigolds and zinnias that grew along the border. Nettles stung my hands, and my nose ran from the ragweed and goldenrod, but I didn't stop until I had cleared every weed and spent plant. I piled the debris high in the alley where folks burned trash. Out by the shed I found an abandoned basket and filled it to overflowing with tomatoes. I don't know why. Gram had plenty for us in her garden, but I just couldn't stop. By the time I finished, exhausted and thirsty, the garden looked respectable again.

I went to the pump and let the cold water pour into my mouth. I took off my shirt and the water ran over my head and down my chest. When I was cooled, I went around the house and sat down on the front porch step feeling low. I watched the sun go down, and still I sat. My brother showed up when it was dusk.

"Time to come home, Harry. We've been waiting for you." He pulled me to my feet and put his arm around my shoulder. I loved him very much at that moment.

32

THE STIFLING HUMIDITY of late summer dragged on and on. I went about my usual schedule at the store and skating rink, continuing to sell appliances from Castle Electric even though my market was drying up. Folks had bought just about everything they could afford to buy. They were getting over the novelty of electricity and all the new ways to use it. I didn't mind winding down. I had a nice bank account to show for my work, and school would start soon.

Sweet letters from Kansas City arrived every few days. My heart seized up each time I saw one in the mail, and I felt all over again the pain of her absence. I answered every one of them and wondered if my letters had the same effect on Carol Ann. In a strange way, the days when I didn't get a letter from her were sometimes a relief because the terrible longing would leave me alone for a while. I learned to keep busy so my mind wouldn't dwell on what I couldn't change.

Russ knew I was lonesome and invited me to go to a movie one night. He gave up a date with Darlene on my account, and I was grateful. We set off for Beaverton in his car, the wind cooling our bodies as we drove. We sang all the songs we could think of as we rode along. "Bye, Bye Blackbird," "Baby Face," and "Always." Before I could get too mopey about that being Carol Ann's favorite, Russ turned to me with an evil grin.

"Harry, do you know what the egg said to the boiling water?"

I looked at him expectantly.

"How can you expect me to get hard so fast? I just got laid a minute ago."

"Oh, brother. That's terrible," I said, groaning. Russ always had a raft of stories and jokes. He just kept going.

"Did you hear the one about the traveling salesman who got lost on the country roads? He stopped at a farmhouse and asked if he could spend the night. The farmer said the spare room was occupied, but if he didn't mind sleeping with a red-haired school teacher, he could stay. The salesman said, 'Sir, I am a gentleman.' The farmer said, 'as far as I can tell, so's the red-haired school teacher.'"

I was roaring with laughter by the time we reached the theater and in just the right mood for Buster Keaton. The movie was *Battling Butler*. It had funny gags about hunting and fishing, but the best part was when Buster tried to learn to box. He was awful at it, but at the very last minute he was able to knock down the villain. We cheered for him with the rest of the audience, hooting and clapping when it was over. I hadn't been out for fun since Carol Ann left, and I felt intoxicated, wound up. I didn't want the evening to end.

We didn't go home right away. The hazy moon, the humid wind that smelled of rain stirred our blood and made us unready for sleep. Restless and strangely exhilarated. We drove around, looking for something, we didn't know what. We wished for some crazy, wonderful thing to release all the energy pent up inside us, but there was only our quiet, sleepy town. After a while, we went out to the Brule, got out, and sat on the bridge for a long time, our feet dangling over the side, smoking cigarettes, talking about the movie, our girlfriends.

"You miss Carol Ann?"

"Something fierce, Russ." I'd felt light-hearted earlier, but now the longing came down over me. We sat quietly for a few minutes.

"I think I'm going to marry Darlene," Russ said.

"Wow! No kidding? Are you really?" I don't know why I was surprised because Russ and Darlene had been going together a long time.

"Yeah, I think so." He sat staring at the water. "She thinks she might be pregnant."

"Jesus, Russ. Are you sure?"

"Well, it seems like she is."

That was something! Russ had been having sex, and I didn't even know it. I wanted to say, "What's it like? When do you do it? How come you didn't tell me?" I opened my mouth to ask, but he seemed so serious and thoughtful, I decided I'd better not. Instead I said, "Why, you old tomcat. Gonna get a wife and a kid. That'll keep you home nights." I tried to laugh, but I was sorry for him, and envious too. I thought how close Carol Ann and I had come to doing it. What if we had ended up like Russ and Darlene!

"Yeah, I guess it will," he said, "but I'm ready. Why not? I'm nineteen, and I've got a pretty good job. Darlene wants to get away from her folks."

"It's hard to imagine you an old married man."

"Oh, you'll be doing the same thing someday."

"I hope so. I hope I marry Carol Ann. Right now it seems impossible." I paused, wondering if we'd ever get back together. "I should probably figure out where my life is going before I think about getting married."

He let out a soft chuckle. "That sounds like you, Harry." He stood up, stretched, yawned, and looked at his watch. "It's almost midnight. Ready to go?"

I nodded, and we headed for home. I went into the house, all the time thinking about Russ. I wondered if he loved Darlene. If he thought he was obliged to marry her. If having sex was worth it. I was afraid things would be different between us now, and that made me sad, but I was relieved in a way. Much as the desire I felt for Carol Ann still stirred me, at least she and I wouldn't have to face Russ's kind of trouble.

I NEEDED TO make one last trip to see Mr. Steele in Sioux City to close my account with him. Gram and Aunt Lida were curious about all the appliances Ty and I talked about, so I invited them to go with me. I laughed to myself to see them come out to the car all dressed up, wearing their old-fashioned Sunday hats.

"Hold on to those," I said. "They're apt to blow off on this trip." The two of them climbed in, giggly as girls to have a place to go and something new to do. They jabbered over the noise of the car all the way to Sioux City.

Mr. Steele saw us right away as we walked into the store. He shook my hand and said, "Well, if it isn't Harry Spencer, my best salesman. Who'd you bring with you?" He beamed as I made the introductions.

"You've got an amazing grandson, ma'am," he said to Gram. "He's outsold all my fulltime salesmen the last couple of months. I could use ten fellows like him with all the opportunities there are right now, the way electricity is changing everything."

She looked at me proudly. "I can tell you he's worked like one possessed, Mr. Steele."

"I know he has," he said. "Harry, let's go back to my office for a minute. You ladies feel free to look around. Ask the floor salesman for help if you need to."

I settled up my bill, and then Mr. Steele said, "What are you plans, Harry?" I told him I intended to finish high school this year. After that I wasn't sure.

"Let me try out an idea for you, Harry. See what you think." Mr. Steele proposed that I work fulltime for him by traveling to towns that had recently gotten power. He wanted me to sell appliances to people the way I had in Richmond. He offered me ten dollars a week plus a ten percent commission on everything I sold, and a gasoline allowance.

"You're a born salesman, Harry. No telling where you could end up with your talents."

I was surprised as all get out. I wondered why I hadn't thought of the idea myself. Mr. Steele's flattery made me feel ten feet tall, and I sali-vated to think about his offer. Why, I could make at least twenty-five dollars a week. Maybe more. I'd be able to buy a car. I'd be able to go see Carol Ann.

But when I thought of her, I knew she'd tell me to slow down. She'd remind me how important it was to finish high school. A degree would help me find a better job in the future. And what would I do if Mr. Steele's offer didn't pan out? I would have wasted all that time and missed out on my senior year.

I was torn. If I took the offer, I could be rich. I'd feel like a man, not a schoolboy. Surely she'd want that for me. It was such an exciting and unforeseen opportunity that it made school seem stale in comparison. But maybe she was right, and I should think of the long-range consequences. Then too, there was the little matter that I didn't own a car, but had been making free use of Granddad's car. I knew I couldn't continue to do that.

I said, "Thank you so much, Mr. Steele. It's a wonderful idea. Do you mind if I take a few days to think about it?"

He seemed surprised I didn't accept his offer immediately. "Harry, you don't get many chances like this in this world. What's holding you up?"

"I...I know, Mr. Steele, but I'd like to talk to my folks about it before I decide." I didn't tell him about the conversation going on in my head with my girlfriend.

"Well, all right, Harry. But don't wait too long."

He walked out to the front of the store with me. Gram and Aunt Lida were admiring the beautiful light fixtures hanging from the ceiling.

"Ladies, I hope you enjoyed the store," he said. "Did you decide on a new sewing machine or stove today?"

"Not today, thank you," said Lida, "but one of these days I mean to have a washing machine."

"If next summer is as hot as this one, I'm going to want one of those electric fans," Gram said.

"I'll tell you what," he said. "Here's a deck of playing cards for each of you with a picture of that washing machine on them. Every time you play pinochle I'll bet you'll think of the washing machine here at Castle Electric."

They laughed and took the cards. We headed for the door.

"I'll be waiting to hear from you, Harry."

"What was that all about?" Gram asked when we got to the car.

I didn't answer but said, "What would you say to a chocolate soda? I'll tell you all about it at the ice cream parlor."

I TALKED TO everyone I could think of about Mr. Steele's offer. Most people thought I'd be crazy to turn it down. "You don't need to go to school if you have a job like that," they'd say, or "a bird in hand's worth two in the bush."

I decided to talk to my dad. He'd surprised me with his bookkeeping knowledge, and I thought he might have some advice for me.

He seemed sulky when I brought it up. "Gonna be a big shot, are you?" he said.

"I don't think so, Dad. It's just a chance I didn't expect to have."

"I don't think you get it, Harry. That man Steele is gonna make about a hundred percent profit on everything you sell. He's the one that's gonna get rich. Bastard will be laughing all the way to the bank. You'll be the sucker."

"Does that mean you think I should go back to school, Dad?"

"How do I know, Harry? I never got a chance to go. I don't know what you should do." He stood up and walked away, and that was the end of our conversation. His behavior irritated me, and I chewed on it as I walked home. A father was supposed to advise his son and help him with big decisions. Then I had a revelation, and my brain lit up. My father was jealous of me! That was why he behaved the way he did. He must feel embarrassed about his own useless life, and my opportunities were just more than he could handle. That explained a lot. I'd have to let it go.

One kernel of understanding did come from our talk. He was right about me making Mr. Steele richer. I'd be just a hired flunky, and I didn't want to do that anymore. I wanted to be on the other side of the business like he was. That helped me make my decision.

After a couple of days I wrote to Mr. Steele to let him know that I'd decided to go back to school. Gram said I shouldn't close the door completely, so I thanked him for his offer and suggested that perhaps I could work for him some time in the future, after graduation.

33

A PACKAGE AND A letter from Carol Ann came at the end of August in time to mark my eighteenth birthday. I opened it and found six handsome linen handkerchiefs, which she had embroidered with my initials, *HLS*. I'd never gotten such a gift, and I was filled all over again with longing for her.

Gram peered over my shoulder and said, "Those are too fancy to wipe your nose on, Harry. You'd better save them."

"You bet I will," I stepped outside to read the letter privately. When I opened it, a color picture of a birthday cake tumbled out.

My dearest Harry,

Happy, happy eighteenth birthday! I found this picture of a cake in one of Mother's magazines. If only I could be there with you, I would make one just like it to celebrate your day. Can you pretend to taste it?

I am thrilled, thrilled, thrilled you'll be going back to school. And so are my parents. You'll never regret it. At least you know your way around. I'm terrified to face the huge school I'll be attending next week. It takes up a whole city block and is four stories high. My stomach crawls when I think about it. What if I'm not smart enough? What if nobody likes me? Oh, how I dread it.

I hope you like the handkerchiefs, Harry. I thought about you with every stitch I put in. Maybe you should tuck them away to save for when you become a businessman. It won't be much longer.

I love you, Harry Spencer. Kiss! Kiss! Kiss!
Carol Ann

P.S. Dad is teaching me to drive the car!

Tears stung my eyes for a moment. I could imagine how scared she was of starting at a new school. Yet I was buoyed up by her thoughtfulness. I vowed to work hard to make myself ready for a life with my sweet girl.

Two days later I was back for my senior year at Beaverton High. It wasn't the same without Carol Ann. We'd always talked over every last thing, and now I had no one like that. At least I got to drive the car to school. I loved the feeling of independence it gave me to hop into the Ford and go where I wanted. After class I sometimes went down to Mobley's Café and had a Coke with the kids who gathered there.

"Hey, Harry. You got a date for the Fall Dance?" Billy asked one day. I grinned and shook my head.

"Still carrying the torch, I guess," he said. "You'll get over it soon enough. Let me know when you're ready, and I'll fix you up."

Sometimes the girls were so bold I could hardly believe it.

"I'll go to the dance with you, Harry," Betsy said.

"Don't go with her, Harry," said Carleen. "I'm lots more fun that she is. And I'm a better dancer."

"If you go with her, I'll tell Carol Ann," said Pearl who had been Carol Ann's best friend.

I laughed. "I think I'd better go to the dance stag. That way I can dance with all of you." I enjoyed their flirting. It was all silliness and we knew it, but without these friends it would be a long slog until graduation in May.

Mrs. Kleinsasser, who'd been my English teacher since my freshman year, had retired over the summer. I missed her. She was tough on us, but underneath, she was kindhearted. I smiled to remember the time I fell asleep in her class. She'd tried to be stern about it, but I could tell she was laughing on the inside.

Her replacement, Mr. Wakeman, made me miss her even more. He was tall and skinny, with pale reddish hair, and a narrow, sharp nose. His shirt hung loosely around his scrawny neck, and he wore the same tie every day. Mr. Wakeman did not smile, nor did his watery eyes behind his glasses ever look at us directly. Even after three weeks, he still had to refer to his seating chart before he could call on us by name.

He had us reading *Julius Caesar* out loud, and I was assigned the role of Cassius. He kept us reading for the whole class period while he sat staring at the book. When the bell rang signifying it was time for lunch, I said, "I have a lean and hungry look." Everyone laughed except Mr. Wakeman. He just blinked uncertainly as we filed out.

I wondered what made him decide to be a teacher. He seemed so humorless and uninterested in his students. How was it that people ended up doing the things they did? So many fellows I knew just happened into their work by chance, not as if they planned it, and they never amounted to much of anything. I didn't want my life to be that way. Day after day as we waded through Shakespeare in his class, I wondered if I'd made a mistake not to accept Mr. Steele's offer. How on earth could studying a play prepare me for a job?

But then in Mr. Hummel's math class, I felt entirely different. He offered a new course that fall. "We're going to use math to learn about the business of business," he said. He told us about banks, about savings accounts, and checking accounts. He made up forms that looked like checks so he could teach us how to fill them out. Most kids' parents paid their bills with cash, so this was new to them.

"I know how to do that," I said. I'd watched Gram and Granddad often enough. But I found out I didn't know as much as I thought.

"You have to write the amount for the check in two ways," Mr. Hummel explained. "Suppose the bill is for $30. First you write it out in words." He wrote "Thirty dollars" on the blackboard. "Then you must write it in numerical form." He wrote "$30.00" on the board.

As always with me, the numbers came easily, but I had to practice with the other students writing out the amounts in words. He made the examples more and more difficult. The last one was for $5,135.26.

Jimmy Harper said, "Wow! I'll never have that much money in my whole life."

"I will. And more, I hope," I muttered under my breath.

When Mr. Hummel was satisfied with our work, he said, "Now I want each of you to assume you have a checking account with seventy-five dollars in it. From that, you should buy ten items, anything you want, and write pretend checks for them."

It was great fun dreaming up all the things we would buy if we had the money, but then came the reckoning when we had to balance our accounts. I was amazed that some kids spent more money than they had.

"Nosiree," Mr. Hummel would say to them. "That's an overdraft. You can't get by with that."

That's when we learned about credit and borrowing money. What an eye opener! Gram and Granddad were so opposed to borrowing, they made it seem almost immoral when, once in a while, they had to take out a loan, but here was Mr. Hummel talking about it as if it were the most normal thing in the world. "Banks charge interest for the use of their money, and they pay interest to savers," he said, "but they never pay out as much as they charge for loans."

At first that didn't seem fair to me, but Mr. Hummel said, "That's where their profit lies, Harry. Otherwise they wouldn't be in business."

I hadn't really thought of a bank as a business before, but now I could see that it was. A bank was in the money business just like Mr. Steele was in the appliance business.

All this talk made me hungrier than ever to have a business of my own. How could I start one? Could a kid like me get credit at a bank? I'd have to ask Mr. Hummel.

❖ ❖ ❖

ONE NIGHT AS Ty and I were getting ready for bed, he told me that Dad's grumpiness was getting worse.

"Sally thinks it's because he doesn't have enough to do now that you don't need him to keep your books. She says he'll go for hours without saying a word. Just sits around looking mean."

I knew that look all too well, but I didn't know what I could do about it. "He needs a job," I said, knowing there wasn't anything in Richmond for him. "I wish we lived closer to a bank. He could keep books for it. I've learned a lot about how they operate, and I think it would suit him just right."

"Yeah, that would be nice," Ty said, "but how to get him near one. Did you know he bought himself a shotgun?"

"No. What's he plan to do with that?"

"Says he wants to go hunting. He goes off for a whole day by himself. Never says where he's going. Hasn't brought back so much as a rabbit."

"I don't see how he could shoot the thing one armed. Let alone hit something."

"I'll tell you something else that's crazy," Ty went on. "I took his clean clothes over there the other day. He was out on one of his rambles, so Sally said I might as well hang them up for him. In the back of his closet I saw his old KKK robe. Couldn't help noticing that the bottom of it was all dirty, so I knew he'd worn it. Even the sleeves were stained with something."

That was an unsettling thought. The Klavern in Richmond had gone out of business three years ago after the store attack. I wondered why he had hung on to the darn thing all this time.

"Do you suppose he just forgot about it?" Ty said.

"Doesn't seem likely."

Ty yawned and began to empty his pockets onto a little table near our daybed. He shucked his pants and climbed into bed. I took off my own pants, and, when I went to turn off the light, I happened to glance at Ty's stuff lying there. Amidst the clutter of his jackknife, matches, a handkerchief, and some change, one of the coins caught my eye. It was about the size of a quarter, but it had a hole in the center of it. I'd seen that coin before. But where? I turned out the light and crawled into my side of the bed, wondering about it, but I was soon asleep.

In the middle of the night I awoke having dreamed that Buster was at the foot of our bed growling at something. How I wished it were true and that I could reach down and pet him. I heard leaves skittering against the window and got up to look. The whiteness of the moonlight made every tree and bush stand out clear as day, but there was nothing suspicious or unusual out there. As I turned to go back to bed, I saw Ty's strange coin glittering in the cold light and realized that I recognized it. It was Dad's coin, the one with the Kaiser's head on it. The one he had shown me so many years ago. How had Ty gotten hold of it? I wanted to shake him awake to find out, but then I thought, "No. It'll keep. I'll ask him tomorrow."

34

GRANDDAD AWOKE IN the morning coughing and wheezing with a recurrence of pleurisy, something that seemed to hit him every year with the onset of cold weather. He sat in the rocking chair, wrapped in a quilt, while Gram built up the fire in the cook-stove.

"Can you boys fix your own breakfast? I've got to get some water boiling. The steam helps him breathe," she said.

I went out to pump a couple buckets of water for her while Ty ate bread and molasses and hurried to open the store. In all the commotion, I forgot to ask him about Dad's coin. It was still early, so I ran over to the store before leaving for school.

Ty was grinding coffee and looked up surprised to see me. "What happened? Is he okay?"

"Yeah, he'll be better once Gram gets the place steamed up. But I want to ask you about something else. Last night when we were going to bed, I saw a coin with a hole in it with the stuff from your pocket."

"You mean this one?" He pulled it out of his pocket. "What about it?"

"Did Dad give it to you? Did you know it belonged to him?"

"No. I didn't know that. I found it a long time ago and just hung on to it."

I told Ty what Dad had said about taking the coin off a dead German and how he'd put a hole in it so he could say he'd put a spike through the Kaiser's head.

Ty looked at it carefully. "Yeah, I can see where the head was." He shrugged. "He's just plain crazy, isn't he?"

"It seems like it sometimes. Where'd you find it? Over at Sally's?"

"No." he said slowly. "I can tell you exactly where I found it. It was the morning after the KKK attacked us. You were asleep on the porch, so I came over here to the store and walked all around." He paused.

I didn't like to conjure up those painful memories, but I wanted to hear it all.

"I got over here by the porch and squatted to look at that big rock where Granddad and Buster went down. One of them must have hit it 'cause it had blood all over it. That's where I found the coin in the mashed down grass."

He stopped talking, and we stared at each other for a long moment.

"You think he was there that night?" Ty breathed.

"I've always wondered," I said. "Now we know. He was there all right! Goddam it, Ty. He was there. Now we know for sure!"

Something hot and hard sprang loose in my belly. I felt its savage heat, and I screamed, "He was there!" I turned and ran wildly from the store toward Sally McVay's house. "I'll kill him" was in my head. "I'll kill him."

I heard Ty's steps pounding behind me, and I ran faster. No one was going to stop me. We'd run a quarter of a mile before he reached me and grabbed my shirt, pulling me to my knees in the roadway. "Stop it, Harry. Just stop it," he said, panting and breathless.

I stood up, breathing hard, and jerked away from him. "I hate him, Ty."

"Okay. I understand. Just don't do anything stupid. He's crazy."

We stood with our hands on our knees, catching our breath.

"I've got to get back to the store," he said. "I left it standing wide open."

I nodded, and after a few minutes, I turned around and followed. A cold wind swept through the empty December trees and dried my sweat. Ty went into the store, and I went over to the Ford. I should have gone to school, but I didn't. I drove aimlessly around the county, reliving the horror of that awful night with Granddad hurt and Buster dead. I was sickened even more to realize my own father had played a part in it. The anger pumped up in me, hot and bitter, and I didn't know what to do. All I could think about was getting away from the pain, away from him, away from this town. I drove and drove, speeding, taking curves recklessly until I was nearly out of gas.

I ended up at River Sioux. The place was deserted, the boats in storage, and the pavilion closed for the winter. The swings on the playground creaked forlornly in the chilly wind. I looked up to the roof where Carol Ann and I had loved each other last summer, and I felt a need for her that was at once so urgent and compelling that it forced me to think out a plan. And after a time, I knew what I must do.

GRANDDAD WAS BREATHING a little easier when I arrived home at the usual time. Gram asked me to deliver Dad's laundry to him.

"I know how you feel about him, Harry, but please don't do anything rash," she said. "Anything you'll regret. We've had enough trouble."

"I know," I said. I went to Sally McVay's and would have handed the laundry through the door, but Dad wasn't there, so I went back to his room. I just threw his stuff on the bed and went into the closet holding my breath, almost afraid to look, but I had to see. It was as Ty said. A dirty white robe and a tall hat standing in the corner. I picked up the right sleeve. It was torn and stained a rusty color. Blood! Granddad's blood. I heard a sound and turned to see my father standing over me.

"What the hell are you doing, Harry? Get out of there." His voice was rough and loud.

Blistering anger surged up in me again. "Why is this thing in here?" I said, pointing to the robe. "You're still a member of that dirty Klan bunch, aren't you? You haven't given it up. You were in on the whole thing, weren't you?"

"Wha… are you talking about? Get out of that closet."

He moved toward me as if to yank me out. "Don't you touch me," I yelled. "I've got it figured it out. Ty found your Kaiser coin right in the very spot where Granddad and Buster went down. I know you were there, Dad!"

He stepped back, his shocked eyes dark and fixated on me. "You don't know any such thing."

"I figured it out, Dad. Before the attack, you never left this house. I saw you once at the church for the KKK convocation, maybe at Gram's a couple of times for Sunday dinner. Otherwise you never left Sally's. You never came near the store. Not ever."

"So what? Where I go, or don't go, is my business. Not yours." His talk was tough, but his voice sounded less certain.

I looked hard at him. "Just tell me this. That coin with the hole in the center. How did it manage to get itself found off the end of the porch where Granddad got his leg busted? Where the best dog in the whole world got his back broke?"

My voice rose as I came closer to him. He lurched back and fell into his rocking chair, his eyes still wide and his mouth hanging open. I stood over him, seething with hatred.

"You can't answer that, can you? That's 'cause you were there that night, Dad. You wore that ridiculous white sheet, and you went there. With that loathsome, hate-filled bunch who burned a cross in the yard and tried to burn down the store." Saliva pooled in my mouth and wet my lips. I had to swallow before I could go on.

He looked stricken and groaned. "I can't…I don't know…" His voice tailed off.

"I'd bet my life you were on the porch with those others when Granddad got shoved and ended up with two broken bones and another one cracked."

I heard the ugly, accusing tone in my voice. I glared as he wiped at his face with his good hand as if to push my words away. He looked down at the floor, and I knew he was guilty.

"I can still see those long, bloody scratches on Granddad's back. We wondered what could have caused them? Well, I think I know. It was you with your hook that did it. Look here." I grabbed the robe.

"It's got blood stains on the sleeve. You shoved Granddad off that porch, shoved him on top of my dog, and then took off in your sheet like the yellow coward you are."

"Stop, Harry. You don't understand. You just don't know," he said, his voice puny now.

"You make me want to puke."

He kept his hand over his eyes and no longer looked at me.

"You dumped Polly and me on Gram and Granddad so you could go do something you wanted to do. Never mind how abandoned we felt. Never mind that those two old people, who'd already raised their own kids, didn't need two more to raise. Never mind that they had to buy our clothes and feed us. And still you came after them because of your crazy, stupid ideas about everything. You hurt them bad. Granddad will never walk right again. You ungrateful bastard."

He swallowed hard. His voice was thick and choked when he spoke. "You got it wrong, Harry. It's not what you think."

But I was caught up in the moment, and I kept on. I wanted to vent all those things I'd stored up in me for so long. I wanted to be rid of it like a bad sickness, and I didn't quit.

"I hate you, Dad. I hate you for leaving us, for not being a father to us, for never even trying to get a job to take care of us. I'm sick of all your rants about everything and everybody.

"Tomorrow I'm going to pack up my stuff, and I'm going to get on the train to Kansas City. I'm going to leave you and Richmond behind forever, and I hope to God I never see you again."

He looked up tears in his eyes. "No, Harry. Hold on…Harry," he begged.

I roared on. "And I'll tell you this. I'm going to do my best to make something of myself in this world. I'm going to do my best to forget about you. I'm never going to think about you again from this day on."

I stomped out of his room and came face to face with Sally McVay. She had a hand over her mouth and her eyes looked frightened. She must have heard everything. I didn't stop but marched out the door into the cold rain. I didn't even feel it.

AT HOME, I told Gram what I planned to do. She pleaded with me not to leave. "You can't be certain about what happened," she said.

"We've proved it," I said. "Ty and I figured it out because Dad lost his Kaiser coin that night. It was right there where Granddad went down. Don't you see? He was there."

"Cal wouldn't hurt Granddad. He just wouldn't. Please don't do this, Harry," she begged.

"I have to, Gram."

I carried on packing my few belongings in an old suitcase. When I was finished, I went into the bedroom to say my goodbyes to Granddad. "I'm sorry, Granddad, but I've gotta leave this place."

"I know," he rasped. "Feeling the way you do, it's probably for the best. Cal hasn't been right since he got back from the war."

That night Ty and I sat up for a long time while I told him what I'd said to Dad. Ty was the sort who just didn't get as mad as I did. Especially about Dad. But I think he understood, in the end, why I had to go.

In the morning he drove me to Beaverton where I closed my bank account and took my cash. We shook hands and said our quiet goodbye at the train station.

35

I ARRIVED IN KANSAS City with all the money I had in this world stuffed like a poultice between my undershirt and my skin, terrified I'd spend it before I got a good job, or worse yet, lose it. I went to a haberdashery where they sold men's suits—two for the price of one. I bought two, figuring I'd need them when I applied for jobs. I got shoes, ties, shirts, and a cap, and hauled everything to my cheap room at Mayme Schwartz's boarding house. Then I spent a quarter and got my first professional haircut at a shop down the street.

Within a day of my arrival, I went to work as a bellhop at the twelve-story Muehlebach Hotel, a grand place with mirrors that covered whole walls and deep, wine colored panels in the dining room. I worked from midnight until 6:00 a.m., but there was blessed little for me to do. Fellows who had seniority had better shifts and made handsome tips running errands and helping with luggage, but most customers were in bed during my shift. Even so, I made enough to cover the $2.75 weekly rent for my room, and I got a hot breakfast every morning. Coffee, with biscuits and sausages. I usually managed to squirrel away some extras for my noon meal.

With my new clothes and a job, even a poor one, I was ready to see Carol Ann. On Sunday, I dressed up and went to find the Bellwood house, planning to surprise them. It was a four-mile walk, and I was so eager to see Carol Ann, I completely forgot that it was winter, and I had no coat. Frozen and shivering in my fancy clothes, I stood on the door-step of a handsome bungalow on Dogwood Street, hoping I'd found the right place.

Mr. Bellwood had answered the door. "Yes?" He blinked and stared. "My God, it's Harry Spencer. Harry, what in the world are you doing here?" He'd offered no welcoming smile, but his wife came up behind him and said, "For heaven's sake, Ed. Can't you see he's freezing? Invite him in."

Carol Ann came running in and threw her arms around me. "Oh, Harry, why didn't you let us know you were coming?"

Our excited talk filled the next hour as we asked and answered all the questions that come up when people haven't seen each other for a while. I enjoyed looking around the home Mrs. Bellwood had created. It made me feel warm and happy. A comfortable green frieze couch filled one living room wall. Ornate lamps gleamed on side tables at each end, and flowered chairs stood opposite. An archway with oak colon-nades separated the living room from the dining room. Photographs, vases, and the like, which I remembered from their house in Richmond, filled the shelves. I was most thrilled to see the telephone that sat on a little table near the door. I made sure to memorize the number.

Mrs. Bellwood invited me to stay for supper. As we sat at the brand new dining room table, I remembered that the only place to eat in their old house was in the kitchen. Mr. Bellwood must be doing well.

"How about work?" he asked. "What do you plan to do, Harry?"

I told them about the bellhop job. "That'll be just temporary until I get better situated."

He thought I should try to get a job at Armour's packing plant where he worked. "Kansas City processes more cattle and hogs than any other city except Chicago. It's huge, Harry. You'd be secure."

I recalled seeing the acres and acres of pens at the stockyards when my train arrived in Kansas City. I couldn't say so to him, but the idea of a lifetime of that work was repugnant. I'd seen enough of that around

Richmond. I wanted something in a more progressive business, some-thing fitting a growing city.

Later, when it was time for me to leave, Carol Ann insisted that I wear one of her father's warm sweaters under my suit coat for the long walk back to the boarding house. We'd hugged and kissed on the front step, unwilling to part. I promised to call her, to come back as soon as I could. The walk home was cold, but I hadn't felt a thing. I could only think about my girl. She was just the same. How I loved her!

THE MONTHS PASSED quickly. Milgram's grocery store was near my rooming house, and I got a job cleaning their refrigerator cases and sweeping the floors after closing time. I knew that business well enough! My shift was from 7:00 to 11:00 p.m., and I made thirty cents an hour.

Neither the hotel nor the grocery store was my idea of a good job, but it was hard to look for something else because I had to sleep in the daytime. Somehow I'd have to find some time to look for different work.

Carol Ann said, "Don't rush into anything, Harry. Make sure you've found the right thing. Some place where you'll be happy."

"Yeah," I said, "and some place where I can get ahead."

One cold Saturday in January I walked from one end of the busi-ness district to the other, not applying for jobs, but just considering where I might work. Rubeck's Jewelry was a beautiful store, filled with pretty baubles, but it didn't seem right. I didn't know anything about gems, or gold, or silver, and the customers inside looked so wealthy and sophisticated, I wasn't sure I'd fit in.

A clothing store might have been an option, but I recalled the fussy little man who sold me my suits. He twittered away about cuffs and lapels, and I could have been a post for all he knew. No. A clothing store was not the place for me.

I came to Lander's Lighting Store and began to perk up. They sold many of the great electrical items that I was familiar with from Castle Electric—lamps, radios, and appliances, but Landers was about three times larger. This was more what I was after.

I couldn't wait to talk to Carol Ann on Sunday. I always looked forward to going to her house for Sunday dinner to eat her mom's homemade food, and be with people I knew. We discussed the Lander's possibility over pot roast with carrots and onions, and piles of mashed potatoes and gravy.

"Oh, I love Lander's store." Mrs. Bellwood's eyes sparkled like her daughter's at the thought. "They have the best selection in town."

"That idea sounds solid," Mr. Bellwood said.

Carol Ann said, "I'll keep my fingers crossed until I hear from you. Let me know as soon as you can."

The next day, I skipped my usual sleeping time, dressed in my gray suit, and went to Lander's. The clerks approached me eagerly until I asked where the office was. One jerked his thumb and said, "Back there," and they turned away. They saw no profit in wasting time with me.

I introduced myself to a big, white-haired man in the office who said he was Ralph Landers. He listened with a bored expression while I explained that I needed a job.

"Any experience?" he asked.

"I sold radios and appliances for Mr. Steele at Castle Electric in Sioux City. And I was pretty good at it." I hoped I wasn't bragging too much.

He looked up a little surprised. "I know Don Steele," he said. "He's a good man."

I nodded in agreement. He looked at me a minute, then said, "I think maybe we'll try you out, Harry, since you worked at Castle. I can always use a good salesman." He said I'd be paid $23 a week, and make a three percent commission on everything I sold.

I was overjoyed. I was able to quit the bellhop job at the hotel and turn in my monkey hat and uniform. To be on the safe side, I hung on to the grocery store work.

I called Carol Ann with the news. "The only bad part is that I won't get that hot hotel breakfast anymore. I'll have to eat oatmeal at Mayme Schwartz's."

"Oh, you poor boy," she said, laughing. "But you'll be able to buy yourself a ham sandwich at noon, I'll bet." Then her voice changed. "I'm glad you found what you wanted, Harry. I'll be so glad to finish high school so I can do something exciting too."

"It'll be over soon," I said. "Try to enjoy it."

"The problem is that my mother keeps pushing me to go to Normal School so I can become a teacher. I don't know if I want to be a teacher. I just know I'm tired of school. I want to be out and about like you are."

"I don't blame you," I said, but as soon as I could provide a reliable living, I'd assumed we'd get married. We hadn't discussed it specifically, but that's where I was headed, and I hoped Normal School wouldn't interfere.

I DOVE INTO the sales work at Lander's, and within a few weeks, I'd earned the grudging respect of the other clerks who vied among themselves for customers and for Mr. Lander's attention.

"Boys, I hope you notice how well Harry is doing," he said one day at a sales meeting.

It was pleasing to be noticed, but it didn't make those fellows like me any better. Even though I made enough money to take care of myself, I wondered if I could advance at this store with all the jealousy. I found out that Mr. Lander's oldest son, who attended college back east, would be home permanently in June and would be groomed to run the store. Two younger sons were coming along who also expected to work in the store. I'd be just another hired flunky if I stayed.

As the weather warmed up that spring, I found new routes to the Bellwood house, and one day I walked through a bustling business area with several small shops. The delicious smell from a barbeque stand outside the meat market excited my stomach. I couldn't pass it by. Kansas City barbeque was famous for good reason. Its deep smoky taste and the tang of the sauce hooked me, and I knew I'd be back for more.

I passed a dry cleaner, a dress shop, and a dry goods store. In the next block, my nose was tortured again by the smell of apple kuchen from a German bakery. I was still hungry, but this time I told myself I must resist. I couldn't afford to let my stomach spend my money

The next shop had a sign in the window in dull gold letters—Sam's Lights. Through grimy windows I saw tables crowded with lamps, short ones, tall ones, some beautiful Tiffanies, boxes of light bulbs, kerosene lanterns, and other stuff I couldn't identify, all jumbled together in an unattractive mix. Why would anyone let his store get into such a mess, I wondered? I thought of all my hard work cleaning Granddad's store, how satisfying it had been to see how the customers appreciated it. If I worked at Sam's Lights, I'd clean it up and make it attractive. If I had a chance, I was sure I could make Sam's store into an outstanding place. In the back of my mind, something lit up and told me this could be the opportunity I was searching for.

Carol Ann was doubtful. "I don't understand. Why would you give up a good position at Lander's? They're so well known here. My folks and I have never heard of this Sam's place."

I tried to make her understand. "There's no opportunity for me at Lander's. I just have to find a place where I can advance."

She finally relented but said, "You better hang onto the job at the grocery store until you see how this works out."

A couple of days later I presented myself to the owner, Sam Rubin, and asked him for a job. He sat on a high stool toward the back of the store—no desk for him. His bushy eyebrows shadowed black, darting eyes that surveyed me up and down. He hopped down from his perch and took hold of the lapel of my suit jacket, rubbing it between his fingers.

"Nice material, Harry. Such nice material. Why would a boy who wears such a nice suit want to work here?"

I was startled at his question, a little fearful of his stern and foreign look. I swallowed and began to talk about my job at Lander's and how frustrated I was. My nerves kept me talking, and I rattled on and on telling him that, if he hired me, I'd be willing to fix up his displays, straighten out the inventory, maybe add radios and appliances, and make the store more attractive for customers. His eyebrows waggled up and down at that, and I was afraid I'd overstepped. I changed subjects.

"My sales record is tops at Lander's, Mr. Rubin. I can sell." I took a deep breath and plowed ahead. "Maybe I could become a manager in your store if I do a good job for you.

His face remained unchanged, just sizing me up. He said, "What else, Harry? What else do you want?"

"Someday, Mr. Rubin, when I'm older, and when I know a lot more, I'd like to have a business of my own." I was surprised at myself, at my sudden nerve. But there it was. I'd said it all.

"You think big, Harry," he said, pulling on his chin whiskers. "You got brains." He laughed a strange high-pitched giggle, showing his little yellow teeth. "Brains, maybe. But money? Not so much." He stuck out his hand. "You like pastrami, Harry?" Without waiting for an answer, he said, "Go next door and get us a couple of sandwiches. On rye. When you come back, we'll talk."

And so it was that I began work for Sam Rubin.

36

RIGHT FROM THE beginning Sam Rubin treated me like an equal. He talked to me about everything—what lamps he should order, how he beat the price down on a shipment of light bulbs, what we, and I mean *we*, should eat for dinner. I loved it. I quit my grocery store job and showed up at his shop at seven o'clock every morning, staying into the evening.

The first week I wore my old work clothes and cleaned the store from top to bottom. The windows gleamed, the lamps were polished, and the floor swept and scrubbed. I could tell the old man was pleased. "So nice," he would say, and his high-pitched giggle would bubble out whenever a new corner was liberated from dust and grime. "It's too hard for me to do any more." Old-time customers noticed the change, and Sam gave me credit. "My new boy, Harry. He keeps things in order."

I was soon emboldened to suggest that we put away the kerosene lamps and add small appliances such as toasters and waffle irons. Ida Klump, who came every month to do the books, sniffed at the change, but she had to admit the store was doing more business than ever.

The windows were bare, so I set up a display that looked just like a living room. I borrowed one of the chairs from Sam's crowded apartment above the store. Then I chose a beautiful floor lamp and a radio console to complete the picture. When customers noticed, I offered to set up a radio in their homes for them to try out. It wasn't long before sales of the new items outstripped lamps.

When the hot weather hit early in the year, I created a window display of fans and attached colored streamers to them. When they were turned on, the ribbons made a bright, swirling display that caught the eyes of passers-by. Sam kept saying, "The juice, Harry. All the juice this takes," shaking his head with worry. But we sold fifteen fans the first day, and he admitted it was worth the electricity to keep them running.

Sam seemed to expect I would eat supper with him every evening. For the first time in my life I ate pickled herring, latkes, and knishes.

"Where do you get this food, Sam? It's delicious. I've never had anything like it."

"Oh, this comes from Hatoffs. The Jewish bakery over by the garment district." He looked up from his place. "You know I'm Jewish, don't you Harry?"

"I…I guess I figured that," I said embarrassed, "but I didn't really know."

"Well, now you do. So eat, Harry. Taste these good latkes. You'll enjoy."

The one dish Sam could make was stewed chicken. Each week he bought a large hen and we would eat from it for days. When the meat was gone, he made matzo balls and dropped them into the hot broth, a warm, satisfying soup.

Over our food, Sam told me of coming to America from Russia with his older brother Isaac in 1882 when he was twenty years old. "So poor we were, Harry. Some days we ate only crackers."

They were lucky, he said, to land in New York in the summertime. "At first we slept outside in the parks until the cops chased us. Then we got a sleeping room." He grinned slyly. "But the landlady didn't like me."

"Why? Why didn't she like you?"

"Maybe it was because I was Jewish, but mostly it was because I smelled bad." He laughed. "Fish skin, fish bones. All day long I handled them working in the fish market. Piles of fish trash, Harry, you wouldn't believe. Hauling bones and skin to the dump truck, sometimes filching some to eat. That's what I did. I couldn't get rid of the smell. It was part of me."

He smiled as he called up the memories. I liked hearing his stories. His life was so foreign compared to everything I knew. I urged him on. "What did your brother do while you were at the fish market?"

"He used the money I earned to buy things for us to peddle. One time he got 120 pairs of men's suspenders for ten cents apiece. We went up and down the streets of Manhattan selling those things for a dollar each. Only trouble was that they clipped to a man's pants, and the clips didn't work very well. We had to run like hell when one old fellow came after us."

We chuckled together, and then he grew serious.

"I had some bad times too. Ike got tuberculosis. He got sicker and sicker, coughing up blood, too weak to work. I took him to a hospital, but they couldn't, or wouldn't, do much for a poor Jewish boy, and he died. I felt really alone after that." His eyes closed under those huge white eyebrows, and he sat with his hand over his face. I waited uncomfortably, and after a bit, he sat up and said, "But you don't want to hear this stuff, Harry. Let's eat."

Over the weeks and months he told me about meeting his wife, Sarah, who worked in a dress factory. How they went to movies whenever he could afford it and how they became fascinated with the Wild West, cowboys, and all the rest.

"We got married and put our money together. I peddled everything I could buy at the right price. One day I got hold of forty quarts of yellow paint—cheap. Out on the streets I went, peddling paint. I tried and tried, but nobody wanted yellow paint. I couldn't give it away. I wore myself out carrying those cans up and down the street. Then I met a fellow who was opening a fresh fruit stand. Said he planned to call it Banana Johnnie's. That gave me an idea. I talked him into painting the whole thing yellow, and I finally got rid of the rest of the paint."

I laughed out loud. "You were clever, Sam." In my mind's eye I saw the piles of apples and oranges, tomatoes, carrots, and of the course, the bananas piled high in a bright yellow fruit stand right in the middle of New York City.

"When I got home," Sam went on, "I told my wife 'I've had enough of this. I want to go west.' And so we did."

WHEN I SAW Carol Ann on Sundays, I was full of tales about Sam, and she wanted to meet him. One Saturday afternoon she came downtown to the store, and Sam took us upstairs for tea and cookies from the bakery.

"Carol Ann," he said when I introduced her. "Such a beautiful name. Just like a melody." She flushed at his flattery and looked at me uncertainly. "Sit, sit," he said as he pulled out a chair for her at his table. "Would you like to know my name?"

I laughed and said, "I think we know your name, Sam."

"You think wrong, Harry. I will tell you. My real name is Schmuel Rubinsky." Over tea he explained how difficult it was for people to pronounce his name when he came to New York. "They called me 'Russky' or 'Polesky.' So what do we do? Simple. We shortened our names to make it easier for them. I became Sam and my brother became Ike. Then just for good measure, we shortened our last name too."

"Didn't you miss using your real name?" Carol Ann asked.

"Sometimes yes, sometimes no. But it was easier for the Americans." He told us how some of their friends went so far as to change their names completely to hide their Jewishness. "We didn't do that. Jews we were, and Jews we'd stay."

His story finished, he beamed at us. "Such nice company. Harry, can you bring us the teakettle and find some more cookies in the kitchen?"

I heated more water and rummaged around for cookies. When I returned, Carol Ann was telling him about her studies at the Normal School.

"We're learning how to teach little kids to read."

"Reading," he nodded. "So important in this world."

The two of them chatted like they'd known each other for years, both clearly charmed. That pleased me. When we finished, Carol Ann tidied up his kitchenette, and he never took his eyes off her.

"A nice girl you have, Harry. You better hang on to her."

She was still wide-eyed when we got outside. "What an experience," she said as we walked down the street. "He's so warm, easy to talk to. I didn't know Jews were like that. Remember that awful preacher at home who told us Jews were trying to steal our country?"

I remembered all right. How could I ever forget Reverend Halsey Brooks whose words set our town on fire. "He was wrong, a hateful, evil man."

She nodded in agreement. "I noticed the woman's picture on the bookshelf. Was that his wife?"

"Yeah, I think so. She was named Sarah, but she got hit by a car just a month after they got here, and she died right there on the street. They didn't have any kids."

"Oh, that's so sad. He must be very lonely."

"Maybe. I think he's glad he has me to talk to. His wife's buried at Rose Hill Cemetery. He goes out there sometimes. Asked me to go with him, but I haven't done it yet."

"You should, Harry. I think it would mean a lot to him."

I CAME TO love the old man. I found I was able to tell him things about my life, about my father. About the hurt and loneliness when Dad came home from the war. I even told him the ugly things about the Klan and the attack on the store. He seemed to understand my anger.

"So young you were for such hard times, Harry. So unfair it was. You got mad, eh?" I nodded vigorously. "They'll eat away at you, those bad times, if you let them." He asked me once what my father did in France during the war, and I realized I didn't know.

"He never talked about it. Only how much he hated the Germans and even the French." I thought for a minute. "I do remember one thing, though. He went out onto the field after a battle and helped load bodies on a wagon."

"Ah," Sam said nodding as though that were a significant piece of information. Later, when the store was quiet for a few minutes, he said, "Harry, have you ever seen a dead body?"

I looked at him puzzled. "Well no, I guess not. Why?"

"Once I saw the body of a man. Thugs beat him up because they thought he stole some bread. Just for bread, they broke his bones, kicked in his face. A terrible sight there in the road with his wife and children crying over him. I felt sick in the stomach, and I never forgot how it was."

Slowly I realized what he was trying to tell me. "You think that's what's wrong with my dad? He saw too many bodies?"

"Think about it, Harry. Every day to pick up the dead soldiers, their bodies bloody and broken. Some maybe your friends. It must do something to a man's soul, that kind of work."

I could see that it would be repulsive to do what my dad had to do, but why would he lose interest in his kids? Go on hateful tirades? I didn't remember things bothering him so much before the war.

"I just know how he used to make us all laugh," I said. "He played games with us. He taught me how to whistle, he was gonna show me how to hunt and fish when I was older, but he never did. When he came home, it was all different."

"I know, but what he saw must have eaten on him. Tormented him." He paused. "I think your father must have had a big soul, Harry, a big soul, and he couldn't help how he acted. Men like that are special, and we need to make allowances."

I started to heat up. I didn't want to think about my dad's torment, and I was a little miffed that Sam seemed to take Dad's side against me. I'd come here to get away from all that, not to wallow in it every day. I just wanted to forget about it. But the next thing I knew Sam was suggesting that I visit the war memorial built to honor the veterans. "Maybe see what your father faced," he said.

Resentment stirred in me. Why? Why should I make myself miserable trying to figure out what was wrong with my dad? I didn't want to think about it anymore. I'd done plenty of that over the years, and I wanted to leave it alone. But Sam wouldn't let it rest. "It'd be good for you to go, Harry," he'd say. He pushed me and pushed me ever so gently, but he didn't give up, and I knew I'd have to do it.

37

THE NEWSPAPERS WERE full of plans for the Lincoln Memorial built on the wide hill near Union Station. President Coolidge and other famous people were to attend the dedication on Armistice Day in November. Even from downtown I could see the tall shaft that rose over two hundred and fifty feet above the city. At night, lights shone in a steam coming from the top and made it appear to be capped by a flame.

One hot Sunday in August, Carol Ann's family went to the Armour and Company picnic. They'd invited me to go too, but I decided instead to visit the Lincoln Memorial and make Sam happy.

I walked up the vast, sloping pavilion where landscapers had not yet finished laying the sod or planting the hawthorn trees that would border the roadway. The sweat was dripping from my face and trickling down my back by the time I reached the tower. I was stunned at its size, far larger than I had imagined, and I stared up at the angels carved on it and read the inscription:

IN HONOR OF THOSE WHO SERVED IN THE
WORLD WAR IN DEFENSE OF LIBERTY

Gigantic marble Sphinxes, one called "Memory" and one called "Future," lay on either side of the tower, and, oddly, both had their eyes covered. They were monstrous creatures, each about the length of three cars and twice as high. The newspaper said the hindquarter stones weighed 17,000 pounds each. They hid their eyes supposedly to forget the war and to show uncertainty about the future. I grimaced because I wanted to forget the war too, but I'd keep my eyes wide open when it came to the future.

Sam would expect me to go to the top of the tower, so I got in line even though it cost twenty-five cents. The ticket seller was a veteran, wearing his old army uniform. I noticed the ugly scars on the backs of both his hands and heard him tell the man in front of me how he got them.

"I dropped my darn gloves on the ground, but I didn't know they'd used mustard gas on that spot. When I put them on again, my hands got burned."

"How terrible," someone murmured.

"The gas got in my eyes too, and to this day, I have to wear colored glasses in bright sunshine."

I flinched to see the raised welts as he sold me my ticket. How painful it must have been.

Along with a few others, I boarded the elevator, holding my breath as it rose to the top of the shaft, its pulleys and cables grinding noisily. From there we climbed a couple of staircases to the observation deck where another veteran, in his uniform, greeted us. I stepped out, terrified to look at anything but my feet, my stomach flip-flopping for a moment. Then the prairie breeze lifted my hair and cooled my skin, and I raised my eyes.

All of Kansas City was spread below: downtown, the Blue River and the Missouri, the rolling hills. It was the most wondrous sight I could ever imagine. No one said a word, as we stood, solemn and awed by the quiet beauty of the view. My lungs filled with the clean air, and I felt a calmness flow through my body. If I weren't so sore at him, I'd have wished my father, three hundred miles away, could be here to see what had been built to honor him and all the others. Maybe it would have brought him the peace I felt.

When we'd had our fill of the sight, we rode back down on the elevator, my head filled with the majesty of what I'd seen. One of the men, an older, sad-faced fellow said, "D'you know why that old vet is up there?"

"No," I said.

"He's there to prevent jumping. You know. Suicide."

"Really?" I was unbelieving.

"Yeah, some of the guys were mixed up pretty bad when they got home from the war. I know at least one fellow who tried to shoot himself."

I shuddered.

I SPENT THE rest of the afternoon exploring the two other buildings that were part of the Memorial. Massive carved bronze doors to the Memory Hall and to the Museum were each flanked by giant urns made of black marble, signaling the grandeur I would see when I went inside.

Flags and banners of all the Allies, the War Mothers and the Gold Star League were mounted in the Museum. Medallions and inscriptions adorned the walls. Cabinets on either side displayed War posters, some familiar to me, and I felt the nobility of this place with all its color and brilliance. I was proud of our country and its great victory. When I studied the glass cases holding relics from the war, I wondered if my dad had handled grenades and rifles like these. Uniforms, sad letters to families, and even a large torpedo from a sub were part of the display.

Eventually I moved on to Memory Hall. A man, taller than any of the others, caught my attention, and I saw he was missing his right arm just like Dad. He wore a shirt that might have fit him once, but now hung loosely on his thin, wasted body. With him was a round, little woman, perhaps his wife or sister. They were strolling, looking at the large, colorful maps of battle sites that covered the walls. Suddenly he stopped and said, "Cora! Cora!" His whole body shook as he thumped his finger against one of the maps. "Look, Cora. This is it. This is the place." He turned to her, begging her with his eyes to see what he saw. "It's the very place, Cora. That place where it...it happened." He ducked his head, but not before I saw tears begin to roll down his cheeks. The woman turned to him with a look of such piercing love and sympathy I was almost overcome. Wrapping her soft arms around him, she said. "Oh, my dear. My dear. Oh, my dear." She kept repeating those words as she held him. Finally she dug in her pocketbook for a handkerchief. I turned away, embarrassed to have eavesdropped.

BACK IN THE city that evening, I climbed the steps to my shabby boarding house room and flopped onto the bed, my arms on the pillow behind my head. I was uplifted by my visit to the memorial, but haunted by the scene with the soldier and Cora. Dad didn't have anyone like Cora to comfort him when he came home from the War. Never once since that sad day when he stepped off the train in Beaverton years ago had I heard anyone thank him or say, "We're proud of you for what you did, Cal."

No. No flags flew for Calvin Spencer. When he came home, everybody expected he would just get on with his life, get a job, and take care of his children. When he didn't, they were irritated and annoyed. They moved him from Uncle Lyle's house to Sally McVay's house like a piece of tired, unwanted furniture. Everyone was sorry he'd lost an arm, but no one saw that a bigger hole had been blasted into him, and that he was not a complete person.

None of this jibed with the idea of the heroic, noble soldiers and veterans that I'd learned about that afternoon. Surely Dad deserved honor as much as any of them. He just never got it. It sickened me to think things might have been different if we'd found a way to comfort him, to understand him better. Why had it never occurred to us to take him to an Armistice Day parade or celebration? Some place where he could have put on his old uniform and met up with other veterans. Let people show their appreciation. Such a thing never entered our minds.

I lay sad and ashamed. Later, as the sun went down, and the sky darkened, I rose and opened the window. A great wash of cool air flowed over me. I watched the silvery moon rise and felt something begin to loosen inside me. It was like a huge boulder being shoved aside, allowing me to see what was behind it. Slowly and clumsily, I began to understand.

I WANTED TO tell Carol Ann about my visit to the memorial, and we met after work at a diner near her school. As we sipped our coffee, I described the tall soldier and Cora. "It made me think about Dad," I said. "How he didn't have anybody like that when he came home."

As she listened, a little pucker of concern formed between her eyes. "Well, he had all of you."

"It's not the same. We all wanted something from him, and we didn't get it. I wanted him to be like my old dad was before the war, and when he couldn't be the person I wanted, I turned my back on him and ignored him."

"You were just a kid. It was natural." Crumbs from the pastry she'd just eaten clung to her lips, and I brushed them away with my hand, just wanting to touch her.

"I suppose. I realize now that he never told us a thing about the war, what he did over there, anything about the fighting. Don't you think that's odd?"

"It is, now that I think about it."

"Instead, he just got ornery. Dad did things he would never have done before. When I think about Granddad and Buster, my blood still boils."

"Do you think that if he'd talked about it, it might have helped him?"

"I don't know. Maybe. Maybe not. He probably figured nobody cared. I just wish he could see the memorial. To see what people have done to honor the soldiers, to show their respect. It would let him know he was appreciated."

She leaned back with a gentle smile. "Harry, you say you hate your dad, but underneath it all, I think you must really care about him."

I looked at her surprised, and then I shrugged my shoulders. "It doesn't really matter, Carol Ann. I doubt if I'll ever see him again."

"That's too bad, Harry. I'm going to hope that things get better between you two."

38

SAM AND I had heard about the expanding development called
Brookside in the Country Club area of town. The men financing the
project were creating a neighborhood of nice homes with shops nearby
so people wouldn't have to travel far for things they needed. That gave
me an idea.

"Sam," I said, "what would you think about starting a branch store
in Brookside? All those new homes going in. Folks'll need the things
we sell."

He looked up, his eyes open wide, surprised at my boldness. Then
he smiled. "Ah, Harry. You're young. Young men want to do everything.
I'm too old to start over again."

"You wouldn't be starting over. You'd just be expanding."

"I don't know, Harry. Business is good here. What more do I need?"

I persisted, and one Sunday afternoon that fall he and I rode the
black and cream trolley to Brookside Station. We walked a couple
of blocks east to Morningside Drive where I couldn't help but stare
goggle-eyed at the mansions, each more extravagant than anything I
could have imagined. The lower floors were most often made of brick
with upper parts of large timbers and stucco. Tall, narrow windows with
small panes blinked in the sunshine. The roofs were steeply pitched
and featured oversize chimneys, sometimes more than one, with deco-
rative brickwork. We walked by one house, the most magnificent of all,

with huge rose trees blooming red and white in the yard, obviously the home of a wealthy man. We recognized the unlikely name—Fletcher Cowherd—etched on a brass plate next to the front door. He was well known in our city.

Just a block in back of the mansions, was a housing development with hundreds of modest bungalows. A large sign crowed:

Built by the Fletcher Cowherd Company
Buy a Cowherd House for One Price
The Right Price

"*Nu*, Harry. Mr. Cowherd's made himself rich building these houses," Sam said as we walked through the neighborhood.

The bungalows had peaked gables like the mansions, though on a much smaller scale. Second-story windows peeked at the front yards from under the gables. Sidewalks lined the streets with inviting walks to the covered porches. Paved tracks between the houses led to garages in back, styled to match the houses. Owners had planted flowers and trees making it as pleasant a place as anyone could want. I imagined myself living there some day with Carol Ann.

"See, Sam. Look at all the customers we would have." I was fired up at the thought of a brand new store with all the latest Ozarka radios and Tiffany lamps to sell to these homeowners.

"Something to think about, Harry."

We returned to Brookside Boulevard and the commercial area. Although most of the shops were closed because it was Sunday, we stared into the windows. The grand array included a flower shop, a meat market, dry cleaners, a filling station, and several others. We laughed at the pictures of women with exotic hair-dos in Fern's Beauty Shop and at their hats in Milady's Millinery.

The Katydid Ice Cream and Candy Store was open and doing a big business. Once inside, my stomach rolled with hunger as we stood in front of bins of chocolate candies, caramels, fruity gumdrops, and toffee. Families were enjoying ice cream cones; mothers were kept busy wiping messy faces.

"Maybe you want something?" Sam asked, and I nodded eagerly. We sat at a little table and ordered chocolate sundaes. I ate mine in a few seconds, and while I waited for Sam, I noticed a shelf nearby with stacks of flyers about the neighborhood. One advertised a scenic route through the Country Club district and its 200 acres of America's most beautiful residential section.

"Look, Sam. It's a map to keep it in the pocket of your automobile to use the next time you are pleasure driving."

He grinned and his high-pitched giggle escaped. "Maybe you know somebody with an automobile?" He knew perfectly well I'd show it to the Bellwoods and hope they'd want a tour.

Our sundaes finished, we went outside and turned a corner onto 63rd Street. "See here, Sam. It's the new Piggly-Wiggly Store. You remember? We read about it in the paper. It's a self-serve store."

"Self-serve?" he said. "How does it work, Harry?"

We stood with our hands cupped around our eyes peering through the window. This was nothing like our grocery store back home in Richmond. A wooden turnstile at the front door led the customer to a line of straw baskets. "See those?" I said. "You take a basket and go around the store putting the things in it that you want to buy. You wait on yourself." Shelves were piled high with goods on every side. Canned fruit and vegetables were arranged in pyramids a few feet apart throughout the store. Two cash registers sat by scales for weighing fresh foods. "And when you're done, you take your basket to the counter and pay."

"I see, Harry," Sam said as understanding spread across his face. "Not so many clerks to run this store. Smart men, these Piggle Wiggle people."

His enthusiasm grew as we continued our walk. "Maybe you have a good idea, Harry. We will think." We even found a possible location across from the filling station.

"We could call the new store Sam's Radio and Electric," I said.

He looked at me smiling. "Maybe we call it Harry's Radio and Electric. Maybe we make a partnership."

My heart just about jumped out of my chest at his words. I danced around in excitement and gave him a big hug. At last, I might have the chance I'd longed for, a chance to amount to something. I just knew we could make a go of it.

WHEN I VISITED the Bellwood's, I could talk of nothing else, and they became excited too. Ed said, "It sounds like a real opportunity for you, Harry. Nothing to lose, as far as I can see." Carol Ann was a little nervous, but she trusted me. I asked if they would like to see Brookside, maybe take the tour that the brochure suggested, and so we climbed into their car.

Carol Ann and I rode in the back seat with her parents in the front. At the last minute her brother Jerry decided to go and crowded in with us. I didn't mind too much because I was eager to sit close and cuddle as much as I dared. It was a nippy fall day and Carol Ann wore her new dark green coat and matching hat that drew out the color of her eyes. Tiny freckles, left over from summer, still showed across her nose even as her cheeks became pink in the brisk air. She had never looked more adorable. I squeezed her hand and said, "Look at these houses, Carol Ann. Can you imagine what it'd be like to live in one?" I wondered how soon I could afford one of the bungalows. It could be our first home.

Her mother said, "They're beautiful, Harry. I can see why you like it out here." Turning to her husband, she said, "What do you think, Ed?"

"What I like best," he said, "is that it's far enough south that you don't get so much of the stockyards smell."

We all laughed, but I thought how glad I was that I didn't work at Armour's where I'd have had that smell in my nostrils all the time.

After we explored Brookside, we parked in front of the Katydid. Carol Ann and I bought some chocolates and wandered down the street looking in shop windows while Jerry and her parents had sodas.

The heels of her new red shoes clicked on the pavement as we walked. Around the corner and out of sight we had a couple of nice, chocolaty kisses before we turned back. I felt so happy and confident; I wished the day could last forever. My dreams were beginning to be within reach.

GRAM WROTE TO me about how relieved she was that I had a good job. She told me about church events, who died, which customers didn't pay their bills on time, all the small town stuff. She said the Feds had shut Granddad down a couple of times, and he paid some big fines, but of course he went right back to selling beer when he figured they'd cleared out. "Stubborn fool," she wrote. Gram never mentioned my father, and I was grateful. I sent her a few short notes about my work and, once in a while, a postcard of Kansas City scenes.

I longed to tell them about my exciting news, but I didn't do it. Gram would tell me not to count my chickens, and Ty might resent being stuck in Richmond while I was having a great time in Kansas City.

I felt a little homesick whenever a letter came, but then I'd realize I was right where I wanted to be. I could see my girl and talk to her. I could hold her and kiss her whenever we could escape her parents. Also, I was wrapped up in the business. When I considered everything, the homesick feeling faded away.

OVER THE HOLIDAYS Ty wrote to me. It was a long letter for him. He'd met a girl named Daisy Vogelzang at a dance, and he'd fallen hard. He thanked me for teaching him the polka and two-step. Rather than describe her, he sent a picture. I was to look at it and send it back. It made me laugh out loud to realize Ty still couldn't find many words for things.

I studied the picture of his gal and decided she wasn't exactly pretty. Her face was narrow and her nose seemed too big for her face, but her smile made her look kind. For Ty's sake, I sure hoped she was.

He went on to say that Gram's knees were plaguing her, and Grand-dad was down sick with his bad lungs. A little flicker of concern went through me. I wondered how they were getting along at the store with Granddad in bed and Gram having to tend him. Surely Ty would be able to manage. Anyhow, there wasn't much I could do about it.

39

D URING THE CHRISTMAS season, Sam and I continued to talk about a branch store. Nothing got decided while we were so busy, but after the New Year's holiday, he had me make an appointment with the J. C. Nichols Realty Company in Brookside.

Sam said, "I'll call Ida Klump to stay in the store. Nobody'll want to buy from her. Ida Klump is such a grump." He giggled at his awful rhyme. "But she's honest. Won't steal from me."

At Brookside, we met an agent, Mr. Rutledge, in the landlord's office and talked about the empty space we'd seen on our first trip. He had all the information—the square footage; the shared cost of a sign; options for finishes including colors, flooring, counters, and all the rest. I was astounded, never dreaming that there was so much involved in setting up a new business.

Mr. Rutledge asked lots of questions. What brands would we feature? Would we need a loading dock? Office space? A toilet room? What kind of advertising did we do in our current location? How would we handle it for the new store? Did we plan to make deliveries? I couldn't think fast enough to answer, but when Sam told him about the success of his current store, he seemed satisfied that we were legitimate.

He told us about the merchants' association and how we'd automatically become members if we rented a space.

"We'll put an article in the newsletter about your store once you sign a lease. It'll announce the grand opening and tell about the fine things you plan to sell. Your business will prosper."

"Slow down, Mr. Rutledge," Sam said. "We have to do some thinking first."

"Well, let me send a copy of our lease home with you. You can read it and call me if you have questions. We'd really like to have your business here, Mr. Rubin."

We headed back to our store, my head buzzing with ideas.

"We should buy a truck now, Sam. I could start deliveries right away."

"Not yet, Harry."

"Should we look for a secondhand desk for the office?" I asked.

"You get ahead of yourself, Harry. First we figure overhead. We have to pay insurance and heat. And telephone, don't forget. They pay the water. How much money to stock the store with all those nice things you want to sell? Quite a lot. Then we see if we can make a profit. See if there's anything left to pay Harry." He cackled.

"And advertising, Sam. We'll have to advertise."

He threw up his hands. "Oy, so much to think about. It makes my head tired."

My head was not tired, however. I got out some paper, a ruler, and a pencil. Whenever I had a free moment, I drew floor plans, figuring where the counter should go, how to arrange the shelves and tables. I had an idea to wall off a small area of the store for radios, where customers could listen and try out different models without store noise. We'd be able to squeeze in some refrigerators and washing machines too, but I hadn't raised that with Sam yet.

"We'll need a cash register," I said. "And some sales books."

"Better make a list, Harry, so not to forget anything."

I raced to do it and gave it to him before I left that day.

"You didn't forget much," he said as he read it. "You even got toilet paper down here."

"Well, we're going to have a restroom."

He looked at me kindly. "It would give me great pleasure just to buy the store for you, Harry, but it's not a toy. It's a business. We have to be sure."

In spite of his caution, it was thrilling to fantasize about our new store, to imagine myself ordering handsome merchandise—lamps, waffle irons, fans, irons, and especially radios. I'd handle the advertising and sales myself. Every night I called Carol Ann and talked over the plans.

"I wish I could be a part of it," she said. "It sounds so exciting. I'd rather help you than go to Normal School."

"Wouldn't that would be great? I'd love it if we could work together."

"My mother would have a fit. She wants me to be a teacher. Ever since I was a little girl, that's what she's talked about."

"You'd be a great teacher if that's what you want, Carol Ann, but I'd sure rather have you with me."

"I do like kids, but the idea of teaching little squirts all day every day doesn't excite me as much as what you're doing."

"Well, maybe your mom will change her mind. After all she doesn't own you."

"We'll see."

That gave me an idea. When the time came, I'd ask Sam if Carol Ann could work in the store. It would take two of us to manage it, I was sure. If I had to make deliveries, she could run the store. And so I dreamed and dreamed, always imagining a rosy future complete with wedding plans just as soon as I could afford it.

A couple of days later, I overheard Sam talking on the telephone to his lawyer friend, Michael Delman. Sam always shouted when he was on the phone, and anybody who was in the store could hear him easily.

"Mike, just see about this lease. Is it okay to sign? Not crooked?" There was a pause, then, "I need a letter, to make a partner." Another pause. "Yes, the boy who works here, Harry Spencer."

It was then I knew it was all going to happen, making me the luckiest fellow on earth! Even though I tried to remain nonchalant, straightening the shelves and adjusting price tags, I could feel my heart thumping inside my chest.

"Maybe we have that new store ready by March or April, Harry."

"That'd be wonderful," I said, bursting with such joy I was unable to say more.

❖　❖　❖

LATE THAT AFTERNOON, the telephone rang, and I heard Sam answer it. "Oh. It's Harry you want? Just a minute. He's here."

"For you, Harry. Long distance it is." His eyes were big as he handed me the receiver. I'd never had a call from anyone except Carol Ann, and a jolt went through me as I realized it must be from home.

"Hello."

"Harry. Is that you?

"Yes. Ty? Is that you, Ty?"

"Harry, Granddad…" His voice faded.

I said, "What? What are you saying?"

Then his voice was back again. "It's Granddad, Harry. He got real bad. He didn't make it."

"You mean he…he died?"

"Yeah. This morning. Gram wants you…" His voice faded away again.

"Can you hear me, Ty? What does Gram want?" I got the words "come home" clearly enough.

"Can you come?"

"I'll try," I said. But he was already gone. I stood stunned, shocked, and unsure what to do.

Sam looked at me, his huge eyebrows humped up. He asked, "What, Harry? What?"

"It's Granddad. He's gone. Dead."

294 | KAREN WOLFF

"Oh, that's bad news. I'm very sorry." He continued to look at me. "It's all right if you need to go home. Maybe you should."

I couldn't figure out if he meant home to my rooming house, or home to Richmond.

"I...I want to stay here."

"All right. That's all right, Harry."

It seemed like I should continue what I'd been doing, so I turned back to the shipment of lampshades I'd been unpacking, but my hands shook. I couldn't think what to do with the shades, and I made a jumbled mess. Try as I might to get control of myself, I just couldn't. My brain wouldn't work right.

Sam took me by the shoulder. "Come. Sit down, Harry. Stay until I come back." He pushed me down onto the steps leading up to his apartment and went to take care of the customers who were in the store.

I was breathing hard for some reason. Granddad's gone, that funny little man I had taken for granted was gone. I'd never see him again. It was hard to absorb.

When the customers left, I heard Sam lock the front door and turn out the lights even though it wasn't yet closing time. That's my job. Why was he doing my job?

He came back to me. "This the first time you lose family, eh?"

"Granddad's not family," I said. "He's my step-grandfather."

"He helped raise you, feed you, gave you a bed, didn't he?"

I nodded and blurted out, "We slept in the same bed. When I was little."

He smiled. "Well, that's family, Harry. Don't ever forget." He went to a little cupboard in the back room and scrabbled around until he came up with a bottle of schnapps and a glass. He poured some and handed it to me.

"Drink. It will help."

I did as he said and felt the sting in my nose and throat.

"I can't think," I said. "Gram wants me to come home. How can I do that?"

"Easy, Harry. You get on the train tonight and go. Your grandmother. She'll need you." He waited a minute, then said, "You call your girl now. Tell her."

The fog in my head began to lift as I reached for the telephone. As soon as I heard Carol Ann's voice, I was on familiar ground, and the shakiness grew less.

Her warm voice filled my ear. "I'm so sorry, Harry. It must be a terrible shock."

"I've never had a long-distance call before. Isn't it silly that it scared me?" That was a stupid remark, and I knew it the minute it was out of my mouth. I should be thinking about Granddad instead of myself.

"No, it's not silly. Are you all right? Do you want me to come down and help you pack?"

"No. I'll be all right. I'm going home now to get my suitcase."

"I love you, Harry. Take care of yourself while you're gone. Take care of Gram."

IN MY ROOMING house, I managed to get some clothes together and tell my landlady I'd be away for a few days. I walked in the cold to Union Station and had bought my ticket before I realized how hungry I was. Sam had tucked a ten-dollar bill in my pocket, and I used some of it for a plate of barbequed pork floating in hot, spicy sauce and some ginger ale. As I spent his money, I remembered I hadn't even thanked him for it. What a hopeless clod. When would I start acting like an adult?

The good food went down easily, and, as I waited for my train, I began to feel more like myself. I could handle this. I had a duty to perform for my family, and I was determined to do it. Kansas City would still be here when it was all over.

40

ON THE TRAIN I crawled into a window seat still warm from the previous occupant. The car wasn't filled, and I was happy not to have to talk to anyone. The Negro conductor came along and looked at my ticket for Beaverton.

"You goin' up north? I hope you like it cold." He brought me a blanket in case I wanted to sleep. I thanked him and fell to replaying all that had happened today, trying to imagine what it would be like to go back home, a place I thought I'd never see again. Ty said Gram needed me. She was so self-sufficient; it puzzled me why she had him say that. I wondered how she felt about Granddad being gone. Their marriage wasn't easy with him so irresponsible and stubborn, yet they must have had fun at some time, maybe in the beginning. She'd miss him, but she'd get along all right.

I recalled everything I could about Granddad. How happy he was when I got my bike, how he egged me on to ask another girl to a dance when Carol Ann wouldn't go with me. And he never once got cross with us kids when we were small.

People laughed at his jokes and loved his fiddle playing. He made friends with everybody. He was such a softie; he couldn't make himself ask his charge customers for payment, but left that to Gram. Yet he was as determined as a mule when it came to his beer. Nobody could stop him when he wanted something to drink.

Did I love him, I wondered? I'd shed no tears, nor was I likely to. I didn't hold a lot of respect for his business sense, but I felt a soft warmth and smiled as I thought about him. Maybe, if he'd been my real grandfather, it would have felt different, but maybe not.

Then came the thought that I had pushed to the back of my mind. My father. Would I see him? How would I behave? I hoped he'd stay away, out of sight. Eddie and Gabe would come for the funeral, and Polly too. My brothers would want to see him, but Dad probably wouldn't let poor Polly near. What a sorry mess our family was.

My mind moved on to more pleasant things—the exciting possibilities I had ahead of me in Kansas City. Sam, wonderful Sam, the new business and a partnership. Would folks think I was bragging if I told them about our plans? Would they be jealous? Or not interested? I decided to play it safe and not talk about it unless someone asked.

The train was a local. It stopped at every little town along the way. Often only one person, or sometimes no one, boarded. Even so, the whistle blew importantly, and the engine pumped steam into the cold night air. So many little towns, like Richmond I supposed, just as boring and dreary.

Ultimately the rocking motion of the car made me drowsy and I fell asleep. I don't know for how long, but when I awoke the first pale light of dawn had appeared. I couldn't see much of the landscape because my window was covered with frost, and I shivered in the cold. The conductor pointed me toward the dining car where I ordered a cup of coffee. The hot steam coming off the cup warmed my fingers and nose, and my sleepiness lifted. I stirred in cream and sugar and figured it would have to serve for breakfast. Using my fingernails, I scraped the frost from the window and gazed out at a bleak, frozen landscape, flat and treeless to the west.

A well-dressed man sat over his breakfast, reading the Omaha newspaper. "How far are you going, son?" he asked me.

"To a little town north of Sioux City." I hadn't spoken all night, and the words came out hoarse and scratchy.

"They've had a big snow up there. I hope you're ready for that."

I nodded. "Yessir. I am."

In a little while we pulled into the station in Sioux City, and I figured my trip would be over soon. But then we sat for another hour. I hadn't taken into account all the switching and moving of cars that would occur there. Eventually, some additional travelers came aboard, bundled in caps and scarves, their cheeks rosy, and snow on their shoulders. "Colder than Billy gee-whiz," one man commented. "It's January, George. What can you expect?" a woman answered.

At last we set off for the short ride to Beaverton. The coffee was working inside me now, and I was eager for this ride to end. A long, lonely whistle announced our arrival, and I got up, grabbed my bag, and prepared to get off, the only person to dismount at this station.

A stiff, icy wind nearly knocked me over as I stepped down from the car. Nobody was on the platform, and I wondered if anyone had come to meet me. Inside the depot, the telegrapher looked up and said, "Are you Harry Spencer?"

"Yes," I answered.

"Your brother was here earlier, but the train was late. He'll be back for you." Then his key started to rattle, and he turned back to his work.

When Ty came in about a half hour later, puffing and stamping off the snow, I was so relieved and glad to see him, I just threw my arms around him. It probably embarrassed him a little, but I didn't care.

"Where've you been, brother?"

"I had to take Gram to the undertaker's. She's there now, trying to get everything decided. We'll have to pick her up and try to get home before there's more snow."

We braced ourselves against the wind and hurried out to the car where Ty had some trouble getting it started. Finally it turned over, and we drove to Westby's Funeral Service. As we stepped inside, Ty said, "There's something I have to tell you, Harry." I looked at him questioningly.

"I got married last week. To Daisy. She's inside with Gram."

"Really," I said. "What a surprise. That sure happened fast."

"We kinda had to," he said, looking down, his face reddening.

"Oh," was all I managed as we walked into the lobby.

Lester Westby, who did every funeral in the whole area, was attired in his usual black suit. He stood tall and thin over Gram and the girl I took to be Daisy. My eyes fastened on Gram. She seemed so small. Her dark dress hung on her, too long and loose. Her face looked more tired than I had ever seen it. Instinctively I went over to give her a hug.

She wasn't much of a hugger, but she said, "Harry. It's good you're here." She turned to the girl and said, "Daisy, this is Harry, your brother-in-law." We shook hands.

"I've heard so much about you, Harry. And I'm so sorry about your grandfather."

"Thanks," I said, unable to think of anything to say.

Gram said, "I think we're about finished up here. We picked out a casket."

"A real beauty," Mr. Westby said, his pale face shining with the glow of a sale completed.

"The funeral will be tomorrow morning at our church," Gram went on. "Lida did some hard bargaining with the minister, but he finally agreed to it."

I knew Granddad hadn't set foot inside a church for years and had even been baptized a Catholic. Good thing Gram and Aunt Lida were such pillars of the church; otherwise the funeral might not have happened there.

Gram shook hands with Mr. Westby who said, "Again, my condolences, Mrs. Didier. We'll bring your husband out this afternoon and set him up in the church."

I got a mental picture of Granddad sitting slouched in a pew, his hat stuck jauntily on his head, grinning his fool head off, but of course I knew that's not what Westby meant.

"To get ahead of the snow," he clucked nervously.

"Let's hope it holds off," Gram said, and we went out into the cold and climbed into the Ford.

AT GRAM'S HOUSE the kitchen was filled with pots of food, enough for an army. The Ladies Aid Society had been busy, and I was ready to make up for my missed breakfast. I piled into scalloped potatoes and ham, green beans and bacon, hot biscuits with rhubarb jam, and a towering chocolate cake. I drank down two big glasses of milk, and then I was ready for more coffee.

We sat at the kitchen table oddly the same as before, but different with Daisy in Granddad's chair. It gave me a sudden pang, and I missed the old man right then. Ty ate his meal and soon left for the store where one of the Beaubien boys had been watching things during the morning. I asked Daisy where they were living.

"We're staying at Sally McVay's for the time being, 'til Gram can get everything settled. My dad is getting old and wants to retire, so Ty's going to take over his farm come spring. We're going to live in my grandma's house just a quarter mile from the home place." She got up to do the dishes, and then she left to join Ty. Gram and I were finally able to talk.

"She seems nice," I said.

"Yes, I think so. Ty doesn't like the store much. He's still shy around the customers, so the farm is probably right for him."

"Was Granddad awful sick?" I asked.

"Not at first. Seemed just like every other time when he got pleurisy. Something was different, though. He was so tired, didn't seem to want to make an effort to cough or even eat. After a week or so, Doctor Brunner came and said he had pneumonia in both lungs. His breathing was bad. He just couldn't get a good breath. We steamed him, and I fixed poultices, but nothing helped. He just got weaker and weaker. Finally he said, 'I'm gonna be leavin' you, Bess.' He just closed his eyes and stopped breathing." She put a handkerchief to her face, but she didn't cry.

"He was an old devil sometimes, but I'm going to miss him," she said.

"Did you love him, Gram?" I said, thinking how I loved Carol Ann and wouldn't be able to bear losing her.

"Oh, I don't know. We were so old. We had affection for each other, I guess you would say. Yes, we had affection."

She stood up then and said, "You'd better unpack, Harry. You'll have to sleep on the daybed. All right?"

"I've done it before, Gram. A lot."

"Did you bring something to wear to the funeral?"

"Of course," I said, proud that I now had decent suits to wear.

"If you're all right, I think I'll lie down for a while."

AFTER SUPPER THAT evening, the neighbors began stopping by to see Gram. I told Ty I'd stay at the store so he and Daisy could visit with them.

Bruno's great black and white body rose to greet me, but, after an indifferent sniff, he padded back to his spot behind the counter. It was a shock to look around the store. The stocks were way down. Big empty holes on the shelves that should have been full of canned goods, flour, sugar, and the like. The floor had been swept, but there was clutter everywhere I looked. Ty must have been trying to do everything himself while Gram took care of Granddad.

Only a few customers came by on this frigid, windy night, so I cleaned out the produce bins and got rid of the shriveled turnips and carrots. By the time I finished, it was after nine o'clock, and I didn't expect to see anyone else. I was tired, but couldn't help noticing the cigarette and candy case sticky with fingerprints. I got a bucket and was washing it when Squint Pickard came in with a blast of cold air.

"Harry," he said, grinning his simpleton smile. "I sure didn't expect to see you here. You been gone a long time."

"Yeah, it's been over a year," I said.

"Is Alfie here?"

"I think you know, Squint, Alfie passed the other day."

"Oh yeah. It's terrible, isn't it?" His one good eye got dreamy and wandered off somewhere. After a minute or so, he said, "Alfie used to let me have some beer. Do you s'pose you could let me have some?"

"Afraid not, Squint. The beer parlor is closed down what with Granddad gone."

"That's right. I guess Ty told me."

I hoped he would leave so that I could finish up and go to bed, but he seemed to be in no hurry.

"How come you went away, Harry?"

"Oh, I just needed to try something new, I guess."

"I heard it was 'cause you were mad at your dad."

"That too." I wanted this conversation to end.

Squint moved closer to me, looking at me carefully. "He didn't do what you thought, Harry."

"What do you mean, Squint?" My skin prickled.

"Cal didn't hurt Alfie. I was there. I saw the whole shebang." His gaze got foggy again as if he'd forgotten what he'd just said.

I felt my head begin to throb. "What are you talking about, Squint? What did you see?"

His eye refocused on my face. "I saw it all. I was standing right there when it happened."

I grabbed his shirtfront and pulled him to me. "Tell me," I yelled. Bruno let out a throaty growl and got up to see what was going on.

Squint looked up at me, fear squeezing his face. I let go of him and tried to calm myself. "Go lie down, Bruno." Then, more quietly I said, "Just tell me about it, Squint. What went on?"

He took a breath. "All them fellas in white sheets 'n pointy hats. They come up over the end of the porch so fast." He pointed in that direction. "They had torches on fire, and they were yellin' at Alfie. I was scairt, I'll tell you. I thought they might kill him and me too."

"What happened next?" I was afraid to move for fear he would stop talking.

"Well, them fellas started pushin' Alfie around on the porch. They spun him around, and he was teeterin' there on the edge, Buster barkin' like a fool. That's when I saw Cal come runnin' up the front steps in his white sheet. Yessir, I saw him."

"You saw him here? How did you know it was him?"

Squint didn't answer me right away, but started walking around, scanning the shelves as if he planned to buy something. At the meat case he stopped and said, "That stuff looks good. I'm kinda hungry, Harry."

My stomach knotted up, but I couldn't lose him now. I cut a few slices of bologna and ripped open a bread package. I slapped the meat between two slices of bread and handed it to him. Then I popped the lid off a Coke for him and said again, "How'd you know it was him?"

He chewed slowly, mushing the food around in his mouth, little bits falling out onto his coat. "I'm tryin' to remember." He stared off again, but finally swung his gaze back to me. "Well, I guess it was them torches. They shined on his claw hook, that's what. That's how I knew it was Cal." He nodded his head up and down. "Yessir, I saw him, and I knew it was Cal." He continued to chew.

My heart was pumping hard, and I felt my breath hot on his face. "What did he do, Squint, when he came up on the porch? Did he push Granddad off? Down on top of the dog?"

"Nosirree, he did not. He tried to save Alfie." He took a big swig of Coke. "Cal's good arm come up like this." Squint raised his left arm with the half-eaten sandwich and waved it in the air. "He pushed them others back with it like this. Then he wrapped that good arm around Alfie."

"Yes? Then what?" I wanted to squeeze the words out of the poor old devil.

"Cal, well he was tryin' to get his bad arm up to hold on to Alfie, but it got tangled up in that white sheet. He couldn't raise it up. I saw that hook slide down Alfie's back, tear his shirt. Next thing I know, Alfie and Buster were on the ground."

I exhaled. Could this old fool possibly know what he was saying? I stood back, scarcely breathing.

"They all run off then, and I fell down in the ditch. I had too much beer."

My mouth hung open, my throat dry. I believed Squint's story, and now I knew for sure that Dad was here at the store that awful night. But he hadn't pushed anybody off the porch. He'd tried to stop the others. He'd tried to do the right thing. I couldn't speak for several minutes.

"I guess I better go home," Squint said. He waved vacantly.

I looked at him without seeing him. "Uh, yeah. You better go. I have to close up." Then I realized I owed this man more, and I said with real gratitude, "Thanks, Squint. Thanks for telling me. It means a lot." He turned to leave. I said, "Wait a minute, Squint. Why did it take so long for you to tell somebody about this?"

He shrugged his shoulders. "I dunno, Harry. I guess I was scairt. I didn't want them Klan fellas to know I was there. Right after that, my sister heard I'd been drinkin' too much, and she made me come up to Portlandville to stay with her. I didn't come back to Richmond for a long time. Not till after the weather warmed up. It was all over with by then."

His short, grubby body went out the door into the cold. I bent over the counter, leaning on my arms with my head down, thinking about Squint's news. Maybe my dad wasn't the person I had thought he was. I stood so long bent over the counter that I was numb, and when I finally stood, the warm blood flooded back into my arms and face, and I breathed deeply over and over. Thank God for that little man who remembered enough. I rejoiced to have heard his tale. Then, just as quickly, I was struck by remorse so deep and painful I could hardly bear it. It doubled me over again. What an evil thing I had done to my father. What a terrible person I was. I had to find him and tell him. I had to make it right.

41

MY BROTHERS, GABE and Eddie, arrived from Westfield with their wives and kids early the next morning, and Gram's kitchen seemed very small. We shook hands and hugged, everybody talking at once.

"Harry, you've grown so much," Pauline said. "And what a handsome haircut." Indeed, I was as tall as my brothers. I felt like one of them in a new way, not like the baby in the family anymore.

The women got busy right away, making breakfast for everyone. We had eggs and bacon, corn muffins, cinnamon rolls that someone had brought, and a big potful of coffee. Ty and Daisy came over from Sally McVay's and joined us. Daisy got introduced all around.

"So Ty's finally got a wife," Eddie teased. "Thought he'd never get around to it."

Esther said, "Now you stop that, Eddie,"

Daisy and Ty blushed with the kidding. She got away from it by taking a tray of food back to Gram who was dressing in her bedroom. I asked Ty if Dad was coming to the funeral.

"Naw," he said. "He knows everybody in town thinks he was in on the Klan attack. He doesn't plan to go."

I was about to tell him what I'd learned from Squint when Vince and Polly showed up with Mary Jo and their little boy, Vincent Harry, whom I'd never seen. It was hugs and introductions all over again. Except for Dad, our family was together for the first time in years. We'd missed out on so much with each other, it made me sad to think about it.

Gram came out of her bedroom dressed in a heavy black dress and her good hat with a black rose on it. Her hair was pulled back into such a tight bun that it seemed to stretch her face taut. We left off bantering and laughing when we remembered why we were there. It was time to go to the church.

Gram had asked that we four brothers serve as pallbearers with Uncle Carl and Granddad's best friend Walter Trometer. Mr. Westby gave us our simple instructions when we arrived. Before the service started, the family walked down to the front of the church where Granddad lay in his satin-lined casket. The smell of fresh-cut evergreen boughs that decorated the altar filled the air.

I noticed right off Granddad's ashy-gray, calloused hands, so incongruous amid the white satin. They were clasped over his chest in the unlikeliest position I could imagine for him. How he would have snorted at that.

"He looks so natural," Pauline whispered, but I thought he just looked dead, and I was filled with a revulsion I wasn't expecting. I remembered Sam asking, "Have you ever seen a dead body, Harry?" Well, now I had.

He seemed small and frail in the vast, white bed, his one good suit too large for his wasted body. My throat tightened when I gazed at his face for the last time. Even though it was puffy from embalming, I could make out the laugh lines that always crinkled up when he joked.

I turned away as soon as it was decent and helped Gram to the side room where we waited with the family. She appeared stricken, her face pale and her jaw clenched, but she shed no tears.

People trickled into the church, their voices hushed, and walked down the aisle to view Granddad in his casket. Olive began playing soft music on the piano. When the procession was over, I led Gram to her seat in the front pew where she sat stiff-backed, staring straight ahead. The church was completely filled; some folks stood in the entryway. I shouldn't have been surprised. People from miles around knew Granddad. They traded with him, and he gave them easy credit. They danced to his fiddle music and knew good times with him. Even his beer-drinking friends were here, slicked up and serious for once. I saw Squint, who had hung a necktie on himself, but otherwise appeared no cleaner than usual.

Reverend Sayles stood up, looking as though he'd sucked on a lemon, unable to let go his disapproval of Granddad's ways even as his body lay dead before him. He offered his condolences to the family and friends of the deceased, reminding us of the prospect of eternal life if we would but accept Jesus. He read Psalm 130. When he came to the line "If thou, Lord, shouldest mark iniquities, who should stand?" his fierce eyes fastened on me for a moment and sent a tremor through my body as I tried to remember any of my misdeeds he might know about. I was relieved to stand with everyone and sing "Nearer My God to Thee."

I wondered if Granddad's soul would go to hell. It didn't seem like he deserved that, but I wasn't too sure he'd get to heaven either. Reverend Sayles cleared his throat a couple of times and delivered himself of a long, cheerless homily reminding us that death was natural and would come to each of us someday. He must have gotten it from a book somewhere because it sure wasn't about Granddad.

Arlo Fitch, who often performed solos in church, sang a grim piece I'd never heard before—"Dust to Dust, The Mortal Dies." I looked down the row and saw that both Esther and Pauline were sniffling and wiping their eyes, but Gram remained stoic. When Arlo was finished, the congregation recited the Lord's Prayer, and we sang one last hymn, "Blessed Assurance." The preacher said another prayer, and that was it.

Mr. Westby crept on silent shoes to close the dark wood casket. We pallbearers rose on his signal and carried its heavy weight outdoors to the waiting hearse-wagon. Snow, falling in huge, fluffy flakes, was already piling a soft blanket over everything.

We walked to the cemetery next to the church, and I stood with Gram at the grave as Reverend Sayles commended Alphonse David

Didier to his god as though Granddad's god, if he had one, were differ-ent from everyone else's, and then his body was lowered into the ground. Gram used her hanky finally and wiped her eyes before she turned to the line of folks who wanted to offer their sympathy, even as they stood in the snow.

I HAD A word with Sally McVay as we were leaving. "Is my father at your house?"

She looked up at me quickly. "Now, Harry. There won't be more trouble, will there? Surely not today of all days."

"No," I said. "That's a promise, but I want to see him."

"He's gone out to the Brule to check his muskrat traps," she said. "He should be back pretty soon."

"Dad's taken up trapping?"

"Yes, he has, and he's making pretty good money at it."

"Well, that's great," I said, pleased about this development.

BACK AT THE house, Aunt Lida had taken charge and had a hot dinner ready for the crowd. All of us piled food onto our plates. We stood, or sat, wherever we could find space—in the kitchen, the living room, and even in Gram's bedroom, right where Granddad died. For dessert we had funeral pies from Crazy Betty Sykes. She brought them to every funeral whether she knew the family or not. It was almost too rich after all the other food, but I did my duty and ate a big piece.

The household was noisy that afternoon with all the children and everyone talking at once. Reverend Sayles joined us briefly, and, with-out Granddad there, he was amiable enough, although I suspected it was because he needed to stay in the good graces of Aunt Lida and Gram.

Eddie and Gabe kept watching the weather, anxious to get started home before the driving got bad. They'd planned to see Dad but decided they'd better not wait any longer. After everyone left, Gram, who hadn't said much all day, sat down with Aunt Lida and Uncle Carl and relaxed a little. They talked over the service, smiling a bit at the stiff-necked preacher and discussing all the people who came.

I made myself busy settling chairs back in place, turning on a lamp, picking up a dropped mitten, and when it seemed they had forgotten my presence, I slipped away to Sally McVay's, eager to see my father, wondering if I could find the right words to say to him. He wasn't back yet, so I went inside and chatted with Sally for a few minutes, but I was so restless, so ready to square things with Dad, I just couldn't sit still.

"You say he's out at the Brule?"

"Yes, he sets his traps in the slew just south of the pond."

"I think I'll go out there and catch up with him."

She nodded. "Be good to him, Harry."

"I will."

42

I BUNDLED UP AND walked west on the road to the Brule. Snow was piling up, but there was no wind, and the temperature had come up a bit. It took me about thirty minutes to reach the slew. Muskrat homes built of reeds, snow-covered now, mounded above the surface of the water. I saw where someone, I supposed it was Dad, had left wet, mushy tracks. I called to him, but there was no answer. Perhaps he had traps farther down the creek.

Daylight on this wintry afternoon was already beginning to wane. I turned my collar up and pulled my cap down as I headed south, but saw no trace of anyone. I returned to the original tracks, trying to figure out where he'd gone. A little kernel of apprehension rose in me. Dad knew this country, and I couldn't understand why I hadn't met him coming back to town.

I began to retrace my steps, paying more attention to where I was walking. It looked like something had been dragged through the snow. Climbing up the bank from the creek, I followed the path made by whatever it was until I came to the road. The path ended abruptly with a large, snow-covered lump at an intersection with a farm road that ran south. Snow was falling furiously, and I had to brush it away before I could see what it was. Underneath was a crude sledge fashioned from a wide board with a rope attached for a handle. Eight or ten dead muskrats were piled on it and tied with a cord. They had to be Dad's, and he must have been hauling them home. But where was he?

I called out, but again there was no answer. Footprints, barely indentions in the heavy snow, left the sledge and led down the farm road to the south. I followed the track for quite a distance to the Snyder farm, but the tracks didn't turn in. Puzzled, I continued down the road another quarter mile or so, until I came to the Blanchard's. The house was dark, and no one seemed to be home. I remembered seeing them at the funeral. They must not have returned yet.

The footprints turned in, but instead of going to the house, they led to the chicken coop. How peculiar. Why would Dad go to their chicken coop? Then I saw the tracks continued on to the barn. I threw open the large door and called out. "Dad, are you in here?"

A figure rose up in the cavernous dark. I couldn't make it out at first because my eyes weren't adjusted.

"Who is it?"

I recognized the voice. "It's me, Dad. Harry." I walked up to him so I could see him better.

He looked at me warily. "Harry, what are you doing here?"

"I came to find you, Dad. I have to talk to you."

"Talk to me. What about?" He turned away. "I don't think I want to hear any of your talk. You shouldn't have come out here."

"No, Dad. You've got to listen to me. I made a terrible mistake, and I need to tell you. I was wrong. I was wrong about what I said to you. It wasn't true, and I know that now."

"What are you talking about?" His voice was filled with contempt.

"Listen to me, Dad. Squint Pickard told me everything that happened that night at the store. He told me you didn't push Granddad down. He said you tried to save him."

He stared at me a minute, then dropped down on a bale of hay, resting his good arm on his knee, the artificial arm hanging at his side. He lowered his head and closed his eyes.

I knelt in the straw in front of him. "Look at me, Dad. I'm so sorry I said all those terrible things. I don't hate you. As soon as I heard Squint's story, I knew I had to find you and make it right. You tried to do the right thing that night. I'm proud of what you did."

He was silent for a few minutes, and I sat back on my haunches, wondering what he was thinking. He heaved a big sigh.

At last his voice came out low and slow. "Well, I'm not so proud of myself. Maybe I deserved what I got from you."

"Why do you say that, Dad? You were the only decent one in that awful bunch."

He looked up and spoke again, his voice raw and grating. "You don't know it all, Harry. I don't know how to tell you this."

I waited for him to go on.

"I was a coward that night. A coward. Don't you see? That Rufus Laycock told me what those fellows were going to do. I didn't see how I could stop it, but, oh God, I wish I'd tried. Instead, I put on my robe and hid across from the store in some bushes. When they came after Alfie, I knew I had to do something. I tried to stop them, but I..." His voice broke, and he swallowed hard before he could go on.

"Alfie went down, and...oh Jesus. I'm so ashamed. I left. I just walked away. I never told anybody. I just went back to Sally's house and sneaked in. I hung up that robe and went to bed." He shuddered. "I've never understood. How could a man do that? How could I do that?"

So that was it. I felt sick to think of the pain and guilt he'd been carrying around ever since that night, and he'd never said a word. That's why he didn't try to fight me when I had cussed him out so long ago.

I sat down beside him and put my arm around his waist and laid my head on his shoulder. "It's all right, Dad. You did what you could do." We just stayed there for some time, me holding on, him not moving. After a bit, he touched my hair with his good hand, and then he began to stroke my head over and over. I felt a surge of love, his and mine, and I was swallowed up in it. I wanted it so much, had always wanted it.

LATER, AFTER WE had collected ourselves and stood up. I said, "What are you doing here, in Blanchard's barn, Dad?"

He smiled a rueful smile. "See this?" He pointed to a box trap sitting on the floor that I hadn't noticed. "Bob Blanchard's been having trouble with a fox that's been raiding his henhouse. He asked me to trap it for him."

I bent over and looked inside. I could make out two bright eyes and a pointy nose. "You got him. I can see him in there. What are you gonna do with him?"

"I don't know. I was just sitting here thinking about it when you came in. I should get rid of him, I know. But I'm havin' trouble doing it."

"Do you want me to do it for you?"

"No, no I don't. I don't want to see it killed."

"Why not, Dad? He'll just keep getting into their chickens."

He stepped to the window, looked out, and spoke without turning around. "One time when I was in France, I was on guard duty. It was quiet where I was in a field near the woods. I saw a female fox come out on the grass to sun herself. Pretty soon about four of her kits showed up. They ran and played, chasing each other, having the best time. It pleased me to see them."

He turned toward me, his sad face lit by the wan light from the window.

"Then the German artillery started up, and I had to duck down. Just as I did, a shell hit and I saw those little creatures and their mother fly up in the air, killed. I never forgot the look of her plumed tail in the air, so red and beautiful. It all seemed so stupid. So hideous."

I nodded, touched by his story. "I see, Dad." I paused. "But if we let it go, he'll be right back in that henhouse. He's a pest."

"I know, but I just don't want to kill it."

I thought for a minute. "Okay," I said. "I have an idea. Let's carry it back home. We can put him in Gram's shed overnight, and tomorrow we can take him somewhere far from here and let him loose."

I picked up the box trap with the scrabbling animal inside, and we started the trek home, stopping on the way to pick up Dad's muskrats. It struck me as curious that we didn't mind drowning those creatures who hadn't harmed anything, but neither one of us could have killed that fox that day for anything. I turned it over in my mind, but decided to keep still about it.

43

MORNING CAME WITH a clear blue sky and the sun casting its lemony winter rays over the foot and a half of snow that had fallen. Snow clung to every tree branch and post, to the well handle, to the weeds against the fence, even to the electrical wires. It hung over the eaves on the house and the store, and all together it created a scene that took my breath away.

My thoughts turned to Carol Ann. I was going to marry that girl, and I decided right then and there to make a down payment on an engagement ring the minute I got home. And dear Sam with our plans for the new store. I laughed aloud as I put on my coat and boots to go out to the shed. Snow fell from the roof down my neck when I opened the door. A powerful musky odor hit me in the face as I brought out the trap with the fox inside. "Oh, phew! You smell awful," I said, hopeful that the fresh air would dilute his odor. "But it's your lucky day," I told him.

Dad met me on the road, and I said, "Good morning, Dad. Isn't this a sight?"

"It is, indeed."

We headed east toward River Sioux on the road. No travelers had broken its surface this early morning, and it was a wide, white expanse all the way to the trees that lined the river a mile away. Walking was a labor, and we didn't talk. The only sound was the crunching of our boots and our breathing. I'd been a city boy long enough to have forgotten how still, how silent, the outdoors can be, and I treasured the quiet along with the beauty.

We came to the bridge across the Sioux River and crossed over to another state.

"I don't think he'll come back from Iowa, do you?"

Dad chuckled. "He better not."

"How high shall we go?"

He pointed to the tallest bluff and said, "Let's try that one."

Climbing was tough. Every few steps, we slipped back, and then lurched upward again. I carried the awkward trap, but the little fox never made a sound. It took a good fifteen or twenty minutes before we came to the top, puffing and sweating even in the winter cold.

I set the box on the ground, and we looked around us. It was hard for me to imagine anything as stunning as the broad view to the west, the flattened prairie under its thick blanket. The snow was already beginning to drop from the trees below us as the sun rose higher, and we knew we'd been witness to a rare moment that wouldn't last much longer.

We gazed our fill, then Dad said, "Well, are you ready?"

I nodded. He flicked open the door of the trap and jumped back. Nothing happened. I hoped the little critter hadn't died on the hike up this bluff. We waited, and then I gave the box a light kick with my toe. The fox flew out like he'd been shot from a cannon. We watched as he ran nearly a quarter of a mile along the crest of the hill, the flowing plume of his tail a brilliant arc of copper and red across the whiteness. Then he was gone. We turned to look at each other, our faces so much alike, our eyes wet. Dad put his hand on my shoulder, and we stood on that shining hillside and smiled.

"That was the right thing," he said.

ACKNOWLEDGMENTS

One summer evening in the midst of writing this book, I sat on our back porch with my husband, two sons, and a grandson. Together we discussed, sketched, and laughed as we figured out how the boys in my story would hoist a baby buggy onto a church steeple. This was typical of the unwavering support I have had from my family throughout the writing of this book, and I am more grateful than I can say.

The completion of a novel is as much about persistence as anything else. The wonderful friends I have found in my writer groups not only provided wise, incisive, and kind critiques of my labors, but they insisted that I carry on when my energy flagged. How could I have managed without them? To you—Eleanor Andrews, Kim Peters Fairley. Ellen Kuper Halter, Donnelly Hadden, Skipper Hammond, Raymond Juracek, Fartumo Kusow, Rachel Lash Maitra, Shelley Schanfield, Karen Simpson, Patricia Tompkins, and Dave Wanty—I owe huge debt of gratitude. I love you all.

I am also indebted to three longtime friends who read early versions of Harry's story: Sondra Peters, Pat Solstad, and Phyllis Kaplan, and to Alice Peck who provided important editorial advice.

ABOUT THE AUTHOR

Karen Wolff wrote her debut novel, *The Green Years*, after a career as a music educator and university administrator. She has also written several short stories. Her novella, *A Prairie Riff*, is a fictionalized account of her grandmother's early life. Her non-fiction articles and speeches have appeared in journals and trade magazines. She served as a presidential appointee on the National Council of the NEA for six years. Wolff lives in Ann Arbor, Michigan, where she is at work on her next novel.